THE BEEKMAN Affair

ERIC CLARK

Copyright ©2025 Eric Clark

ISBN: 978-1-957917-82-5 (paperback)
ISBN: 978-1-957917-83-2 (e-book)

Library of Congress Control Number: 2025914994

The main characters in this book are fictitious and bear no resemblance to actual people, living or dead. Portville, nestled along the Ohio River, is, likewise, a fictitious town created for the purposes of this novel. The psychotherapy sessions portraying various mental health concerns are intended for the sole purpose of character development. Dialogue and analysis during these sessions should not be used for personal insight into one's own mental health issues. It is always advised to seek professional mental health consultation for appropriate therapy.

All rights reserved. No part of this book may be reproduced, stored in a retrieval system, or transmitted in any form or by any means without prior written permission from the author, except for the use of brief quotations in a book review.

Cover design by Judith S. Design & Creativity
www.judithsdesign.com
Published by Glass Spider Publishing
www.glassspiderpublishing.com

*I dedicate this book to my father,
whose quiet benevolence
has been a guiding inspiration.*

Preface

I grew up in New York City, a melting pot of mixed cultures of the 1960s and '70s. On my block alone were both Italians and Puerto Ricans, Irish and Jamaicans, and still others who blended in without distinction, all vying for their definition of happiness. Many of us were immigrants or second generation, and our success in life depended on how well we could find commonality in others. We didn't see the world from the same viewpoint and our language spoke a different blend of English, yet we more than survived. We found solace in a shared sense of purpose.

In *The Beekman Affair* I was compelled to tell a story of two people who disagree on a fundamental societal issue. These two people would know each other quite well, and would be significantly invested in each other such that simply walking away from the conflict would not be a choice. In this setting, I wanted to have two souls defend their position and their actions in an effort to persuade their mate that theirs was the noblest. In doing so I hoped to reveal the essence of human nature, that is, our innate inclination to adhere to a view of the world that may be contrary to what others espouse.

I chose a single issue with which to seed this conflict: America's inveterate troubles with otherism. In this case, race. To be fair, it could have been any "othering" that would have sufficed. Race, however, was an issue already well defined and the arc of its struggle was self-evident.

My point of view in this protracted debate was from the outside looking in. It was a perspective with inherent limits. For the most part, this debate excluded those who were at the center of the conflict, the actual people being othered. But the issue of race in America affects everyone and understanding it from everyone's perspective, I thought, brought value to the discussion. *The Beekman Affair* sidesteps the views of those treated harshly to focus on those instigating the harsh treatment. Arguably, this perspective may seem to be of trivial value compared to the real pain suffered by the victims of othering, but those perpetrating the offense don't usually see the issue with the same deference, and they, undoubtedly, are the ones that ultimately change.

I liken all human interactions as a derivative of two basic impulses: give and take. And while it would seem too simplistic to distill our humanity—or troubles—into binary terms, it is, nonetheless, my feeling that give and take is like a DNA strand with only two amino acid codes. The sequencing of give and take codes in one's DNA would thereby determine one's action in any given place at any given time.

The Beekman Affair is a story of our DNA, of *give* and *take*, and an American search for true happiness.

Prologue

In the hour before midnight, a black sky shrouded Beekman in hot humid purgatory. Faces floated in space, illuminated by a glow that beckoned, and we came like flies to a fire, drawn by destiny. Glum and stricken, we gawked at a reality we were not surprised to see.

We knew something was bound to happen; we simply had no idea it would be this. We were Beekman homeowners, proud and assuming, caught in a brewing storm brought on by things we said and did not say, by things we did and did not do.

I took hold of Peter's arm, but in a mindless fit he pulled free and began to pace, as if there was something he could do to stop what was happening. I feared for his safety, feared he would be next.

Though Beekman's eyes were transfixed, I knew what lay beneath: a menacing, restless hunger. My Peter was the traitor, and retribution was due. That these were once my friends—my allies— didn't matter. I no longer trusted them. It had all gone too far.

When it was all done, when the worst of Beekman had unleashed itself, I hoped Peter and I could make amends, find solace in each other, but it was false hope. In the aftermath, our suffering diverged.

While I was eager to move on, to leave the past behind, Peter was not. In this tragic opera he sang solo, and in an octave more sublime. Thus, his fall was all the more solemn—a descent that would entomb him in guilt and uncertainty, haunting him for years to come.

1

"Clare! Chai tea latte."

It sounded like a jury foreman announcing a verdict: Guilty! And I was. My choosing to stand in the corner of the coffee shop didn't help. The attempt to blend in was a feeble one at best. A long brown suede overcoat, brown wool scarf, and matching brown beret was a monotone madness—but next to the equally dreary decor, I was hardly noticed. The color scheme was a faux pas I normally avoided, but it had only been seven months since the event and I needed to get out of the house. My self-imposed exile was suffocating, and I needed air. But everyone still knew me. My face had been plastered on the front page of the local papers: The wife of the man who stood alone against the mob. The wife who stood against her own husband. *The wife.* That was me.

"Clare!" The barista was growing impatient.

Seven months hadn't been that long. I was certain people still talked about it—the Beekman affair. We had done what any sane community would do. But how easy it is to judge in hindsight. I knew they were watching. Customers nodding in conversation, but I knew the subject... and the main protagonist. Funny how easy one descends the ladder of fortune. Schadenfreude is a slippery fate.

It wasn't supposed to be this way. I wasn't supposed to be on this end of things. There shouldn't have been a "this end of things." The whole affair had come out of nowhere, upending our entire world in the space of a few months. One day, PTA meetings. The next… well, this: a grown woman hiding from the world.

It all started in the spring, such a wonderful time of year. Everything was in bloom. All of the bulbs I'd planted before the coming frost were now on full display. All was right with the world. The worst of winter had long passed, and the Ohio River ran swift and wide from runoffs in Appalachia toward distant lands far and away. A restless Beekman stirred to life. Lying on a plateau two hundred feet from the water's edge, its breath was steady and sure, its heartbeat determined and strong, as any creature intent on living and having every right to exist in its own space on its own terms.

Beekman sat on a prominence where the Ohio genuflected in its meandering from east to west—a pretentious protuberance no doubt ordained by a higher order and referred to by some as simply the Cape. It stretched only three blocks, but they were long and serpentine and hidden from wayward travelers, just as we preferred.

Rarely contemplated, rarely seen, and rarely the focus of conversation, its repute was the envy of most, though few would ever admit it, even to themselves—an envy that revealed an unseemly, unbridled desire. In coffee shops around town, reference to Beekman was whispered across tables. In the few boutiques dotting our small-town square, a simple upturned eyebrow or tilt of the head toward a known Beekman member told the story by those witnessing providence in their presence. Ours was the idyllic suburban community, the type featured in movies with gorgeous young actors driving quietly down the middle of the road, their blue-eyed chiseled features sitting side by side, smiling in nonchalance to worldly cares.

Beekman was not central to anything in the city of Portville—the town in which it was hidden—so you would have to know how to get there if we invited you. Its lone street was lined with unassuming two-story homes, well-manicured lawns, and garden beds teeming with meticulously chosen roses, geraniums, lilies, and azaleas in a perfect spring parade of colors. Oak trees bordering the wide avenue formed an arboreal tunnel of branches and leaves walking arm in arm in brotherly love. It was a beguiling enticement for all who visited. But its charm could be found in the seemingly ordinary. The homes were large enough but not too large, just adequate for genteel living without an ostentatious snub. The yards were spacious enough to indulge the art of horticulture without the appearance of being a spectacle. Beekman was the quintessential picturesque neighborhood that anyone could easily fall in love with, and those of us fortunate to live there knew we were the pride of Portville.

The image of such a setting could have only one meaning: Peter Davidson, my husband, was a lucky man, perhaps deserving, or maybe simply destined. Whatever divine or happenstance reason had brought him to this point in his life, there could be no mistaking its appearance. It was a grace of fortune. Our wealth was not material in any sense of the word; our means were neither extravagant nor trivial. We had more than sufficient financial standing not to concern ourselves with balancing checkbooks or putting funds aside for the unexpected. We purchased what we wanted when we wanted, within reason. Financially speaking, it was a comfortable life. The real truth to Peter's wealth lay in his circumstances. He married well—just my opinion, mind you. He had two adoring children, and we lived on Beekman. It was not a plan that had been pressed into fruition, but rather an afterthought, a life simply lived, meandering any which way and ending up exactly where it was. Or so Peter thought. Choices had been made to get to that point in life, but attending to granular details was never his forte. Many of the particulars were my doing. Still, he knew he was blessed in one way or another without obsessing over the reasons why.

On one particular day in spring, as the afternoon glow descended on Beekman, Peter turned the final corner of his drive home from work. He crept along in his usual way, mindful of children still at play or toddlers chasing errant balls. The paralyzing months of Canadian cold fronts invading from the north had finally given way to a warm embrace that unshackled the young from months of confinement. No encouragement was needed; nature had set them free. The wide avenue was their makeshift playground, with hopscotch squares and football goal lines marked in colorful bold chalk lines down the middle of the road. It may only have been fifty degrees, but that was enough for spring to feel like the beginning of summer.

Peter eased into the driveway of our white, two-story colonial home. It was accented with a centered deep-blue door and bordered by twin Greek-style columns supporting an entryway overhang. Flowers cascaded from the portico in an array of colors and scents. It was such an inviting sight and an even more delightful aroma that Peter often lost himself in meditation. In that moment of tranquility marking the end of a long workday, he saw our neighbor wave in greeting.

They shared a perfunctory smile, but before Peter could return the wave, our neighbor turned and went back into their house.

While outside brimmed with kids caught up in spontaneous amusement, the inside of our home was a quiet sanctuary. I didn't hear his entrance, but Peter would usually slip out of his blue sport coat and drop his leather briefcase unceremoniously on the first step of the stairs leading up to the bedrooms. It was the same routine, five days a week. He was punctual, predictable, and usually practical—the three P's of suburban life. He always called when he left work and usually found a way to let me know if he was running late.

Before long, he made his way quietly to the master bedroom entry. With arms crossed, he leaned against the doorjamb, watching me type on my laptop. I was sitting in bed, likely looking determined as ever, undoubtedly engrossed in what was sure to be a literary feat. Peter knew the look. I was in a trance, ideas forming as fast as my fingers could type them. The creative paradox was not his area of specialty, so he simply stood there, admiring his genius wife at work. A minute later, I paused, reread what I'd just written, and closed the laptop.

"Thank you for the moment," I said with a smile.

"I'm always amazed at how you can create something from nothing."

I'd heard his flattery on many occasions, but it still made me blush. I quickly changed the subject. "So, how was your day at work? Same ol', same ol'?"

"Same ol', same ol'. How's the article for the magazine?"

"It's coming along. I'm pretty much done with it."

"What was the subject again?"

"Interest rates. The title is *How to Navigate Interest Rates for Personal Finance*."

"Ah, a subject near and dear to my heart. Do you need any accounting facts to spice it up?"

I smirked. His droll humor was often on display and rarely worthy of encouragement. Despite his accounting background, my finance degree put us on equal footing. I had an open invitation to contribute articles to several women's magazines, focusing on what women should know about managing their finances. It was a pivot once both of our kids were fully occupied with school. Being a stay-at-home mom was also a pivot from my work in finance consulting at the Bank of Portville. Indeed, I knew as much about the subject as he did—perhaps even more.

"Uh, I'm not sure anyone would consider accounting a spice to anything—really." I flashed a mischievous smile. "And, as I recall, interest rates aren't really your thing."

"Hmm… I don't know what you're talking about," Peter said, avoiding my gaze by staring down at the carpet as if studying the oriental pattern for consistency.

"Don't play coy. You know exactly what I'm talking about. That's why Dr. Jordan gave you such a hard time back at Ohio State. Remember? Nobel Laureate and Chair, Professor Jordan? You botched interest rates in our microecon class when you had your chance. Ha!" I couldn't resist another haughty laugh.

Peter finally looked up and met my eyes with a sheepish smile. "She had it in for me. It wasn't fair of her to single me out. I was minding my own business in the upper deck of the auditorium when, out of the blue, she called on me. I doubt she could even see me in the dim lighting."

"Oh, she saw you well enough. She saw you not paying attention. What were you looking at, anyway, that got her on to you so?"

"Haven't we rehashed this enough times already?"

"I don't know. Sometimes a little reminder helps keep you honest. I forget, why were you so inattentive in that class? Hmm… checking out the architecture? Studying other classmates?"

"Let's just say I was clearly distracted. The wall lights were flickering, people walking in late, my neck had a god-awful crick in it—"

"Nice, nice. Yes, that's how I remember it. You were looking everywhere *but* at the professor. And, oddly enough, you were always looking in my direction. Go figure." I smiled again, this time with an endearing warmth.

"Yeah, yeah. There was a major distraction just two feet away. Rather unfair, I'd say. A distraction like that deserved a lighter sentence. Dr. Jordan was way too harsh."

"What'd you say? 'Um, I—I guess… if the dollar is weak… I wouldn't be looking to buy a house or car'?"

"An accurate assessment."

"Only you left out the part about interest rates. Dr. Jordan wanted to know the impact of the dollar value *on* interest rates. You flubbed it. I gotta say, I'm surprised I let you get to first base after that."

"I saw you enjoying my inquisition with a big grin on your face. I guess you couldn't resist my humor."

"What—the 'I'm P-P-Peter, Peter Davidson' response when Dr. Jordan asked you to identify yourself?"

"I was acting. Trying to show off a little. Otherwise, you would have forgotten me in a heartbeat."

"Hmm. Well, maybe that part actually worked. I did laugh about it with my friends later."

"See? In the end, it was all good. What's that line? All's good that ends good?"

"Close. You're a real comedian."

Peter took it in stride. The jibe about his lack of finance skills and the inherent dullness of accounting wasn't new to him. I often ribbed him about his failed performance on that day back in college and regaled friends with the story during social gatherings, clearly still amused by his natural attraction to me. As for being an accountant, well, I was not the first to reflect on accounting's less flamboyant nature, and Peter had long grown inured to such ridicule. Accounting required a steady demeanor, and he felt it suited him well.

He was in the process of unknotting his tie and kicking off his shoes when I interrupted. "By the way, you may not want to change. We have an invite across the street at the Johnsons' for dinner."

"In the middle of the week?"

"Indeed."

"I saw Jordan outside when I was on my way in. He waved but didn't hang around to chat. Seemed a little weird, but I just figured he had a busy day."

"Well, Sarah called me earlier and they invited us to dinner—tonight. Seems out of the ordinary on a school night and all, but maybe there *is* something going on. I think they have a lot on their plate, what with him losing his job down at the factory. I can't imagine being Sarah right now, having to carry the load on just a teacher's salary. They must be burning through savings."

"Layoffs suck! You never see it coming. Jordan's a talented guy, though. He should easily bounce back."

I wasn't so sure. Peter was always a glass-half-full sort of guy. I was a realist. I heard the foreboding in his voice, as though he were trying to hide something. This was a topic that could veer off into a deep, dark corner of uncertainty. The kind of uncertainty we always avoided like the plague.

2

Session 1

"Mr. Davidson, you may go in now."

The receptionist's voice jarred him from his reverie. It had become a preferred escape to someplace safe, someplace less complicated. Reality seldom held his attention for long. It was as if he were living on the periphery of his own existence. Daydreaming was an indulgence, maybe even an addiction. That much he was willing to concede. But he didn't think it would be a problem for anyone other than himself. Or so he believed.

The possibility that his life was slipping away, that he was veering off into some other realm—a psychosis, maybe?—was not quite apparent. He had agreed to do this, to partake in actively dismembering his life. To a total stranger, no less. It was the only way forward, his wife had decided. They'd reached an impasse, and this was the only way out of it.

He didn't entirely object to the idea, though there was some part of him that rebelled. Despite his willingness to first look inward for anything amiss, he yearned for affirmation that his view of things was more noble than hers. Confrontation, however, was not his forte—just as agreeing to disagree was not her virtue.

He knew he was no longer himself. The outgoing Peter had turned recluse. The event that had stopped time five years ago was a quake that shattered his moral compass. He had misstepped—a cavernous leap, in his mind—leaving life and trust and faith as promises betrayed. It was all his doing, a consequence of his emotional weakness. He couldn't bear to believe the truth back then, that the Beekman that had nurtured his fledgling marriage and growing family could turn inward in such a grotesque delusion of preserving values.

His misstep had been in choosing between right and wrong, between outcast and neighbor, between virtue and wife. Deceit had consumed him. It was how he saw the past, and it weighed on him—stones carried aloft in a Sisyphean effort toward redemption. But it was all to no avail. Now he was here, at an office for therapeutic intervention. A scientific approach to a crisis of courage. An odd solution, he thought, but who was he to say?

Peter's eyes regained their focus. The dieffenbachia embracing the corner behind the receptionist, stiffened back into shape, its defining green and white accents throwing the receptionist in sharp repose.

"Er, uh, thank you, ma'am. Through this door?"

The receptionist smiled, glancing over her silver half-rimmed readers, and pointed approvingly to the wood-framed door with frosted privacy glass and "Session Room" stenciled in cursive. She wore a nonchalance that could easily be dismissed as someone preoccupied with other particulars. He couldn't shake the thought that her insouciant grin belied a dull curiosity about him. She must have wondered about all the weak-kneed patients shuffling to and fro. Did she foster imaginings of anxiety attacks, impulsive hand washings, and belligerent outbreaks? She'd no doubt seen them all. He wondered if she secretly listened in on lunatic ravings, hiding smirks when the patients passed her on their way out.

He knew this line of thought wasn't helpful. But obsession was his calling card, and limiting its boundaries was a new task that had so far proved elusive. He returned her smile with a knowing bow of the head. He was on to her.

―― ··· ――

"Hello, Mr. Davidson. I'm Anna Dietrich. Please, have a seat."

She stood behind a glass-topped desk and wore a subtle smile that put him at ease. Her voice was pleasant yet maintained a lingering air of authority. It was a delicate balance that enticed him to follow along.

He greeted her with a smile and looked around the room. It was a place in which he expected to spend a lot of time—time spent talking about things he hadn't spoken of and wasn't sure he was ready to share. That he was still optimistic a shrink could rescue him from the misery of his situation was laughable. Just the thought put a smile on his face. He chose the left of the two leather chairs, hoping his smile appeared appropriate and wouldn't make him seem like an idiot.

The office was long and rectangular, sparsely furnished, simple and elegant. A sofa bordered one end of the room while the desk and two chairs occupied the other. A few tall plants were decoratively placed, and two oversized artworks of Mexico City's Zócalo Square and Paris's Le Pont Notre-Dame hung on the wall behind him. A large window sterilized the room in bright light, as if preventing any truths from hiding. Anna Dietrich reached out her hand, and he politely extended his for a brief, uninspiring shake.

"So, Mr. Davidson, what brings you in today?"

Her start was direct and professional: *Let's get to the point here.* He had a sudden feeling of walking into a furniture store with a salesperson eager for a commission. It was a brief adjustment that settled into a mild panic when he realized, for the first time, that someone genuinely cared about what he had to say. Years had passed by with Peter evading his wife and obsessing in private. Now he had to put words to feelings. It was awkwardly deliberate, as if two worlds were about to collide: oil and water, earth and space. Would they mix? Would it make sense?

His mind began to race with anxiety, the whole ordeal another uncertainty he couldn't control. "Uh, well… uh, I've never done anything like this. I'm not sure of the protocol." He sat with his hands in his lap, every bit the grade-school student in the principal's office.

"That's quite alright. It's the first time for most of my patients. Let's lay some ground rules. First, call me Anna. The fewer boundaries between us, the better. May I call you Peter?"

"Sure. That works." Maybe this was a simple business transaction instead of a painful tooth extraction. Maybe the sales commission analogy was apropos. He smiled on the inside but suppressed its effervescent rise to the surface.

"Okay, Peter it is. There, that's a start. Now, I'm here to help you with whatever you'd like. I may not always have an answer for you. The process is often slow, and it's not always obvious things are improving. Patience is required. Sometimes, situations are like peeling back an onion. I know it's a tired metaphor, but it applies. Over time, we can both see and understand more about the source of whatever it is you'd like to understand. It's only at that point that we can decide what course of action to take. I'd like to emphasize the *we*. This process is not a passive one. You have to work at this, and any solution to your problems, if you have any, we will solve together. Your feelings and opinions have value. They'll shape how we move forward."

"Okay, Doc. Er… Anna. Sounds fine by me."

He was beginning to loosen. The tension in his shoulders melted away, and his teeth gradually unclenched. He was convinced he would stay in control of the situation. After all, it was his life, his story, his pain. But he was being usurped. She was taking the helm, and for the first time, he felt a true sense of real release.

"So when you say 'together,' what do you really mean? Is it negotiable? Can we arrange that you do more of the heavy lifting, and I do the pensive staring?" He smiled, but part of him still looked like someone in mourning.

Anna smiled in kind but made no comment. Instead, she pressed on. "It's usually best to start with something simple, something obvious. You decided to make an appointment. Why?"

His face soured. He'd known the question was coming, but still it took him by surprise. For as much as he'd prepared himself for the probing to come, it seemed perhaps he hadn't prepared enough. It was as if a hypodermic needle was coming at him from across the room. He knew what it was for and who it was for, and as it got closer and closer, he had to resign himself to the fact that it was going to be in him in short time, and that he needed it, and there was no arguing the fact—to save the patient, the patient had to take the medicine. It was a simple truth, a commodity he'd forgotten and was now rudely reminded of. He needed to say something so as not to appear the fool.

"Well, I'm really doing this to save my marriage. My wife and I… I guess we see the world differently, and I guess I'm rubbing her the wrong way. She sees it as my problem and feels this is the way to get back on track."

Wow! Peter's own frankness surprised him. That was easy enough, but maybe it was too easy. He drew a dividing line between himself and his wife, and it gnawed at him—but the danger to these sessions was now obvious. There was nowhere to hide. And there was no way to plan his answers in advance. He had no idea where Anna would mine next, and his response was expected before he fully understood the weight of what he would say. It was effortless and cathartic, but the guilt soon followed. He was selling out his wife, plain and simple.

"Do you agree that it *is* your problem?" Anna asked.

He felt something in the recesses of his mind, lurking in dimly lit alleyways. These were things he never shared with Clare. He never felt the mood was right, or that her temperament was willing or that their marriage could survive the frankness. Anna's style of probing empowered him to say the things he often left off the table, things that were off limits for discussion or just too toxic. In a way, this might be a welcome outlet. No beating around the bush with, "How does that make you feel?" It was the classic line he expected from a therapist. He found himself settling back in the chair, the anxious threat of some horrid exposure receding into his subconscious.

"I don't know. I mean, I don't know that I'm the problem. I have my issues like anybody else, but she thinks I'm not letting go or moving on with my life. She thinks I obsess too much over stuff I shouldn't care about."

He looked Anna directly in the eyes to gauge her intent. Was she on to something already? Was she taking sides? Whose side was she on?

"And you think your take on things strikes a reasonable balance?"

"Yeah, I do," he blurted out. Embarrassed, he paused to appear more reflective. She smiled quietly, as if giving him space to rephrase his words. "Well, maybe there is something to it, I'm not entirely sure. Maybe that's why I'm here. My wife set the ultimatum, but I do have my own demons, and maybe another opinion would be helpful. The ultimatum may not entirely be unfair."

Peter watched her play with her pen. She flipped it one way, then the other. He wondered what she would write about him. How weird was he? Or maybe that was all she used the pen for—to flip while strategizing her next move against him.

"So," Anna finally continued, "it may be fair that your wife asked you to see someone?"

"Yeah, that's possible."

"How long have you and your wife not seen eye to eye?"

The implied accusation stung. What she meant to ask was how long they'd had marital problems. He was sure of it. The calm in the eye of the storm was over. He was already beginning to wonder where this would end. Maybe he'd shared too much. He'd expected to be probed, to be prodded and pinched, and even piqued—but he hadn't expected Clare to be a part of it.

Maybe it was his own naiveté. In some odd way, he felt the need to protect her from blame. This should be his albatross to bear, not hers. "We've, uh… been married for nearly… twenty years." The words came slowly as he looked for landmines along the way. "I think, for the most part, we've had a good marriage." He paused. There was more, but he was stuck mid-thought, mesmerized by the glare of the large window.

"But you feel there are still issues between you, right?" Anna said.

"Well, yes," he finally succumbed, begrudgingly coming back to life. "But all marriages have issues, especially after twenty years. Don't you think?"

"True," Anna willingly agreed. "But I sense… something between you and your wife keeps coming up. As you said before, she thinks you're obsessing over things, maybe a bit too much?"

The sparring match had begun. It was inevitable that her probing would eventually draw blood.

Anna lunged in with her foil, taking an initial stab at the heart of an issue. He parried with denial and obfuscation to deflect exposure of a painful truth. Her riposte then cut further to the core, the more denial on his part merely pointing to the heart of the matter. All the while, she stepped hesitantly around in his mental abode, trying to avoid knocking over precariously placed vases or sharp objects.

In the end, the sparring was supposed to help unearth buried treasure, the painful experiences lost and forgotten. Although it had its risks, denial and obfuscation were not the only parry he might muster. Anger and belligerence for being undressed in public, the sharp objects sometimes lurking in plain sight, could set him on edge for an unknown amount of time. Trust lost would need to be fostered anew. It was all a fine line to tread.

"I've had trouble letting go of some things," Peter said, "but I think some things can be life changing, and to ignore them is to ignore… well, to ignore a piece of who you are."

Anna arched a brow. "And what you value as life changing, your wife does not?"

Peter's left hand closed in on itself, squeezing 'til his nails dug into the soft flesh of his palm. He welcomed the pain; it was alive in an existence apart from him. He released and felt a calm energy flow up his arm and descend into his chest and abdomen.

"Things happen, Doc—uh, Anna—and I don't expect my wife and I to see everything eye to eye, but I think…" He broke off, realizing he might have traveled too far down a wrong alley. "I think she's sometimes too insensitive. I mean, she can sometimes be too dismissive."

Peter's voice wobbled slightly as he pleaded his position.

Anna knew marriage issues were fraught with the usual he-said-she-said battle lines. It was often nearly impossible to really know what was going on with a couple. Much of what one shared in therapy was a perspective shaped by an underlying insecurity; her job was to find the events that triggered that insecurity and the resulting poor coping skills. That there were poor coping skills was a given; they wouldn't be sitting in her chair if they coped well with life's vagaries. Her work was usually a sticky dissection of past events, intentions, and outcomes that ultimately drew a landscape of how one saw the world and engaged with it.

For now, at least, she noted that Peter sat calmly and maintained a direct gaze without looking away. There were no facial tics, fidgety hands, or noisy feet. He was likely not hiding anything. He was telling his version of the truth. She was not used to this so early in therapy. It was a welcome relief. Usually, it took a few sessions to build the kind of trust that allowed a patient to be candid instead of treading around the periphery of their life's angst. She took this as a sign to probe further.

"Is your wife dismissive of you, or just the things you care about?"

Peter shifted in the chair but kept his gaze on Anna. "Doc, the truth of the matter is that she only cares about herself." He took on a professorial look, his fingers tented, head on a tilt with a sarcastic half-smile.

Is this his confident, in-charge look, or is it a façade? Anna didn't know him well enough to be sure. *Do I scratch the veneer and see what's lurking below? Is it too early?*

"And you?" she asked.

"Well, I kinda feel... I'd say I'm normal... average," he declared. "I care about things—about people!"

Anna didn't respond. It was an intentional choice to let that statement linger in the room for a while. No doubt it was provocative, and while she would normally have probed further, she decided not to push him too far.

"Peter, I think we've covered a lot of ground for our first session. I'd like to build on this progress next week. I do need to ask one more question just to complete my thoughts on this issue. Can you give me an example of what you care about that Clare does not?"

Peter's confident gaze dissolved into a vacant stare. The question hit a soft spot, and dead air hung in the space between them. He squirmed in the chair as if some perfect spot would end the inquisition. His hands began to fidget as he turned to stare at the floor.

"Peter, if you'd like to end our session at this point, it would be okay to do so. We don't have to cover every detail in one sitting."

The silence spoke. Peter's hands knotted, fingers worming in motion, his eyes locked on the slats of the hardwood floor stretching off into the rectangular distance. Anna held her gaze for a long, agonizing minute. Finally, he murmured something—something inaudible.

"I'm sorry, Peter, I couldn't understand you."

"Beekman!" he sneered with the pithiness of an obscenity. "That damn Beekman!"

"Who is Beekman?"

Another pause followed. "It's not a who," Peter finally said, "it's... it's a *where*. A place—a *thing*." He finally looked up, his vacant eyes staring in her direction. "They call it... the Cape."

3

An hour had passed before Peter and I were finally sitting across from Jordan and Sarah. The kids were off in other parts of the Johnson house, doing what teens do while their parents entertained the more mundane aspects of life. It was a language that reliably sent kids scattering from the dinner table. Megan belonged to the Johnsons, and Sandy was ours. Both wasted no time finding other pursuits. Matt was fourteen. He was our eldest, and he lingered a bit longer than his sister. He fancied himself mature enough to listen in on adult conversation as if he were one. But ennui eventually beckoned him to a TV game console more suited to his demeanor.

The mood began with the usual friendly banter that accompanied these types of dinner gatherings, especially since we considered one another the best of friends. This was especially true for me and Sarah. Our attachment was especially unique since I was an only child, and Sarah easily filled the role of the sister I never had. Given my penchant for proper living, Sarah also served as mentor. I admired her classy way of doing things.

Their house was beautifully landscaped on the outside and well-appointed on the inside. Imported furniture was scattered among the domestic in a perfect balance of sophistication that was still approachable. The Johnsons' choice of simple yet elegant Wedgwood China, Gorham silverware, and Italian napery left no doubt that Sarah had been raised in a proper home. While her cooking skills left one wondering if teaching was really her first profession, it was her manners that stood above all. She always exuded an effervescence of politeness and consideration, even remembering birthdays with a phone call or a nicely chosen card.

Probably where Sarah shone most was her dinner parties, an annual event held in high regard by the Beekman community. These were not pedestrian affairs. No, that would never suit Sarah's taste for the de rigueur. Her evening soirees began with a stylish invite left in one's mailbox, complete with ribbon and bow—Sarah style.

She greeted everyone on arrival and was the perfect hostess, moving among the guests with poise and equanimity—refilling wine glasses, offering an amusing or witty comment, with never a negative sentiment. Where others would occasionally get pithy with an observation here, an opinion there, or an off-color joke in an attempt to be the life of the party, Sarah was seemingly above it all, effortlessly keeping the ruffles of life smooth and palatable, like a wine aged to perfection. It was just who she was. You admired her without envying her; envy carried the bitter aftertaste of wanting to be her equal. Somehow, it was okay for Sarah to be alone on that pedestal, a singularity of purpose disposed to sincerity, kindness, and grace.

The gaiety, however, had come to an end. The spontaneous dinner party had a purpose, and that purpose was now upon us. Jordan was the first to speak, stating the obvious—he had been jobless for six months. The prospects were grim. With Ohio rooted in the Rust Belt and manufacturing jobs having left for distant shores, the economy had soured. A likely turnaround was not in sight. The future for Jorgan and Sarah was not on Beekman, not in Portville, maybe not even in Ohio. They would be putting their house on the market.

I saw in Sarah's face a noble effort to wear a smile, composed as usual, despite having every reason to be demoralized, or even angry. Clearly, they were being squeezed by the forces of fate, and yet Sarah seemed to be taking it all in stride. I knew better. I knew that this was Sarah's breeding. It was always distasteful when people left their angst at your doorstep. Sure, sometimes they couldn't help it. Life can be a bear. But again, I saw in Sarah something to emulate.

I slid to the edge of my chair and leaned forward onto the dining table, my eyes fixed on her with plaintive hopes. I hoped my body language didn't betray my anxiety. "Sarah, this place will never be the same without you, and I don't know what I'm going to do with myself. My heart will ache seeing anyone else move into your home." I glanced at Peter, then gazed down at the table as if trying to find a comfort that refused to be found.

"Where will you go?" Peter asked in his effort to lift my spirits with something concrete. "I mean, once you sell. Chicago? Milwaukee?"

"We're open to either at this point," Sarah said. "We just need to settle for a while and get the finances in order. We're going to stay with Jordan's brother in Evanston once the house sells, so we'll be closer for job hunting. I wish we could do it from here, but we don't want to accept something and leave the house vacant. The housing market is down, and it'll have even less appeal with just bare walls to look at." She sighed. "We thought about just leaving Beekman altogether and renting out the house, but no one's looking to rent. Not in this market."

"You know," Jordan added, "my factory closing is just the tip of the iceberg. Factories have been closing in Ohio for the past decade. I guess I just kept my eyes closed to what I didn't want to see. I'm part of management. You'd think I'd get a golden parachute or something. Well, I didn't. Two months' severance. That's nothing, not after what I gave them. All these Midwestern companies are chasing shareholder profits. It's significantly cheaper to do what I do overseas."

I was quietly seething at this point. This shouldn't be happening to a Beekman. To see Sarah suffering the indignities of raw capitalism at play was simply unfair. I knew there were others in Portville who were also victims. I was sure of it. But I always put Beekman above the rest. For that matter, the idea of Sarah and Jordan selling their house—their *home*—meant someone else would eventually become a Beekman. That idea was even more unsettling. It was akin to coming home and finding someone taking up residence in your living room.

I locked eyes with Peter as though seeking refuge in a safe harbor. He met my gaze from the other side of the table with a sympathetic nod. I was clearly disappointed, lost in a hollow solace. And I wasn't alone. I knew the whole neighborhood believed as I did, that keeping Beekman *Beekman* was as important as life itself. The name had become a pronoun, a living creature with its own persona. It was a fortress of integrity, auspicious values, and justifiable pride. Like a rare species threatened with extinction, it needed to be preserved.

"So, Jordan, when does it go on the market? The house?" Peter asked, again seemingly determined to find terra firma.

"Soon. We've already interviewed a few realtors, but none were optimistic. They begged us not to sell. Not in this market. We're actually thinking of selling it ourselves. Sarah and I have to move on. We can't stay in limbo forever."

I finally surfaced from my moribund state. An idea had sprung, and my face gleamed with new confidence and true purpose. I looked at Peter, who seemed unable to divine my intentions. Then I turned to Sarah, who returned my newfound smile.

"Sarah," I said, "Maybe we can help you find someone to buy the place. This way we can sort of give them the once-over, make sure they're Beekman material?" I looked at Peter with an obsequious smile. "It's too bad we don't know of anyone who's looking to buy. How nice it would be to pick our new neighbors."

"Hmm," Peter said. "You know someone who's looking? Are they a former client?"

"No. I was thinking *you* could find someone—someone at work."

"What!?" Peter waxed pensive. "I guess that would be nice, if I knew someone was already looking, but for me to go around and find someone, when does *that* ever happen? Aren't we being a bit too selective? I've never heard of anyone actually *choosing* their neighbor."

"This all sounds interesting," Sarah said. "Anything that gets us out of this mess we're in makes it easier on us."

"I don't know," Peter said, "some things come just as they are: colleagues or classmates. It's like your family, handed to you on a platter of fate. Life asks us to treat fortune and misfortune the same. We just have to deal with whoever the new owners are."

Peter's preaching annoyed me. It was ill-timed, and my frustration simmered. "There's nothing wrong with grabbing the bull by the horns," I pressed. "That's how we do it in my business. There must be someone down at your company that would be a good fit for Beekman. The price is right, right?" I glanced around the table. "Jordan will see to it."

Jordan looked at Sarah, and they both nodded. "The house *is* priced to sell," Jordan said. "We're definitely not asking fair market value."

"You see!?" I said.

While I had been out of banking for many years, I still could smell a good deal. It was the investment hound instinct of raw survival in a world of uncertainty. When I had a prospective client in the crosshairs, I was relentless in closing the deal.

Peter was unfazed. He barely raised a brow. "Yeah, yeah, but still, how would I do that? Put it on a bulletin board or something?" He lifted his hands high as if preaching to a crowd of thousands. "Wanted," he said sardonically, "a sophisticated couple for an exclusive neighborhood, children an added benefit. Respectful manners a must. Should be successful, well-traveled, and, uh, not be unscrupulous in any way."

He smiled, obviously pleased with his spontaneous antics.

"I'm just not sure of this," Peter continued. "It's way out of my comfort zone—acting like a realtor at work. My reputation is built on objectivity, not solicitation." He raked his fingers through his hair, a telltale sign he was the one now on edge.

I was familiar with all his tics and knew he was backpedaling. "I was just hoping we could somehow keep the nice neighborly feeling we've got in our little part of paradise."

"It's a fantasy," he replied, "but I get it. Who could resist picking neighbors that share your values? But I think that anyone moving into this neighborhood will be happy with what we've got here. I think they'll blend in easily, especially if they have kids. I just think exclusivity shouldn't be by choice. It should be by some sort of fate or kismet."

"I kinda agree with you there, Peter," Jordan said. "It would be nice, especially if we had a lot of lookers. We could pick the best fit for Beekman. But the way things are, we'll be lucky to get *any* buyer. They'll have to become Beekman, after the fact."

"Don't worry," Peter said to me with a grin. "We'll roll out the red carpet to the new owners, and they'll be overwhelmed by our hospitality. After a few dinner parties and the football Sundays coming up, they'll be Beekman material in no time."

His humor was meant to reassure me, but once again, his timing was off. I wasn't in the mood to be trivialized. This whole situation was shifting the foundation on which we'd built our life. Changes like this weren't in the plans. Not that anything could be done about it, but I at least expected a healthy sense of anxiety from him, not some reflexive attempt at disarming humor.

"Tell you what," Sarah finally interjected, turning to me. "When we get a buyer, we'll keep you in the loop. You'll be the first on Beekman to know who they are, where they're from, all the sordid details. Maybe that'll make the transition for you—and them—a little easier."

Sarah seemed to grow excited as the idea knitted together in her mind.

"Maybe I can introduce you to them," she continued. "You know how these things go. There's a lot of back and forth. Since we're selling it ourselves, we'll be involved in all the legal stuff—title documents, inspections, all that. It's all a process. I'm sure somewhere in there, we'll find time for a little meet-and-greet, maybe a lunch party. Just the four of us and the buyers."

I blushed. My wide grin probably said it all. I loved Sarah, and this was the exact reason why. She knew just what to say and just what to do. She read my emotions like a twin sister.

"Thank you so much, Sarah. You have no idea how that makes me feel. It puts me so much at ease." My eyes welled up, and I hurriedly excused myself from the table.

4

Session 2

"Hello, Peter." Anna smiled and gestured to the chair he'd previously chosen. She was hoping to disarm any anxiety from their first session. She knew all too well that sometimes, second visits could be more stressful than the first since the client knew what to expect, their defenses sharpened now that the rules of the game were out in the open.

Peter had arrived on time; he was neatly dressed and well groomed. He showed no hesitation in his stride or greeting. Anna took note of these small details. While their first session had its turbulence and almost ended on a down note, Peter eventually shared what he'd meant by "That damn Beekman—a place, a thing." Enough so that Anna had reason for a guarded optimism that today would be at least productive.

It was mostly a wish on her part. She knew quite well that therapy takes on a life of its own. You might start on an issue you'd like to explore, but probing unearths relics of emotions and suggestions pointing in an entirely different direction, and all a therapist can do is delicately walk through the landmines of someone's memories, insecurities, and triggering issues with uncertain consequences.

The soft spot she'd happened upon in their first session was not expected, but it was also not by chance. She felt he was gradually leading her to that very question: *What does he care about that Clare does not?* She'd contemplated not going there, that with a brand-new therapist maybe he wouldn't trust her enough to be frank about what was really bothering him. But she took the leap on the grounds that if he *was* leading her there, what kind of therapist would she be if she didn't read him properly? It was a dilemma she chose to act on by following her instincts. So far, all evidence pointed to it helping rather than hurting.

"Hi, Doc," Peter said as he sat.

"Anna is okay with me. No need to be formal."

"Oh, right. Forgot. It's been a week. I'll try to remember."

She had mentioned this before, but it was worth mentioning again. This was yet another effort to soften his defenses. She wasn't fond of titles. They created the very boundaries she was trying to erode. While Peter may have felt she was simply being modest, she was staging an atmosphere where he would interpret her probing uncomfortable memories as friendly chatter and not the surgical excision of a cancer. The cure might be the same, but with therapy, the ends do not justify the means. An aggressive excavation of deep-rooted memories could shock a patient into an unwillingness to continue therapy. If it came to that, you were left with someone walking around with internal organs exposed to the world—as if surgery had exposed the problem but didn't excise it. The gnawing knowledge of one's emotional frailties, probed and then left untreated by a therapist, could cause more damage than if you simply left them hidden from view.

Peter settled into the chair and glanced about. Anna gave him all the time he needed; it was the final lynchpin to help patients relax and make her job that much easier. After a while, she was ready to begin.

"At a certain point last week, we were talking about differences. Differences between you and your wife."

She paused to gauge his reaction. He had none. He sat fully reclined, feigning indifference, as if this were a discussion about someone else's affairs.

"Yeah, sorry about that," he said. "Must have hit a nerve. I didn't realize that topic was gonna set me off like that." The confession was neutral in tone, almost as if it were someone else's problem. He wasn't denying it nor trying to disown it.

"That's quite alright, Peter, we're just peeling the onion, right? Somewhere along the line, we expect to hit a nerve or two. The good thing is that these nerves are like signposts pointing in a direction we need to go if we're to find answers that matter. We don't have to travel that road immediately, but eventually we'll need to circle back and explore what lies in that direction. I don't want you to think my probing the sensitive areas reflects callousness on my part. If you ever feel hesitant about something, let me know. I'll make a note to circle back another time."

Peter seemed unperturbed. If he was at all wounded by their last encounter, there was nothing to show for it. "Got it." He sounded like he was accepting a job offer.

Anna smiled and pushed forward. "So, to put it simply, you care about people, and your wife doesn't. What did you mean by that?"

The awkwardness of that admission was nakedly apparent. She knew it sounded absurd and gave him all the time he needed to find a delicate response.

"Ah, yes." Peter blushed. "That… that's a little embarrassing. I didn't mean to say it that way. Just to be clear, I love my wife. I couldn't imagine a life without her. We've been married a long time, we have two beautiful kids, and she's the center of everything I do. So you'll have to take my criticisms with a grain of salt."

"Certainly." He was obviously hiding something, but Anna had no intention of challenging it. "Please, go on."

"Okay. Well, I guess what I was getting at is that she's very protective of the status quo. She likes the way things are and doesn't see a reason for change—any change. I, on the other hand, I'm less stressed by the idea."

"Any change?"

"Well, yeah, most any change—from what she expected—the way she planned." Peter struggled to find clarity. "But it's just her way of looking at the world. She's, I don't know…" With a frustrated sigh, he gave up.

Anna sensed he was avoiding an issue. She decided to pivot. "Tell me about your background. Your home environment growing up, parents, siblings, that sort of thing. Paint me a picture."

Peter raked his hand through his hair and took a brief glance out the window but returned to meet Anna's gaze. "Oh, the old Freudian mother-son thing?" he asked with a modest dose of cynicism. "You think my problems are from some childhood scar, like I've been harboring some demon from my past?"

"Humor me."

"I was expecting this type of interrogation last week. I have to say, I was surprised when you just cut to the chase and dove right in. I was a bit taken aback, but it was refreshing. The surprise of it all, I mean."

"Well, I'm glad I impressed you in our first session, but I guess this 'interrogation' is going in a different direction today." She threw him a disarming smile to ensure he understood they were mutually jesting. "Do you think you can handle it?"

"Well, alright, let's see where this goes." Peter readjusted himself in the chair. He had begun to slouch, and so he made an effort to sit upright. "There's not much to tell, really—a mom, dad, brother, no crisis issues to speak of, just a boring childhood."

"Were you close with your brother?"

"Dave? Yeah, he and I were buds for most years growing up. By our mid-teens, our three-year age difference—he was older—felt like an eternity. Ninth grade versus twelfth is a big difference. He was driving and had a bigger circle of friends. We still got along, but we didn't share stories like we used to."

"And your mom and dad?"

"They were cool. No issues I can remember."

"How did they interact with each other?" Anna probed.

"Hmm, that's kinda hard to say, from a kid's perspective, anyway."

"Well, did they get along pretty easily? Was it a happy marriage?"

Peter looked down at his shoes. He wore brown penny loafers that matched the same walnut stain on the hardwood floor—slats running off in the distant emptiness of the long room. While still gazing off in that distance, he murmured, "My dad... my dad was a funny guy, always finding the humor in a situation."

Anna watched him stare at the floor. There was something there, in the reference, otherwise he would have looked her in the eye. It was as if he wanted to hide something, and looking away was the best he could do. He was trapped with no way out.

"What situation?" she asked.

Peter looked up at her, then shifted his gaze to the wide window, where a brightness filled the room as if trying to penetrate his mind. He looked back across at the sofa on the far end of the room. His shoulders slouched as he slid back in the chair. The session had already taken a few unpredictable turns.

"Peter?"

"Sorry." He looked up, a bit embarrassed. "What'd you ask?"

"Situations. You mentioned your dad used humor in certain situations."

"I guess," he started, sheepishly staring back at Anna, "whenever things got stressed around the house. My parents didn't argue much because my dad never let it happen. He always found a way to defuse things."

He fell silent, like a submarine slipping back below the surface, leaving a swirl of interest in what had been. Anna had watched the confident Peter—who arrived on time, well-dressed and spontaneously engaged—devolve into a slouching heap of emotions, bottling up memories he clearly didn't want to talk about. She knew it was the right path to stay on.

"So your dad used humor to deflect—situations. He was sort of nonconfrontational? Is that what you're saying?"

"Well, it wasn't like he was shy or afraid to make a point. Making a point was something he excelled at." He leaned forward in his chair, finally showing renewed interest. "Everything was well thought out, almost like a lecture. But then he would end things with a joke or something witty."

"And your mom, how did she cope with these 'situations'?" Anna was hoping to squeeze as much out of his renewed invigoration as possible.

"I guess, between the two, she was more the instigator, the one driving the ship. Most often, we did things her way. I can say that, looking back on it, but in the moment, at the time, I never felt stress or any major conflict. I mean, I often saw my friends' parents argue, so whatever happened at home seemed the same. Back then, it all felt normal." Peter tried to appear unfazed by the topic. He readjusted himself in the chair but maintained eye contact.

"I'm sure it was," Anna said, hoping to put him at ease. "It's never a perfect science, this thing about childhood experiences and how they affect our adult lives, but there may be connections between you and your wife and your mom and dad. You probably won't find this too crazy. I'm sure you may have thought of it yourself."

Peter smiled nervously. "Well, this should be interesting. This is gonna answer all my problems, then, huh?"

"Well, probably not," Anna said with a half-smile. "More like just scratching the surface. There *are* some links between your father's handling of stress and your current situation. So, what I hear you saying is that your father deflected stress by using humor. Whenever conflict arose, often because your mom had a strong personality? Should we say your dad chose to find a funny perspective and then just go along?"

"Are you saying my dad's a wuss?" Peter snapped.

"No, not at all. Why he chose to handle those conflicts in the way he did may have been for good reasons. It may be that he understood your mom and felt it best to choose that approach. Rather than being passive, you might consider his actions to be proactive. My point is what you saw was your mom defining the terms of life, and your dad accepting it with humor. He was nonconfrontational. Sure, maybe he was running from the confrontation, but maybe it never really stressed him. Maybe these things just didn't get under his skin. This is not a value judgment. It's just what it was."

Peter gave Anna a sarcastic I'm-not-buying-it glare. "Okay, I hear you, but I also never thought of my mom as bossy or pushy. I don't see her that way."

"I'm not surprised. We rarely see our parents for who they are. If they don't leave memorable scars, then we grow up passing it off as a normal family life. However, you did say your mom was more the instigator, which is an interesting choice of words. You may feel that was random on your part, but things are never really random, at least not when it comes to therapy. I must at least conjecture, if not assume, that your mom had her way of doing things, and somewhere along the line your dad decided it wasn't worth the fight. He was, or is, a smart man who chose humor as a way to preserve his integrity, at least to himself. Why he chose not to fight it out with your mom on a daily basis is something you'd have to ask him."

"This feels like you're reaching, Doc." Peter squirmed a bit in the chair.

"It could be that I'm way off track. I am that other opinion you were looking for, though," she said. "Allow me to continue. You might be wondering how this plays into your current situation. Well, this is how I'd put it together. I think in some ways, your wife and your mom are very similar."

"What?" His distracted look of willful disengagement suddenly sharpened. "What's that you said? My mom and my wife are the same? What the… What are you getting at? You're saying I married my mom? Are you calling me a pervert or something?"

"No, no, no!" Anna said, blushing a conciliatory smile. "That didn't come out right." It was the response she was trying to avoid, but she'd chosen her words poorly; she muffed it. "It's sometimes necessary to make comparisons between parents and spouses. Though I know no one wants the two mentioned in the same thought. It's a delicate area to tread since the incestual implications are too close for comfort."

A sticky issue still needed to be reconciled. Peter had been *told* to get therapy; he hadn't asked for it himself. There seemed to be a power struggle, or simply an imbalance of influence in the marriage. The similarity seemed too obvious to gloss over.

Anna tried again. "The idea of mothers and wives—or for that matter, fathers and husbands—having commonality is not a shocking occurrence in psychology," she explained. "People like familiarity. Whatever traits your mom has, you're likely to be drawn to as an adult. It's all subconscious, but it's rather common. Some have conjectured that it allows us to solve the unresolved issues of our childhood. The important thing is that your wife is not your mom, so you have to find ways of relating to her that may be different from how you related to your mom."

Peter crept forward to the edge of the chair, raking his hand through his hair again. The issue was obviously getting complicated.

"So," Anna continued, "your wife has her moments when she won't budge on an issue. Maybe she's not an 'instigator' the way your mom was, but there are times when she digs in and wants things her way. I suspect she's a strong-willed individual. The coping skills you learned from your dad was not to stress things, and I wonder if not stressing the small stuff has allowed your wife to feel emboldened to fill the void. She's become more and more comfortable calling the shots. Only something isn't right anymore. Something or some list of things has been happening that you're refusing to let go of, to borrow your words. An important 'life-changing event' as you said, that should not be easily dismissed."

Anna was hoping that last line might prompt Peter to talk more about whatever the event was that had caused the problem.

"I'm guessing you're a proud man and you've drawn a line in the sand," she continued. "On some level, your morals won't allow you to dismiss this one issue, and your wife is not happy with you all of a sudden standing up to her. She's hoping therapy will convince you that you don't need to fight back so much—that maybe you'll go back to just following her lead."

The room fell back into a familiar silence. Peter's expression of curiosity changed. His vacant eyes looked lost in despair. In just two sessions, Anna had him pegged. He turned away from her, as if doing so would undo everything she'd just said. He slid back in his chair and slumped to one side as if dethroned, a condemned man guilty as charged, a glare of reproaching light streaking through the window having revealed all.

5

Children charged through the large wooden doors one after another, a prison break of young'uns with eyes darting left and right assessing the grounds for an adequate hideout. It was the usual first sign that services had come to a close at Saint James Episcopal Church. Eventually, the doors were propped open and the men and women of Portville, wearing their Sunday best, sauntered down from the narthex.

The older ladies, some with canes in hand, paused to smile up at the middle-aged pastor, who was still robed in white, green, or whatever color the season required. Each of them, in single file, reached for his hand and gave it a shake. On occasion, one leaned in to whisper in his ear. Possibly it was a compliment on the sermon, but more likely it was a criticism of how he was trying too hard to accommodate the young ones and needed to keep more to tradition.

The pastor's smile never left his face. His was a job of diplomacy. He was liked by everyone, though he never really pleased anyone. That would have been an impossible job, a Faustian bargain with certain reckoning. He knew better. The job required more people skills, not more religious fervor. The latter often had a short lifespan; congregations quickly grew tired of all the piety and felt insecure in their own spiritual states of mind. Though a congregation wanted to be led, following was a prerogative they exercised at will. If there wasn't a suitable balance, it wouldn't be long before minor pastoral shortcomings became a small rumbling tremor in the middle of the ocean—seemingly innocuous at first, but gathering strength over time until they reached the shore with tsunami-like force. Likewise, a whispering campaign of small dislikes would succumb to hyperbole and become the very reason a pastor would need to be replaced.

As Peter and I gradually made our way to the front door of the church, the high-noon sun beamed deep into the narthex and blinded us for the few seconds it took to reach the pastor. It was a light of biblical proportions, disorienting those who were eagerly formulating their critique of the sermon, a divine intervention to cleanse the soul before yielding to temptation. As we stepped through the doorway, Pastor Smith was dutifully receiving praise and condemnation with equanimity, his smile a permanent fixture of appeasement.

He turned to me as we approached. "How are you, Clare?" He was charming as usual when he took my hand in his. "How stunning you look in your peach chiffon dress. Doesn't she look just darling, Peter? My, you are a lucky man. Better keep her happy. Not likely to find another like this pretty gem."

Pastor Smith always laid it on thick but knew just how long to lather before letting go of a hand and shifting the smile to the next in line.

He looked at Peter. "How are you doing today? Thank you both for coming down for service. I know you're both regulars, but I don't take your generosity for granted."

"Thank you, Pastor. You're too kind," I said, squeezing his

hand before he could release it. "I thought your sermon was inspiring. You sure have a knack for channeling God's message."

My attempt at holding his attention yielded mixed dividends. Pastor Smith turned to Peter while still locked hand-in-hand with me.

"Thank you, Pastor, for your kind words," Peter said. "We don't deserve the flattery."

"Please, Peter," I said. "I believe Pastor and I were sharing a moment."

Pastor Smith blushed, only then realizing he had blurred the lines. His eagerness to appease stepped all over his earlier praise of my peach chiffon dress. It was only my pride at stake, but there was more to come. Unaware, Peter extended his hand as if nothing had happened. Pastor finally released my hand and pulled Peter in close for a confidential word. Pastor whispered and Peter nodded.

"...I know, they told us they were going to sell," Peter said in a voice loud enough for me to hear. "Just last month, in fact."

"Well..." Pastor continued while craning back into Peter's left ear, the side farthest from me. I watched them despite trying not to, deciphering only bits and pieces of what was said.

"I'm surprised he didn't lean on me to help out," Peter finally mumbled to himself.

I found myself staring at the two men in conversation. It was a scene reminiscent of the many times in my career when men had pulled other men aside and whispered deals that required the necessary genes to be included. The exclusivity soured my mood, and my expression probably said as much. I wanted in on the details, but we were in public and I had my wounded pride to protect. I didn't want to appear unseemly or insecure, especially not after Pastor Smith had said such nice things about me. I resigned myself to standing a few steps away, my hair pulled back in a chignon with the sun beaming down on my dress, casting me in a luminous glow. My countenance alone, a disapproving frown, said everything.

——— ... ———

The car sped down the side streets of Portville, navigating neighborhoods that told their own stories. First were the homes built in the late-1800s that bordered Saint James on the outskirts of the older part of town. They were simple two-story homes lacking the distractions of architectural triumphs or colorful adornments of seasonal flora. With no real yards to speak of, these were homes that served the basic purpose of providing a roof and four walls. An occasional American flag adorned a window frame, reminding passersby of the community's national fervor. Otherwise, these homes were a staid statement of simple means and simple tastes in keeping with the austere living of the early 1900s. The homes were laid out in a circular pattern surrounding St. James, forming the nucleus of an early Portville.

What followed was an aging industrial park with factory buildings dating back fifty or more years. Most were still in use and employed many of those living in Portville. I took in the familiar surroundings, a vivid reminder of my days in banking and development. The factory expansions and renovations still helped to keep the commerce side of Portville relevant.

I was curious to see if anything had changed, but in truth my mind was elsewhere. I was simply trying to distract myself with the past. The issue with Pastor Smith still irritated me, and I was doing my best to keep it in perspective.

A row of Victorian homes came into view, adding some much needed color after the drab brick and concrete of the business community. Homes wearing their sun-faded blues and reds and yellows with accented window frames and doors almost turned my stare into a half-smile. Soon, the Portville village storefronts were upon us. I began to fidget and squirm. I looked back at the kids at least three times, trying to find something more to distract me. Finally, I gave in.

"So are you gonna tell me about your special chat with Pastor Smith?"

Peter glanced quickly at the kids in the rearview mirror. "Now's not the best time, hon. Kids and all."

I resigned myself to a longer wait. The drive home was all of twenty minutes, and Matt and Sandy were in the back seat dutifully plugged into their iPods, listening to their favorite music. I had to admit, the appearance of distracted kids was always misleading. Although it looked safe enough to discuss sensitive issues, they were always listening.

The final meander through the last few neighborhoods began the ascent to more elaborate living. Homes were larger—stately, even. Artfully designed architecture with manicured front lawns became a common theme. In some areas, no two homes looked alike.

Finally, we made the last turn onto Beekman, and Peter slowed the car to an unnatural creep. The kids paid no mind, but I stared at him in confusion. Peter ignored me, maintaining a constant gaze at the homes across from ours. As he finally spun the car into our driveway, I saw that the "For Sale" sign across the street at Jordan and Sarah's house was gone. How long had it been missing?

My initial thought was that some kids must have grabbed it as a Saturday-night prank. That would have been unusual for our neighborhood, but I was reaching for an explanation, and my mind ran wild with possibilities. I thought maybe Sarah and Jordan had decided to hire a realtor, which would likely require a change of signs. It hadn't been that long since they'd put the house on the market. Could they have changed their minds so soon? Unlikely. Had they chosen to postpone selling for a year or so? Also unlikely. It would have ruined their finances.

We parked in the driveway and the kids immediately tumbled out. "So," I said to Peter, "what did the pastor have to say?" It came out calm and casual. I'd had my time to settle, and not a hint of eagerness was detectable.

"Did you notice the difference with the Johnsons' house?" Peter asked.

"Yes! The sign is gone. Is that what you meant?"

"Yeah." Peter got out of the car, walked around to my side, and pulled the door open. I stepped out, and we both turned to stare at the Johnsons' home. There was no car in the driveway and no evidence anyone was there.

"The sign is gone," Peter mumbled.

"Was that what Pastor Smith was telling you?"

"I'm not so sure what happened. Did Sarah say anything to you this week? Did you see her at all?"

Sarah and I usually saw or spoke at least two or three times a week, but I hadn't seen her for a while. "Come to think of it, no."

"Pastor Smith told me Jordan came to see him last week about a tough decision he had to make. He apparently was afraid of hurting our feelings with whatever that decision was."

"That doesn't sound good," I said. "I wonder why Sarah didn't talk to me. She knows we can talk about anything."

"I think she's hiding from you the way Jordan's hiding from me." Then, with a resolute nod, Peter said, "I'm gonna go knock. Wanna come?"

I nodded hesitantly. His choice of the word "hiding" circled my mind with dubious intent.

We knocked and rang the bell. No one answered. Peter peeked in the front bay window while I remained on the walkway where my heels wouldn't catch in the soft grass. "The lights are off," he reported, "but the sun is shining into the front room. The furniture is still there, pictures are still hanging, a vase with flowers is on the table. I even see magazines and newspapers strewn about. It all looks normal. Wait! There are some boxes on a kitchen counter farther back in the house. But I don't see anyone."

"I guess there's no mystery here," I said as we crossed back to our house.

Peter had nothing to add. His sour, pensive expression said enough. He was always skeptical, unwilling to accept the obvious.

I strolled into the kitchen to find Sandy making herself a peanut butter sandwich. At twelve, she already bore a striking resemblance to me. She had my shoulder-length auburn hair and round hazel eyes, but her small upturned nose was all her own. When she smiled, her eyes lit up her face and turned her fair complexion rosy. I admired Sandy's self-sufficiency. She reminded me of myself at that age. She made her own snacks, did her chores, kept her room clean, and got her school projects done on time without any parental nudging. Sometimes, I thought of her as a child on autopilot.

"I see you're making yourself a little something," I said.

"Yup, would you like one?"

"No, but thanks for offering. Can I ask you something?"

"Sure."

"Did Megan tell you anything this week at school about her family moving?"

She answered nonchalantly, dipping her knife into the jam jar. "No." The knife scuttled around the bottom of the jar, creating a cacophony of sounds as she tried to rescue the last bits of raspberry.

The kids both knew the Johnsons were planning to move at some point in time, so Sandy's indifference was no surprise.

"She wasn't in school for most of the week," she said. "Just Monday and Tuesday. She said they were taking an early summer vacation and were leaving before school let out. When she didn't show up on Wednesday, I figured they left. Why?" Sandy delicately aligned the two bread slices and cut the sandwich diagonally, as was her preference.

I hesitated. The mom in me instinctually wanted to protect her friendship with Megan. The last thing I wanted was unnecessary anxiety over a friendship abandoned, especially if no such thing had happened. "Oh, nothing really. Your dad and I were trying to catch up with Mr. and Mrs. Johnson, but they weren't home. We hadn't heard anything. Just thought I'd ask if you did. A vacation explains it. Thanks. Can I get you some milk to go with that?"

"Sure. Thanks, Mom."

Just then, Matt strolled into the kitchen, spinning a football in his left hand while gripping his iPod in the other. "Are we going on vacation?" he asked. "Florida, maybe? Or California? That'd be cooool!" As always, he spoke with an earnest smile, always hoping to steer a decision his way.

"Not this summer," I said and watched Matt's eager smile melt into a puppy-dog frown—his way of always manipulating a discussion. His antics were predictable. "We're just discussing the Johnsons and *their* summer plans."

Matt shrugged and decided to flip his interests from vacation to something more immediate and winnable. "How about a sandwich for me too, Sandy?" he said.

At fourteen, Matt was already the consummate salesman. His five-foot-nine stature was likely on its way to six feet before eighteen. Tall with long, wiry blond curls extending to his well-defined cheekbones, Matt was winsome in looks and character. He knew it, and he used it to every advantage.

"You can make your own sandwich, honey," I told him. "Stop relying on your sister to cook and clean for you."

I went soft on him, but my words still held a scent of frustration. How could you not love a son's ambition to mold the universe to his every whim? And yet, I also detected budding traits of male pride I knew would need winnowing in the years ahead, lest he become an intolerable narcissist.

"I don't mind, Mom," Sandy said. Her generous offer was to be expected. She was ever accommodating to her older brother. While they were opposites in character, with her more the introvert, Matt's gregarious nature meant she didn't have to work hard to be popular on her own.

Besides the obvious charm he spread like butter at every opportunity, Matt was a constant for Sandy. She grew up knowing him as her protector, problem solver, lost-doll finder, and someone who didn't mind keeping her company when Mom and Dad were too busy to keep them engaged. Matt had a selfish streak, to be sure, but that ended when it came to Sandy. Was it Matt, who showed an isolated generosity toward his sister for some unknown reason? Or was it Sandy—sweet, unassuming, and always generous in her own right to everyone she met? Peter and I never quite understood why they bonded so well.

"Sandy, you're too nice to your brother." My frustration was palpable, but this was an old subject, hashed over for years. It was hard to take my chiding with any real seriousness. "He has to learn to stand on his own," I added, hoping for some traction.

"Mom, this is between Sandy and me. Our sibling love runs deep. No need to interfere." Matt's tone was instructive but softened with an affectionate smile.

I wasn't sure what to say next. Matt had a disarming way of leaving one speechless; continuing the argument was pointless. He was manipulative to a science. Sometimes I just didn't know how to handle him. Standing three inches taller than me with a politician's confident grin, he was more than a match when it came to debating issues. I decided to concede the verbal rally and left.

Peter was changing his clothes in the bedroom closet when I came in and stood in the doorway. My mind now free of Matt's exploitation, the Johnson issue came bobbing to the surface.

"Well," I said as Peter pulled on a pair of jeans, "Sandy spoke with Megan at school, and it seems the Johnsons just went on an early vacation. No crime committed. I guess we're getting all hot and bothered over nothing."

I wasn't exactly hot and bothered, but I knew he was. It was generous of me, to be sure. But in my mind, it helped make up for the ill will I harbored over his secret talk with Pastor Smith.

Peter paused, one leg in his jeans, the other still out. "That's interesting. I guess the whole sign thing and his talk with the pastor could all be just a coincidence. It makes sense that if you're selling your house, you don't want buyers coming by while you're out of town."

"That's what I think."

"I still don't get the weird, 'He's got a decision to make that may offend us,' thing. What do you make of that?"

"I don't know, Peter. He's your friend. You'll have to figure that out yourself. Sarah probably didn't talk with me because there's nothing to talk about. They were planning a vacation while selling the house, and it's near the end of the school term. I'm sure she had a lot on her plate."

I hoped that would put the issue to rest, but it didn't.

Peter finished pulling on the other pant leg and followed me out of the closet. "Yeah, okay," he said. "Maybe. I hope it's nothing."

And then, standing in the middle of the room with his hands on hips, he stared at me. Or so it appeared. He seemed lost in thought, his gaze fixed in my direction. I didn't take much notice and climbed into bed with a book in hand.

Finally, he released his irritation. "I just wish he'd have called or something. Pastor made it sound like he was really troubled—about us—and we live right across the street. I don't get it. Something doesn't add up."

For all intents and purposes, I had already moved on. I opened my novel to the bookmark and ran my finger down the page like I was already lost in prose.

"Maybe," I said, as if reading aloud from my book, "but I think it's just a guy thing. You'll find out eventually and probably laugh it off."

Peter hovered. Nearly a minute passed before I finally took notice. I looked up from the book and saw he was more than just a little bothered.

I knew my point of view made sense, but apparently that wasn't good enough. Peter and Jordan were pretty tight. They shared everything. Now Peter looked like a toddler left alone in a park—abandoned.

"So, what's eating you?" I asked. "You're not buying the vacation bit?"

"No, not really. I can't square what Pastor said, and how he said it, with a sudden vacation. He made it sound like Jordan was really disturbed. Jordan went to see him for advice but wouldn't tell him what it was about. And whatever it was, Jordan was sure it was going to upset us. Now, all of a sudden, they're on vacation? My sixth sense says there's something fishy. I don't see a happy ending to this."

"I don't know. I think you're reading a lot into this."

"Well, you may be right, but the obvious isn't obvious… to me, anyway."

6

Session 3

"Welcome back," Anna said, standing behind her desk as Peter came into the session room and strolled toward the chairs.

"Hi," he replied flatly. The tone of his greeting was uninspiring. It was as perfunctory as passing someone on a sidewalk and feigning politeness.

He took the chair on the left. As usual, he was dressed neatly. His shirt was tucked, his buttons aligned, and his hair was combed. There was nothing about him to suggest a person losing control of the basics. It was the thought that registered as he looked at his reflection before leaving for the appointment. The one thing he didn't control was his face. It was a bland, neutral look more befitting a bust in a museum than a person about to bare their soul. It betrayed nothing of whatever was brewing inside.

"Sorry about the last two weeks," he said. "I needed time to process."

Two weeks since their last session. Or had it been three? He hadn't even called. He'd just no-showed. Peter wasn't sure how common that was in Anna's line of work, but he felt sure she expected some kind of excuse, something like a bronchitis or a business trip, or the more common lame family obligation.

"It's quite alright," she said with indifference. "It's important to know when and how to de-stress. So, how do you feel?"

Peter almost smirked, but he smothered the impulse. It was another classic therapist question he'd expected on the first visit, only Anna hadn't gone there. Her using it now seemed anticlimactic, even though it was probably appropriate. He had to admit, he was developing a lot of respect for her style. She was always direct, and never condescending or trite.

"I'm okay. For the last two weeks, I kind of went from thinking you were way off-base to thinking maybe there *were* some truths to realizing you were very close to my situation. Maybe even too close for comfort. I needed time to be sure I wanted to keep going down this road."

"Should I take your being here as a sign you want to proceed?"

"Yeah, I'm ready." It seemed the thing to say. Admitting there was trepidation, that his willingness to get therapy was now riddled with anxiety about what he'd find out about himself, betrayed his need to preserve his manliness. Even though he didn't define himself as a control freak, he reserved the right to appear genuine and responsible, not timid and weak.

"Are you certain, or are you a little ambivalent?"

Her timing was freakishly on cue. He squirmed and hesitated. "Well, uh… let's say I may change my mind at any time." It was a relief to be honest. At least it was some kind of progress.

"Fair enough. So do you have any thoughts you'd like to share about your last three weeks? Any conclusions you've drawn?"

The smirk he tried to smother reared its head again. She knew. Her subtle confirmation that it had been three weeks—despite him saying two—must have meant she was onto him. She knew he was hiding something. Maybe that was why she kept probing, pushing, trying to get something out of him. His lie spoke in ways he hadn't anticipated. And, of course, he didn't have an exit strategy for this predicament—nor did he know how big an issue it was in the grand scheme of things.

Peter tried not to let embarrassment get the best of him. All he could do now was plow on. "Well, Doc, I've been all over the place on how I feel. But I think I'm feeling better about the issues that brought me here. I mean, I wasn't sure if obsessing over some issues was justified. Now I'm wondering if it's actually okay to obsess. Maybe a little."

His newfound optimism surprised him. They hadn't really solved anything yet. Did he sound naïve? Was this just a mind-play on his part, something to make him feel better? He studied her response to see if he'd gotten a rise out of her, but she wasn't giving up much. She had that perfect stoic look that said nothing when she wanted to say nothing. In any other place—not in a therapy chair—a person would have showered him with accolades of support. Not here, though. Here, he was unaware if he was making any sense at all.

After what seemed an eternity, Anna finally asked, "And why do you feel okay about it today as opposed to, say, a month ago?"

"I think my wife has been on me so much about living in the past that I actually wanted to believe her and not so much myself regarding how I feel about things. What you brought up at our last session made me realize maybe my feelings have merit."

"And why do you think they have merit?"

Peter leaned forward in his chair. The more he shared, the lighter he felt, like a burden was being lifted off his shoulders. "I think I've been stressing this whole thing for five years, and if it won't leave me and I'm using all this energy to cope, then maybe it's not all a waste. Maybe I'm just being true to myself."

Anna finally smiled. "You know, Peter, I held back on saying anything about your obsessing so much because I didn't want to mislead you with my observations. Obsessing *is* a coping mechanism, so in the short term, it can be helpful, as you seem to have realized by what you just said. But you did come here to stop obsessing, and it would be reasonable to expect that any obsessing that goes on for five years and affects a marriage is worthy of some evaluation. Without taking your wife's side on this issue, I'd have to say at the least, your coming here is a reasonable effort to get to the bottom of something that needs clarifying. I think we need to get to the kernel of what's causing the obsessing."

"Only then can we tell if I'm curable?" Peter quipped.

Anna smiled again. "Curable… well, yes, I think you get the gist of it."

They sat and stared at each other for a moment. Anna seemed to be strategizing her next move. She flipped her pen back and forth around her thumb. Peter wondered where her next line of questioning—probing—would take them. He was aware of how their other sessions ended, and a repeat of that was a foreboding that hovered.

Momentarily lost in thought, Anna smiled to herself.

"I'm a handful, Doc, aren't I?" he asked.

Her smile disappeared. "I'm so sorry. I was trying to figure out what direction we should go. I'm hoping to end the session on a high note this time. The last two didn't work out well."

"Pain is gain, right?"

She nodded and paused briefly before continuing. "I notice that you use levity quite often, maybe as a way to handle stressful moments. I'm wondering how that came about?"

"I don't know. It's just who I am, I guess." He felt a tingling in his scalp. He raked his hand through his hair.

"Do you think you subconsciously pattern it after your father? I may have alluded to that possibility in our last session. You mentioned previously he used humor as well. The reason I ask is because my smile made you feel something, maybe something uncomfortable. It was unprofessional of me, and I apologize again for it. It was quite reflexive. But your response wasn't what I would have expected. I would have been quite prepared to hear a rebuke for essentially laughing at my patient's problems. You didn't do that. You internalized it then put on a smiling face to handle what should have been a stressful moment. Do you see what I'm getting at?"

"Ah, yeah. I think so." What else could he say? What did she expect him to say? He was embarrassed. Undressed would be more like it. All he could do was nod in agreement.

"The reason I bring this up is because it's an avoidance issue. You may be using levity to avoid the uncomfortable, which is usually a confrontation with someone. If you feel you disagree with someone's opinion, instead of confronting them, you avoid them, sometimes with humor. If I'm right about this, then it's certainly something we'll want to look at more closely. By that I mean the issues you may be avoiding at home. For now, how about we pivot and discuss the obsessing? I'm not entirely sure what you mean by obsessing. I'm not sure if you actually are obsessing or if your wife is the one who thinks you're obsessing and you're simply passing on her diagnosis."

It was an easy question, but he hesitated to respond. Keeping track of things was becoming a chore—Clare, levity, avoidance, and now obsession. The chivalry thing was also rearing its head again. He wanted to appear in control, and getting into the granular details of all this more than highlighted his lack of it. That lack of control meant the problem was not so much Clare but him. Sitting there whining about the details was not the manly image he wanted to project. He had already violated this male maxim in the two prior sessions. Now he found himself hesitant to appear hapless and helpless. Especially as undressed as he felt from her last comment. Another way forward would have been a timely inspiration, but one never came. Divulging all the sordid details seemed the only way out.

"Believe me, Doc, I'm… obsessing."

"In what way?"

He stalled again. The water was cold and deep, and he needed to jump. "I… I have nightmares, on and off," he finally said. "I seem to do things that intentionally upset my wife, but it's always about the same issue. And it's now five years later, and I'm still daydreaming quite a bit about things—the same things, over and over."

Anna didn't respond, intentionally slowing the exchange to a crawl. Peter expected her to pounce, but she didn't. Finally, she calmly asked, "I guess the elephant in the room here"—another pause—"is, what are we talking about? What happened five years ago that caused this obsession?"

Peter stared at her but didn't say a word. He felt the urge to look away, to avoid her eyes by gazing at the floor or out the window. But he didn't. He felt the chair soften beneath him—he was sinking, ever so slowly. His mind was playing tricks. His hands trembled as he tried to fight it by staring intently at the instigator. It was his rail to cling to, to stop sinking into oblivion. He held the stare.

"Take your time, Peter. Share whatever you feel comfortable sharing and no more."

Peter's fingers began wrestling with themselves in a feeble attempt to control his emotions. They caught his eyes and he stared at them, mesmerized but unable to stop the twisting and knotting folds of flesh. They were the outside of the churning on his insides. He sank further.

"It was a long time ago." He cleared his throat. "But, God! I remember it like it was yesterday." It was a sudden offering, but he paused again, this time looking down at the floor, rearranging himself in the chair and releasing his hand to rub his forehead. "I let someone down. Someone who depended on me. He was a friend, and… and I can't forgive myself for it. It's a monkey on my back that I just can't shake loose."

"Go on."

"That's it," he said, finally raising his head. "I'm unreliable and untrustworthy. Someone depended on me, and I let him down. Why should anyone trust that I'm the kind of person who will stand by them when they need me?"

"Is this you speaking, or your wife, if I may ask? She wanted you to see a therapist, so I just want to be straight on whose opinion I'm listening to."

"This is me talking." He was now seething with frustration. "Clare doesn't want… she's tired of me putting myself down. She thinks I'm making a mountain out of a molehill, as she puts it." He grew louder, his voice trembling with intensity.

Anna plowed on. "So you're saying you betrayed a friend in their time of need. Well, I can see being disappointed in yourself. But we've all come up short from time to time when our friends need us. We're not always strong enough to be everything to everyone—all the time. Why would you hold onto this—for five years, no less?"

Peter pressed his forehead against the heel of his right hand, each wrestling with the other, trying to banish a thought that refused to be banished. His frustration finally boiled over.

"You don't understand, Doc!" he blurted, tense and agitated. His face flushed red as he perched on the edge of his seat, his right hand now fisting clumps of hair on his head.

"Help me understand, Peter."

"It's... it's all because of *me*," he stammered. "I killed someone!"

7

"Clare! Clare!" Peter burst into the house, yelling frantically. "Where are you? Clare!"

I came to the top of the staircase to find a panting, disheveled Peter standing in the foyer, pacing impatiently. "I'm upstairs. Why the yelling? What's got into you?" I had a stack of folded clothes tucked under one arm and a clump of socks, already segregated by size and purpose, in the other hand.

"They're gone! They're gone!" he said, lowering his voice when he noticed the front door still wide open. "The Johnsons…" His breathing, anxious and heavy from racing across the street, now demanded restitution. After two sighs, he continued. "The Johnsons, they're gone."

I was looking down at the socks, satisfied that one more chore was completed, barely paying attention to him. "What do you mean?" Then, showing a little interest, I said, "They're on vacation."

"No. No. No!" he bellowed again. "They're gone, for real." He paused again to catch his breath, and a calm soon settled over him. "They moved out," he said in a more measured, deliberate tone. "Their house is empty."

I gasped, and as my hands reached to cover my mouth, the clothes I held dropped and tumbled down the stairs, unfolding in a playful display of freedom. "What... how... empty!?"

"Yes! After my run, I noticed their house looked abandoned. I had a weird feeling, so I went to take a look, you know, through the window like we did last week. All their furniture is gone. Boxes are gone. Not a thing in the house."

"Holy shit," I mumbled under my breath. I plopped down onto the top step and burst into tears.

―― ... ――

We sat in the kitchen, mourning as if death had paid a visit. We held each other's hands as if holding onto a stillness, to the past and the known. But it was an illusion. What we were truly left with was a new reality—the unknown, the uncertain, and the unpredictable.

"I can't believe this is happening to us," I groaned, realizing Peter's instincts had been right all along. "What does all this mean? What do we do now?"

He was still focused on our interlocking fingers, lost in melancholy, no doubt reminiscing about the good old days with Jordan. The sudden turn of events seemed too final to accept. "I'm not really sure," he finally said. "What's clear is that Sarah and Jordan wanted out, and they apparently didn't want anyone to know about it. I mean, it's great that a month after they decided to sell the house, they were able to find a buyer. But I just don't get all the secrecy."

A few minutes passed in silence. Peter grew antsy and went to the kitchen for a glass of water. I blew my nose, rubbed my eyes. Again, tears ran down my cheeks. I was a mess. Peter watched from the sink, his expression tightening as if the weight of something heavy was settling in his stomach.

"I just don't understand," I said, shaking my head as if signaling disapproval could right a wrong. My sadness was retreating; a tsunami of anger now gripped my emotions. "We've been their best friends for years. Why? Why would Sarah do this to me?"

"You know," he said, "it's interesting that there's no *Sold* sign up. Don't they usually put one up when a house has been bought?"

I glared at him, confused. "What? I don't know. You're asking the wrong person."

"Just wondering. The whole thing seems odd."

"Maybe if there's no realtor, there's no *Sold* sign," I said bitterly, resenting the distraction. "They cost money, don't they? What's the purpose, anyway? It's probably just to drum up more business for themselves. I'm guessing the Johnsons didn't want to advertise that they're good at selling houses."

"I think you're absolutely right," Peter said, sounding like he wanted to change the subject. "It doesn't serve a purpose when you're selling your own home. I wonder who the new owners will be?"

I looked at him with a blank stare and burst into tears.

―― ... ――

Later that morning, we went into town for groceries. It was mostly a diversion, a need to just do something to feel normal. Peter backed out of the driveway, and we took off down the block. As we turned onto the main thoroughfare into the heart of town, I rolled down the window and felt the wind against my face, my hair trailing off as if I hadn't a care in the world. I'm sure I looked peaceful, but my mind was in turmoil. I felt Peter look at me and sensed his longing for the old days when we were so carefree and in love. Back when nothing really mattered as long as we had each other.

"Penny for your thoughts?" he asked.

"I don't know. Just depressed, is all. A month ago, things seemed so perfect. Now they've all gone to hell."

My words came out mumbled. I was defeated and disinterested. Last month, my best friend was still my best friend. The cocoon of Beekman seemed invincible. All of the people and the things that mattered were in their right places. The world orbited on a correct axis. But that damn fate had flown in on a spring breeze and seeded Beekman with uncertainty. The axis had shifted ever so slightly, and that made all the difference. Things could never be the same.

"I'm sure we'll come out alright," Peter said. "I know you think I'm trivializing things, and I am upset with Jordan, but I just got a hunch that it'll all be okay. I don't know why, but I wish I could somehow convince you of it."

I didn't respond. I didn't care if he knew I heard him or not, if I was daydreaming or had tuned him out. Peter decided to leave well enough alone and just drive, which was fine by me.

The business district of Portville was three to four miles from Beekman. Its main intersections were already bustling in a way peculiar to Portville. A few shoppers were stranded on street corners waiting to cross while others meandered in and out of the local stationery store, pharmacy, or one of the few boutique shops. The town was happily too small for the large, trendy chain stores found in bigger cities. These were mom-and-pop shops, independent owners thriving off the local community.

I stared at earnest shoppers seemingly intent on filling their Saturday morning with favorite indulgences. The sight annoyed me. I shook my head. "These folks have no clue, do they? Real changes are happening in Portville, and these mindless fools have no idea that she's gone."

My voice quavered, and I held my fist to my mouth to stifle my emotions, but another wave of anger crashed again.

"Someone who used to be an important person here is gone!" I yelled out the window to no one in particular. I turned to Peter. "Beekman will never be the same, and all they care about is spending money."

I closed my eyes and allowed the sway of the car to shake my head from side to side. I could feel Peter's eyes. He'd never seen me this way, distressed to the point of lashing out at others.

A minute later, he pulled into the large parking lot of the local supermarket. I looked up in time to see someone exit the Bank of Portville, which shared the same block with the market. My eyes brightened as an idea took hold. My sour expression turned hopeful.

I turned to Peter and betrayed a sly smile. "Peter, whaddaya say we go see Sally at the bank and pick her brain on the Johnson house? Maybe she can tell us something."

He didn't need to mull it over. "I like your thinking. Let's do it."

Sally was in a corner office with clients, but it looked like things were coming to a close. They were already standing, nodding, and smiling.

Handshakes ensued, followed by Sally escorting the young couple out of her office. It appeared she was planning to go as far as the front door, but I made eye contact, and Sally said her goodbyes and turned to her old friend.

"Clare, Clare, Clare," she said in an almost singsong manner. "How are you? My, my, how long has it been? A year, maybe? Has it been that long? It was the Morgan dinner party, right? For the holidays? Since you stopped working here, you've forgotten all about us!"

Sally spoke teasingly with a wide grin. She turned to Peter, exuding even more charm.

"Peter, you haven't changed a bit, looking all tall and handsome." She leaned in to give us a brief, businesslike hug. Peter blushed, even though he knew this was all for show. Like Pastor Smith, Sally was used to lathering affection, maybe more so. They were both in marketing—one did money, the other redemption.

I also felt a little embarrassed, as if I didn't belong or was imposing. This used to be my place of employment. I was the one greeting clients, shaking hands, and giving out business hugs to my regulars. That was a long time ago—before kids, before Beekman, before everything important that would come to define me.

I cringed when Sally went on and on about my rare appearances at the bank. These were my old stomping grounds from back in the days when life was simple. When my circle of friends was totally different, when going out for drinks in tawdry bars and staying up late in Cincinnati nightclubs was the thing. But that was then. Sally was still part of that circle, and my leaving it all behind meant leaving her behind. It shouldn't have been, but moving on was an all-or-nothing proposition. That was how I saw it and how I played it. My life choices were not the kind of thing I ever doubted. I was always sure about who I was and what I wanted in life. Still, I cringed. It stung hearing the subtle hypocrisy of my allegiances laid bare in the niceties of Sally's greeting.

"So, what can I do for you fine folks on a beautiful Saturday morning?"

"Well," I said, "we were wondering if you could help us out with something. Something kind of personal?" I sounded tentative and unsure. The tables were clearly turned; I was now the client. It couldn't have been any less natural for me to be in this position. Peter must have noticed because he held my hand for encouragement.

Sally studied me for a brief moment, apparently sensing my discomfort, and replied with a very professional, "I most certainly can. Why don't you both just come into my office, and let's get to work on what you need."

Her office was a glass enclosure, with windows along the back and glass walls on every other side. When she closed the glass door, total silence prevailed. You could barely hear the traffic outside.

"You have a very nice setup here," I said, dabbling a bit in the lathering. "I envy you."

"Why, thank you, Clare. It's not a large office, but it works fine for what I do. Most times, I'm here alone. So, tell me what you need."

"We've got a peculiar situation. Our neighbors, very close friends of ours, up and left town. Quite a surprise to us… or anyone, really." My voice quavered again, and I paused to calm my emotions. "It's… it's a house across the street from us. The Johnsons. Sarah and Jordan Johnson."

"Beekman, right?" Sally asked as she turned to her computer. Though she already knew, appearing empathetic seemed the right tone for the moment. "Such a nice little community. I'm not sure of the number, but it was a sale-by-owner house. Might that be it?" She turned the computer screen for me to see.

"That's it! 1345 Beekman." My excitement was palpable.

"I'm actually surprised someone's selling on Beekman. Once you're on Beekman, you usually don't leave." Sally's business side slipped in momentarily. "However, a lot of homes are up for sale these days, what with the factory closing and the job situation. It's making for weak home values, so I hope you're not thinking of selling anytime soon."

Sally turned the computer back, pulled up another page, and began typing away, nails clicking on the keyboard at lightning speed. She ran her finger down the screen, scrolling through a spreadsheet list. "Here it is. Oh. It just sold last week, on Wednesday or maybe Tuesday. Either way, what can I tell you? Do you want to know the purchase price?"

I froze, still processing the reality, the truth of the matter. It wasn't that they had sold the house. It was that they had moved. Moved without telling their best friends. I felt the knife in my back push in deeper.

Peter noticed my blank stare and finally spoke. "Uh... what do you know about the buyers?"

"The buyers are, uh..."—nails clicking and clacking—"Jerome and Margaret Robinson. They're not from here. They're actually from right outside Cincinnati. Norwood. I think they had some issues up there a while back. Factory plant closings laid off quite a lot of people. I thought they—"

"What kind of name is that?" It came out of nowhere. I didn't know anything anymore. Things were moving too fast. I was losing control—losing grip. I needed something not to change. I looked at Sally as if she were the culprit, squinting with a raised brow of distrust.

"I... I don't know." Sally was taken aback.

It was clear our plan of sleuthing through Sally's records to find out what was happening on Beekman was no longer a secret. She was onto us. But I couldn't restrain myself. A surge of anger boiled over from within and spewed out with no filters. "So they're not from around here? They're not... one of us?" I shot back, my tone notably agitated.

"Uh, no," said Sally, sounding surprised. "I... I guess not."

"How could they do this to us?" I mumbled under my breath, still loud enough in such a small office to bounce off the glass and reverberate. Peter and Sally could hear it all, as if I was speaking with intent to be heard. "How? How? How!? It's so selfish. So selfish!"

I didn't want to believe it. My best friend. We saw the world through the same lens—shared values, shared wants, shared dislikes. It was all more than I could handle.

The last thing I remember was staring at the floor. I heard Peter's voice, but I wasn't listening. I wasn't really there at all.

The next thing I knew, I was walking toward the entrance of the bank. Peter and Sally filled the air with gratitudes.

"What are friends for?" I heard her say.

"We must have you over for dinner some time. It's been too long," Peter said, returning the kind gesture.

——— ... ———

Peter decided to skip the market on account of my altered state and headed straight home. By the time we got there, I had come around—sort of. I was certainly more animated than the catatonia I'd fallen into at the bank, although the awakening process was gradual. It started as an occasional grunt or sigh as I repositioned myself in the car on the ride home. Next were the mumbled irritations about trash containers left at the curb by neighbors. Garbage collection was the day before. It had always been a pet peeve of mine—the appearance of one's home was sacred. It reflected a belonging, a shared community value that homeowners had an unwritten but expected obligation to maintain.

By the time we pulled into the driveway, I was in rare form. I railed against everything, including skipping the store, and launched a few ad hominem attacks on Peter. His body odor, in particular, so annoyed me. He had jogged that morning, hadn't showered, and had ripened throughout the day. He was ready for harvest, and I was quite willing to cut and slash indiscriminately.

"I think we should leave the windows open to air out the car," I said with exasperation. "It stinks."

"The car? Or are we talking about me now?" Peter said, biting the bait. I'm sure he regretted it as soon as it spilled out of his mouth. He usually knew not to feed my agitation, especially in rare states like these. It was a long day, though, and I'm sure he was tired of walking on eggshells. The early morning run had likely worn off, and he was emotionally defenseless, so he jabbed back. "What's gotten into you, anyway?"

"Me? I'm fine. I'm wondering why *you* don't really care about what's going on around here."

"Look, Clare, I care. I'm pissed that the Johnsons treated us like they never knew us, that Jordan felt he couldn't confide in me, and that they snuck out of here like they were being chased. But I can't do anything about it. I'm certainly not gonna go around calling people names because of it."

"What about the *Robinsons*?" I demanded.

"What about them?" He was in full fighting mode. We sat in the car glaring at each other. He refused to blink.

"Aren't you at all bothered about who they are?"

"I'm curious that they somehow came into the neighborhood and looked at the house and we never got to meet them or even see them come and go. It's like some stealth secret operation or something."

"Exactly!" I shot back. "Exactly."

"So you see something suspicious going on, huh? Remember,

you're the one who said it's just a vacation, and the reason Sarah never called was because she was busy."

"Well, it's all pretty clear now, isn't it?"

I had the last say, but we both knew our limit. It wasn't an argument either of us could win without losing on some other level.

―― ... ――

Two days later, when Peter arrived home from work, I met him at the front door. I'd eagerly awaited his arrival. No sooner had he entered the foyer than I thrust a flyer at him.

"Look what someone put in our mailbox today," I said.

Peter put down his briefcase in the usual spot and sat next to it on the lower step of the staircase. He read the flyer once and read it again, aloud.

"Beekman neighborhood meeting to discuss 1345 Beekman. Let's take action to preserve our community. When: Wednesday, May 20, 8 p.m. Where: 1265 Beekman." Peter stared at it as if it were a language he had to decipher. He looked up at me with the sun in his eyes from the arched glass window at the top of the front door. "That's Fred's house, isn't it? What do you think this all means?"

He was blinded, but I saw clearly. He had no sixth sense about any of this. He was the innocent child wandering through life without a care in the world. I wondered when he had become so freewheeling about things. It had never been my way. It was not my instinct. I couldn't understand how we'd ended up so deep into a marriage with him ultimately going soft on me just when a crisis was upending everything we'd worked so hard for. I was growing more than just frustrated with him. Anger was creeping into the equation. Dad would never have tolerated this. Heck, if I had met this Peter years before, we might never have gotten married. I admit I couldn't help myself. I'd lost enough already. Peter's ignorance was a sign of weakness, and I lashed into him.

"What do you mean, what does it mean? It means we're gonna do something about the Johnson house. Someone finally realizes that something has to be done. We need to take action to preserve our neighborhood."

Peter looked surprised. "Finally… take action? You say that like I've been the one stalling some great plan or something."

"Well, you have to admit, none of this seems to upset you. Why should we just let anybody move onto Beekman? This is our street, and we need to protect our home, our family, our kids."

"Protect? From what? What do you think is going to happen here? This is a nice neighborhood. I know that as much as anyone. But people adapt to a neighborhood. They absorb the culture of a community and become like it. They don't change it."

"Peter, I don't think you realize what's at stake here. You're too naive. You're like a Boy Scout who's never grown up, and I, for one, am glad that Fred Mason gets it. We need to do something before our way of life is over."

8

Session 4

"Hi, Peter." Anna remained seated as she greeted him. She was eager to change something in their session, even if it was leaning superstitious.

"Hi, Doc... Uh, Anna. How's your week coming along?"

"It's well, thank you. And yours?"

"Okay, not bad, can't complain. Or maybe I can. Got an hour to spare?"

He grinned, and Anna returned a smile. She was impressed he hadn't skipped a week or two like he'd done before.

Under normal circumstances, she wouldn't let the last session lose its traction since it was difficult getting to that level of trust. Peter had proven to be quite a challenge. His deeper emotions were elusive. He circled and circled but never let go of the pool's edge.

They'd made progress, to be sure, but they'd spent too much time avoiding the real issue. He was refusing to let go. He pulled his hair, wrangled his fingers, even went catatonic at times while standing on the precipice, looking down into the deep—unwilling to leap or step or even crawl toward clarity.

Anna fully expected to peel the onion, but that metaphor was for getting to the "why" and not the "what"—she still didn't know the "what." What had brought Peter to her office aside from his wife telling him he must? Despite all that, Anna decided against the temptation to plow headstrong into the last session's revelation. She opted instead for a lighter touch, a less threatening subject matter, a gradual sinking in to the heavier, more serious topics.

"So, Peter, our last session had quite a revelation. One might say a rather difficult revelation. Was talking about it difficult for you? By that I mean, did you have any thoughts during the week you'd like to discuss?"

She had mastered the neutral. While a bit of elation and back-slapping was in order for having reached a breakthrough in the last session, you wouldn't know it from her demeanor. Despite how she felt about a patient, you'd never detect any frustration—or excitement, for that matter—in the tone of her voice, or even a wrinkle of the brow. She was rarely critical and never overly complementary, and certainly never exuberant. Sometimes patients gave her ample reasons for frustration, like when they kept repeating the same impulsive behavior that they knew would sink them deeper into a depression. And sometimes, when elation was apropos, like when a breakthrough to a deeper understanding finally surfaced for a patient, she was emotionally meager, giving only a nod or half-smile. Mostly, through the good and the bad, the progress and the disappointments, she remained neutral. She followed the maxim to never allow a patient to feel good or bad because of her emotional state of mind. Their progress needed to come from within themselves. And maybe it was because Anna was such a blank slate that Peter was prepared to engage.

"It was cathartic, I suppose," Peter answered. A pensive pause followed. "I guess it's always difficult to admit the finality of what happened. I know you know I've been skirting the issue that brought me here. We've talked about it, but we haven't *really* talked about it if you didn't know *that* detail."

"I would agree with that," Anna said. "That kind of holdout is important. It's difficult to move forward when you know we're not really addressing the full gravity of a situation. I also realize, however, that full disclosure in therapy is not like a contract situation. One doesn't start therapy and disclose everything on day one. The most painful events for us don't just surface on demand. It usually takes time to find the 'when' and the 'how.' Just finding the right words to share something that personal isn't easy."

Peter nodded. "I felt a little lighter all week."

"Good." Anna nodded, offering one of her rare, approving smiles.

"This is the first time I've ever talked about this. It's been bottled up for years."

None of this was new for Anna. After a few sessions, her patients usually began to feel the benefits of talk therapy. "Getting it out is always very therapeutic. Now, we don't have to start where we left off, though I would like to circle back and discuss with you exactly what it means, circumstances and all, about the fact someone died."

She deliberately softened Peter's words—from "killed someone" to "someone died"—hoping it might help ease him back into talking about it when the time was right. She stayed cautious for now, not wanting to press too much, too soon.

"I hope you don't mind if we go in a different direction for a bit," she said.

"I'm good with that, Doc. You're the expert." Peter crossed his legs as if settling in.

"Tell me, how do you spend your time? What do you do for fun?" The question was innocuous, but Anna had ulterior motives. She wanted to know if he had a release valve. Now that he felt he had a right to obsess, she expected more tension at home, maybe some pushback by Clare.

"Well, you know I'm an accountant. That keeps me busy enough, especially during tax season."

"You work for yourself, or in a large company?"

"I used to work for a manufacturing company in Portville, but I'm on my own now."

"How did that come about? Was it by choice?"

"Well, truth be told, the company was downsizing, and I got the axe. I initially freaked out. I went into a depression for a few months, but I got back on my feet. I restudied the basic individual tax laws and picked up a few clients in the neighborhood. They told friends, and the friends told friends. Eventually, we stopped dipping into savings. I even got lucky and picked up a few corporate and nonprofit clients with more year-round tax needs. I'm doing okay."

"Does your wife work?"

"Clare, yeah. She didn't while the kids were young, but she does now. She went back to work at the bank in town. It was where she worked before we had kids, so it was easy. She still had connections. All I can say is, when things got tight, she never hesitated to chip in."

"Well, it's nice to hear the two of you worked together to stay afloat," Anna said, aware that future sessions might offer few chances to praise Clare.

"We're a team. We can rely on each other, if that's what you mean."

"Any hobbies, spare-time activities? Do you get involved in any kind of sports?"

"Hobbies? Nah. I jog a bit, but not with regularity. It has to be nice outside. That means only half the year, and if you eliminate rainy days, overcast days, or any days over eighty degrees, you get the point. I mostly do it to get out of the house."

"Boredom?"

"Maybe. Sometimes. Sometimes I just need to get out."

"Clare?"

Peter paused but kept his gaze on Anna. "Yeah, sometimes I just need a little space."

"Well, she recommended you get another opinion, should we say? It wouldn't be a surprise that occasionally a little tension surfaces between you two."

After a momentary pause, Anna decided now was the time.

"I'd like to remind you that I'm not your marriage counselor. I'm not here to patch up issues between you and your wife. I'm here to help you help yourself. I don't know what the future has in store for you, but I want you to know if I need to make uncomfortable observations about Clare, I intend to make them. My observations, if I'm good at my job, should only be about how she interacts with you, particularly her expectations of you, anything I feel is an unreasonable stress that you may be internalizing. I feel I have a responsibility to bring these types of issues to your attention. I should not, as a professional, make blanket attacks on Clare, or anyone, for that matter. My criticisms should strictly be about her actions or comments, not about her as a person. So if you hear me say anything regarding Clare that sounds offensive, or defensive on your behalf, think first about whether my observation is about her personally or about her position on a situation. Hopefully, you'll find it's the latter. But if you do feel uncomfortable or offended in any way at any time, please tell me so I can clarify."

"Got it, Doc." Peter shifted uncomfortably in his chair, then settled down.

"So you work, and you sort of jog on occasion. Do you do anything for fun? Do you volunteer somewhere?"

"Yes, I do that," he said quickly, as if he'd just hit the jackpot.

"Yes to doing things for fun, or yes to volunteering?"

"I volunteer."

"Go on."

"One of the nonprofits I work with is a small company called the EAG. Stands for Eaton Advocacy Group. They're located in the Cincinnati area and advocate for LGBTQ issues."

"Oh, that's interesting. Have you been connected to the LGBTQ community in the past?"

"No. But I was doing the corporate taxes for Eaton, and the more I got to know the people, the more interested I got. Eventually, something came up, and they asked if I could help out. It was very therapeutic. I enjoy the people there."

"Volunteering *can* be very therapeutic. I'm glad you found that outlet. What about their issues?"

"Well, I have to admit, I really knew very little. In fact, for me, it was just another paycheck. But they're just people, you know. I don't see what everybody else sees. They struggle just like all of us, and we have our support groups, so I see no reason they shouldn't have theirs. In fact, their issues are not all that different from ours. Sometimes I tease them about that. I remind them that straight people have some of the same problems. Not everyone gets the job or the pay raise or the vacant apartment. I have to remind them that bullying is not limited to LGBTQ. Of course, I know they have a difficult time of it. This country has not been very hospitable to anyone different, be it ethnic, racial, or sexual orientation. I'm really just pulling their leg when we're sitting around having a beer or something. I've become friends with all of them. Not too many straight people are willing to work in an LGBTQ organization these days."

"Why do you think that is?" Anna asked.

"We're just too polarized in this country. People don't want to see beyond the nose on their face. It sounds cliché, but it's all about 'me' and less about 'us.' I don't know when it all happened, but we're knee-deep in it now."

"Sounds like you should be giving lectures," Anna joked.

"Nah, I get passionate sometimes about the things I care about. But I'm no soapbox kinda guy. I'm more on the quiet side. I lean introvert."

"And Clare? How does she feel about your volunteering?"

"She doesn't mind."

"She approves?" Anna pressed.

"I wouldn't go that far. She, uh, tolerates."

"Is she not an LGBTQ advocate?"

"She's, well, not *against* the group or the people behind the group. She… she sees it more as a distraction from the important things in life."

"Which are?"

"Us."

"So, anything outside of the Davidsons is energy not spent well?"

"You could say that."

"How did that realization make you feel?"

"Add it to the pile."

"So, just to be clear, you expected that she would not approve?"

"Yeah."

"But you did it, or do it, anyway?"

"Yeah."

"It doesn't bother you that your wife doesn't support you in what you consider an important activity?"

"I think a number of years ago, it might have. But now, I gotta do what I gotta do."

Anna thought that sounded flippant but decided to go along for the ride. "Well, I can see how you might feel the need to just move on with things. It's nice to hear, once again, that you value yourself enough to do things for you." She paused for a moment. It was time to probe a little deeper. "With your work at Eaton, is Clare's dismissiveness about this activity, which is something you care about, similar to her dismissiveness about the person, the friend you let down, the one you've been obsessing about?"

She was circling.

Peter started on his routine again—squirming in the chair and fidgeting with his hands. "I guess you could say so," he finally admitted.

"Would not volunteering at Eaton improve things with Clare?"

"Maybe. Probably."

"Does she ever mention the friend and Eaton together?"

"Well, Doc, to be honest, she thinks they're part of the same obsession."

Bullseye! Anna suppressed her surprise. "And you?"

"I'm just living my life. I'm doing what I wanna do."

"When you were having a tough time, trying to build your tax business, how did you go about finding these corporations and nonprofits?"

"Phone book, essentially," Peter said nonchalantly. "I found a list of businesses and looked them all up and made unsolicited visits."

"So you visited Eaton and learned all about them before you decided to work for them?"

"Before they decided to *let* me work for them," Peter corrected.

"I'm just wondering if your Eaton work is purely selfish motivation, which would be fine, or if it's possible that, at least partly, you're motivated by a passive-aggressive, nonconfrontational way of getting back at Clare for not supporting you in the first situation—the friend. Any thoughts?"

She knew this was a lot to take in; it was a connecting of dots he had never contemplated.

He slouched in his chair, his right hand propped under his chin with his forefinger tapping his cheekbone, Rodin's *Thinker* come to life.

"I… I'm not sure," Peter finally said. "It's not obvious to me how this is doing something to get revenge on Clare."

"Well, you chose Eaton before they chose you. There may be a reason someone with no family or friends who are LGBTQ, at a time when people don't see beyond their nose, as you say, would choose a group that is focused on being there for others, for being reliable and trustworthy for people in need. That reason may be to relive the incident, over and over, and this time, get it right. You said it's therapeutic, and I don't doubt it, especially if it's helping confirm that you *are* reliable and trustworthy. This is a coping mechanism, to be sure, but there's nothing wrong with it. The problem is that the one person you're relying on for validation isn't buying it, and that person is Clare. What's more, it seems you may be torn between wanting her validation and wanting, possibly, to just irritate her."

Peter heaved a big sigh. A simmering tension was clearly building during Anna's summation. "I'm having trouble following you, Doc," he said, his bemused look now also betraying exasperation. "You're saying my volunteer work is good for me, but you're also saying I'm doing it for revenge, to purposely frustrate my wife. It seems it can't be both."

"It can. Take my word for it. We're complicated beings, and we often have conflicting reasons for doing what we do in life. In this case, if I'm correct, this one activity accomplishes two important goals for you. The crisis event is an obsession you need to set right. Someone died, and that's tragic. It calls out for redemption. We can address whether you really are the one responsible here, but it's clear you feel responsible, or at least partly so. On the other hand, your wife doesn't share your values, doesn't share your compassion. This is a central part of our being. It's who we are. When Clare dismisses your responsibility for the tragic event, she is, in essence, dismissing your humanity. That's a heavy burden to bear, especially coming from your wife. It's no surprise that a part of you needs to push back. And you're doing it by continuing to volunteer at Eaton, knowing she disapproves."

"Well, maybe I should stop doing the Eaton work if I'm using it as a weapon," Peter conjectured. "It doesn't seem to be all that therapeutic since I'm not really getting any better. If what you said is true, that I might have subconsciously taken the job to relive the crisis event, to give to people in need to make up for when I didn't give in the past, then why am I still obsessing?"

"A good question. An excellent question, actually. I can't open a book and turn to a page and find a pat answer. People are complicated. It could simply be that you're waiting for your wife's validation, which may never come. It could be that the event was tragic enough for you, that you will struggle with this guilt for some time, maybe your whole life. That sounds horrible, but people can harbor a dark past and still move on and have a fulfilling life. There are many soldiers who return from war who did horrible things they were told to do, things they knew they had to do to survive, and they come home and go on with their lives. There's a dark spot somewhere deep they never want to talk about, but you'd never know it by how they live their lives."

Peter's vacant stare locked on Anna. She wondered how much of what she'd just said had registered with him. He slouched deeper into the chair, looking defeated. "Where do I go from here?"

"I think you should continue to volunteer. You like what you do, you have friends there, and you're making a difference in people's lives. There's nothing more noble than that. It's consistent with your humanity, so you're in sync with yourself. It's your balance. The challenge for you will be to learn not to depend on your wife's validation. You'll also need to confront the issue with her directly—without humor, otherwise working at Eaton might always be in part just to spite her. You should have no reason to believe she can't support you if she feels your motives are sincere and not part of some obsessive distraction."

"And what if she still doesn't?" He looked defeated before he'd even started. It seemed he had little confidence in Clare making any changes.

"Then that's her issue, not yours."

"Well, Doc, I see you're full of optimism today. I'm glad I didn't skip this session." Anna smiled. "There is one thing I want to make clear," Peter added. "Today sounds like a lot of heavy lifting—for me. But this thing about my possibly not being responsible, forget it. I was there. I know." He paused, noticing the slight tremor in his hand. "I could have and should have done more. Things didn't have to turn out the way they did." He looked down at the floor and then slowly looked back at Anna. "I have blood on my hands, and it's nothing like going to war. People sign up for that. They confront that. What I did is like turning your back when the enemy's approaching. It's cowardice, plain and simple."

Anna remained silent for a while to let Peter recover. She sensed he was pushing himself beyond his comfort zone. "Fair enough, Peter. I won't deny your stepping up and owning your actions. But, if you'll allow, let me share a different perspective on this. There are people who do things and have no remorse, and there are people like you who are confronted with a crisis that none of us ever want to confront, and we sometimes fail. But we have remorse, and that remorse makes us a better person. It makes us do better things and touch other lives. I believe in redemption because without it, life isn't worth living. Let's face it, we're all doomed to failure for one thing or another. I know your one thing or another is pretty serious—tragic, even. But that's the beauty of redemption. It doesn't ask the *what*. It asks the *how* and *when* and *where*. How are you going to make a difference from now on, when are you going to act, and where will that action be? Redemption is about ownership and action. It's about moving forward, while not denying the past, but still wanting to do better. It doesn't matter what it was. It matters what you do with it."

Peter was now the one smiling. He sat up, fully engaged as Anna shared her perspective. "Talk about a soapbox, Doc. I think *you* need one. That was pretty good stuff. I hear you. Those are kind words from your mouth to my heart. I just need to get my mind around it." His need for levity was palpable. Anna could feel it.

"It's work, Peter, hard work. And it takes time, sometimes a long time. In this business, you don't measure success by time. You measure it by daily, incremental progress. Sometimes it's two steps forward and one step back. Sometimes it's two or three steps back.

The hope, the goal, is to have more steps forward than backward. And if you're functional, able to carry on with healthy family and work relationships, then we have all the time in the world."

She smiled reassuringly, quietly pleased the session had shown progress and ended on a gentle note.

9

Two tense days passed in the lead-up to the meeting. While Peter was in purgatory, I was excited—so much so that I unknowingly gave him a reprieve of sorts. The small, and not so small, irritations that had piqued my discontent with him went unnoticed. The marital divide had been put on hold. My lack of outward frustration with his tepid concerns about Beekman's fate was all the evidence he needed to know I was pleased with the plans afoot.

For him, it was all eggshells. He went jogging both days but apparently couldn't break the grip of foreboding about the meeting. Dinner conversations might have been the only respite. It was that last bastion of family dialogue where anything could be said, and everyone had an opportunity to speak their mind.

Matt and Sandy were a bright, witty duo that didn't easily bite on a parental offer to converse. The subject had to have more than just a teen perspective for them to emerge from their shell of adolescent preoccupations.

Often, I would ask about a teacher of Sandy's that Matt had when he was in her grade. I would bait them with who had the more difficult midterms or term papers. The kids eventually bit, and the conversation would devolve into a revelation of funny stories like, "Remember that time when—" or "I hated when Mrs. Holbrook always—"

Peter could reliably angle in a football-related event, either a game they'd watched recently or one of Matt's own games. It all served to lighten the mood. But not today. Peter's dour mood must have finally rubbed off on me, because try as we may, our knack for engagement missed the mark.

Whatever conversation started ended just as quickly. A simple "yeah" or "nah" or "I don't know" seemed to bring any parental probing to a quick conclusion. We suffered through it as our meal slipped away in total silence. Peter and I caught each other's glances. A painful look said, "I can't wait till this neighborhood thing is all over and we can get back to normal."

I sensed Peter knew me well enough to know I wanted the best for the kids. That there was no ill intent, no spite for anyone in particular, despite my recent frustrations. I was just a mama bear protecting my cubs. And it's true, I considered him naive in his belief that Beekman would survive whatever lay ahead. Truth be told, we probably still had a nagging pessimism about each other, a doubt that lingered in the air between us.

After dinner, with the kids firmly occupied cleaning up the kitchen and tending to homework, Peter and I strolled the block or so to the Masons' house. The evening air was warm and calm, and the sun shone near the horizon, blanketing the neighborhood in a golden hue. The smell of fragrant hibiscus from a neighbor's front garden wafted past us as we noticed a few other couples also making the trek. I wondered if other homes on Beekman were fraying at the edges over the Johnson conundrum. We gave a perfunctory wave and smile as we all slowly converged on the only brick ranch-style house on Beekman.

The Masons' home was adorned with a typical color-splashed

flower bed, a perfectly manicured lawn, and a fashionable deep-red front door featuring a fleur-de-lis glass inlay. Phyllis Mason greeted us at the entry, and we joined what appeared to be a friendly neighborhood social. It seemed we were one of the last to arrive. Our ten-minute fashionable lateness was actually very late compared to the many couples already in attendance. What we both expected to be a somber discussion of Beekman unity was instead lively clusters of nodding smiles and backslapping laughter, with everyone enjoying their choice of wine or beer and nibbling on decoratively arranged meat and cheese charcuterie. For those not able to dine in advance, something could be found to hold them over.

"Wow," I said. "Now this is how you throw a block party."

"The Masons always do it right," Peter said. "No matter the cause, their functions always have that special… something. Something special. What am I trying to say here?" He looked to me for help.

"Je ne sais quoi?"

"Yeah, that." He grinned.

I shook my head and rolled my eyes. "I'm glad you're enjoying yourself, and you've only just arrived." Indeed, for a moment there, I think Peter had forgotten this wasn't just a social outing.

We studied the room to find a grouping suitable to our respective energy levels. I sauntered over to two other neighbors from our block on Beekman.

"Hi, Clare," Maggie said, "so glad you could come tonight. I didn't think you would."

"Hi, Maggie, so nice to see you too. I didn't realize we were late until we walked in. I guess this issue has everybody on edge."

"That, or everyone loves a Mason party," added Alice.

"So, ladies," I asked, "what's new with you two? Any summer vacation plans?" While I saw them both at least once a week, the setting begged for a formal start to the conversation.

"Dennis and I are taking Jeffrey to Disney World next month," Maggie said.

"Ah, the Happiest Place on Earth. Matt would love to join you. He keeps begging for an adventure somewhere, anywhere but here. Maybe we can work something out," I said jokingly. "We have no plans. I think Peter is a little nervous about the plant closing and what it may mean down the line. He says he's secure in his job, but I think he's hedging his bets by keeping our expenses less indulgent. I guess it's the prudent thing to do."

"Maybe a driving trip for a few days up to Lake Erie would be a nice compromise," said Alice.

"Problem-solver Alice," I replied. "You know you're our favorite travel agent, therapist, anything the situation calls for. I think that's a great idea. I'll start campaigning as soon as the kids get out of school. It will definitely be nice to get away for a while. The stress is killing me."

"Now, now, Clare," Maggie said soothingly, "things will be okay. Just wait and see."

"How can you be so sure? It's really out of our control at this point, isn't it? I mean, I really want us to do something about the Johnson house, but sometimes I just don't know. Peter is totally disinterested, so I'm trying to keep up a strong front."

"When did they actually move?" Alice asked.

"Yeah, when *did* that happen?" I added.

"I'll tell you something funny," Maggie said in a half-whisper. "I heard a truck driving down our street that Monday night, a couple weeks back. It was three in the morning. I was up to use the bathroom, and coming back to bed, I heard a gear grinding noise of a truck driving by. I would have looked out the window, but our bed is on the opposite side of the room, and I figured it'd be gone by the time I could find out. At the time, I thought it weird for Beekman, you know. But it was a truck, so I didn't think anything nefarious was afoot. Now I think that may have been them, the Johnsons, making their grand escape."

"My Sandy told me Megan went to school that Tuesday, but maybe that was a front, a ruse, intending to throw us all off. I was so upset when I found out they snuck off. I couldn't figure out when. Peter and I checked their house on Sunday, and all the furniture was still there. By Saturday, it was empty. I was so depressed and angry with Sarah." My voice betrayed a seething disappointment.

"Sarah told me a couple weeks ago they were taking a long summer holiday," Alice said. "Naturally, I tried to get details, see if I could make any suggestions. Sarah was all mum. She beat around the bush without giving any details. 'Oh, our plans haven't been firmed up yet. Oh, we're just gonna wing it. We may go west, or maybe east.' She was all over the place. I figured they simply hadn't planned it yet. Little did I know."

"That was all a lie," Maggie said. "Who takes a long trip when their house is up for sale? That's crazy and too expensive. Jordan lost his job, for heaven's sake. They're living off savings, and Sarah spins tales of leisurely summer holidays. That's rich—really rich."

I smiled at Maggie's pithy comeback, especially knowing I had fallen prey to the same delusion. My mood had mellowed to the point I could laugh at myself. I was halfway through a glass of chardonnay and was finally feeling at ease. Something about Maggie's frankness appealed to me. Unlike Peter, who was too analytical, Maggie got straight to the point. Making the comparison reminded me I was not there alone.

I glanced around the room to find my other half and was pleased to see he was happily engaged by the unlit fireplace, leaning on the hearth with his obligatory bottle of beer. His grouping had Maggie's husband, Dennis, and Scott Hildebrand, the neighborhood pediatrician. I figured with Peter's wide grin and occasional laugh, they were probably discussing sports or some other guy talk, not the Johnsons. It put me even more at ease. Peter was happy, at least for a while. For one night—maybe.

I turned my attention back to the clan. I so needed this night to lean on my *other* best friends. "Hey, you guys have any idea what Fred has up his sleeve about the Johnson house? You know Fred. He doesn't just gather people up to take a poll. He has something in mind, I'm sure of it."

"I'm with you on that," Maggie said. "He can be a little cagey sometimes, like he always has a secret agenda. But with this whole Johnson house thing, I think we ought to let the rottweiler off the leash."

Alice and I grinned while holding our wine glasses aloft for a silent cheer.

"Where are your husbands on this?" I asked. "Peter is kind of noncommittal. He thinks we're making a mountain out of a molehill. I told him he's too naïve, that we need to protect our neighborhood."

"Dennis and I are on the same page," Maggie said. "Block the sale or do something until we know just who these people are. I wish we could form a block association that required membership. Like some of those condos in the big cities, where you need to apply and be interviewed by a committee. That's what we need: a Beekman committee so we can have our say."

"George and I haven't really talked much about it," Alice said. "But we see eye to eye on almost everything. He was excited about tonight, but I think that was mostly just to get out and have a beer with everyone. He's such a socialite. It's a good thing we have kids.

Otherwise, he'd be pushing to go out every night. That man never seems to age."

"That's because you're doing all the work around the house. Raising kids is no walk in the park, Alice, and George doesn't help you nearly enough." As always, Maggie's direct candor shone through. Alice and I knew we could count on her to speak her mind no matter what the situation.

I looked around for George, and sure enough, he was happily engaged with Fred Mason and a couple of other neighbors. I happened to notice Fred pull away from his group and head toward the bay window. Once in position at what looked like a perfect spot to address the crowd, he tapped his glass delicately with a spoon that he had hidden in his pocket for just the occasion. The man was organized.

Ting, ting, ting.

"Can I have everyone's attention for a moment? Phyllis and I are very pleased with such a strong turnout from Beekman. I hope you're all enjoying yourselves. Enjoying what makes Beekman the pride of Portville. This..."—Fred spread his arms in reference to the crowd sitting and standing before him—"...is what makes our little community special. This is what we should not take for granted. We have every reason to be proud of our neighborhood, and there's no shame in wanting to protect it. Look around you here." He gestured left and right with his wine glass hand. "These are the people we share our lives with. Our children build lasting friendships from this neighborhood. Our very culture and way of life begins and ends here."

Fred was a portly fellow in his mid-forties, about five-eight. His receding hairline and graying temples belied his youthful vigor and gave him an authoritative presence. He was used to being in control of neighborhood activities, or at least having an important say in how things were going to shape up. His wife, Phyllis, was likewise a proud and direct woman who spoke her mind freely. While some may have thought a go-getter like Fred would have married someone more passive, someone less inclined to challenge his whims, he'd married a woman very much his equal. His law practice thrived despite economic hiccups that threatened Portville; Phyllis sat on the Portville city council for several years, had a failed run for state office, and was now the principal at Portville High.

Now Fred pointed his wine glass hand to the floor in front of him. "We have an unprecedented situation brewing here on Beekman that requires equally unprecedented resolve to protect what we hold dear. The Johnsons were forced to sell their house—a distressed sell, I might add—and we were all caught unawares."

"He screwed us!" someone yelled from the back of the room.

"I won't argue with that sentiment," Fred responded quickly, trying to tamp down any chance of the infection spreading. "As I said, we were caught unawares, but we need to act quickly if we're to prevent irreversible consequences."

The room stirred with scattered mumbles and a few nods. Phyllis stood in the back of the room closest to the kitchen, ever ready to juggle the hosting job with emotional support for her husband. She stood firm, arms crossed with a smile of approval.

"So," Fred continued, "I took the liberty of doing a little investigating."

Maggie nudged Clare. "See what I mean?" she whispered. "Let the rottweiler do what he does best."

I smiled back at her. "Touché," I whispered in approval.

Fred's eyes canvassed the room as he laid out the details. "I asked a contact of mine in Cincinnati to look into this Jerome Robinson, the listed buyer of the Johnson house." He glanced down at a paper that had all the particulars then returned to canvassing.

"Here's what we know. He's a middle-aged man with a wife, Margaret, and one child. He's an electrical engineer and was recently hired by the McGuire Corporation. My guy staked out his house to get a look at him, and this Jerome Robinson appeared to be a well-groomed, professionally attired man living in an apartment with his family just north of Cincinnati."

"Okay, so what's the rub here?" Dennis grumbled from the hearth. "Everything you said sounds pretty decent."

"You're right, Dennis," Fred said, "all does sound good. There's one additional detail, though. The Robinsons are Black."

"African American Black?" someone called out.

"Is there any other kind?" Dennis asked.

"Well, there's also Caribbean Black and even African Black," someone else offered.

"Same thing," came another voice.

"I think we all get the gravity of the situation," Fred quickly cut in. "Now, we're all good people here, and we mean no ill will to anyone. But there's no reason to experiment with our community. Like I mentioned earlier, our way of life begins and ends here, on Beekman."

The room fell silent for what seemed an eternity. I scanned the faces for Peter. We both caught each other's eyes simultaneously—two hearts seeking refuge. Or so that was my first thought. But Peter's expression changed, and my worst fears were realized.

I hoped he was going to finally get onboard with the rest of Beekman, but his look said otherwise. He was actually in shock. Was it Fred's investigation of the new neighbors, or was it what people in the room were saying in response? I didn't know. But the look on his face meant one thing for certain: The divide between us would only get worse.

I looked away, pretending to appear distracted by something

else in the room. His earnest stare was too painful to watch.

"This can't be good for property values," Maggie said. I supported her with a quick rub of her shoulder. My eyes were again drawn to Peter, but he turned away in apparent disgust.

"So what are our options?" someone else asked.

"Well," Fred began again, "I think a reasonable approach is to keep things professional and courteous. I suggest we make an offer on the house, a generous one. Maybe fifteen, twenty percent over the Robinsons' total expenses in this matter. I believe reason will prevail. I'm certain, with the right approach and a generous offer, the Robinsons will take the money and consider it a quick investment turnaround. Not many people make forty to fifty thousand dollars in one month. There's no reasonable person that would turn that down."

"And if the Robinsons don't bite?" came a skeptical query.

Fred's eyes tracked to the voice with an instinctive look of disapprobation. The outburst, of course, had weakened his authority, but he was too late in identifying the culprit. "There's no reason to get ahead of ourselves here. I deal with contracts and negotiations all the time," Fred quickly explained. "If you treat people with respect and courtesy, and if you especially make the terms very favorable to them, well, it's a win-win. Happens all the time. Basic contract law 101."

Peter abruptly stormed out of the room, thrusting his glass at Phyllis with a, "Here!" I assumed he'd gone to the bathroom since he walked past Phyllis and the kitchen and was soon out of sight. The front room continued despite the sudden awkward departure.

"That's an expensive proposition," came a voice.

"Isn't that a bit extreme? I mean, isn't there another way, a less expensive way?" Dennis asked.

"Folks," Fred said with a calm, convincing tone used by

politicians trying to win your vote, "you have to trust me with this. If there's too much back and forth in this negotiation, we'll lose. The Robinsons will get frustrated and fall back on their original plan, which is to move onto Beekman. We need to be quick, decisive, and generous. Very generous. The more generous we are, the more sincere we look. And we are sincere here, aren't we?"

"Sounds more like we're desperate," a voice chimed in. "Maybe we can handle it another way. Maybe we send a couple of guys over to Cincinnati to pay the Robinsons a visit. You know what I mean. There's more than one way to convince a man."

"We don't want Beekman to become a target," Fred shot back, his frustration now on full display. "If we handle this in a rash, impetuous way, we run the risk of retaliation from all sorts of people. The evening news may show up interviewing our kids one day while we're at work or something. Imagine how embarrassing that would be. Imagine a camera crew greeting you on the steps of Saint James. The Feds could also get involved if this leaks out. There's a Fair Housing Act, you know. Or worse, even—Beekman's on the map. What's to prevent friends and family of the Robinsons from coming to pay *us* a visit, only not a friendly one. You know what I mean. It goes both ways. We have family at risk as well. And these are not the lynching days where you can just do what you want and they'll be too scared to retaliate. We have to be calm, respectful, professional—"

"And weak," another voice finished.

Fred was losing grip. The meeting was spiraling out of control, and his ego would not abide it. "Okay," he interjected before another outburst could claim real estate in the room, "who here has a state license that certifies them to work?"

Half the room raised a hand.

"I'm looking around at the hands that went up and you know

what I see?" Fred paused for effect. "I see a few medical licenses at risk after a felony conviction. Physicians and nurses can't have felony charges against them. Same with teachers, bankers, lawyers like myself—you get the point. There are some engineers here, too. If you work for the city or state, then your state license is also at risk. Folks, again, I say we have to be subtle here, very subtle. There's nothing wrong with a group of people making a counter-offer or, in this case, offering to outright buy any house anywhere. There's nothing illegal about it. I know the money thing is an obstacle. How do fifteen to twenty couples collectively buy a house? Well, I've done my homework. That's why I invited you all here. I've already spoken to my contacts at the Bank of Portville, which is how I learned of the Johnson sale."

I was listening but perked up even more when I heard Bank of Portville. Sally Jennings had likely had another visitor that Saturday.

"For us to make an offer," Fred continued, "all we'd have to do is divide it twenty ways and pay five percent of that amount as a down payment. The remainder would simply be guaranteed by the equity in our homes. It's really not a lot of money we're talking about. You could even take out a second mortgage on your home to cover all the expenses. A four-hundred-fifty-thousand-dollar offer, divided twenty ways, amounts to twenty-two thousand dollars per couple. Five percent down is just over a thousand bucks. A second mortgage can cover that thousand, and any mortgage payments, until we sell the property. That's essentially no out-of-pocket expenses. It's just signing a few papers."

I thought the logic of Fred's argument was airtight. But the room was filled with blank faces that seemed not to get it, and Fred knew it. He looked deflated. Phyllis, from her defensive position as rear guard, stood in the back of the room with her arms crossed, looking every bit the sentry and standard-bearer. Seeing her husband's growing dejection, she unfolded her arms and stood with her hands on her hips, glaring at the room with frustration.

"What's wrong, people?" Phyllis chided as she stepped into the center of the room, replacing the soft touch with a strong slap in the face to get through to them. The feeling in the room said they were all in agreement to do *something*, so half the battle was done. "Does someone have a better plan? Did you folks come here just to sing 'Kumbaya'? I thought we all knew we had a serious issue. All the families on Beekman are sitting right here in this room. That means there's not a person on Beekman who disagrees. You all know we have to do something. As Fred said, you can do it like the old days and probably end up getting arrested and embarrassed in front of your kids and the rest of the city, which I think is a stupid way."

Her eyes moved across the room as she regarded everyone present.

"That's right," she continued, "it's stupid. And I, for one, am willing to call a spade a spade. Or there's a smart way, a twenty-first century way, to make it happen. That means hiring a lawyer, private detective, and a bank loan officer. Done, done, done. All the heavy lifting is done. We've done all the hard work, and we're serving this horrible situation with all the problems solved up on a platter. All you have to do is fill in the blanks and sign on the bottom line. We're all sticking our necks out a bit here, but everything we're suggesting is legal. We don't even know if the Robinsons will accept the offer. They may not, as some of you have expressed. In which case, we'll need a plan B, a reasonable one."

"What will that be?" Dennis asked.

"Well," Phyllis said, "we'll have to meet again to decide. It may be that we lose this whole thing, and we'll have to live with the consequences. But I for one want to know I've done everything I can—everything I *legally* can—before I'm forced to accept a reality I don't want."

Phyllis looked around at everyone. Expressions varied—a furrowed brow of skepticism, a half-smile of tepid commitment, or a rebellious failure to make eye contact. Faces tell stories, and these faces seemed to be softening up. A few nodding heads and some whispering to folks left and right was much better than the blank, staring faces from just a few minutes ago.

Driving it home, she said, "Come on, guys! Let's stick together on this. It's doable, *and* it won't interfere with our day-to-day lives."

Fred stood quiet for a minute, allowing his wife's appeal to marinate. It was clear that Phyllis was the real rottweiler in the family; Fred was more the poodle. The thought made me smile, which I quickly covered by kicking back the remains of my chardonnay.

"So," Fred finally said, "we'll make an offer. If they take it, great. If they don't… well, we'll cross that bridge when we get to it. On the table in the foyer is a manila envelope with your name on it. I had the bank prepare the necessary loan forms in advance. It's a simple form to complete since they already filled in names and addresses, all the stuff that's already in the public records. The respective loans are essentially all preapproved. It's really a small amount for each of us, so the bank is willing to cover it without any credit checks. And, just to put everyone at ease about tonight, we won't pull the trigger until we hear from the Robinsons. Pardon the choice of words," he finished with a grin.

Peter had returned to the room but remained on the periphery by the kitchen. He stood where Phyllis had earlier watched him storm out. It seemed he'd caught the last bit about bank forms and pulling triggers, and Fred's grinning dismissal of it. The room slowly began to murmur, then whisper, and eventually a regular tone seeped back into many of the conversations.

I turned to Maggie and Alice and offered to refill their wine glasses. They were both ready for something to take the edge off, and wine bottles had been strategically placed within arm's reach all over the room. I finished by topping off my own, and we all cheered to less stressful times.

Peter approached me from behind, but Maggie's periscope warned, "Possible enemy at six o'clock."

I turned to greet him with a smile and a kiss on the cheek. The meeting was successful for me, which meant it hadn't been for him. I knew that and wouldn't rub his nose in it. I simply hoped that in time he would come around. For now, my strategy would be to disarm him with nonchalance and distractions. Since there really wasn't anything for us to actually do, I felt there was no reason to keep the subject alive. I would let it just fade into the background.

"So," Peter said, his irritation as palpable as scales on a crocodile, "looks like you kind of expected all this." His right eyebrow lifted with skepticism.

I took a few steps away from my drinking buddies and glanced around the room. "I have to say, I didn't expect such a turnout, and I certainly didn't expect such strong feelings. You are right, though. I did hope something could be done about this. I just want it all behind us." I leaned into him with one hand on his shoulder, the other holding onto the chardonnay. "Can we just agree to let this whole thing pass? We're not doing anything illegal. And actually, we're not really doing *anything*. For now, anyway."

"Clare," he said, "let's be real with each other. I think it's what you do best, right? I'm making no promises about how I'm going to react to all this because it's all new territory for me. And not to be a killjoy or anything, but there's a difference between an illegal act and an immoral one. Some people are bothered only by the former. You know me well enough by now to know I put a lot of weight on the latter. In fact, I know you do too. So I'm hoping that our values will prevail in this matter. Moral values, that is."

Peter slipped out from under my hand on his shoulder and wandered back to Dennis and Scott, taking up his former position listening to Dennis pontificate on some order of business. He'd had a few drinks by now, and you could hear everything he had to say.

"Did you see that special on Reggie Brown?" Dennis asked Scott. "Man, oh-man! That guy is a beast. I'm telling you, no one runs like he does. It's in the genes. I don't care what anyone else says. That guy was bred to run."

"He is fast," Scott murmured, seemingly hesitant to join the point of view.

"I mean, come on, you're a doctor—a scientist," Dennis said. "You know these things better than I do. There's no way you can tell me that one of ours here in Portville could ever run like that guy. I hope we can draft him for our own Cleveland Browns. They'll never make the playoffs with the guy they have now. He just doesn't have what it takes."

"Isn't he from the same town Reggie is from?" Scott asked.

"I know, I know. I think that Archie Sanders guy is done, though. Used up. Like a horse that was run too hard and doesn't have anything left. You need a new steed in there. And yes, maybe from the exact same breeder." Dennis chuckled. Scott smiled along. "What do you think, Peter? You're a football man. Reggie Brown? The proverbial RB at Ohio State. Running-back extraordinaire. Is he not the greatest?"

Peter looked no more interested in the subject matter than Scott. He glanced about the room and caught me gazing in their direction. "Sure," he said, "I think he's pretty good. Not sure if he wants to stay in Ohio, though."

"Why not?" Dennis asked. "He's got his people up there in Cleveland. He'd feel right at home." Peter sighed. "What, you don't think we need RB on our team?"

"I just find this topic ironic, given the meeting we're in and the plans afoot." He quickly glanced back at me. "If this guy Jerome Robinson was Reggie Brown looking to buy here on Beekman, would we be meeting like this?"

"Hell, I'd buy the house outright and give it to him, if he played for us," said Dennis.

"Right! Exactly. A little hypocritical of us, don't you think? Complaining about this guy who's highly educated and successful in his own right, but turning a blind eye to someone like Reggie Brown."

"So you think Reggie Brown wouldn't be a good mix for Beekman?" Dennis asked. "I can respect that."

"No!" Peter said. "I think both Reggie Brown *and* Jerome Robinson would be fine on Beekman."

"Ah, I see. So you're in favor of this Jerome guy?"

"As you are with Reggie."

"Well, come on, Peter. A guy's gotta have his allegiances, right?" Dennis patted Peter's shoulder with his beefy hand in a familiar offering of friendship and communal values. "You think we ought to roll out the red carpet for this Jerome Robinson? Welcome him and his family to the neighborhood? Throw caution to the wind and all? Is that right?"

Peter looked to Scott for moral support, but Scott fidgeted and turned away. Peter looked back at Dennis's large, cherry-red face. Dennis wore a grin from ear to ear, as if he had settled all the world's angst and was delighted with himself.

"Fair is fair," Peter said. "If Reggie is good enough, Jerome should be more than good enough."

"Well, you're entitled to your own opinion. I won't begrudge you that. A man's gotta stand up for what he believes. Right, Scott?" Dennis said, and Scott nodded in affirmation. "I guess it doesn't hurt to make an offer on the house. After all, it's just a business proposition, right? It happens all the time, just in different scenarios. Take for example a business that doesn't want competition in their community. They may buy the only lease space available to prevent a competitor from getting a foothold. And landlords always reserve the right to rent to whomever they want. I mean, it may be a legal slippery slope in some communities, but sometimes it's just hard to tell. My cousin in New York said for many years, some neighborhoods wouldn't let you rent or buy if you weren't the right nationality. Italians didn't want Poles or Greeks, and vice versa."

"Something tells me that Blacks weren't wanted by any of them," Peter interjected.

"That may be," Dennis said, "but I suspect that Blacks weren't too keen on outsiders either. They may have liked their community just the way it was."

"Makes sense to me," Scott said, finally offering an opinion. "I'm not a big-city guy, but I like living with people who think the way I do, whose family values are similar to mine and like my kind of music. And yes, they must be an Ohio State or Cleveland Browns fan." He grinned.

"Absolutely," Dennis added. "Well said."

Peter looked around to see if anything had changed since he'd stormed out earlier. The crowd was thinning; some had already left. Those that remained were pouring themselves more wine. He noticed I was still drinking with my threesome but was mostly looking in his direction, hanging on his every word. My nonchalance plan wasn't going too well.

"Nothing you guys have said is new to me," Peter said. "I've heard it all before. Blacks don't want to live in integrated neighborhoods, and nobody likes strangers in their midst. Maybe I'm overreacting. It all seems benign. But is it? I think this sophistry is all one sided." He turned to Scott. "So what if the Robinsons do move to Beekman? And what if, say, they come to you as a pediatrician? What are you going to do with them sitting in your office?"

"I don't get it," Scott said. "They're patients. I'd care for them."

"Oh, so you don't see any problem trying to keep them out—property values and family values and all the stuff people are talking about here—but making money off them in your place of business?"

"Well, I'm a doctor. It's what I do. If they have the insurance, then I have the time. Same as anyone else."

"And if they have the money and the desire to live on Beekman, is it still 'same as anyone else'?"

"Well, I think you're twisting things around a bit, aren't you? I mean, one is a place of business, as you said. The other is my home—my family. A guy's gotta draw the line somewhere, right?" Scott looked to Dennis for support.

"I'm with you on that," Dennis said.

"And Dennis," Peter pressed, leaving him little time to get his bearings, "if the Robinsons show up with a five-thousand-dollar order at your lumber yard to renovate their new house, are you going to stick with keeping them out, or is it business as usual? Is it always business first, societal rules second?"

"Five thousand, huh?" Dennis chuckled. "That would be nice." He smirked at Scott, seeking his assent.

Peter glared back at him. "Good ol' capitalism, alive and well," he said with a pejorative air. "Certainly, guys, don't let earning a buck get in the way of your moral irreverence—or maybe I should say moral irrelevance. Your immoral high ground only takes a back seat to making money. How proud you must be." He faked a laugh. "It's funny. I haven't given this whole issue much thought because, frankly, it's never been a problem for me. We've lived in all-white communities since college—not by choice I might add, but because we always went for what our money could most afford. Nicer homes, better schools, right? But when I think about shared cultures and all that family values stuff, it seems to me that we're all sharing quite a bit."

Peter must have shifted into second gear because a defiant prosecutorial tone had seeped into his rhetoric. At the same time, Dennis looked weary of the whole discussion and glanced over his shoulder to see if they were attracting unwanted attention. It was becoming obvious that Peter was the lone holdout at the meeting, and fraternizing with the enemy might make Dennis guilty by association.

"We love their music, don't we?" Peter said, jabbing like he was aiming straight for the heart of the matter. "Dennis, I know you're into jazz. And let's be honest—rhythm and blues, soul—that's the music we grew up with. Maybe our parents were unsure when they first heard those new sounds back in the fifties and sixties, but it didn't take long before they were mouthing the lyrics and humming along. That music became part of who we are. It shaped us in ways we didn't even realize."

He paused for a second, then added, "And even if it's not your thing, I bet your kids are listening to it. Every generation has gotten more used to Black culture being woven into our lives. Hell, Elvis built his whole career off Black music—plagiarized it, even—and from there, it opened the door to all those pop songs we play at parties and weddings. It crept in slowly, almost unnoticed, but we were all part of it. The more we engaged with it, the more it became a part of us." He gave a shrug. "Honestly, all that noise about integration back then seems like just a lot of hot air—because it's happening anyway."

Peter's earnest look stood out among the few guests still sipping their last round of wine. He was the sole standard-bearer, marching into battle on an issue that everyone else had already put behind them. I found myself surrendering to his rhetoric, eloquent as it was.

"I can't stand the hypocrisy," he went on. "We'd never teach our kids to act the way we do as adults. At least not nowadays. It's obvious you guys don't discriminate against Black baseball or football players. You cheer them on just like the white players. If your kids were watching you at a game, they'd come away thinking all the players were important people. They'd think you valued every one of them—equally, as players, teachers, doctors—neighbors, even. You think our kids aren't watching, but they are. They're learning what we accept and making it part of who they are. We've all played a role in the progress of racial equality just by allowing people of color into our lives, on any level. The Robinsons moving here is very much a part of that change. You, Dennis, are guilty of helping to bring about this progress, and now you stand here and act like what the Robinsons are doing is appalling. I don't know how you live with yourself."

I couldn't help but smile. I followed it with a quick swig of wine. Peter had paused for a moment like an orator waiting for his ideas to sink in before continuing, looking as if he was ready to make another point.

Scott furtively took a look about the room, clearly hoping for refuge. He and Dennis were two kids trapped by the principal in an unconscionable act of self-indulgence, and they were being lambasted in the public eye. Scott saw in the faces of those still in the room what was clear for anyone to see—we were all listening and were probably glad not to have been caught in the same predicament.

"And I think I know why you do it," Peter finally continued, aiming his stare at Dennis. "Why you're so hypocritical about race. The truth of the matter is that you know you're already Black—culturally, literally, linguistically, musically. And the simple fact is you can't live with yourself while being reminded everyday of who you really are. That's who the Robinsons are to you—a reminder of all the shared experiences, shared likes and dislikes. They are you, and you are nothing without them. Instead, you'd rather be the ostrich with your head in the sand. You're running from yourself."

Dennis stood frozen, giving no sign he understood, but the shock on his face showed he'd heard the word "Black" as an accusation—the worst kind of insult, in his eyes.

His soliloquy done, Peter shook his head. I was sure at that moment any hesitation he may have harbored about the Beekman affair was gone. He was Beekman's only choirboy, and if he was naïve, it was because he believed that other people cared—but they didn't. Back then, a real fear had gripped the community, and one ignored it only at their peril.

10

Session 7

"So, Peter, what should we talk about today?" It was an anodyne question cloaked in ambiguity. Peter knew well enough by now to see the trap being laid out before him. Only the naïve would take an open-ended question from Doc and assume simplicity.

In the past two months, he had come to realize that therapy was not a passive, benign process. Anna had warned him there'd be work, but he'd had no clue what she really meant. Like most people, he thought therapy would be like visiting your family doctor: You tell them what hurts and they tell you what's wrong, and off you go with a prescription to fill at the pharmacy. A week later, you feel fine. A transactional experience with few demands.

Therapy definitely was not that. Not even close. He found himself not only working—exhaustively excavating emotions—during his sessions, but he also found himself at home trying to understand his impulses, second-guessing his decisions or insecurities, trying to understand how it all fit with what was going on during his sessions.

Was his personal life informing his sessions, or was it the other way around—his sessions making sense of his personal life? He didn't really know. But he often found himself trying to figure it out, and in the process, he appeared out of touch with the goings-on at home. It was a distraction that deepened the chasm between him and Clare. Anna's open-ended question stirred those feelings of uncertainty, an uncertainty he had become accustomed to. It took him a while to reconcile these thoughts, but finally, he made an offer.

"Well, for the past few weeks we've been kicking around the idea that I need to unlink my expectations from my wife's approval."

"Do you feel it's an unreasonable expectation? I'm not sensing you've made any headway with this, which is why I wanted to open the discussion with what interested you most."

"It just seems I leave here all pumped up to forge my own path, but the reality at home brings me back to a truth that's not easily dismissed."

"And what might that be?"

"Well, Clare is my life partner. We share everything, including time and space. It's hard not to have expectations. She has them of me; I have them of her. If you live with someone, it's not easy to divorce them from your intimate needs. What's more, I think my attempts at 'emotional independence' if you can call it that," he said, punctuating his words with air quotes, "are pissing off Clare. I think she's pulling away."

"Okay, that's not an unreasonable feeling to have, and I apologize if I presented it as a necessary next step to improvement. I think, however, you'll have to be realistic about how much improvement you'll make while linking your personal growth with marriage expectations. I know you have to live under one roof and all, but personal growth is… well, personal. I can't help you make progress unless we identify the impediments to you overcoming your issues. And you've identified Clare as an impediment—maybe the only impediment. But that's something we can explore. *Is* she the only impediment? Are we laying all the blame on Clare when it should be spread around a bit?"

He had no response. It was yet another line of questioning he had never probed, so the door needed opening. He tried to give a pensive look, like he was thumbing through the files of his life, but he came up blank.

"I don't know, Doc. Nothing comes to mind."

"Well, let's explore in another direction."

"Oh, boy. Here we go. Hold on for an e-ticket ride."

"E-ticket?" Anna's bemused look begged for clarification.

"It's the ticket for the craziest rides at Disney. Maybe I'm dating myself here."

"Well, then, let's hope I don't disappoint." Anna smiled, and Peter's anxiety subsided. "We spoke a month or so ago about your dad, and how he handled confrontations with your mom."

"Yeah, you said I may have picked up some of his coping skills."

"Everyone is different, but our parents *do* influence us, at least subtly. So there may be something to that. This time, I'd like to focus more on your mom."

"The mother-wife thing again?" Peter said, his tone unmasking a hint of derision.

"Yeah, moms are important, are they not? I think we should explore your first relationship with a woman to understand your current relationship with your wife. So, how about your mom? Did she ever discipline you? Do you have any memories of serious conflict with your mom?"

"You guys always spend a lot of time with childhood conflicts, don't you? That stuff is years in the past. How is anything that old going to help me today?"

Anna smiled. "It's what they taught us in therapy school: Start from the beginning. I know patients always feel the old skeletons should stay buried wherever they are. No need to resurrect them. But it's wrong to think that having skeletons means you're damaged goods. If that were the case, then we're all damaged and you'd be in good company. The reason to start from the beginning is that childhood is when seminal events occur. It's when things get seeded in our psyche and go on to affect the rest of our life. I like to use the analogy of pouring cement. When you're young, you're surrounded by wet cement. It's moldable, in good ways and sometimes in bad. By mid-teens, the cement is beginning to harden. By our twenties, it's pretty much rock-hard. The ability to make changes later in life requires a hammer and chisel. That's what I do. I used the analogy of peeling an onion, but I more often peel with a hammer and chisel. Hopefully, I can help a person mix new cement and place it in new molding to help them get on with their life. So tell me about you and your mom. Anything stand out?"

Peter fumbled with his fingers while looking down, denying Anna eye contact while trying to decide whether to come clean or find a way to play dumb and make up something trivial.

"Well," he finally started, "my mom was definitely more strict than my dad. She disciplined more regularly, the same way, no matter where—in the house, in the car, on vacation, and in front of anyone. It could be a little embarrassing sometimes. But there's nothing that stands out too much."

"What stands out the most to you?"

He locked eyes on her, feeling annoyed by her persistence. "You're really digging here, aren't you?"

"We're in this together, Peter. Were all the times you got disciplined the same?"

He let his eyes slowly wander to the window behind Anna and lost his gaze in the bright light. More work, more exhaustion. He'd rather spend a full day crunching numbers as an accountant than spend an hour searching his soul. He methodically went through his youth like a Rolodex, flipping through each year, going back further and further. Everything seemed so benign. Boring normalcy. But then—bingo.

"There was a time, actually, yeah. There was a time I actually *didn't* get into trouble. I expected to be read the riot act, but I got out of it. Got lucky, I guess."

"Sounds interesting—do tell."

Peter sat back and stared over Anna's head in an attempt to collect his thoughts. It was some time ago. He wondered if he remembered all there was to it. He wasn't quite sure how much was just feeling and how much actual memory of the events.

He was about twelve when he and his brother, Dave, rode their bikes down to the river by Shawnee Cove, something they weren't allowed to do—too many stories of kids drowning, some mysterious belief in Native American retribution at play. But if you tell a kid not to do something, you might as well lock 'em up, because they're gonna do it.

Well, he and Dave were horsing around by the edge of the river. Their plan was to go fishing or something, but they forgot their rods and decided instead to skip stones. At some point or other, Peter crept closer to the edge of the river embankment to get the advantage of releasing his stone at water level.

It was the best throw of the day. The stone skipped six times. He missed the last skip when he lost his balance and fell in. It was probably what happened to all the other kids that had drowned out there. Some parts of the riverbank were like quicksand, and the ground just gave out from under you. Next thing you knew, you were underwater with mud on top of you.

He remembered an old oak tree nearby. It sat right on the edge of the riverbank. When he fell in, he discovered what he was never able to appreciate from looking down on the river from up the embankment: There were roots, lots of them, snarled in large loops like snakes wrapped in a tumultuous wrestling match. He became tangled in that wrestling match and it held him pinned, unable to surface.

It didn't matter that he was a decent swimmer. The whole thing happened so fast. All he could remember was that he couldn't get free. His arms were caught, and his head was scratched every which way whenever he tried to move. All he could do was kick, but that only propelled him into more roots. Eventually, he realized this was the end. He freaked and thrashed even more 'til he finally gave up. But then the hand of Providence reached in and pulled him out and up the riverbank.

It was Dave. He was all matter-of-fact, like, "No time for swimming today, buddy," while all Peter could do was cough his brains out. It took them a while to make it back home. Peter was in no hurry, seeing as how he was pretty scratched up and probably still in shock. He also knew what was waiting for him. His mom was certain to be apoplectic, and he would definitely suffer the worst of her ire. At a minimum, he would be grounded for a month—maybe a year. This was something he would never live down. His mom had a way of holding onto things. When you thought she'd forgotten about something, she'd bring it back just to keep you off balance. All he knew was that he never wanted to go home. But home he went.

His mom was outside gardening, and his heart began to gallop like a racehorse when she saw him. The world shifted on its axis. She came to greet the boys at the fence with a smile, but her pleasing motherly demeanor changed to a hung-jaw, wide-eyed fright. It was quite surreal.

Peter watched the muscles in her face slowly morph, not unlike a horror movie. He had no idea what he looked like, but apparently he'd been to hell and back. His clothes were wet, actually still dripping in places. Mud-smeared patches streaked across the front of his T-shirt and pants, and his hair looked like he'd had an encounter with a crazed hairdresser. And, of course, there was the blood. Gashes on his head leaked, and remnants of oozing cuts ran down the sides of his face. Dave was obviously not savvy enough to put him back together.

His mom screamed holy terror, "What happened to you?!"

Peter couldn't respond. Too many not-very-artful lies came flooding into his head so fast that he couldn't pick any of them. "I... I..." was all he could get out. He must've looked a sorry sight, all scratched up, his clothes mud-stained and torn, his hair a mess.

Dave, apparently unfazed by the whole ordeal, simply blurted, "Oh, he just rode into a pile of shit and skidded off the road into a wet ditch."

Peter looked at his brother in disbelief. *What?* His mom did the same. Peter wasn't sure if she was shocked by Dave saying "shit" or his riding into shit and taking a fall into a ditch. Whatever went on in his mom's head, the result was the same—her face slowly shifted into a smile, then a chuckle, and finally, uncontrollable laughter. Then she realized she shouldn't be laughing *at* him because she certainly wasn't laughing *with* him.

Despite Peter's sorry state—scratches, dried blood, and mud stains—she put her arms around him and gave him a hug. She asked him if he needed any Band-Aids, and then she warned him to clean the poop off the wheels before putting his bike back in the garage.

"That was my expecting discipline that never actually came," Peter said, sliding back in the chair. The retelling had put him on edge. The emotions related to the incident were just below the surface, still quite raw.

"That's an interesting story, Peter."

"Just your usual kid-getting-into-trouble story."

"Not so," Anna said. "I asked you to tell me something from early childhood, and you pulled this story from deep in your memory banks. It's the only one you found important enough to share, or the only one you chose to remember. The brain is peculiar that way. What it chooses to hold onto is often an unresolved issue or something that's changed us in some way, even if we don't recognize it. It becomes something of an *après-coup*, a term we use to refer to events that have meaning beyond being a simple timeline in our past. When a twelve-year-old almost dies, is saved by his brother, and *not* scolded by his mother because of a bald-faced lie—that is a life-altering event."

Hearing his story summed up in such a way encouraged Peter to nod his approval. Still, his curiosity prodded him to ask, "How so?"

Relieved to come out of the story unscathed, he was now pleased to entertain the psychology of it on a more intellectual plane—sort of like he was sitting with Anna examining some other poor fool who couldn't keep his life in order.

"Well," Anna obliged, "aside from being forever indebted to your brother for saving your life, you learned at an impressionable age, cement-still-wet age, that reward can come from telling a lie, or maybe just not telling all of the truth. That can be a confusing realization for a kid that age. An adult can say, 'I just got lucky,' when things take a surprising turn for the better, even if the facts were a little shady. They don't necessarily assume that the normal rules of engagement are forever altered. Psychopaths excepted, people generally have a sense of right and wrong. Being *rewarded* for doing wrong, which is essentially what happened in this story, is not something a twelve-year-old processes like an adult."

Anna paused, regarding Peter, before continuing. "By the way, did you ever get a chance to pay it back to your brother?"

The question caught Peter off guard, and a pregnant pause ensued. When it was becoming too obvious, he finally replied with a muted, "No."

"Why not? Seems like you owed him one after he saved you at the river *and* saved your neck at home."

"Well, you know, I was a few years younger. By the time I got old enough to pay it back, he wasn't around. He died in Afghanistan. 2007."

"Oh, sorry to hear that. How old were you then?"

"Fourteen," Peter responded unemotionally.

"Hmm. So he died not long after he left high school?"

"Pretty good math, Doc."

"How'd your family take it?"

"Not good, as you can imagine. A lot of crying. My mom was beside herself, almost angry about it all. We all grieved in our own way. Mom was the loudest. Dad became more of a recluse for a while."

"And you?"

"I… I wasn't sure how to feel. I thought I'd be tearful and all, but it just didn't happen. There were times I thought I wasn't mourning in the right way. I was afraid my mom would hassle me for not showing respect to Dave's memory because I was still hanging out with my friends, going to movies, playing hoops. Let's just say things were tense around the house for some time."

Peter adjusted in the seat, seemingly uncomfortable. Anna was asking him about feelings he never dwelled on, let alone shared with anyone. It felt like yet another diversion. Something of consequence only to him. He had no idea why they were exploring the outcome of a war on the other side of the world. Once again, Anna's curiosity left him confused, but he had already given up on resisting her will. He was now used to following her lead and found himself compelled to simply follow along.

His long pause made him self-conscious, so he finally continued. "A couple months after we got the news, this guy showed up on our doorstep. A guy Dave served with. It didn't seem he'd had enough time to make friends, but I guess when you're out in the middle of a desert, relationships intensify pretty fast. He was a Black guy decked out in military uniform, said he knew Dave, served with him in Afghanistan. He was friendly, walked with a bit of a limp, made me wonder if he was still on active duty. My parents invited him in, seeing as how he came all the way from Alabama just to see us. That afternoon is seared in my memory. Earl was his name. Earl Benoit."

"Earl Benoit from Alabama," Anna repeated.

"Anyway," Peter continued, "he told us about Dave's last day. There was this firefight. I guess that's where everyone is shooting at everyone, and all you see are tracers of the bullets flying by. It was hot as hell, and so arid you could choke on your own saliva. They were on patrol out in the middle of who-knows-where. He said things didn't go well. He got hit, shot in the leg. It was bad. He was bleeding out and couldn't walk. They were far from base, and…"

Peter paused again, his voice quavering. Anna maintained a supportive gaze as he took a moment to regroup.

"They were far from base," Peter began again, "and Dave carried him—ran with him—all the way back. All the time, they were being shot at from all sides. It was crazy when you think about it. Nighttime. A half-moon was the only light he had to go by. 'I weigh a hundred and sixty without any gear,' Earl said. 'I don't know how he did it, but he saved my life.' "

He paused yet again, but this time his emotions overflowed. His face blushed. It seemed he knew this part of the story might set him off. Finally, he continued.

"Those words, 'I don't know how he did it, but he saved my life' have stuck with me ever since. There was a problem, though. Dave took a bullet to the chest somewhere in all that, but he never gave up—he kept on running with Earl on his back. When they finally made it back to base, he collapsed and died. His last deed in this world was done."

Peter sat back with a glum look about him. Telling the story wasn't new to him, but it was exhausting nonetheless. He sat perfectly still, betraying nothing.

Anna reached across to her box of Kleenex, pulled a tissue, and dried her eyes. She looked up after a moment, hoping to appear professional. She cleared her throat and proceeded. "So, Peter, you were just fourteen at the time. Do you feel like you've come to terms with it all, as best one can?"

"I believe so. I loved my brother, for obvious reasons. By fourteen, he was already a hero in my book. That bike ride wasn't the only time he saved my neck. I always had a way of being in the wrong place at the wrong time. I wasn't a wayward kid or anything. Just bad luck, I guess. The way he died simply put a shine on someone I already admired."

Anna studied him as if something wasn't right. "Have you ever really mourned your brother's loss?"

Peter's bemused expression was the first betrayal. It was the real answer.

"Your story about Dave is very compelling," Anna continued, "and it seems your mother and father both had their own way of mourning. But you admit you didn't mourn at all, and you felt bad about it at the time, and you still seem to harbor regret. Why didn't you mourn?"

It was a silly question, akin to asking why he hadn't cried. Peter knew well enough that no one can control their emotions. Just the asking suggested he'd done something wrong.

He continued to stare, his expression a weary mix of confusion, innocence, and apathy. To look at him, it could have been someone else's life—he was merely a bystander watching an eastbound train pass by, the faces in the windows absorbed in the full panoply of life's angst, while he sat completely detached from it all.

The uncomfortable silence was enough for Anna to know this line of questioning would not bear fruit. She gave him a smile as an olive branch to move on. "I must admit, I admire your endurance. I realize now how much you've been through and are still struggling with, and I admire your tenacity for not giving up."

Anna's accolades were well meaning, but Peter was still tentative. His emotions swung from confidence to near despair with each session. Nonetheless, he knew she was making a difference. He was finally feeling a comfort level that he'd never felt before. He'd crossed a chasm that proved he belonged; he'd trusted the doc with one of his most cherished memories. He had no idea what lay ahead, but he was less anxious about taking the next step.

"Well, Doc? Now you know everything that's anything about my youth. You think I've got a chance of getting this monkey off my back?"

Anna looked him square in the face. "Well, I mentioned that the bike ride experience may have primed you to subconsciously think you can get away with bucking the rules now and again and not really pay a price. The risk-taking as sort of a reverse-reward thing, remember? Your brother's death, and how he died, certainly intensifies things a bit more. It makes anything in your life that he was a part of even more special. But the bike ride and Dave's death are not the only significant moments in your life. You have a lot of competing experiences to dilute the impact of these incidents. We don't really know, as yet, how these experiences play out in your life. We're still peeling the onion. I have to admit, though, the bike ride itself *is* an entertaining story." Anna smiled as if wanting to lighten the mood.

"I'm glad I can provide some comic relief, Doc," Peter said and chuckled. "So you don't see any obvious link between my mom and my wife, then, huh?"

"I sense that you're still anxious about this issue of mothers and wives. The Freudian response would be that you marry someone who is somewhat like your mother. There's probably some truth to this, but it's not always obvious. We talked about this before. What someone feels comfortable with in a mate *is* related to what they experienced as a child, but the connections can be rather deep and subtle. Sometimes, finding the link doesn't help with whatever issues you're dealing with as an adult. We're all very different, even though we're alike. Sounds like a rather prophetic way of saying we therapists just take each case one-by-one and try not to make assumptions. Regardless of whether your wife is similar to your mom in some ways doesn't alter the fact you need to find a productive way of engaging her. Have you ever been to a marriage counselor?"

"No."

"Have you ever discussed needing a marriage counselor?"

"No." It was a drawn out response, as if he didn't want to admit to a wrong answer.

"So, prior to this whole event—the situation where someone died—you and Clare had a happy marriage?"

"Yeah, pretty much."

Anna's penetrating stare made him even more insecure about his answer. He had total respect for her ability to see what he might not want to say. She was that good. He also had come to trust her and would never want to intentionally lie. He still wondered, however, if maybe he was minimizing his issues with Clare—or maybe he was in denial and not even in touch with what was really going on.

"Went out on dates?" Anna asked.

"Yeah."

"Held hands?"

"Yeah."

"Expressed affection for each other?"

"Yeah." The inquisition was beginning to feel weird.

"Had sex often?"

Peter paused. "Yeah," he finally responded. "Maybe *often* would be more like *occasionally*, or sometimes. We do have two kids, you know." He smiled, and Anna smiled in kind.

"Do you still have sex—sometimes?" Anna asked.

Peter thought about it. It had been a while, but he hadn't been craving it much himself, so he wasn't sure if it was a fair question. "Not much."

"Dating?"

"No."

"So, this obsession thing *has* changed your relationship?"

"You think?" he asked. "I mean, my relationship with my wife seems fine enough."

"Well, maybe the change happened some time ago. It's been, what—five years? But what you describe sounds like a change. Affection and humor are the hallmark of a healthy, balanced relationship. You're describing less of that. Maybe it's been very gradual and you don't notice it much, but it seems like a growing emotional disconnect. I'm wondering if it's your choice—subconsciously, that is—or if it's Clare's. Again, subconsciously. I'm not sure."

"Are you telling me my marriage is failing?" Peter said, getting more animated.

"I'm not here to hide what I think, Peter."

That glum facial expression glared back at her again, then to the floor. He played with his hands some more before looking back at her. "So, you're gonna tell me what all this means?"

"Well, let me ask a couple more questions. Then I'll tell you what I think. Does Clare argue with you as much as she did, say, a few months ago?"

Peter thought for a bit before yielding a relieved, "No."

"And you, Peter. When you're volunteering at Eaton, the LGBTQ group, are you at all concerned about Clare and what kinds of comments she's going to make when you return? Is she on your mind at all?"

"Sure, Doc. In fact, I'm often wondering what she's doing without me around. I'm not jealous or nervous, but I do think about her."

"I'm wondering, based on what you've told me, if Clare *is* emotionally distancing herself from you—not you from her. When we argue with people, we care about them. Or at least about the issue. When Clare used to complain or argue with you about your volunteer work or about you obsessing a lot, she cared. At least enough to complain. She was hoping for change. She was invested. But this obsession thing has been going on for five years. That's a long time to stay invested and not see results. So now she's either tired of fighting and has given it a rest, or she just doesn't care. It may be that you're alienating her by not stopping the Eaton work, or by not stopping the obsessing. Either way, it would seem she's taking a breather."

"I'm confused. I thought her not arguing as much was a sign of things getting better?" Peter asked.

"Not in this situation. If it were, she wouldn't have requested—or demanded—that you get a second opinion with me."

"Shit!" Peter began the raking of his hand through his hair. "Is this something I can fix, Doc?"

"As I said at a previous session, my responsibility is to you, not Clare. I'm not here to save your marriage. I'm here to point out issues and help you take control of your life."

Peter jerked himself upright in the chair with new determination. "Well, my marriage *is* part of my life. I want to control what happens to it." His voice was laced with defiance.

"It's not that easy, Peter. Your motives for doing what you're doing can't easily change on a dime."

"What!? What motives are you talking about?" Peter's voice had risen, and he was nearly yelling now.

"Well, for starters," Anna said evenly, "you've said in the past that working and volunteering at Eaton was something you just 'gotta do,' to quote your words, despite it being a hindrance to your relationship with Clare. It seemed a little glib when you said it, but I believed you meant it. You've said, 'I'm just living my life, doing what I want to do.' Remember, we talked about this as well, the idea that you may have dual motives at Eaton—to relive the experience and prove your humanity, but also to irritate Clare for denying your humanity, for being dismissive about what's important to you. Well, those words, the glib response, they don't sound like someone who should be surprised his wife may—and I stress the *may*—be pulling away from him. And after you told me the story of the river, the near drowning, feeling petrified of what your mom would say, and then the relief from having it all disappear under the ruse of a lie...Well, it stands to reason."

"What? What stands to reason? I'm lost," Peter barked, his face red with exasperation.

"It stands to reason that maybe, just maybe, you've developed a habit of engaging in undesirable activities despite the consequences. You know Clare is unhappy with Eaton, but you do it anyway. I think that's because you subconsciously get a thrill from the reverse-reward conditioning from childhood. Usually doing bad things brings punishment. But you experienced a seminal moment in childhood when the rules were reversed. A negative behavior was actually rewarded, in your case, with no punishment. You're repeating your childhood experiences, so changing your behavior requires undoing an impulse that originated in childhood. It's not impossible to do, but it's not that easy, either."

"Shit! Shit! Shit!" Peter grumbled and looked away in denial. "I knew that story would come back to haunt me."

"Sorry, Peter. You won't like this next point, either. When people have a behavior they can't stop doing, it's often because they really don't want to stop. It has somehow become an integral part of their psychological balance. The fact that they don't stop means they've become dependent on it in some subtle way. It fills a hole in their psyche. You can't stop obsessing and you won't stop volunteering, despite knowing your wife dislikes both. Making Clare angry may be the very reason you keep doing it. Now, with the story of your mom and the river incident, the reason for all this may be obvious. You like taking risks. You like the adrenaline and dopamine surges that come with it. Fortunately, you don't seem to have a severe case of it. That is, you're not putting yourself or anyone else in immediate danger. But this reverse-reward thing, doing something unacceptable without concern for the consequences, defines your behavior with Clare."

"I can't believe all this is going on inside me and I have no clue about it. It's like finding a key to a door with a ton of skeletons." Peter glared at Anna, frustrated. "Why am I doing this, Doc?" he said, his anger giving way to a plea.

"Why? I don't know. Maybe it's because she doesn't care about something that you care quite a bit about. Maybe you're punishing her for not being more like you, having your sensibilities about things. Maybe her sense of humanity offends you. We can go back and figure out if it's related to your mom. Maybe some hidden or suppressed anger that went unresolved is now being transferred onto your wife. In your stories about your childhood, your mom stands out as the enforcer, the 'instigator,' as you said. You could be harboring anger from your youth, resolving your mom issues with someone more accessible—Clare. I don't know if you noticed, but you describe them in similar ways. It would seem that one part of you delights in hurting Clare, while the other part of you eagerly wants her validation, like you would have wanted from your instigator mom. You're trying to have it both ways, maybe even confused by your attempts to have it both ways. But as we discussed before, you need to let go of depending on your wife for validation. I know you think it'll interfere with your marriage, but your marriage needs a healthier foundation, and that requires you to find a path that works for *you* first."

The room fell silent. Peter wore a sullen look of guilt—not unlike a boy who had disappointed his mom.

11

The summer sunrise in Portville began with an orange glow over the distant hills east of town. Its morning dance of colors, rivaled only by the equally brilliant sunset, made these two hours of the day the only times worth strolling the side streets of Beekman. The slight breeze off the Ohio River tamed the humidity while the solitude of the neighborhood made for a peaceful meditative escape. All seemed possible at this time of day. Yesterday's defeats were forgotten; today promised new opportunities.

The women who had been part of my threesome at the Masons' a few weeks earlier and I were about to set off on our Sunday sunrise jaunt. It was a debriefing of sorts, an hour for talking about the day's plans, for summer day trips, picnics, the latest kid-friendly movies, and possibly a dinner date with the hubby. It was also the hour for catching up on the neighborhood gossip. It was a Sunday ritual that usually began in June when the kids were out of school and their weekend sporting events came to an end. The ladies and I would meet until September, when the beginning of school meant the return to the usual marathon of weekend activities.

The three of us rendezvoused at our usual spot: the corner of Beekman and Jackson. Our walk would take us into the surrounding neighborhoods, allowing us to compare and contrast the benefits of Beekman with the less fortunate. It was never stated as such, but we all hinted at that reality in one way or another.

Our strolls were often peppered with, "That's such a cute house," or "I love the way they do their garden." The truth of the matter was these strolls often resulted in us finding the occasional random jewel of architecture or landscaping that we later brought back to our own dwellings on Beekman. It wasn't, of course, seen as co-opting others' ideas. Not at all. That would be an acknowledgment that betrayed the premier status of Beekman. If anything, co-opting was thought of as *improving* on an idea, bringing it up to Beekman standards with more exclusively sourced materials—though the final product would often be identical.

I strolled the short walk to the meeting spot and found my comrades already stretching, sporting the usual T-shirts, tights, and trainers.

"Hi, ladies," I said with a slight wave of the hand.

"Hi, Clare," Alice responded.

"Good morning, Clare," said Maggie. "Ready to get sweaty?"

"You know it, girl," I shot back with a smile.

Despite my bravado, I had an unsettled pit in my stomach. This was the first time we would be walking without Sarah. I felt the sting like tugging on a paper cut. It was always uncomfortable—painful, in fact—whenever I thought of her, which was often. The angst over how to deal with new neighbors was just the kind of frustration that she and I used to sit and discuss over an afternoon cup of tea. Much as I liked Margaret and Alice, Sarah was really my sister. Emotionally, I always defaulted to her. Only later would I check myself, remembering that Sarah was the reason we were in this mess to begin with.

We began our power walk headed in the usual direction, down

Jackson for six long blocks. From there, we would turn onto Franklin and wind through several neighborhoods that were quite beautiful in their own right, though always considered less desirable than Beekman. It was ironic that Franklin was always a required segment of our Sunday ritual. Though boredom or curiosity sometimes itched us to turn a block early or head in a totally different direction from the prescribed route, Franklin was the only mainstay. Its elegant homes were sometimes referred to as the sister of Beekman. If Beekman was too expensive, or just as likely had nothing for sale, Portville realtors offered Franklin as a consolation.

"It's our other beautiful gem," they'd say, hoping to keep a buyer interested in making Portville their home.

After Franklin, there were a few hills timed perfectly to coincide with the last leg of the power walk, after which we wound up back at Beekman. The whole affair was usually about three miles.

Portville's rise from slumber was evident as we began our stroll. The misty dew sparkled in the sun's early glow, soon to evaporate in the heat of midday. The clarion call of wrens, finches, and sparrows—chirping, singing, and occasionally squabbling—was usually loud enough to replace any need for an alarm clock. Their morning ritual of catching the early worm was also a required part of nature's call. The classic double-foot shuffle disturbed the neatly groomed flower beds with the hope of unearthing a morning delight, leaving the telltale marks of random holes and dirt debris sprayed onto walkways. The occasional car scurried off on an early errand, racing down a side street; early morning joggers or cyclists sported their usual harlequin colors; and homeowners sipping their morning brews appeared on steps to retrieve their morning papers. These were all signs that a new day had dawned.

"So, Clare," Alice asked at some point during the first half of our walk, "are you and Peter still planning on just hanging around for the summer? No vacation plans?"

"It's a touchy subject now," I said. "I dare not go there. What with this possible new expense, the house offer on the table, I think Peter's not willing to entertain anything that'll cost money. Funny thing is, he's made it clear he's not planning on us participating in what he calls *the neighborhood scam.*"

"Scam?" Maggie interjected. "Really? Where'd he get that from?"

"He thinks we're all hypocritical for wanting to protect our neighborhood. He gets all philosophical. It makes no sense to me."

"He's a good man," Alice said. "You've always had good things to say about him, and he always makes time for the kids. I wish George could be more like him."

"Yeah, yeah. Somehow that all just doesn't seem to matter much right now," I said. "I just wish he'd fall in line with everyone else. I hate being the odd couple out."

We continued on in silence for a while, but after another block had passed, we slowed to admire daylilies in full bloom. Each of the us took turns sniffing the sweet aromatic scent from the red trumpet-shaped flowers beautifully arrayed in terra cotta pots of varying sizes and shapes. In all, they formed a long serpentine border around the front garden of a Franklin competitor. Hummingbirds flitted from flower to flower, gorging on the abundant nectar. This was the home that often delayed our weekly journey. The owners were a husband and wife in their seventies with an apparent green thumb that was the envy of many.

"I met them once," Maggie said, taking her turn at drawing in the aromatic dew.

"Who?" Alice asked.

"The folks who live here. It was a chance meeting last year. You guys were out of town, remember? It was just me and Sarah. Late

August, I think. Beatrice and Virgil. They had such a cute English accent. They're from Barbados, if I recall."

"English accent? From Barbados? Don't you mean Caribbean accent?" Alice asked, trying to hide her indignation. Everyone knew that cultural ignorance was the one thing that set her off. Her infectious politeness turned chilly in the face of the faux pas.

In response, Maggie's prickly irritation also surfaced. She was unaccustomed to correction and appeared slighted from Alice's intrusion. Their friendship would prevail, however, as Maggie quickly glossed over the matter. "Oh, I don't know. I can't keep up with all that stuff. All I know is they were different. *Sounding*, I mean. I remember they were decked out like they worked at a botanical garden—hats, scarfs, gloves. She worked a trowel digging up tulip bulbs, and he had shears, trimming back the roses. They were quite the pair."

"From Barbados, you said? Here, on Franklin?" I was surprised.

"Go figure," said Maggie. "Anyway, Beatrice was so nice. We got to talking about what they were doing and how we always enjoy passing by their place and all, and she even gave me a dozen of her favorite tulip bulbs. They're the ones I have growing by the mailbox."

"How nice," Alice said, quickly warming to the conversation. "The fuchsia ones?"

"The very ones."

"I guess that was a nice gesture," I added. "Are you going to gift something back?"

"Never thought of it," said Maggie. "Seemed to me more like one of those one-off kinds of things. What do you think, Alice? Do I need to bring over a Bundt cake or something?"

Maggie seemed sincere in her ask, and Alice appeared to move on from the earlier tiff, so she responded with no hint of sarcasm.

"Oh, that's always a tough one. I guess you just have to follow your heart on that."

"Well, it's been a year, so maybe I missed my opportunity." Maggie went on to say how she found the couple quite charming and neighborly and quite willing to part with little tidbits on their gardening style, like how best to care for the bulbs and when to plant them for a spring bloom. It was high praise coming from a Beekman. "Beatrice and Virgil are both retired and enjoyed gardening, as any true... Caribbean?"

Alice piqued again with a raised brow but chose to say nothing. I smirked.

Indeed, the gardening talents of the Barbados couple spoke for themselves. Their flowers bloomed in a steady performance throughout the summer season. Every week or so, a new blossom appeared, right on cue: early blooming azaleas, followed by spring's ranunculi and peonies, then summertime daylilies, roses, and irises—until fall brought crocuses, daisy sunflowers, and the return of the azaleas.

Sometimes a rare dahlia or plumeria species, hidden from the winter frost, would emerge to stop the power walk in their tracks, and a slim pocket camera would emerge to quickly archive any new specimen. Later, we'd consult with our local nursery expert, who would name a plant simply by studying its leaves. Beatrice and Virgil's home became a therapeutic way station along our weekly journey. One couldn't help but abandon all thought of life's more compelling chores or angsts and simply bask in the aura of nature's colors and scents, its synergy, diversity, and inclusion, all concentrated in this one little hamlet. Who knew immigrants could be so talented? *Barbadians.* Go figure.

We continued our walk with a temporary blissful countenance. With our floral meditation behind us and the hamlet now half a block away, I could no longer contain my anxiety about the Johnson house. "Does anybody know how things are going with Fred Mason? I haven't heard a thing, and I dare not talk about it at home."

"I think Fred, or someone he's got on retainer, presented the offer this past week," Maggie said. "The hope is that the Robinsons will jump on it quickly, seeing as how it's about sixty thousand above their purchase price."

"George told me that Fred made the drive himself," Alice said. "He apparently wanted to put a friendly face on the offer and answer any questions in person. He was hoping to make things look like... well, a business deal, you know? Keep it from looking too shady."

"Are there any plans for a follow-up? Like, are we supposed to just wait indefinitely, or should we make a show of being serious about the whole thing?" I prodded.

The topic always made me edgy, so I sought closure on as many issues as possible. The idea that an offer could be left on the table, so to speak, without anyone knowing what the Robinsons were thinking, was unacceptable. It would mean an open timetable, the idea of which was already grating on my nerves.

"Well, usually escrow is only so many weeks. I'm not sure what it is for the Johnsons' sale, but I'm guessing it's likely to be shorter than longer. We don't have much time to ratchet things up—*if* there's a next level, that is. We didn't really spell out a plan B at the Mason meeting."

"Why do you think the escrow is likely to be shorter?" I asked.

"Because," Maggie answered, "my guess is that the Johnsons wanted out, and they didn't want things lingering. They likely wanted maximum assurance that, financially, they could cut the cord quickly and leave little chance for the Robinsons to change their minds. Just my guess, since they did sneak off in the middle of the night."

"Makes sense," Alice said. "I gotta say, the whole thing sounds so sneaky."

"Sneaky but necessary," Maggie retorted.

"Don't get soft on us, Alice," Clare chided.

——— ... ———

Saint James Episcopal Church sat on a small grassy knoll not more than a hundred feet high. Contrary to its old tradition of being in the center of town, Saint James was now on the outskirts, away from the hubbub of traffic and other activities that keep a town alive during the intervening days between Sunday worship. If you didn't make the trip, you would never just happen to stroll by it. That said, the church was a fine specimen of nineteenth-century architecture, first built in 1852 and renovated to its current stature in 1951, just in time to celebrate its centennial. Its ivy-covered gray brick façade, with a Gothic arch entry, central tower, and a spire rising 150 feet high—along with a classic long nave, small transepts, and an apse behind the altar—made the church feel as though it had been plucked from old Europe and planted along the Ohio River. It was pleasing to the eye from any angle, and its parishioners held it in high esteem. It was their pride and joy and made any thought of moving from Portville a nonstarter.

On this Sunday morning, most of Beekman, along with the many others from Portville, sat shoulder to shoulder at morning service.

The day had grown progressively hotter, but the congregation stuck to the expected semiformal attire—the men in suits and women in long dresses with covered shoulders. Perspiration was already evident on a few of the parishioners and promised to infect many more before the hour ended.

The usual service cadence was unfolding with greetings and prayers, hymns and readings, and finally came to that pivotal moment that most in attendance found the primary reason for coming: the sermon. If it wasn't clear to the Beekman clan that Pastor Smith had gotten wind of the Beekman affair, it became abundantly obvious when his sermon strayed from the biblical readings assigned for that particular Sunday. Though the most prominent passage talked about feeding the masses in first-century Jerusalem, Pastor Smith pointed to other readings that had to do with social outcasts, particularly the Samaritans, a people often shunned by first-century Jews.

"I've been hearing a little bird tweeting in my ear these past few days," Pastor Smith began at the pulpit, "and I have to say, times like this challenge a pastor to, well, do the right thing. Usually, doing the right thing—that is, saying the right thing—is an easy task. Usually, the right thing is obvious to everyone, even if it's not that apparent at first. As a pastor, I take comfort in knowing that, though I may disturb some consciences by revealing the truth behind a biblical message, believers will see *the light*, as they say, and open their hearts to a better way."

Pastor Smith reached under his heavy mixed cotton-polyester robe for a handkerchief, which he used to wipe his brow. The beads of sweat on his forehead were growing in number and size as he stood under the direct glare of an overhead spotlight and a beam of sunlight shining through the window, timed perfectly for this very sermon. He was essentially standing in a proverbial spiritual light. One could reasonably wonder if his sweat was from the summer heat or from the obligation to venture where few religious leaders dared go, especially from the pulpit.

"I think it timely to remind parishioners about a recurring theme in the Bible," he continued, "a theme of inclusion, of *giving* to our fellow brothers and sisters. I don't mean the relative ease of comforting a family member or neighbor in need. That's almost like providing for your own children. It's expected, and thus, not really rewarded in a great way. Indeed, we feel good about helping our neighbor, but its uplifting quality soon passes since it's almost a daily expectation. No, that's not the kind of *inclusion* I'm talking about. My idea of inclusion is a difficult one. It requires us to reach deep. To stir the settled emotions of our day-to-day lives into a vortex of discomfort and sometimes confusion.

"My idea of inclusion is a *costly* inclusion. You may lose the favor of your family, your friends, or your neighbors. It may even feel as though there is nothing instinctual about this kind of inclusion. It goes against your grain and feels like your energy is wasted on the undeserving. You'd be wrong. Costly inclusion is actually more valuable than an inclusion with someone you already know or someone who is like you in every obvious way. The very cost makes it more valuable.

"It may seem counterintuitive, but once you step out of your comfort zone and cross the divide, you'll find there is, indeed, life on the other side. You may have alienated some who couldn't see the merits of giving, but the grace you feel is enduring. The impact of giving to family and friends may easily wane with the ebb and flow of your life, but the costly 'give' of making someone whole, the sacrifice of time and service to someone not like yourself—an outcast, a Samaritan—that kind of give will change your life. You don't do it out of fear or to earn special favors with God. You do it because you feel a calling to see God in someone seemingly unlike yourself."

The pastor wiped his brow a second time and shifted from his left foot to his right. He felt he was hitting his stride. The words were coming easily. It was as if he had prepared the sermon days in advance and practiced every line for emphasis and effect—although he hadn't. He didn't have the time. The truth of what was evolving on Beekman had revealed itself slowly throughout the week. It took time to piece it all together because his sources didn't want to reveal that they were part of the scheme to buy back the Johnson property. He looked beyond the front rows to the back of the church to feel the energy level of his congregation. He wanted everyone's attention—and by all accounts, he had it.

"Jesus' time was no different than ours," he continued. "The outcasts were many, maybe more than what we have today here in the States, even in our state. Back then, an ailment that wouldn't go away was enough to cause someone to be shunned. Today, we pity those with incurable diseases. We have fundraisers for them to help with hospital bills and to advance research to find a cure. Those outcasts of the early-Christian era are today embraced, mostly because they're our brothers and sisters, our moms and dads, our neighbors. The outcast of Jesus' time that *still* exists today is that of the Samaritan. Though they were Jewish, their cultural evolution had long before split them from traditional Judaism, and they were considered illegitimate in the eyes of God. These were people similar in every way except culture, and that was enough for them to be ostracized.

"Jesus, however, did not. Sometimes, a Samaritan questioned Jesus' cultural obtuseness. You may remember the readings on the woman at the well. Imagine that. He deigned to talk to her, a woman *and* a Samaritan. It was something that never happened, and she ridiculed him for violating custom. It would have been much easier for Jesus to just follow along with cultural tradition because the inclusion of Samaritans was costly.

"People not only challenged him outwardly, but they also murmured behind his back. They questioned the authenticity of his message, his reason for being, solely because he included Samaritans in his quest for redemption. Even his hand-chosen disciples, his closest friends, chided him for reaching out across the divide. It was foolish, a waste of energy, and against tradition. What could be the purpose? Yes, my friends, Jesus defined the word costly. He did nothing that was easy. He always challenged the status quo because the status quo, by definition, was the easy way, the cheap way, the way of the world. But we believe he was not of this world."

Pastor Smith heard a cough, followed by some rustling. These were the beginning signs. It usually meant he'd been talking too long. If he ignored the signs, they usually increased in frequency until one might as well start chuckling at all the movement and clearing of throats, as if to say, "Okay, already, let's wrap it up, Pastor."

Today, however, his sixth sense told him it wasn't the length of his sermon causing the stir. It was the content. He was making some in the congregation uncomfortable. He had crossed over into that netherworld where pastors seldom venture. He had pierced the soft underbelly of their shell and exposed their hypocrisy.

"Let me tell you of a town and a people that is more current and closer to our way of life. This is a town and a people that had a choice to make, and now, reflecting back on history, those people are a proud representation of what this country is all about. In the 1840s, this country was suffering from a plague that devastated its land, its people, and its culture. While the plague had been long in coming, its cure was evident, right here in Portville."

The pastor paused for a bit to see if he had hooked the crowd back in. He had. All was quiet.

"Yes, my friends, Portville. Your Portville, my Portville. *Our* beloved Portville. This plague was slavery, a tragic blight on a people not of their making. What many of you may not know is that Portville stood proud in helping runaway slaves who were making their way to freedom in Canada. The epicenter of what we all know as the Underground Railroad ran right through Portville. Your forefathers and mothers chose to include. It may have been a costly choice, but they made it anyway. Runaway slaves crossing the Ohio River were given shelter, new clothes, and food; they were resupplied for a journey that would take them north to freedom. It was against the law, punishable by imprisonment or a fine, or both. The deterrent was strong enough that not everyone chose to make a difference in the lives of those who needed it most. But enough did for it to be written into history. You may not read about it in your children's textbooks, but if you scratch the surface, maybe go down to the public library, you'll find the truth spelled out in black and white. Pardon the pun, though it is timely."

He smiled.

"The people of Portville have a proud history in this country, and many of our homes dating back a hundred and fifty years were homes used to make freedom a reality for those who chose to see the face of God in someone who looked different. I'm asking you today, my friends, to look beyond the ones we see sitting next to us in the pews. Look to the people we don't see very often here in Portville, the ones that most choose not to see, the ones it would be 'too costly' to see, and see them. Include them. Honor them as a brother and sister in Christ."

The pastor stepped back from the pulpit with a look of satisfaction. The Beekman issue had been simmering in his conscience in the days leading up to this very moment, and he felt blessed that somehow the words had come to him. An unprepared sermon was not his usual, especially on such an important subject. He would know soon enough if he'd hit the mark. He sat in his chair on the altar, wiped the sweat from his brow one final time, and bowed his head in prayer.

——— ... ———

As the congregation filtered out into the hot, muggy air, Pastor Smith stood at attention, greeting the older congregants in his usual style. A few "tsk tsks" were murmured as limp hands were offered up by parishioners who, out of habit or guilt, felt obligated to greet the pastor every week after service, regardless of his performance at the pulpit.

When Peter and I came by, I didn't slow my pace—just walked past, offering a quick "Hello, Pastor" almost as an afterthought. Peter reached out and shook the pastor's hand with a strong squeeze of affirmation.

"You outdid yourself today," Peter said, smiling. "We may lose you to some mega-church in Cleveland or Cincinnati if you keep it up."

"Thank you, thank you, thank you," Pastor Smith replied. "You're the first one to say something positive, if you can believe it." He pulled Peter in close, as he usually did, for a personal word. "I guess the Jordan dilemma is obvious. At least you can take solace in the fact that he cared enough about you to struggle over the decision. I'm not sure if his final motives were generous or selfish, but it does seem like he values your friendship."

"I appreciate what you're trying to say, Pastor. At times, though, it seems like putting lipstick on a pig."

They both laughed heartily while I stood by, doing my usual act of nonchalance. The pastor slapped Peter on the back as a way to say thank you, see you later, and move along. He was gracious and diplomatic. He knew the line was growing long, but he wanted Peter to know he respected his insight.

———— ... ————

As the afternoon wore on, Peter continued to feel upbeat. He seemed to think the sermon was an affirmation that his moral compass was not off the mark. At least someone was in his corner. I, on the other hand, was confused. It was as if my head and my heart were pulled in opposite directions. I never verbalized doubt or compromise, but I'm sure others could tell something was not sitting right with me.

After a late outdoor lunch, we continued to enjoy the usual temperate weather at that time of day by sitting out on the back patio, away from the sun's glare. The beginnings of the late-afternoon breeze broke the stifling humidity. Beads of perspiration ran down the side of our iced tea, which sat between us on a small round table.

"You and Pastor Smith seemed quite chummy there after church. Found a new comrade in arms, did you?" My tone was tainted with curiosity and disdain. I kept a steady gaze away from Peter, out over the distant property line.

"Well, you have the whole neighborhood seeing this thing your way. You can imagine how I feel on the outside looking in. Don't begrudge me a little camaraderie with the pastor." He studied my profile to see if I betrayed any sign of contrition. I didn't.

"He's not supposed to take sides in these nonreligious issues," I shot back, still no eye contact.

"Do you hear yourself, Clare? Nonreligious? What in this world is nonreligious? Philosophically, everything is religious. Going to the bathroom is religious, if you want to get granular about it. Come on, don't be a sore loser."

"I haven't lost anything, Peter," I snapped, my voice dripping with sarcasm as I gave him a whale-eye glare.

"You sound like someone who's on the defensive. Is it possible that somewhere deep down inside you feel uncomfortable about something? Like something's just not right about all this? Just an inkling?"

"No!"

"Okay, my bad. I guess Pastor and I are the odd ones out here."

"Then why do you have a grin on your face if you're still in such a minority?" I was now staring him down with both eyes.

"Because I'm in good company. The majority isn't always right."

"Says you!" I said, growing testy.

"We're sounding like kids here, Clare."

"Don't insult me!"

He decided to let it drop.

——— ... ———

Later that evening, once dinner had been cleared, the family settled into the family room to watch a favorite sitcom. The widescreen TV sat centered in a floor-to-ceiling cherry wood entertainment center. The room was dotted with family photos on surrounding bookshelves and end tables. The happy smiles in photos from our travels painted the picture of a strong, intact family. But behind the smiling faces in the photos were the real Davidsons—claiming our favorite seats for watching TV or the occasional board game. The latter was something we still engaged in despite the electronic revolution taking place in homes across the country.

Mobile phones and other computer games had disrupted the family bond in ways unpredicted, and we were no different. We had all the latest in electronic gadgetry but I held fast to tradition.

Well into the evening, the house phone rang. Sandy sprang to her feet, ever hopeful it would be for her. This time, she was out of luck.

"Mom, it's for you," she said with a sulking frown. "It's Mrs. Thompson." She held the cordless phone out for me with palpable disappointment.

"Oh," I said as I leaped from my favorite spot on the loveseat. "I wonder what she's up to?"

I walked out of the room to take the call and was gone almost twenty minutes before I returned and plopped myself back down on the loveseat. Normally, Peter would have asked how things were going with Maggie, but he must have sensed from my look that whatever we had talked about, it wasn't good. He decided not to venture into the emotional quicksand that was a common danger at that time.

As the night went on and memory of the call faded, a wall of emotion overcame me. The call was, indeed, not good news. I tried to contain it, but it spilled over. A tear broke free from my left eye and I quickly wiped before it could scramble down the side of my face. The required sniffle followed, a rub of the eye, and I then got up and left the room.

——— ... ———

A half hour after I escaped to the bedroom, I was reclined on the bed reading the book I'd been trying to finish for close to a month. It was an indulgence that usually needed less than a week, but recent events had changed all that. My usual refuge of retiring early to the quiet of the bedroom and traveling to faraway places—London, Paris, Rome—with heroine characters, determined and brave while preserving honor and pride, was now undermined by calls to and from neighbors with updates on *the offer,* as it was now referred to.

The unpredictable confrontations with Peter over moral turpitude and philosophical destiny didn't help matters. It wasn't that I didn't have the time. My days certainly had their quiet moments to escape, but it was my mind suffering an onslaught of possibilities and probabilities of the offer. I was in such turmoil throughout the day that escaping it all in a book had slowly faded from my list of joys to a needed distraction, and then its demand for calm and focus meant I no longer was in the right state of mind to read at all.

At that very moment, I really had no intention to read. The phone call churned my insides and frayed my nerves. I looked about the room, trying to find something to occupy my mind, to distract me from the offer. The unfinished book sat on my nightstand, beckoning to me. For some reason, it pulled me in. It was a drug that fed my anxiety and sank me deep into wants and needs that could never come to fruition.

The drug was *The Optimist's Daughter*, and I had reached that momentous point in the novel when Laurel Hand finally remembered that her mom and dad, both deceased, were not the perfect parents she had always remembered them to be. They had their flaws, but they were the kind of flaws one only appreciated as an adult glancing back at one's youth with the salve of time. It was a subtle blindness, an inability to see what was always there. Eudora Welty weaved this hidden truth throughout her novel. Imperfect though they were, Laurel still loved her parents, and that balance of truth and childhood optimism allowed her to accept their passing and begin anew.

For me, the novel incited intense longing for my own parents, who were also deceased. But unlike in the story, their memories sat ever so perfect in my imaginings, and they were sorely needed to shore up my failing confidence in the Beekman affair. I was not blind. I saw the reality of life as it was—as it was meant to be. I read and reread those passages, over and over, stuck on rewind, sinking deep into a netherworld of false truths and assuaged memories.

Peter eventually made his way up to our bedroom. He was quiet and tentative, no doubt sensitive to whatever I might be going through. Despite my efforts, I'm certain he'd noticed my tearful escape. But what he saw did not comport with what he expected: a woman besieged with preserving some Beekman fantasy of exclusivity, all by her lonesome.

Did he misread something along the way? Was he wrong? Was *his* vision marred? What he did not see was that his stubborn, recalcitrant wife was now a ship foundering near rocky shoals, the specter of despair seducing the woman he fell in love with so long ago. Would he surmise that my need for escape was at a crisis point—that by finding refuge in my book, I had hoped to conjure up memories of better times than these? I doubted it.

He sat next to me on the edge of the bed and gazed into my face, waiting for acknowledgment. "Clare?"

I avoided him.

"How are things with Maggie? What did she have to say?"

I ignored, but he persisted.

"Clare? Come on, talk to me."

"Nothing, really," I relented.

"Hmm. That 'nothing, really' seemed to upset you."

"I didn't think you'd care about it." I was annoyed with his persistence.

"Well, let's see."

"She was just passing on information."

"And?" he prodded.

"Maggie said news was traveling around the neighborhood that Fred Mason followed up with the Robinsons in Cincinnati to see about the offer. He tried to visit them this morning. He knew they were home because his hired guy had been tracking their whereabouts. Well, they wouldn't see him. Apparently, they wouldn't open the door." My tone grew defiant. "And they wouldn't give him an answer when he asked them through the door. They just totally disrespected him. What kind of people are they? They have no sense of normal decency."

The tears returned, and my lips quivered. This time there was no hiding it. If I was blind to anything back then, it was the irony of it all—the phone call and my distraught despair of realizing our meticulously hatched plans a few weeks ago at the Masons' had all gone sideways.

Peter likely saw what I refused to see. He had that look. He wanted to comfort and appease me, but he was hiding a smirk that said he wasn't surprised, like he knew all along this whole thing was a bad idea. Sure, the Robinsons were not negotiating with *proper* decorum. Meanwhile, all of Beekman conspired to legally block their hopes and dreams from finding fulfillment in Portville. We hired a private investigator to track them down and spy on their whereabouts. And I'm sure Fred Mason, our attack dog let loose, lacked tact. He probably gave no foundation, no reason by way of explanation why the community found itself in need of making the offer. It was likely a cold, plain business proposition. *We want to buy your property. Sell it to us, and we'll throw in a little something extra, just for your troubles.* It was not a surprise the proposal fell flat. The irony was obvious to anyone not blinded by self-preservation.

"I get it, Clare. The Robinsons are playing hardball. But it's all part of negotiating deals like this. I don't see why it would upset you so."

"No, you *don't* get it, Peter. Of course, you don't get it. You and Pastor Smith are clueless. Your heads are in the sand, and you're out of touch with reality. Right now, I'm the only one holding this family together, and sometimes it's just irritating. I just wish this whole Robinson thing would go away. They're not welcome. They should know it by now. Why be stubborn about it? Why move to a neighborhood where you're not welcome? You'd have to be a glutton for punishment to ignore what's going on. I'm just so frustrated."

Another tear ran free, and my congested nose sniffled in vain to open a passage. Peter handed me a tissue.

I had become my mother's daughter in more ways than I'd care to admit. Peter's teasing to that end was always met with a disapproving glare. But he had heard enough of my childhood story to know he wasn't far from the truth. My idyllic upbringing, something I could hardly dispute, came from two doting parents and no siblings to rival. While an only child often longed for a sister to play with—dolls, tea parties, imaginary adventures—I was not of that ilk. I was content in the limelight of total parental devotion. Some thought my parents were too indulgent. But in all fairness, isn't that what children are for? To spoil? It was my parents' defense when friends teased them. Indeed, they hovered with every activity, and I easily accommodated their needs. What's a daughter to do?

Such was the hardship I endured growing up in the upper-class Bexley suburb of Columbus, Ohio. I wore embroidered dresses with matching patent leather Mary Janes for playdates while my friends dressed in jeans and sneakers. Peter had seen the photo albums and teased me for my precocious upbringings. I managed a whole cast of American Girl dolls when my friends were elated to have just one. Visits to the pediatrician were peppered with every concern my mother could conceive to prevent the most esoteric of diseases. A fever might be malaria, a cough could mean diphtheria, and diarrhea—cholera. Doctors heard about the latest article on tropical diseases not from their monthly journals but from my mom, ever diligent in keeping no stone unturned.

These were stories I was proud to share. My parents had taught me to have ambitious standards and not accept compromise. For example, teachers second-guessed themselves when issuing semester grades, fearful that my mom would launch interminable complaints of foul play. Their attempts at touting the benefits of allowing the occasional B for mediocre performance went unheeded and were derided as ineffectual parenting if she were to allow it. Even college professors had more than chance opportunities to meet my mom. We were both similarly strong-willed, and it surprised neither of my parents that I intended to get my business degree and join the family's financial consulting firm.

Such was my focus, determination, and pride. That pride was long-lived and touched everything I cared for. It was why the Johnson house, and the possibility of new neighbors—*different* new neighbors, to be precise—was such an obsession with me. It ran counter to my need for order, predictability, and decorum. This was simply me attacking the things I cared about with pride and determination. I knew no other way.

Peter gave me all the time I needed. Talking about the issue seemed to calm me. I was on the verge of tears when he first came into the bedroom. Now, I was more animated and engaged in proving a point. I looked him in the eye when I spoke, as if I were trying to convince him that my cause was noble.

"What's so wrong about wanting the best for our kids, for wanting the idyllic magic that makes Beekman Beekman to remain unchanged?"

Of course, Peter always felt that my intentions were noble. But he also felt they were misdirected. "I don't know," he said, "maybe I'm wrong and you're right? I just can't believe that protecting the family from the unknown needs to be an exclusive proposition. I don't know what to expect any more than anyone else on Beekman. I just don't fear uncertainty."

I rested my belief in what was known, what was tangible, what was history. I knew of no other suburb as nice as ours that had Blacks living among them. It just didn't exist. Why should we acquiesce to experimenting on our family? It just didn't seem prudent. Certainly not something a mother would allow for her children.

Peter sat next to me and held me in his arms, and it occurred to me at that moment that the day had taken a turn. Sunrise and sunset were not the two hours of glorious golden colors on a canvas of our making. Quite the opposite, in fact. For me, it was the hour of hope and the hour of reality, the hour when expectations were made and the hour when they were deferred—a time when all seemed possible, and a time when I just had to get on with life as it was.

12

Session 9

Peter entered the session room and flumped down in the left chair with a sigh. He offered no salutation and ignored Anna's. He sat motionless for a while, staring at her, then staring out the window, which had a soft glow. It was overcast, and the usual bright sunshine was hidden. It seemed appropriate for his mood. After a while, his eyes returned to Anna. She sat and waited and watched.

"Well, Doc, you called it," he finally said. "She's leaving me."

It came out as a matter-of-fact statement, but it also had a tinge of blame, like he was holding her responsible. She remained silent while he wondered what she thought of his declaration. He expected she was quietly—smugly—pleased with herself. He didn't know why he'd come to the session at all. He'd canceled the last two just to spite her. Something, however, was pulling him in, like a fish on a hook. He had taken the bait like a fool and was now helpless to go where he wanted. She had him in her snare. He could cancel now and again, but he knew he couldn't stay away indefinitely. He'd heard of the codependency between patient and therapist, and he always felt he was too independent, too intellectually strong, to let it happen to him—not unlike the person who says they can never be hypnotized, but then it happens. The ones who deny it are the first to succumb.

He was hypnotized. He didn't want to need her, but it was an addiction, a dependency that deepened with every session. There was no denying it. His life told a story in a language only she knew. It was complicated. Apparently, more than he could ever have imagined. Anna peeled back that onion, layer by layer, and there he lay, bare, naked, exposed, and hurting. He tried to fight it, to fight the direction she was pushing him. To improve, she said, he had to be independent—of her, of Clare.

He wouldn't. He couldn't. He outright refused. Instead of turning away from Clare, he would try instead to make amends, only an impulse would surface and pull him in a different direction. He could never follow through. Clare must have noticed his attempts on occasion, his bursts of energy to plan a trip for just the two of them or a dinner party for Beekman friends, but eventually he would mention some new tidbit about a friend from his forbidden Eaton crowd, or Clare would find him brooding alone in the cellar, clearly not one with himself. She must have thought he was simply teasing or taunting her, playing with her emotions. After a while she grew irritated, probably believing that his mind was not in the right place. These were two ships passing side by side, neither knowing the other's destination. He was at a loss and had resolved to go it alone. He was gradually giving up—only he thought it was Clare who was pulling away.

"Did you hear what I said?" Peter said, trying to fan the flames of his indignation. He wanted a sparring match with Anna over whose fault it was that things were turning sour in his marriage. Her prescient warnings had come to pass, or so he believed, and in his emotional state of loss, he felt she deserved the blame. "She's leaving me. I just know it."

"How does that make you feel?" Anna asked.

"How do I feel?" Peter shouted as he bolted out of his chair and hovered over her desk. "How do I feel?" His voice grew even louder, his face injected with red rage. "I feel like shit, that's how I feel!" He was panting and looked every bit the wild man.

Anna gasped. Her eyes went wide, pupils dilated in shock. She stared at Peter without emotion. His outburst was real, and she feared what he would do next, but she also needed to remain outside his issues. If she showed anxiety, she would lose objectivity. Ultimately, she would lose perspective. So she waited, looking as dispassionate as possible, hoping he would settle.

That this caught her off guard was an understatement. Peter usually denied or wallowed or became catatonic when he was frustrated. He never yelled. He was clearly on edge, maybe on *the* edge. She had been here before with other patients, but Peter was different. He seemed to pride himself on control. Other patients often declared their volatility early in therapy. She usually had a chance to acclimate. Peter, however, threw her a curve; her need for delicacy was now critical. Anything she said or intimated could be misinterpreted as insensitive or too aloof, igniting him into a rage. She needed to allow time for the air to cool, for Peter to regain his composure. Words were weapons that could pierce like a saber or soothe like a salve, and she would have to choose them with care.

After another minute, he finally sat down. Eventually, his breathing slowed to normal, his hands stopped fidgeting, and his glare softened.

There was a soft knock at the door. It repeated before Anna reacted. "It's alright, Mrs. Chu. Everything is okay."

As Peter settled, so did she. Her composure finally returned.

But now she had to make a quick decision on how to proceed. Should she address this incident and what it might mean in the grand scheme of Peter's coping abilities? Was this the beginning of a turn, a weakening of resolve? Would there be more of these? She had no idea, and so she decided to let Peter determine what importance it should play.

"Peter, I'm sorry you feel the way you do. Can you help me understand what has happened over the past month to make you feel Clare is giving up on the marriage?"

"She's pulling away from me. I… I can feel it." His anger was gone; dejection was all that remained.

"Well, we discussed this a few weeks back, didn't we? We talked about the possibility that Clare was growing tired of the obsessing after five years, or possibly irritated by you still going to Eaton."

"It's gotten worse."

"Okay, then, give me more."

"More? Like what?" he sneered, jerking his head up to stare at her.

"How is she pulling away? What happened before she started pulling away? Did she simply wake up one morning and change how she behaved, or did something happen?"

"Well," he said, pausing to put his thoughts together.

Engaging him thus was like stroking his ego. He felt obliged to give exact answers, and he'd always put his emotions aside to excavate whatever he thought was the truth of the matter. Anna knew it and played it.

"She's not talking to me the way she used to. Our conversations are just the basics, nothing more. *Hi. Bye. What time will you be home? What do you want for dinner?* That sort of thing. We hardly even touch each other."

"What kind of conversations do you *try* to have with Clare?"

"I don't know, just anything, I guess. It all used to be easy. We used to joke around a lot, tease each other, kiss hello and goodbye. Now it all seems like work. And it's not going anywhere. I think it's because she's pulling away."

"So more of the same, just worse?" Anna asked.

"Yeah."

"I assume you're still volunteering?"

"Yeah."

"So she's still frustrated, then," Anna concluded.

"I guess," he said, now looking defeated and lifeless. "You know, I've been coming to you for four months now, and nothing has changed at home. I'm sure she expected some improvement by now, and things are pretty much the same as they were last summer. I haven't gotten any better."

"How do you know you haven't gotten better?" Anna said. "What's your definition of better?"

"My marriage, for one. I hoped to have this obsession thing well behind me by now, but I think Clare senses something. Sometimes she searches all around the house looking for me, and when she finds me, she turns and walks away. I think—I know—I'm a big disappointment to her."

"What are you doing when she finds you?"

"Nothing much, just lost in thought."

"Is that new for you, pensive moments in quiet places?"

"Well, I've felt a little detached lately," he said, looking surprised to hear himself say it. Then he quickly tried to backtrack. "What, with the emptiness between us and all."

"Are you feeling frustrated with yourself or maybe conflicted about something?" Anna asked.

"I don't know," he said, still sullen. "Maybe. I'm certainly frustrated with Clare."

"Why Clare?"

"I didn't mean it... I didn't mean it that way. I'm not frustrated with Clare, just the situation with Clare is frustrating. That's what I meant."

Anna gave a skeptical look. "You know, it's not uncommon for us to misjudge other people's motives, especially if we're not really communicating well. You may very well be attributing feelings to Clare that are inaccurate, maybe even projecting your own feelings onto her. I mean, it could very well be that Clare is confused about you as much as you are about her. It could be that she feels the void between you just as much as you and is at a loss to find an answer. It could be that she's just giving you space. Someone who searches you out to find out what you're up to doesn't do that out of hate or disappointment. They do that out of concern, maybe even love. I don't want to credit Clare too much here. This is, really, just conjecture on my part, but your version of things may only be one view. But if you'll indulge me here, I have another take on this. Look at her actions. What reasons have you given her to distance herself from you? None, really, that you've told me. *You* may be distancing yourself from her as much or more than she is from you. It may be *all* you, but your guilt doesn't want to own it, so you project it back onto her and make her the villain. I know she sees an event in your past differently than you, but that doesn't mean she's the villain in this marriage."

"So I'm the villain, then, huh?" Peter said, suddenly snapping back to life.

"Why is it that you have a knack for finding the one word that I use to paint a different picture and bury yourself with it? I know you don't see yourself as the villain here. Are you just looking for sympathy?"

"Why not? I'm confused. Freaking confused."

"When are you not confused, Peter?"

Peter fell silent, looking like he didn't know what to say.

"Did I catch you off guard with that question? You know, I sometimes come at you from left field. I apologize," Anna said, keeping a more friendly, professional air in play.

"I wasn't sure how to answer," he said. "I mean, when I'm at work I'm not stressed or anything. But that's work. It probably doesn't count. The kids aren't at home anymore, and I don't socialize with the neighbors much. So I guess the times I enjoy most are when I'm at Eaton."

"Isn't that work for you?"

"It is, but I've become pretty social with some of the folks there. We chat a bit after I run the numbers for them, and part of my time there is volunteering, remember?"

"Yes, that's right. It's more a volunteer job than an accounting job. So when you're at Eaton, you feel at ease. You're calm and most like yourself?"

"Yeah, it's like the old days. I can just relax, joke around with everyone like I really fit in. Except, of course, I'm not gay or anything."

"No harm if you were," Anna said.

"I wouldn't be trying to save my marriage if I *were* gay, now, would I?"

"I've seen stranger things, so I don't assume. But yes, I didn't take you for someone with latent sexual ambiguities."

"Well, when you put it like that, it sounds like I have a disorder or something."

"Sorry, it came out wrong. Just the therapist in me. But I can't help observing that the way you describe your time at Eaton as similar to how you describe what your marriage was like: fun, easy, spontaneous, lots of humor and teasing. It's almost as if you've transferred your emotional life from home to elsewhere. You're essentially creating a new family."

Peter's angry, disturbed features were long gone. He was now fully back to his old self. "Uh, well, maybe there's something there. What exactly are you implying by that connection, Doc?"

"It's pretty straightforward here. I'm not trying to uncover some hidden secret or anything. It's just that you enjoy the company of the people you volunteer with. You've chosen to put your energy elsewhere. I thought it was a very healthy outlet for you. I thought it when you first told me about it, and I still think it now. It does make me wonder, though."

"About what?" His ask was quick and defensive.

"Well, I'm wondering, but I don't know the answer yet."

"Answer to what?" Peter stammered.

"I'm wondering if it's you beginning to pull away from Clare since you've found another outlet, someplace you feel more accepted, that's low-stress and fun. A place that makes you feel… well, like you."

Peter's head hurt. He had worked himself up in the exchange and was on the edge of the chair, waiting for Anna to get it all out. And now, in the aftermath of her revelation that he was the instigator in all his recent emotional agony, he slid back in the chair and stared out the window, much like he had when he'd first come in for the session.

All was quiet. A soft glow of the overcast sky still illuminated the room with a subdued ambiance that allowed Peter to lapse into reverie, like a stone falling through water. It was hypnotic, and he was transfixed—once again having fallen under her spell.

13

I rolled over in an early Saturday morning slumber to find Peter had already risen. My eyes were still heavy, and the bright lights of the summer sunrise made keeping them shut all the harder. I tried to doze off, but I'd had enough sleep to make dozing an unlikely dream. As I lay there with the hope of another ten or fifteen minutes of shuteye, the world became ever-present, poking at my senses like stabs from a thorny bush. My spirit was unwilling, but I could not deny the new day its due. Birds chirped outside, aggressively staking their claim to a limited supply of worms; the smell of eggs and bacon, Sandy's favorite, wafted upstairs like a winged temptation of breakfast in bed; Matt sang his heart out to Michael Jackson on a radio barely audible; and cars zipped by as if Beekman were a four-lane thoroughfare, which it certainly was not. I was conflicted with the acknowledgment that everyone else had already accepted the inevitability of the new day and a frustration that I must do the same.

I was lying on my back, pondering the day ahead, when I heard the distinct sounds of a conversation. It was Peter and—someone else. It was barely audible. I tried to lock in, as if mental focus would amplify the sounds. It didn't.

Initially, I dismissed it as nothing more than chatter between neighbors. But after a few minutes, a loud laugh by the other mysterious person sat me up in bed. Who was that? I knew all the neighbors well enough to know that voice was not a Beekman regular. Was it the postman? Too early. A delivery? None expected. Who was it?

I jumped out of bed and in two strides was at the window, laid bare, most likely by Peter when he decided to join the day in progress. With the drapes sidelined, the sun's glare blinded me, making it impossible to look down on Beekman. I squinted and held my hand along my brow as a visor, but nothing worked. I had to wait for my eyes to adjust.

Eventually, I spied the two figures across the street in front of the Johnson house. It was Peter, and the other person was undeniably Jerome Robinson. My chest galloped. A pounding fullness swelled my ribcage. My left hand clenched the gingham drape. My breathing grew heavy. The room soon lost its shape. I wasn't given to panic attacks, but I was certain this was one. I slowly released the drapes and slid to the floor for a safe landing. I sprawled out on my back and breathed, in and out, in and out.

——— ... ———

An hour earlier, Peter had gone through the same process. Only when he looked out on Beekman, he saw Jerome and what must have been his teenage son negotiating a large piece of furniture off the back of a truck. The teen seemed unsteady. He was tall and wiry but all of thirteen years old. Peter sprang into action and was downstairs, exiting the front door in a matter of minutes.

I wasn't surprised when I heard his side of the story. He's always been a knight-in-shining-armor sort of guy. I shouldn't have criticized him during his telling of it, but by then I was wired to find fault in anything he did.

As it turned out, he arrived just in time. According to Peter, father and son were struggling to keep the large sofa from falling. Peter came up behind Jerome's teenage son, who flinched in surprise.

Peter smiled and said, "Let me lighten your load, young man."

It was just the kind of thing he would say. The father finally secured his end of the sofa and started the walk backward to the curb, slowly lowering the load so his arms were fully extended. In doing so, his head peaked over the top of the armrest, and it was then that he clearly saw Peter's smiling face.

"Hi, neighbor," Peter said in greeting. Jerome was still staring some five seconds later when Peter added, "I don't know about you, but this sofa isn't gonna carry itself into the house, and my arms are pulling out of their sockets. How 'bout we get this thing inside?"

Jerome jolted back to life. "Yeah, yeah, sure, thanks."

After several trips from truck to house, much of the load was finally inside. With the cursory pleasantries of introduction behind them, the two men stood on the porch looking out on Beekman, wiping away the perspiration from their early morning workout.

Peter welcomed Jerome to the neighborhood. I'm sure he made it sound official, like it was on behalf of the Beekman Block Association—which, of course, didn't exist. Jerome was gracious and appreciative, as any new neighbor would be. I didn't give him points for that.

Jerome's attention seemed drawn to the tree-lined block. As it was a beautiful morning, Peter knew it was days like these that featured Beekman at its best—its wide thoroughfare, wider than most residential blocks in the area; the perfectly manicured lawns and vibrant flower beds in perpetual bloom; and the beginnings of children out and about on bikes or skateboards or jumping rope.

It was as if Jerome were taking it in for the very first time. "I wasn't sure if this day would ever really come to pass," he said. Peter asked what he meant, and Jerome went on to reveal all the sordid details of Beekman's other side. "It's been... how should I say? An interesting last month or so." He punctuated his words with a chuckle, as if the story had a humorous side.

"Okay, Jerome, you've piqued my curiosity. Interesting?"

Jerome told Peter how, after getting the job at McGuire, he and his wife, Margaret, had started looking at property values all around town. There was a lot out there, so it was definitely a buyer's market. He'd heard something about a factory closing but figured he had a good salary—why not invest? One day, they took a turn onto Beekman and the wow factor was real.

"This," Jerome said, holding his arms open wide to encompass the neighborhood, "is special. You don't see this too often. We expected nothing to be available, and even if there was something, we fully expected it to be out of our reach."

That was when they'd seen the sign: "For Sale by Owner." They couldn't believe someone was actually wanting to leave this block. They took a shot and stopped by to see if the sale thing was real. Jerome said the owners were a little shocked to see them at their front door, but they'd been down that road before and weren't fazed by it.

Jordan had invited them in and was very pleasant. He and Sarah offered them drinks and snacks and made them quite comfortable. That part of the story I could believe. Sarah was hospitable and gracious under the most trying of circumstances. Jerome went on to say that the Johnsons seemed pretty genuine, really nice people.

"I'm a pretty good judge of character," he said, "especially when it comes to race issues, and they treated us like relatives. They showed us around, pointed out the unique features of the house, the areas they'd improved on, you know, all the usual stuff. Jordan showed me what needed looking after, what might give us problems in a few years—real honest about the whole thing. Sarah spent as much time with Margaret, too, showing her the kitchen features, what doesn't work well, or the things she knew Margaret would get a thrill out of. They laughed and smiled and even hugged us at one point."

When the time came to talk numbers, the Johnsons said they were willing to negotiate, but the Robinsons already knew the asking price was in line with homes in other neighborhoods. They'd fully expected at least twenty percent more for Beekman. Margaret and Jerome had looked at each other and tried their best not to exchange high-fives.

Just to show they weren't pushovers, they bickered with the Johnsons over something trivial, but they had clearly done their homework. "We knew we were getting a deal," Jerome said, admitting he felt guilty trying to knock the price down after the Johnsons had been so friendly about showing the house.

Peter said the only odd part of the story was when the Robinsons left. Once they all agreed on a price, the Johnsons toasted them with a pour of champagne—a nice touch that had Sarah's fingerprints all over it—but when they went to show them out, Jordan and Sarah refused to step outside, as if someone were watching.

Jerome let out a deep, hearty baritone laugh that took Peter by surprise. The voice didn't match the body. Jerome was about six feet and lean, a hundred and eighty pounds at most, yet his laugh sounded like it belonged to a three-hundred-pound opera singer. He was in his late thirties, his eyes were a pleasant almond shape that gleamed when he smiled, but his voice had a quality that spoke for itself: "Don't mess with me."

Peter laughed along, although he felt stupid doing it. It hadn't been intended as a joke; Jerome was simply making fun of the Johnsons' predicament.

"It was like right out of a movie set," Jerome told Peter, "and I knew something must be up. Maybe we were in hostile territory. You know, that's a reality for us in many places. We don't want to ruffle feathers—well, not any more than necessary. This was a good deal, too good to pass on. But we weren't surprised when we got the Beekman calling card."

This time, Peter simply raised a brow.

"The buyback offer," Jerome said. "The Beekman community buyback offer, to be precise. I suspect you know all about it, being that you *are* a Beekman."

Peter was embarrassed and immediately said, "For the record, I'm not one of them. In fact, I might be the only one on the block who's not one of them."

"I believe you," Jerome said, "but you shocked the hell out of me when I looked up and saw your mug looking back at me. I thought, oh boy, here we go, these people are gonna get under my skin from day one."

Peter smiled and suppressed a laugh. "Sorry, I should have introduced myself first. But there didn't seem time. That couch was on its way down."

"I appreciate your thoughtfulness," Jerome said with a chuckle. Then his face grew serious. "As far as offers go, it wasn't that bad. They added twenty percent to our costs and offered to pay our moving expenses… to any other destination."

It was Fred Mason's signature card at work. Fred always did what others would do, plus a little something extra. That offer of paying to move the Robinsons to any destination of their choosing would have cost only a few extra thousand, but it might have been what tipped the scale. It didn't.

"We said no," Jerome told Peter. "It didn't go over too well. Within the week, some other guy showed up at our door trying to get us to change our minds. They offered another five percent, told us the neighborhood wasn't our kind of place, that we'd be happier in another community, that Beekman might not be too friendly to outsiders. It just kept getting darker and darker after every no. It seemed in the end they were outright threatening us."

Peter apologized for Beekman, though he was in no position to speak for us. At the time, we were on a mission, and Peter stood as a lone coyote doing his own thing. Still, he tried to be reassuring.

"Well, now you're here, and it's all behind you," he added, as if the bitter pill had been swallowed. In truth, that pill was now traveling through the whole system and would need to find an exit... somewhere.

"*Is* it behind us?" Jerome asked. The answer was obvious by his tone. "I don't know what we're in for. I just hope the Beekman bark is bigger than its bite."

Peter offered help out in any way he could. "I know we just met and all, but I feel I've been fighting this fight for the past month or so. I've got a stake in whatever happens."

"You and me both."

Peter admired the man who stood down Fred Mason purely on principle. Jerome wanted what was best for his family and would not be bought off.

At that moment, Peter looked across the street and saw me come outside. I looked around the front garden without any attempt to look their way. He knew that I knew. It was my way of sending a message—another chess move to neutralize any advantage he might have gained by befriending the Robinsons against my will.

——— ... ———

Minutes before walking outside, I startled back to wakefulness. I was on my bedroom floor. I had drifted into some other state of consciousness. I had no idea how long I'd been out. I didn't want to get up. Just lying there felt peaceful. My nerves had calmed, and my breathing was barely noticeable. The smell of bacon clung to the walls, and the wrens and finches were still chirping, now a more singsong melody than the territorial squabbling from earlier. The sun's glare shone through the window, illuminating dust particles dancing in space. I lay there in the shade of the windowsill, mesmerized by the atoms in motion. All was quiet. No talking.

When rest was no longer restful, I got up and peered out the window, hoping things would look the way they had the week before: just a regular Saturday morning on Beekman. But the moving truck was still there. The reality everyone had dreaded was now at my doorstep.

I could see Peter talking to the man I assumed was Jerome Robinson. They stood on the Johnson porch directly across the street, but this time I couldn't hear their words. The two men looked like old friends rehashing old memories. The way men spoke always piqued me to annoyance—the constant comparisons, the braggadocio, and one-upmanship.

As I watched, their animation ceased, and their laughter gave way to silence—pensive thought unencumbered by awkwardness. It was then that I realized their conversation was not superficial banter. They had already scratched the surface of frivolity and were now on to more serious matters.

I wondered if I was one of those serious matters.

Was Beekman and its rejection of the Robinsons the subject at hand? Peter was connecting with Jerome, and I knew he was liking it. It was what he really wanted—if anything, just to prove a point. But rather than feel bitter, a deep emptiness consumed my gut, like I had been betrayed.

Peter making friends was his pulling away from me, and worse, drawing close to someone else. Jerome Robinson might as well have been another woman. It was marital infidelity, plain and simple.

What was equally offensive was that now I would have to explain Peter's flirtation with the new neighbors to the rest of Beekman. This was as damaging to me as it was to Peter. Maybe more so. I had the reputation on Beekman of being a Sarah Johnson disciple. Much was expected of me, not only because of my tutelage under her impeccable reputation, but also my own accomplishments.

My journalism had burnished my reputation on high-class living. Those articles to women's magazines covered more than just personal finance or retirement planning or mortgages. I also occasionally wrote about lifestyle choices, particularly choices that maintained a certain image.

The gentrification of my readers was the primary goal. But between the lines, as few Beekman homeowners ever admitted, my prose defined a list of dos and don'ts. Do pick partners that will permit you to stay home and raise your own children; pick homes where local schools rank highest on state testing scores; choose the more durable though more expensive items to furnish your home.

Of course, it was imperative to steer clear of excess: indulgences such as smoking, alcohol, and recreational drugs—dietary control being the paramount theme. Avoiding unambitious men and those who flirt with every skirt were subtle suggestions hidden among the more prosaic concerns.

Needless to say, choosing clothes, cars, and even friends all said something about who you were or wanted to become, and it was all covered in my articles.

While I'd never put myself on Sarah's level, I still believed Beekman had two highly regarded examples of fine living in their midst—one *told* you how; the other *showed* you how. Ironically, with Peter's elopement, I would now be forced into the disappointing camp of Sarah Johnson, who had already betrayed Beekman.

I decided enough was enough. I threw on my summer walking outfit and ran downstairs. Sandy heard me coming and called out, "Mom, want any eggs?" I ignored her, hoping she'd assume she wasn't heard.

I just needed to get away, to see nothing that would remind me of the house, the truck, the neighbor, or Peter. I needed out, to keep my nerves from fraying any more than they already had.

As I shut the door behind me, the new day tempted me from the mission at hand. The Lincoln roses in the front garden were in full bloom. Their scented sweetness melted over me like a soothing balm. I was drawn to them in an unconscious desire to linger in their aromatic hypnosis.

I indulged myself by stepping through the front garden, admiring my handiwork—the perfectly laid flagstone path winding through the flowerbed, bordered by white and purple sweet alyssum, overgrown poppies, bearded irises, and delphiniums, with hollyhocks lining the back and roses standing sentry at the front.

It was a delightful synergy of landscape, colors, and scents that imitated the style of an English country cottage I so much envied. This was my home, my creation. It had taken years to imagine, plan, and curate to perfection.

And in one month—one day—it was all threatened. The realization brought me back to my right senses, and I stormed off down the street, taking notice of no one, my mind in a frenzy of confusion and frustration.

14

Peter watched from across the wide Beekman expanse as Clare marched past. He couldn't help but feel sadness from the growing disconnect between them. He also couldn't understand why something that seemed so natural to him could be so objectionable to her. If they were ever soul mates, that time had passed. Was it the Robinsons, or was there a growing cancer in their marriage that he had not noticed, something lurking behind the scenes waiting for the right moment or some provocation to surface and wreak havoc on what he once thought was the proverbial match made in heaven?

It was a sinking reality for him that his marriage was no longer what it once was. The evidence was marching past him as he leaned on the Robinson porch railing, his wife, his first real love, emotionally separated from him as much as the Beekman expanse that separated them in that moment. He had violated his marital vows. He allowed something else—*someone* else—to come between them.

In that moment, he felt he would do anything to make amends. He owed it to her, to their marriage, to their vows of fidelity. He was committed to Clare's happiness, and he knew he could never be satisfied unless she were, indeed, happy. Only he knew what that meant—and he was not prepared to go there. He knew it was selfish, maybe even arrogant, to think that his view of things was right and hers wrong. Persisting in his current acts of infidelity could not possibly bode well over time.

He reached his hand up and dug his nails into the top of his head, imagining he was tearing at his mind, trying to scramble his stubbornness, to give way, to acquiesce.

Peter was lost in thought as Jerome's wife, Margaret, came outside and greeted them. "Gentleman, can I interest you in a fresh glass of orange juice? Iced tea seems a more social beverage, but it *is* still mid-morning."

Margaret smiled at Peter as she offered him a tall glass filled with orange pulp and ice cubes. He kicked it back, forgetting his manners, and let out a satisfied "Aah." It was refreshing.

"Thank you, Margaret," Peter said. "It tastes like fresh-squeezed. Could it be? I know you couldn't have whipped up something like this in between all the unboxing."

"Don't underestimate me, Mr. Davidson. I've been known to do more with less," she said with a guileless smile.

"You're amazing, and please call me Peter."

Jerome looked on with an approving smile. He knew he had a good thing in Margaret and didn't need to sing her praises.

"So, Peter, which house is yours?" Margaret asked.

"We're directly across from you," he said, pointing. "There, with the red roses, my wife's pride and joy. Along with our two kids, of course."

"What a pretty home you have. They're all beautiful homes on this block. What I like most is that they're not ostentatiously huge or anything, but they are all uniquely built and well-appointed, if you know what I mean," Margaret said.

"Very observant," Peter said. "It's what we like most about

Beekman. Every house has that special something."

"And you have two kids, you say. How old are they?"

"Matt is fourteen, and Sandy is twelve, though you'd think she was sixteen by the way she handles herself. She's quite precocious, but then again, many girls are these days."

"We have a son, Julian, he's thirteen. Of course, you met him when moving in the furniture. Where *is* he? He's always off somewhere with his nose in a book. The minute we don't need him for something, he's hiding, doing his own thing."

"Could be worse," Peter said. "You got a thirteen-year-old that likes to read. I say let him be."

"So," Jerome said, "that house there is yours? Was that your wife we saw leave a few minutes ago?"

"Yeah, she's a bit upset with me at the moment. We're not exactly seeing eye to eye on some things."

Peter spoke with a calmness suggesting it was an issue long in coming and he'd grown used to the predicament. The Robinsons were silent. It seemed they knew well enough to leave it alone. It could have been his own issue—he and Clare—or it could have been them. Either way, it wasn't their issue to deal with.

"Tell me something," Peter said to Jerome, "did you and Margaret ever have issues like the one here on Beekman? I'm just wondering how these things usually settle."

"Well," Jerome said, giving Peter a curious look, "our last neighborhood wasn't always friendly. People were skeptical when we first moved in . It helped that we were renters, not buyers. Something about the impermanence of being a renter was less threatening. It seemed everyone was reassured our financial depth wasn't on par with the rest of the community. Also, as renters, you know we're ultimately going to leave. The community bided its time. But time always has a way of working miracles. At least that's how I've seen it play out. Time in people's faces usually softens the heart. Gradually, people became hospitable. A few were even pleasant, and an ever rarer few were quite neighborly."

A lull in the conversation allowed the indelicate issue of family strife to drift away. As if on cue, Julian appeared.

"Well, there you are. We were just discussing your disappearing act," Margaret said teasingly.

Julian glanced at Peter and chose to remain quiet. It appeared to Peter that even though they had moved furniture together, he was instinctually shy or easily embarrassed and wouldn't chide his parents in mixed company.

He had his dad's narrow face and features. His hair was cropped very short—military style—and he sported a magnetic smile that revealed a brilliant array of perfect teeth. Julian was destined to be a favorite among the ladies, if he wasn't already.

"I have to compliment you on your work ethic," Peter said to him. "You were quite focused this morning with all the lifting and organizing." He spoke with the kind of pride one reserves for their own flesh and blood. "Margaret, your son wasn't just a passive worker here, he actually orchestrated a lot of what got moved and how. He's got an eye for physics. You might have an engineer on your hands. I see an expensive college tuition down the road."

Margaret leaned into Julian and gave him a hug. "He's our young man of the house, this one here."

"Do you play any sports?" Peter asked.

Julian hesitated then looked at his mom, as if asking permission to participate in their adult conversation. She nodded. "I shoot hoops a bit with my cousins back in Cincinnati, but I'm not on a team or anything," he said. "I'm not really into sports that much. Everyone thinks I am because I'm tall for my age. I always get asked to play. I don't mind playing, it's just not my favorite thing."

Jerome pulled himself away from appreciating the Beekman views. "I make him play. He needs to learn a team sport. Life is a team sport, and if you don't learn early, you don't develop the skills to interact with others—to know when to lean on others for help or when you should keep the ball, so to speak, and take your own shots. There are a lot of life lessons in sports that you don't get from hiding in your room." He finished his words with a gruff grunt and then turned back to look at the oak trees, which were now in an early bloom, their leaves small and bright green.

Peter, who had turned to listen to Jerome's soliloquy, now turned back to Julian to see what his response to his dad's admonition would be. But there was none. It seemed to be another tired aphorism parents unleash on their kids and kids just endure.

"So, what keeps you busy on a Saturday morning when you're not moving furniture?" Peter asked.

Julian broke a timid smile. "I like to read, mostly." His tentativeness subsided as he became more animated.

"I see you have a book there." Peter nodded to the book tucked under Julian's arm. "Is that something you'd recommend?"

"I like it." He was painfully polite while showing the book cover to Peter.

"*The Count of Monte Cristo*," Peter read. "I believe there's a movie version that I saw some time ago. I hate to admit it, but I'm not much of a reader. My wife, on the other hand, can't get enough hours in the day to read. That's like a classic, isn't it? What do you like about it?"

Peter enjoyed engaging kids as adults. While their opinions might not have been sought after much, he knew those opinions were a kid's pride and joy—and Julian apparently preferred this avenue of discussion to the prior one on sports. He needed no further prompting.

"I like books with a lot of action," he said, shyly amused at the attention, "and people stuck in tough situations. This book has all of that. It takes place in the early eighteen hundreds, and it's about a guy that gets sent to jail—though he was innocent, and everyone knew it. The cool thing is that he escapes and gets revenge. He becomes rich, and everyone treats him like royalty, even the people who put him away. They don't recognize him because he's got a ton of money, and all they see is someone they want to impress. It's amazing how cruel people can be," he added, betraying his naiveté.

Julian basked in the attention, while Peter watched him closely, hanging on his every word. Julian paused to let his thoughts settle. Then he added, as an afterthought, "Oh, and I also think it's kinda cool that the author was the son of a slave from the seventeen hundreds."

"Dumas, right?" Peter asked, even though he already knew the author. He had done some research on him back when he'd seen the movie.

"Yeah," Julian said.

"Yes," Jerome's emphatic tone corrected.

"Yes," Julian repeated without a beat. It was obviously a correction he was used to.

"There's an interesting story about him you may or may not know," Peter said, "about the dad Dumas, not the son."

Julian's eyebrows arched, his quizzical look appealing for more.

"Well," Peter continued, "Dumas' father, the former slave, had become a general in the French army. He was quite tall, muscular, and very successful on the battlefield. Napoleon Bonaparte didn't like him. Some thought he was threatened by General Dumas because Dumas was a rising star and had the potential to someday rule France and push Bonaparte to the side. If you've seen a picture of Bonaparte, you can't miss that he had a rather short stature. I think that may have made him easily intimidated by taller men, especially if they excelled in his area of expertise—on the battlefield.

"Dumas and Bonaparte had an argument after the French army invaded Egypt. Dumas was against going to war in Egypt, thinking it would be a difficult place to conquer since you had to cross the Mediterranean. Well, the French did have a very difficult time, and Dumas was proven right. Soon after, Dumas' ship had problems crossing the Mediterranean back to France. They were forced to land in Naples, where he was taken prisoner. Napoleon intentionally left him there for two years, during which time he reinstated slavery as legal in France.

"It was only after that when Bonaparte got Dumas out, but by then he had no rights as a citizen and was no longer a threat to Bonaparte. What happened to the older Dumas certainly makes the son's *Count of Monte Cristo* an interesting story. I've always thought of it like, 'What would Dumas senior have done if he'd escaped prison and returned to France with enough money to get revenge?' Interesting, huh? All those nobleman characters that the count plots against might actually represent Bonaparte himself in real life."

Julian smiled. That there was even more meaning to the story than he'd thought clearly cemented the book as a holy grail. A secret had been revealed, and he was now the new keeper.

"Do you have a favorite part of the story?" Peter asked, intent on keeping Julian in the spotlight.

Julian grinned as if he'd hoped for that very question. He gleefully opened the book like a student who had already done his homework and was expected to recite it to the class. It was pride, to be sure; he was in his element. Something he loved was being validated by a complete stranger. He found the page by first going to the back of the book and scanning what looked to be a list of page numbers he'd listed as an index to different parts of the book.

He found what he was looking for, turned to the right page and paragraph, and read aloud. "There are men who have suffered and who have not only gone on living, but even built a new fortune on the ruins of their former happiness. From the depths into which their enemies have plunged them, they have risen again with such vigor and glory that they have dominated their former conquerors and cast them down in their turn."

Peter studied Julian's face. His sharp, focused eyes looked up at Peter with a devotion that bordered on zeal, his furrowed brow and faint smile breaking across a soft, supple jawline that belied any trace of innocence. Was this the same Julian who had sheepishly appeared in the doorway just minutes before? Peter was mystified. He glanced back at Jerome and Margaret. They simply smiled. What more was there to say? Julian had spoken.

"You read well," Peter said. "It goes without saying, that's a rather deep book. Justice is always a gratifying theme. Sometimes, it may take a while for justice to reveal itself. I'm sure your parents would agree that it can take a few generations before a bad situation begins to change."

"Arc of the moral universe," Jerome interjected. "King said it first." He was leaning on the porch railing, pontificating to the unsuspecting Beekman audience.

Julian's face drew a blank, having missed the import of his father's exegesis. "That's another way of saying that progress is slow," Peter explained to him.

Peter also wanted to add that sometimes justice never calls, that bad things happen in life and recompense is a fool's errand, but its realism was more than he cared to share with a thirteen-year-old. Preserving Julian's innocence was a fatherly impulse at play.

"It's unfortunate," Peter continued, "that people haven't changed much over the years. You could probably say people's instincts never really change—at all. I'm sure your mom and dad would also agree, we're all still motivated by selfish desires. That book could be written today and still be relevant, if you know what I mean by relevant."

Julian nodded while his mom kept a supportive gaze. "Amen to that," she said. "And I believe, if I'm not mistaken, that Theodore Parker was the one who really said it first when he preached against slavery. Martin Luther King borrowed it when he preached against segregation. Two men. A century apart. Same evil."

"Hmm," Jerome muttered, nodding an approval to his wife without looking away from studying the arching oak trees joining hands down the middle of the road in a natural display of neighborly love. "The problem with people," he finally said, "is that the law doesn't matter. What matters is what the majority wants, not what the Good Book says, or Rousseau opines, or King preaches. People can get away with just about anything if enough of them decide it's what they want."

Peter studied the small family. The love between them was palpable, though each had a unique way of showing it. He'd only just met them but somehow felt he really knew them. Jerome had a gruff, matter-of-fact exterior but could read people and expected everyone to rise to their potential. He'd known Peter for only the better part of an hour and yet already trusted his intentions by sharing his own dreams of a better life tempered by real anxieties about Beekman. He certainly held his son to the same high standards. And he immediately—and respectfully—bowed to Margaret's correction on the primacy of King versus Parker. Peter sensed Margaret was a generous soul that only knew giving as a way of living. And Julian was a kid with hopeful expectation that his family's love was exactly what the world had to offer. This was a threesome in sync with themselves, not just as a family but as a spiritual unit and a people looking out at the world through a singular lens.

Mesmerized by this epiphany, Peter felt the discomfort of being out of his depth and the inability to understand the centuries of endurance that had brought the Robinsons to his doorstep. He also felt a sense of calm and knowing that here, in this place, on this porch, there was a right order to the world. This was the philosophical center of the universe; one needn't look any further to understand right and wrong, good and evil, and a just pursuit of happiness. The irony was that it was all happening within arm's reach of a people least interested in understanding.

A pensive silence lingered for a while before Peter succumbed to the anxiety of stillness. "I have a twelve-year-old," he finally said. "She's also an avid reader. Much like her mom, actually. She's obsessed with a book about sorcerers, witches, and magic, by way of children learning the meaning of life. She's totally engrossed, but I have to see if she can handle this *Count of Monte Cristo*. Maybe in a few more years."

Margaret beamed proudly over her boy. The promise in her eyes spoke volumes of what she expected of him. Peter learned that Julian was their only child, their cherished prize that almost never happened. Despite coming from large families—Margaret one of five sisters and Jerome one of three boys—they had spent years trying, without success, to start their own. Their hope was barely a flickering ember when Julian was inexplicably conceived.

"Like I said before," Peter said, feigning a serious tone, "let him be. This here is a diamond in the rough."

Margaret, still holding onto her son, leaned into him until their heads were one.

15

Two days into the following week, an impromptu meeting was held at the Masons. I attended; Peter did not. There was no argument about it. I expected the dueling allegiances since Peter had already committed himself to befriending the Robinsons. I resigned myself to a respectful détente between us.

At the meeting, most of the prior attendees were present, and I found comfort in my closest friends, Maggie and Alice. All of Beekman was a whisper about the goings-on between Peter and the new neighbors. They had all heard about Peter's impromptu Saturday morning social with the Robinsons and the occasional greetings on the days that followed. Peter felt it was the minimal courtesy that most would have shown to any of their neighbors, but that did not immunize him from the scorn of being judged through a different lens.

There was no explaining the Beekman perspective to rational people. To the Beekman clan, Peter was compromised—damaged goods. One of *them*. And everyone knew who *them* was. When it came to clashing cultures, the *them* were the undesirables. The Samaritans, as Pastor Smith had already preached. Some knew their place on either side of the divide, and others didn't, straying over the line to be with—*them*. They strayed because they thought they were *better* than their own. They believed they understood something others didn't—or that they could somehow bridge the divide or ease the tension. What they didn't understand was that the line, the clash, was a desired status quo. Social justifications, advantages, or benefits existed by keeping things just as they were. These do-gooders, violators of the culture war, became the enemy of some while serving the interests of the others.

Peter had chosen to cross over. Beekman had no choice but to make him pay the price—to shun him. I knew all this like I knew how to nurse my own children at birth. It was instinctual. My Peter would be the traitor on Beekman, and even though I was married to him, my lot would not be thrown in with his. I was determined to forge my own path, the path that all of Beekman would now decide.

Maggie and Alice knew all this just by my decision to come to the meeting. That was how things were about these kinds of issues. One needn't ask forgiveness from friends for a wayward spouse or friend. People knew your allegiance by your presence. I was greeted with hugs and smiles. Someone offered me a place to sit and fetched a glass of wine. Maggie and Alice gave the endearing smile and pat on the shoulder. It was all understood. Sometimes, people surprised you when it came to that one issue. You never knew, until you knew. Some stayed in their place, and some didn't.

"Okay, folks, settle down," Fred Mason said, intending to get everyone's attention. "Once again, thank you all for coming on such short notice. I know you have families at home and things that need to get done. Fortunately, it's a summer evening, so homework isn't one of them," he said with a chuckle. "You all know why we're here, and it's not to share the obvious news."

Fred paused and paced a bit, rubbing his chin while staring at the floor. It seemed by his abrupt stop and his body language that he was choked up about the whole ordeal. The circumstances could easily bring one to that level of despair. But Fred was an overly cautious man. Maybe it was the lawyer in him, or simply his temperament, but he always tread lightly and deliberately. His pause was him finding the precise words to convey his frustration with the matter before us.

Assuredly, he felt he had let down the Beekman crowd and we all had every right to hold him responsible. He had been overly confident during our last meeting. His plan was definitive, as he put it to us then. All would be good. The matter closed. He clearly never expected the need for the meeting he now found necessary, and though he took the lead, suggesting he was the most incensed by the circumstances at hand, he was also the most cautious. He knew all too well how things like this could spiral out of control. He didn't want to be the ringleader of anything that resulted in law enforcement looking for a lawyer to hold accountable. In short, he was frustrated and scared that *he* was in jeopardy.

While all of Beekman was there to be enlightened, Fred Mason was already covering his tracks. Of course no one knew of his duplicitous allegiance, the cause at hand pitted against his own survival instincts—except for Phyllis, whom he strategized with as things had unfolded over the past month. Phyllis was his sounding board, moral compass, and grounding wire all in one. She was not a lawyer, but being a principal of a high school and former city council member gave her the perspective that Fred needed to steer their ship true north, even if everyone else might be veering off in a different direction. His dilemma was to lead but not be the leader. One could argue it was a distinction without a difference, but Fred felt it a necessary one, nonetheless.

"The obvious news being that we have new neighbors," Fred

continued. "No, that is not why we're here," he hastened to add.

Fred noticed me sitting almost directly in front of him. I squirmed in my seat while discreetly looking around me, hoping I would not become the focus of attention—that I would not be part of the news.

"We are here to make a plan of action that can still accomplish our goals. We simply need to push the goal line back a few yards. We need time, and as long as we're all patient here, I see no reason why we can't cross the goal line by the end of the year."

"End of the year?" Dennis shouted. Maggie's husband was not one to be shy about his expectations. "That's crazy!"

"Now, now, Dennis. There's nothing to be gained by being too rash about things. As I said at our last meeting, there's a right way to do things and a wrong way."

"We need definitive results, now," another voice yelled from the rear of the room. "If my property values drop one dollar, I'm not likely to be a patient man."

"What would you have us do, then? Violence is not a reasonable choice of action," Fred stated. "I think you all need to calm down and hear me out."

Fred paused, hoping the room would settle without any more outbursts. Now that the wild cards had gotten the bitterness out of their system, he was optimistic that reason could now prevail.

"The long game, as I like to call it, is one of patience." Grumbling became audible from different factions in the room, but there were no outbursts. That was good. "I believe, if we simply make living on Beekman inhospitable, in a *social way,*" he emphasized, "the new neighbors will likely choose to leave."

Fred knew his choice of words had a double edge to them. The "likely choose to leave" might not be strong enough for the growing belligerence of some in the room. He needed to be measured, however, and less definitive than before—but by being so, he opened the door for those who wanted a quick fix by taking matters into their own hands. All he could hope for was a collective memory by those in attendance that his approach was a nonviolent one.

"I say," Fred continued, "that we do not speak to, make eye contact with, play, or in any way socialize, assist, or approve of the new neighbors' existence."

Fred had consciously distanced himself from the Robinsons by not referring to them by name. It was the first step that was necessary to successfully isolate them. If they had no name, they didn't exist. Simple. More grumblings followed, but still no outbursts.

"This guy is working over at the McGuire Corp, isn't he?" Scott Hildebrand chimed in.

"Yes, he is," Fred said.

"Do we know anyone over there? If this family is moving here because of a job, it stands to reason: no job, no house. They'd likely move to wherever else they get work next. He's probably going to be on probation for a year or so as a new employee. If we know anyone that's sympathetic to our cause, it might be an easy way out, in addition to the social pressure and all."

"Excellent idea, Scott," Fred said. "I might have some legal friends with contacts over there. If anyone else has a direct link, I encourage you to drop some hints, subtly. You want people to help you without you directly asking them to. See, this is what I'm talking about. There are indirect ways to get our message out. We don't have to get heavy-handed in the matter."

Fred was pleased with the period of reflection that followed, but it was soon interrupted.

"This is pussyfooting around, plain and simple," Dennis finally interjected. "There are no guarantees in anything you've laid out here. A social plan? Really? These are people used to being ignored, and you're gonna what—ignore them? Come on. Let's get real here. They can spend years being the only Black family on Beekman and be content to just be here. I'm sure after our offer to buy them out, they came to Portville knowing they're not welcome. They're prepared, I'm sure, to hunker down and be shunned for however long it takes for one of us to buckle and say hi to them one morning. That'll crack the ice, and next thing you know, a flood of good intentions will come their way. Hell, it's already started. Poor Clare over there has one under her roof, no fault to her."

I cringed and kept my head down, staring at the carpet's swirling semicircle pattern. *What would Sarah do?* I wondered. *What would Sarah do?* The thought kept bashing against my head in my desperation not to be the center of attention. I wanted to close my eyes and be anywhere else, but I didn't want the appearance of surrender. That would have been the worst. My pride could not tolerate it. I cursed Peter under my breath. He was the reason I was in this predicament, and where was he? Hiding at home. While I was fighting the good fight, he was at home planning more excursions to visit the new neighbors. My anxiety was reaching epic proportions. I breathed a heavy sigh. It was probably too heavy. Someone must have seen it. I sat still and stared at semicircles.

"That McGuire thing," Amy, another neighbor sitting in the back corner, added with a little hesitation, "seems even more unlikely." She stood up as she addressed the gathering. Amy was a tall, slender woman, nondescript in every way. I saw her as the type least likely to indulge an article in a woman's magazine, let alone flirt with ideas of tasteful dress, elegant house furnishings, or evening soirees. But here she was, preserving class distinction. Who knew?

As an engineer, Amy dressed the part, which meant she didn't dress for style but for practicality. Little to no makeup, chinos, and a simple blouse served almost every situation. She was also a no-show for our weekend warriors. She and her husband, Ketan, also an engineer, lived two doors down from us, and their eleven-year-old daughter, Tamarai, was one of few girls in the neighborhood Sandy took an interest in. Though Amy and I were never close, oddly enough, our two girls were similarly bookish and less inclined to the cliques that were becoming a thing in middle school.

Amy surveyed the room like she was embarking on a corporate presentation, making eye contact with as many as she could before she continued. "I work at McGuire, and it's a big company. We know nothing about what kind of guy this new neighbor is. For all we know, he got the job because he knows someone. Now we're supposed to find someone else, close enough to his work area, that can what? Plant contraband or say they heard him say something crude or harassing?"

Her voice was growing more strident and more determined. "That's a stretch. A he-said-she-said kinda thing. It means they have to put their neck out to damage some guy's reputation and hope they don't get their own neck chopped in the process. It's an HR nightmare, and it's not gonna happen. Trust me, that's not how things work in big companies. Scott, you're a pediatrician. You spend your whole day in one room, maybe two. You're the boss, and everything is straightforward and easy. You can't take that experience and apply it to a corporation with several thousand employees. And Fred, you're no different, no offense. You both live in an insular world where you control the outcomes of the things that matter most: who you employ, and your income stream. I'm telling ya, if you want to make a difference here over the next few months, you'll need to come up with something pressing, something that makes it clear what they're up against."

"Like a rock through a window or a burning cross?" a defiant voice said from somewhere in the crowd. Everyone turned to look, but the words had come out quickly, and only someone sitting next to the instigator would have known who had spoken.

Those words silenced the room. The idea conjured up the wrong kinds of images, and no one wanted to touch it or go near it—for a while, anyway. But, like all unattractive options, when your back is up against the wall, they look more and more agreeable, especially with few alternatives that were not likely to make a difference. The proponent of such actions might normally be shunned for even broaching the idea—but when things get desperate, the masses find themselves gravitating in that very direction. They stand behind that person as a unique leader needed for these special times. It's guilt by association, to be sure, but now you're likely to be in good company. One certainly feels less guilt when many are involved with an immoral deed versus going at it alone. The growing mob mentality was becoming palpable, and I locked eyes with Maggie for reassurance. She stood off to one side, nursing her own glass of white, seemingly as bemused as I was to the defiant tone seeping into the meeting.

"Fred, I'm sure your idea is well intentioned," Amy concluded, "but I'm trying to be real here. Change doesn't happen without a push—a real push. Anything else is just playing with perception. It looks good on the surface but doesn't get the job done. What I'm saying is that you shouldn't be surprised if things fall off the rails and some people take matters into their own hands. It may not be the official plan, but sometimes you just need to light a fire under something to get it started, so to speak."

The room fell silent, and I could feel the mood change like an oil tanker making its massive slow turn in the open sea. Fred had lost control of the ship, and someone else had taken the helm, pushing him aside.

"Thank you, Amy, for your sanguine take on the issue," Fred finally said in jest. "I just want to state that I have no intention of being a part of any malfeasance in this matter—just for the record."

With that said, he took his leave from the front of the group and made for the kitchen, ostensibly to refill his wine glass, but I think it was with the intention of relinquishing the responsibility of any further discussion to someone else.

Whispering murmurs slowly began to ripple through the gathering and, in time, gradually grew into more casual exchanges with smiles and laughter as folks began discussing the weekend prior or the weekend ahead. The topic had obviously become too toxic, and people's sensibilities were either slightly offended or simply on edge; they needed to decompress and act as if none of it had really happened. But the seed had been planted.

Someone somewhere now had a kernel planted in their subconscious—and it would grow.

16

Session 15

Peter's grin was plastered on his face like a badge of honor when he entered Anna's office.

Anna returned the smile as she took her seat. The handshakes were now passé. Their conversations had evolved to the familiar, the casual, the weekly updates. "How have you been?" she asked.

"I'm feeling pretty good these days. I think something you said a while back is beginning to pay off. It was that thing about how Clare won't respect me until I stand up for myself."

"How so?"

"Well, I've been sticking to the things I want to do, as you recommended. It hasn't been easy. I mean, I get the guilt trips from time to time. I feel like the power can go to my head, and I might be tempted to do what you thought I was doing, intentionally distancing myself from Clare just to spite her. I try to keep it in check."

"What about her ultimatum that you needed to change—or else?"

"I don't know. Either it was all a charade, which I doubt, or maybe Clare didn't know what she wanted out of all this. I mean, maybe it was my doubting myself that was the problem all along. I've been letting her opinion of what I value dominate the relationship. I've been afraid that if I push back, I might lose her. I'm realizing now that either things are very complicated and I have no idea what's going on in her head, or she's changing her expectations. That as I express myself in no uncertain terms, she's reevaluating what it is she really wants from me."

"You sound surprised that she's more invested in you than she let on."

"Well, of course. It's been years of nagging and final ultimatums."

"When you got upset during one of our earlier sessions and we concluded it was you—not Clare—creating the distance between you, that was likely your first real sign of progress. The first sign that you were finally acting in your own interests. I know it seems like that's turning your back on your marriage, but I think you needed to create some separation from Clare, to be less dependent on her for validation." Anna hesitated for a moment before continuing. "There is another angle here that's maybe less flattering of Clare, and I hesitate to mention it."

"What's that, Doc?" Peter's response was quick, a sign that tension was lurking below a façade.

"Well, in the spirit of full disclosure, you could say that divorce is a poor option for her if she really wants to remain in her current situation. I'm making an assumption here that despite pulling your career back together after the layoff, you're not raking in big bucks. That you live comfortably, not excessively—despite the nice house on Beekman, that is."

"That would be accurate."

"So, a divorce would force a house sale."

"Yeah."

"I'd have to also assume, then, that Clare is not likely to do anything that would force a move from Beekman. It's likely the one thing she covets most. Aside from you, that is. Essentially, she has two reasons to tolerate the status quo: a hope that you two can fix the marriage, and keeping her home on the Cape, as you referred to it."

Peter didn't respond. He sat expressionless with a gaze on Anna, feeling the sting of Clare being undermined, her intentions dishonored. The hidden message was also clear: He wasn't Clare's primary interest, the house on Beekman was. He thought he should come to her defense, if anything to defend himself by inference, but something in him couldn't. It was a disconnect between what seemed like the natural thing to do—defend his wife—and what he wanted to do: just let it go, let Anna's cold, heartless attack on his wife ferment and bloom. He could not deny the real possibility that Clare was over him even if she couldn't leave him… or Beekman.

"I'm probably not worth all the effort," was all he could muster.

"Well, don't get down on yourself, Peter. We don't know that for certain. She's shown a lot of patience with you thus far. She's more than tolerating you, I'd say. The point is, we don't know Clare's motives. This is really all about you, that your stake in all this is valid, your interests, your values, your commitments, they're all valid. Your need for her approval is causing you to sell yourself short. *You* have value. You needn't walk on eggshells hoping to appease someone who has her own agenda. You can't control her. You can only control yourself, and you seem to be coming along nicely, thus far."

Peter had deflated. The confident air was gone. Pessimism crept back in. He hadn't quite gotten used to Anna's pure objectivity, that she would often say things or give perspectives that ran contrary to an opinion he'd just bought into. The end result was always a scrambled sense of confidence in making any progress.

"This is all a bit confusing," he said. "Where do I go from here? Are things getting better? Really? Or is Clare simply making the best of a lousy situation?"

"It would be fair to say that Clare's investment in the marriage is only something the two of you can discover by either personally discussing it in a sincere moment or going to a marriage counselor who can help you navigate the particulars."

"How do I reconcile myself to someone whose humanity, for lack of a better word, is so different from mine?" Peter asked. "I mean, I really have issues from what happened, yet I… Clare…" The words seemed to have escaped him.

Anna could see he was struggling. "It's not so easy. If it were a friend or a coworker, I could just say not to expect everyone to have your sensibilities. When it's the person you share a life with, however, it can be a wedge issue, something that stands in the way of natural attraction. But, having said that, I'd have to also acknowledge that people stay together for a lot of reasons. You might not fall in love with someone whose humanity you disagree with, but staying married to that same person is a whole other matter. People stay married because they've had an opportunity to see many facets of someone's persona. There are things about Clare I'm sure you are very much attracted to. This one, her humanity, is only one thing. It's a big one to be sure, but whether you two can survive together is dependent on how many other things you have in common. Though this particular conversation is very marriage counselor-like, I'd hazard a guess that Clare isn't ready to give up on you. In fact, one might say she's always been invested in you.

Maybe not your actions, but I wouldn't be surprised if she doesn't admire you for your very 'limitation,'" Anna said, putting air quotes around the final word.

"What *limitation* are we talking about?"

"That you care about things that she doesn't. She might very well admire in you what she knows she doesn't have in herself. That you make her uncomfortable with a quality she envies, that she wishes she had, but just can't find in herself. This may sound weird, but it's almost not her fault that she doesn't feel the way you do. Her complaint may very well be that she doesn't like living with the comparison and coming up short every day. The more you obsess, have pensive moments, or do Eaton volunteer work, the more you remind her of a quality she doesn't have. It's speculation at this point, but as I mentioned earlier, intentions matter. Understanding Clare's motives can be helpful in one way that I neglected to mention. That would be for you to understand the limits of her empathy. Initially in our sessions, I needed you to focus on you. I can see now that you're ready to look at Clare through a more analytical eye. Her view of things is not necessarily the right view. In fact, from your perspective, it's definitely the wrong view. Others on Beekman may agree with her view, but they don't count, do they?"

"I guess not," Peter said a little sheepishly.

Sometimes, Anna's forays into his complicated life felt like quicksand. He could barely keep his head above ground. All the while, something pulled him deeper into the vortex. It was all a lot to take in and left him unsure of what to believe or do next. But that was probably Anna's point—to stop trying to decode other people just to validate his own values. Live the way you want to live. Just *do*.

"Look, Peter. Love Clare for who she is, warts and all.

Understand her limitations and her strengths and decide if she's the woman for you. It's that simple."

The seesaw continued. Peter's optimism had been cast down into a pit of despair, and now he was up again, breathing fresh air, feeling like he could conquer anything.

"It's strange," he said, "how all along I've seen her as being in the driver's seat of our marriage. Now I'm realizing that *I* may be in the driver's seat."

"You were always in the driver's seat. You just didn't trust yourself. Maybe the driving metaphor is not really accurate. A marriage has two *players*, and you've been abdicating your values to Clare. You saw your actions as a weakness instead of a strength. Even though you failed your friend that one fateful day, your remorse is your real humanity, not your actions on that day."

A pause followed. This was not like the agitated Peter from the past, angry with himself and the world. There was no anxiety in this silence. He ruminated on everything they had just covered—a thick textbook of desires and disappointments, longings and loss. He knew the next couple of weeks would be spent trying to digest it all. That was what his daydreaming had become.

Often, when he found himself in an empty room of the house, it wasn't obsession with what had happened that tormented him. It was the revelations that Anna had challenged him with. It was a different kind of obsession, like he was editing an essay and needed to find the logical thread that kept his story intact. Anna usually gave him just enough to unravel that he spent all his free time trying to make sense of it. And then, of course, he needed to apply it to his life—to Clare.

It was exhausting work. Anna had warned him about that in their first session. But progress was being made. He could feel it. He was more in control. Their sessions were now every two or three weeks instead of weekly. The morass of lost, sinking feelings was almost nonexistent. This part of finding himself was more illuminating, and certainly less depressing.

    He sensed a light at the end of the tunnel. He could see it, off in the distance. It had a warm glow, as if it were where he was meant to be. He just hoped Clare was on the other side of that light. Life without her was not something he was willing to accept. She was his life partner. He knew that like he knew his name. He saw nothing that could change it. That might have been why he had tolerated years of angst, both from her and from himself. He could have left her, but he didn't. He had no choice in the matter. His heart and soul were still hers.

17

Peter woke tense and conflicted. He had retired the night before feeling much the same way but hoped it was the fatigue of a long week. I suggested to him it was pessimism about the whole Beekman affair. I had shared the salient details of the meeting on Tuesday evening, and had nonchalantly mentioned the "no contact" plan.

Peter nervously chuckled; he was already in violation. He began to fret over what the consequences would be, blind as he was to what it meant to cross over. He may not have understood the term, but he had transgressed, creating a wake of commotion among the people he called friends and neighbors, not to mention me. It was clear he couldn't have it both ways. He had the clarity to see the other side of this culture war and had the courage to act on his beliefs, but it was now also clear that there would be a penalty for crossing over.

I didn't say as much, but Peter inferred from the way I demurred when he pressed for more details of the meeting. Being an ambassador for change was not without its consequences. Peter still hoped that some, at least, would understand. Unfortunately, history hadn't been kind to these ambassadors of societal woes.

Peter was relying on his good standing on Beekman, that people would not be so petty as to hold a grudge. Why would they? He was *Peter*, after all. There were many shared poker nights, dinner parties, and Super Bowl celebrations. He thought that all had to count for something.

His interactions with the Robinsons had been simple hospitality. It was naïve, and I told him so. But he was stubborn.

"Beekman was not the first community in America to integrate, by far, and the Robinsons *are* nice people, the whole neighborhood would eventually see that—in time," he'd say. He was simply the first to reach out a hand of welcome.

He envisioned including the Robinsons in future dinner parties, much the way the Johnsons had also taken part. It was a simple swapping out of one family for another. His naiveté in any other scenario would have been endearing, but under these circumstances, it was dangerously ignorant. The powers at play on Beekman were real survival instincts. Raw emotions had been unleashed at the recent meeting that one would never have expected. Yet Peter still thought it was all seemingly benign.

There was nothing I could say to change his mind. He had his head in the sand. He didn't want to know what he didn't know. He was content to wake every morning and go to work and let the neighborhood grumblings peter themselves out. Given a little time, it was how he expected things to evolve. There was no reason to get emotionally invested in a social quandary that he believed was anachronistic and unsustainable. I at least forced him to admit that he might have lost any objectivity in the matter. In just the past week, he had come to like the Robinsons. He said they had a transparency and earthiness that seemed to elude the Beekman community. He was not crediting it to their race so much as just having a different take on life. He even went so far as to hope they would not become more Beekman-like with time—which made him wonder if we had changed much from who we were to who we had become since moving to Portville. In just one month, the lens on our life and marriage seemed to change focus.

The kitchen was a beehive of activity. I flipped pancakes while sous-chef Sandy sliced strawberries and bananas for toppings. Matt, on the other hand, read a sports magazine in his usual dining spot. His Majesty, apparently, was waiting to be served.

"Good morning, everyone." Peter's greeting was upbeat, a determined attempt at changing something in the current tide of events. The wide grinning ornament of a smile was almost too much to be taken seriously. He tousled Matt's hair affectionately then went over to scrutinize Sandy's culinary skills. "Nice, honey. Careful of your fingers."

Sandy lifted her head to acknowledge his cautious complement with a quick smile then she was back at work.

"How're you doing, Clare?" Peter asked me. "You got up and out early this morning?"

"Yup, we needed eggs and maple syrup, so I made a quick trip to the store. I hope you didn't need anything."

"I don't believe I do. Don't we have a store-brand syrup in the garage?"

"The kids won't touch the stuff, you know that. It's real maple syrup or nothing. Otherwise, we only have bacon and eggs. They're spoiled on the good stuff, the expensive stuff." I threw a smile his way to acknowledge his interest.

"Oh, yeah, I guess you're right about that." He looked back at Matt, who was still nose-deep in his magazine. "How'd we get that imitation stuff, then?"

"It was something left over from an event I went to. No one

claimed it, and I didn't want it going in the trash. I thought at the time the kids wouldn't mind. Well, as it turns out, they do. I don't know what I'm gonna do with it now. I need to find a food donation service I can give it to."

"That's very thoughtful, but it's just syrup. Isn't that a lot of hassle?"

My thrifty impulse over the syrup seemed to intrigue Peter. It seemed out of character. "Maybe," I said. "I just can't bring myself to throw out perfectly good food. Fortunately, it has a long shelf life. I'm in no hurry." I looked over my shoulder intermittently as I poured and flipped pancakes on the wide frying pan used only for this purpose. With my keeping busy and Sandy doing her thing, Peter looked at Matt and realized the division of labor was a little askew.

"Matt," Peter said, "wanna help me set the table?"

Matt sat motionless, staring at a page in his magazine, studying a photo of a football player diving for an errant ball. It was as if he were absorbing a technique through the photograph for later use on the school playing field.

"Matt," Peter barked.

"Huh?" He barely looked up as he finally flipped the page.

"Place settings. Let's get a move on."

"Oh. Okay, okay. Just a sec."

Peter got up to start the process. He and I had a gradual squeeze technique of parenting. We suggested the *required* activity and gave the kids room to fit it into their decision-making process—the hope being that when they acted, they took ownership, and the deed might take root as something they would consider doing again.

It worked well if you had the patience to wait it out. Sometimes it required several reminders and sometimes just doing it yourself with an expression of disappointment that they let you down. Of course, this applied more to Matt more often than Sandy. Where he strived for independence from the home dynamics, Sandy fit like a glove, enveloped in family life, enjoying her role. Her needs were simply different from his.

Same home, different personalities. Peter and I tried to make allowances for the divergence.

As Peter grabbed the plates and started setting them out, he reached out and tapped Matt on the head. "Hey, silverware. Come on. The magazine isn't going anywhere."

"Yeah, yeah. I was just at a good part," Matt grumbled as he rose to do the deed.

The table was now set with a serving plate piled high with pancakes, surrounded by bowls of blueberries, strawberries, and bananas.

"So what's on the agenda for today?" Peter asked.

"Maggie and I are going to the garden nursery to stroll around, see if anything new came in," I said.

"And you, Matt?"

Matt forked five pancakes onto his plate and reached across the table to grab the maple syrup sitting in front of Sandy. "I'm gonna shoot hoops with some friends over at the rec center."

Peter raised a brow. "Hey, you should invite Julian, the Robinson boy. I heard he plays basketball."

Matt stabbed at his pile of pancakes, poking holes in the top of the mound as if they needed airing out. It seemed to be a mindless chore with no end in sight.

"Matt?" Peter repeated.

"Dad, stop!" Matt snarled.

"What?" Peter said.

I looked at him with a blank stare. There was meaning in it, though it took Peter a few seconds to divine my message. *Don't go there.*

"I'm going with *my* friends," Matt said.

"Julian seems like a nice kid. I met him last week, and he said he shoots hoops with his cousins all the time. He might give you a run for your money."

"I'm fine."

"It would be a nice gesture, you know—the new kid on the block, your age just about, an opportunity to meet other kids before the school year starts. Makes a lot of sense," Peter said.

"Not to me."

Matt's quip sounded more defiant than irritated. Peter looked his son directly in the face. Matt stared down into his lap just as he let loose his mutinous comment. There was guilt in his body language, but it was anybody's guess if he truly believed what he was saying. Maybe he was simply embarrassed. Peter seemed at a loss. He had no idea what was going through Matt's head.

"Matt, what's gotten into you? You've invited new kids over to the house before. You're certainly not shy. Yet you're intentionally being dismissive here. This just doesn't sound like you. What gives?"

Matt kept his eyes down, fumbling with his blue-striped cotton napkin, which matched the table's napery and place settings. Sheepishly, he added, "I'm just not interested in meeting the neighbors, that's all. That's your thing, not mine."

"Help me out here, Clare. What's going on?" Peter asked, looking puzzled.

"Let Matt do what Matt does. It's his life," I said.

"Let Matt do what Matt does?" Peter repeated. "This all sounds conspiratorial." Peter looked at Sandy to see how far the conspiracy went, but she had a blank look and he didn't want to drag her into something he saw was heading in a distasteful direction.

"Dad, you know you're not making things any easier on us," Matt said finally.

"How's that?"

"Well, you're over there chumming it up with those people without caring about the rest of us. You know people are upset and ready to burst, and you act like nothing's happening."

"Caring about the rest of us? What does that mean? Stop being so cryptic here. What's bothering you? You don't like that I'm talking to the Robinsons? You don't like that I'm being neighborly? I've greeted newcomers before, you know. They're not the first to move into the neighborhood since we've been here. But somehow, I'm cramping *your* style, am I?"

"Yes," said Matt. "Exactly. I don't like being the butt of my friends' jokes about how my dad is the n—" He didn't finish. He must have known where to draw the line. One can only push their father so far without being terminally disrespectful.

"Wow, the nerve of this kid!" Peter said, looking at me for support. None came. I kept on eating as if this was all to be expected. His crossing over was bound to have consequences.

It seemed to crystallize for the first time. His making friends with the new neighbors was not putting the household in the best regard with our friends. The expectation was that he would choose his family's social standing over the Robinsons. But of course, I knew he could care less about the Beekman social standing.

A surge of frustration came over him, anger percolating to the surface. He pushed his plate away with pancakes stacked three high and got up from the table.

"This family can go to hell!" he yelled and stormed out of the kitchen.

Peter burst into the front yard, seething—as if a conspiracy had been hatched, the trap laid, and he'd walked right into it, just as everyone had planned. He needed to run—whether physically or metaphorically, it didn't matter.

He ran—first down Jackson as far as it went, then looping around to the river and following it for a long stretch. He kept at it until he could feel his frustration subside and some sense of perspective return to him. He, at least, understood Clare. Even if he felt a détente had been reached, a little flare now and then was to be expected. Matt troubled him, however. This was his son, a product of his fathering. How could he turn out so insensitive—so uncaring? Had it been there all along?

Am I raising a kid who'll turn out to be like Dennis or Scott? He asked himself. *I can't believe it!*

He tried to find justification. Maybe Matt was simply insecure and couldn't handle the social pressure of being the odd one out. He was just a child, after all. The idea sank in and calmed Peter's anxiety. But it didn't sit well for long. Matt had not come to him about the issue. The way this should have played out was a dad-and-son chat about the ways of the world. Matt should have wanted Peter's perspective, especially if he was feeling confused about something.

Peter ran on, his head still swirling, trying to come to terms. Maybe, just maybe, Matt wasn't as confident as he let on. Maybe he was the star athlete at school but it was all a veneer he was unwilling to shatter for the moral high ground. A disappointment? Sure. But still very true.

Matt lived in the real world just like everyone else. The idea that your kids inhabited a fake world until you sent them off to college was an illusion parents liked to delude themselves with. It maintained their belief that they controlled their kid's entire universe. In reality, Matt was fighting for survival and acknowledgment, no different than his dad.

Peter finally circled back and ran his wounded pride back home. This was certain to change things. He'd have to figure out how to interact with his genetic offspring who was essentially conspiring against him. He'd have to be vigilant about when to discipline or give advice. He'd have to make sure he didn't overreact with too much criticism, or too little, or unknowingly distance himself. *He's only a kid, after all*, he told himself. It's easier not to hold a grudge against a friend or coworker than your own flesh and blood.

He turned the last corner onto Beekman and decided to walk the rest of the way. A limp favored his left leg. The hard run betrayed the aging knee problem he always protected with the right pace, terrain, and distance. This time, he'd run too hard up the last hill and ignored the telltale sign that something was amiss, his mind all the while frantic with the goings-on at home.

The sun rose higher and grew hotter as beads of perspiration covered his forehead. He wiped them away with his T-shirt, leaving a large sweat stain that marred his appearance. He, of course, paid it no mind. His style when exercising was never a concern compared to some on Beekman.

As he walked the last block, he spied Jerome moving boxes around on his front porch. Their eyes caught each other, and they exchanged waves. Peter then noticed the covered car in Jerome's driveway.

A car worth covering, he thought, *now that has to be something special.*

His curiosity got the better of him, and he stopped by for a quick visit. "Hey Jerome, how goes it?" Peter reached out a hand for the perfunctory shake.

"Beautiful morning, what can I say?"

"I see you still have boxes to unpack, huh?"

"Yeah, it's a process. One I can't stand, but what am I gonna do?"

"If you have any more heavy lifting, don't hesitate to ask."

"Thanks. It's all small stuff at this point. Nothing Julian can't help me with."

"I see you have a bigger item over there that Julian *can't* help you with," Peter said and pointed to the covered car. "Whaddaya got hiding under there?"

"That, my friend, is my pride and joy. A 1965 Chevy Corvair Corsa convertible."

Peter raised a brow. "Holy shit! Oh… excuse me."

Jerome laughed. "No, you're right. Holy shit."

"A Corvair. My dad had one of those. Rode in it all the time as a kid. Back then, no one expected them to become collectibles, though. He got rid of it and went with a Mustang. I guess that was the serious competitor back then."

"You know your Corvair history," Jerome said, sounding impressed. He strolled over to his hooded gem and gently peeled back the cover, folding it neatly and tucking it away on the porch. You could tell by the way he handled just the cover that this car really was his pride and joy.

"Holy shit," Peter repeated. "This is incredible."

Awestruck and mouth agape, Peter stared at the pristine yellow Corvair with white convertible top. Sunlight dappled through the trees and danced off the front fenders, while the hood glistened as if it were the center of its own constellation. He started his walk, as all inspectors of classic cars do. He circled to the rear and came up on the driver's side, checking out the trim, emblems, and redlined tires. Then he leaned through the driver's-side window, gawking at the wood steering wheel, multi-gauge dashboard, and white leather interior. Peter was impressed. He rubbed his hair back from his forehead in disbelief.

"This is incredible," Peter repeated. "Gorgeous. I'm so jealous. This takes me back to my childhood. My dad's wasn't this nice. It was a blue '63 coupe. Not bad, but definitely not this. The badge on the trunk says 140. I'm guessing that's the horsepower?"

"Yup. Turbocharged, too. This baby can fly. For a classic, that is. It was Chevy's idea of racing on city streets. Hence the name: Corsa. It means 'race' in Italian. Did you notice the floor shift manual? Four-speed."

"Very, very nice, dude. Not many can handle a manual these days. I'm one of the few, so if you need someone to take care of her for a while, it's alright by me."

Jerome chuckled. "You got it, man."

"I like this color, sort of a subtle yellow."

"Goldwood Yellow," Jerome corrected. "Original issue."

Peter looked back into the driver's-side window to check things out, and Jerome came over and unlocked the door. "Have a seat," he said.

Peter's grin was permanent, like a kid on his birthday with the one thing he'd always wanted. Jerome tried not to notice. Peter figured Jerome was used to gawkers since the car really was nice to lay eyes on.

As Peter slipped into the driver's seat, his hands naturally caressed the firm wooden steering wheel with chrome attachments to the steering column. He inspected the gauges: 6,000 tachometer, 140 max speed, engine and oil temperature, vacuum, and fuel. It was pure perfection in an automobile from the 1960s.

"You probably know already about the air-cooled engine in the back, storage up front, four-wheel independent suspension. I could go on and on. I won't bore you with all the particulars," Jerome said. "Some of the concept was patterned after the VW Beetle, but the independent suspension was the Italian racing mindset."

"Jerome, I will never bore of stuff like this. It's too rich for my pocket, but I sure appreciate the work, the detail, the charm."

"It wasn't too bad. I'm pretty handy. Did most of the restoration myself. As an engineer, I was used to the technical jargon. The one thing you need with projects like this is patience. There are a lot of Corvair parts available all around the country because most people thought they were too cheap, not worthy of refurbishing. Well, the tide is changing. There are niche markets out there where these cars are hot. But you gotta put out the word to all the restoration shops and tell 'em what you're looking for. They'll get in touch if anything comes in. I've had parts shipped to me from as far away as California."

"So there's a whole secret network of guys trading parts for old cars?" Peter asked, still sporting his childish grin.

"Not so secret. Once you scratch the surface, the whole thing opens up like a dictionary. It's incredible how organized and efficient the whole business is. And you're right, sometimes you do trade parts instead of buying them. If I have something someone needs, we swap. The best part is, no one cares who you are. If you understand the business and have a passion for the art and science of classic cars, people treat you like you're one of them. Unlike this Beekman crowd, color means nothing. People respect the talent and the final product. When I wheel into a classic car show, I draw the crowds. People slapping me on the back, asking details about how I did this or that, where'd I get that part from, how'd I think of doing it this way or that way. We share stories about stuff that stumped us and learn from each other. People become… just people. If you spend time in this business, you realize how nice it is to be appreciated for what you do, not so much for what you look like."

"Cool, I get that. It's nice to hear that somewhere," Peter said, affecting an exaggerated look up and down the block, "somewhere, people get it."

As he was talking to Jerome, Peter noticed a shadow over the passenger window that blocked the sunlight. He looked over to see Sandy staring in. His prior world came racing back, and he realized how much chatting with Jerome helped him put his family issues on the shelf. But why was Sandy here?

"Hi, sweetie, is everything okay?" he asked.

"Yeah. I just saw you from across the street and wanted to come."

"Well, that's perfectly fine. Jerome, this is my youngest, Sandy. I believe I mentioned her to you last week. She's my reader."

"Hello, Sandy," Jerome said. "Would you like to get in and sit with your dad?"

She nodded with a grin, just like her dad had been doing since Jerome unwrapped his beauty. She had no appreciation for the classics, of course, but she liked the idea of being included, and she no doubt sensed something special about this car by the way her dad was fawning over it.

"Sure," Sandy added, trying to hide her shyness.

Jerome opened the door for her, and she quickly got comfortable in a passenger seat that almost swallowed her up. She was petite for her age, and the seats were bench-style—wide on the bottom and wide on the backs.

"I think she likes the car as much as you do," Jerome said, admiring his admirers through the passenger window.

Peter massaged the manual stick shift and put it through its paces, depressing the clutch and feeling the gear play from first to second, second to third (which was often a sticking issue with some gearboxes), and finally third into fourth. It was all smooth as pie. He looked over at Sandy and saw her caressing the smooth leather seat.

"You know, hon, shifting gears is like a metaphor for life," Peter said, waxing philosophical. Sandy's eyes gleamed with the excitement of sitting in something she knew was special. "You gotta learn to walk before you can run. It applies to everything we do. It taught me to take things slow, get comfortable with the pace, then shift into high gear. Lessons from Grandpa on our Saturday morning drives. He taught me to shift when I was a boy. I'd listen to the engine, feel the pull of the car, understand the strain of not enough gas, or the gearbox holding back an engine wanting to go faster. You have to pay attention to your car with a manual shift. You become one with it. If you ask me, it's the only way to drive."

Jerome nodded an assenting smile. "You know your cars, Peter."

The small talk went on for some time before Julian spied them from the second-floor window. In no time, he came outside to join the fun. "Hey, Dad, Mom's been looking for you."

"Well, tell her I'm entertaining classic car enthusiasts." Jerome smiled at Peter and Sandy. "Hey, Julian, come over and meet Mr. Davidson's daughter, Sandy."

"Please, Julian, he can call me Peter."

"Na-ah, Peter. He's been schooled to address adults in a formal way. We think it's the best way to show respect for elders and be treated with respect in kind. Just some necessary rules for survival, if you know what I mean." Peter nodded.

"Hi, Sandy." Julian's winsome smile was ear to ear.

"Hi," was Sandy's sheepish reply.

"Julian, tell your mom I'm out here with Mr. Davidson, and

maybe you can show Sandy around the house. Give her the royal tour. If that's something you'd be interested in?" Jerome said, addressing Sandy.

She looked at Peter with a searching look for approval. "Go ahead," he said, "enjoy."

The kids headed inside, and the dads turned their attention back to the Corvair.

Jerome seemed lost in thought. Then he laughed. "You should have seen the condition this was in when I bought it. It was an eyesore. Margaret nearly flipped out when she saw it. It was a rust bucket with missing fenders and bumpers. The tires were shot, the convertible top was long gone, and the engine was a mess. I essentially had to start from scratch. I kept it in the backyard of the house we were renting."

"Wow, to look at it now, it's hard to imagine," Peter said, again gliding his hand over the creamy white leather seats.

"It's an addiction," Jerome said with a hearty laugh. "Once you get started, it's near impossible to stop. Every day, you find yourself scouring parts catalogs and Chevy repair manuals. You learn as you go, and your head is always planning the next fix. It's actually pretty relaxing because hardly anything bothers you at work or anywhere else. Your mind is always on *the car*."

"Well, that's my kinda problem," said Peter. "I've never taken to any one hobby with that level of intensity. I guess it's like being an artist. You get the inspiration to create something, and you can't stop 'til it's done. I don't think I have that kind of creativity."

"You do, Peter," said Jerome. "I think we all have it on one level or another. Problem is, life gets in the way and squashes those impulses. We feel we need to put food on the table and that should take precedence. The reality, though, is that life itself will suck the life out of you if you don't find a passion that can keep you up at night. Sounds backwards and all, but it's been my experience that life doesn't begin until you stop letting life get in the way."

"Profound words, there, Professor Robinson," Peter said, imitating a regal voice. "I get the point, though. Slaving away earning money will squash any passion for creativity."

"Exactly," Jerome said. "You know, I usually hold off committing to friendships until I can gauge a person's response to this very subject. Many just don't get it. Making money is all that matters to them, and expensive hobbies that sometimes have you living week to week are considered foolish. I value life differently, and I can't spend time with people who waste away their lives accumulating stature without creating texture."

"Amen to that," Peter said and climbed out of the car. He strolled back around to Jerome's side, admiring the workmanship at every step. The car was genius work, a Michelangelo of classic cars. "I don't know if I have it in me. This is so out of my class. I'm just amazed at what you've done with what you started with."

"Everyone finds their own expression. Cars happen to be mine. You may appreciate it but choose to get into something else. It's more about the opportunity to express yourself. It's the process more than the product. I can't tell you how many times I ruined perfectly good parts that took me months to find. I'd simply start all over and plug along. My mind wasn't on this." He pointed to the Corvair with his thumb. "My mind was on the satisfaction I felt figuring out the next step. The endgame was never in sight. The motivation had to come from within."

Peter walked around the car, trying to absorb its meaning, to hold onto the experience for some kind of inspiration. It was a prophet telling a story in a tongue he didn't understand, but he hoped being near to it meant he would experience something transformative. It was a meditative moment for him. Jerome was the master, and Peter the disciple—the car was life itself.

Jerome shifted, and his tone changed. "Hey," he said, "as much as I can talk about cars all day, I've got a gnawing issue I want to pick your brains about."

"Shoot," Peter said.

Jerome sighed. "I'm just wondering what Margaret and I are in for with this Beekman crowd. I figure if the block was organized enough to make a buyout offer, they're organized enough to plan for a failed buyout offer. There must have been a meeting after we refused to sell to decide what to do next. We expected some pushback, like being ignored and whatnot. We certainly didn't expect people to be bringing over pies and whatever else a welcoming committee does to make a new family feel at home. Hell, we didn't even expect to get hellos or any acknowledgment at all. We *have* gotten some pretty mean stares, and one day someone even used the N-word."

"I can't believe it," Peter said, pulling back in shock. He then remembered his own son, who'd almost used the same word at breakfast. He quickly suppressed the thought as something that had never happened.

"Now," Jerome continued, "I'm no stranger to that kinda attitude on display, mind you. But it seemed strange coming from this community. I mean, just look at this place." He gestured down the block in the direction of the most picturesque tree-lined part of the neighborhood. "This isn't a block that gives off a backwards vibe. This place looks like intelligent people living in harmony, spending good money to keep their homes looking beautiful. Ignoring us is one thing, but using the N-word is something I expect from a run-down neighborhood, not this one."

"I'm so sorry that happened, Jerome." Peter fixed him with a steady look. "I don't know what to say. This whole thing has no precedent here, and I guess I don't even know my own neighbors. If I had to guess, though, I think these people are not all that bad at heart. I think they're just in shock, maybe."

"Shock, huh?"

"Yeah, I think the whole thing went down so fast that they haven't had time to adjust."

"Adjust to us?" Jerome clarified.

"I know, it sounds bad. I'm not proud of them, believe me."

"I believe you on that point. But I'm not so sure they're just shocked. I'm wondering if you're putting lipstick on a pig here, maybe trying to be too optimistic. You don't have to spare me, Peter. I'm asking 'cause I want to know. I want to prepare my family. I want to protect Julian from the worst of what they plan to do. So, my question to you is, what's the worst they plan to do?"

Peter studied Jerome's face. It was strong with resolve. Jerome was asking, but from a position of confidence. Whatever Peter planned on offering up, Jerome was not planning on backing down. He was strategizing his defense. Peter thought about the last time he'd used that line, "lipstick on a pig." He had been chastising Pastor Smith for making light of Jordan avoiding him and skipping town in the dead of night. Back then, he preferred a more direct approach—honesty, transparency. He never got it.

It was now taking too much time for Peter to answer, and his raised-brow expression all but suggested he was in a tough spot.

"I don't envy you," Jerome said. "I know I'm asking a lot. There may be details no one is sharing with you. I get that. After all, I'm sure they see you as a traitor and want to keep you in the dark on whatever they're planning."

Peter was struggling with exactly that—what he knew and what he didn't. He knew the neighbors were upset. He knew they'd never planned on things getting this far, that they had hoped for a soft landing, so to speak, by making a generous offer to buy back the property. But that hadn't happened. He had hoped they would let bygones be bygones and leave it alone. That with time, things would mellow, and all would be well. Time was all that was needed.

But Peter hadn't attended the last meeting. He didn't know how and if things had escalated. How mad were people now? He didn't know. He and Clare were not inclined to discuss it—at all. For what would likely be a brief interlude, they were enjoying a small respite from the tension. Until that morning, when things had gone bad. Things were no longer contained to just a few adults on the block. Now the kids were involved. People were picking sides—or maybe he was on one side and everyone else was on the other.

Then Matt's comment, "upset and ready to burst," stormed back into Peter's consciousness. What did that mean? Who was bursting? Was it just talk? Was it just a kid using too much hyperbole to get a rise out of his father? Peter didn't know. There was a lot he didn't know, and the last thing he wanted was to look stupid or lame by just saying *he didn't know*. He had to pick a side. He had to be firm.

"Jerome," Peter finally said, "we knew the Johnsons pretty well. They were our best friends here on Beekman. And just saying 'they were' our best friends kinda says it all. We knew they were selling because of dropping housing prices and realtors having no interest in selling in a down market. Jordan decided to sell it himself, and he and Sarah both promised to invite us over to meet the new owners for a meet-and-greet, maybe on a return inspection or when signing papers or something. It put my wife at ease knowing she could at least prepare for whoever planned on buying the house. Well, none of that happened. Not only that, but Jordan and Sarah never told us they had a buyer, never told us they were moving out, or when, for that matter. They just up and left. The neighborhood got wind of things just by chance. We all noticed the house was empty. One thing led to another, and by the time you got the offer, the block had already been through its paroxysms. It's not reasonable by any stretch of the imagination, but it is what it is. That's why I'm saying that folks here need time to get over being upset at the Johnsons and get used to neighbors they hadn't prepared themselves for."

"Hmm," Jerome murmured. "I feel like a dangerous exotic animal people have never seen. We do live in America, don't we? We've been around since the early 1600s. What's there to get used to?"

Peter had no response. He had touched the nerve that white people usually tried to avoid when talking about racial prejudices, especially in the company of someone so often the victim of such prejudices. He felt embarrassed as an awkward silence fell between them. A part of him felt indignant, that he had no reason to be embarrassed. After all, he alone had carried the torch in defiance of Beekman's moral illiteracy and turpitude, and he didn't want to give his neighbors the excuse of inheriting their backward ideas of segregation. But he also realized the social awkwardness he now felt was the requisite aftermath. He didn't really know Jerome, and Jerome didn't know him. Peter tried to hold his gaze, locking eye to eye, hoping to show he was merely the messenger and not the cause of the racial outbreak. He hoped it would eventually seep in that the Beekman crowd was likely to move on—only he had nothing to go on. In fact, if anything, there was more evidence to the contrary.

In the end, Peter felt being totally sincere about the situation was more harmful than remaining positive—that being real meant admitting even his own family were instigators in what might befall the Robinsons. It was hard to admit it to himself, let alone to

Jerome. So he pivoted, turning his back on truth in his need for hope, denying anxiety for want of calm. He succumbed to ignorance, ambivalence, and shame, choosing to dissemble instead of admitting that Beekman was filled with people afraid for their very survival, and like a cornered wild animal might do anything to preserve their way of life.

When he finally spoke, Peter didn't recognize his words. He had no idea how it would all sound to someone wanting to know how to protect their family. "Jerome, trust me, you have nothing to worry about." It was a lame start, so he decided to double down to be more convincing. "I know these people. For many years, we've been like family. You and yours will be fine. This will all blow over."

Jerome looked at Peter with a serious glare. Peter couldn't tell if Jerome was feeling scornful or feeling scorned. After an interminable moment, he smiled and let out that hearty laugh that resounded so unlike what should be coming from his lean body. He slapped Peter on the back in a friendly manner.

"Peter, you've got the look of a man staring into the face of God! Sorry to put you on the spot like that. I may have taken advantage of your good nature to appease my need to know."

Peter tried to show levity in his demeanor. It wasn't easy. He was the one dangling over a cliff with a thousand-foot drop, the feeling of death all but certain, only to be snatched away at the last second. And now he was expected to move on with a calm resolve.

"No worries, Jerome," he finally said, sounding timid. "It's all good. I'd do the same if I were in your shoes."

"Let's hope that never happens," Jerome said jokingly, reigniting that deep baritone laugh.

Sandy and Julian emerged through the front door, laughing over something one of them had said. They had passed the awkward stage of politeness and moved on to a newly found friendship. Julian stood much taller than Sandy, his eyes fixed on her with newfound admiration.

"Hi, honey," Peter called out as the kids approached the driveway.

"Hi, Dad."

"How was it?"

"Oh, you know, I've been in there before. Sleepovers with Megan, remember?"

Peter's thoughts raced back to all the times they'd spent in the Johnson home. The old memories were still there, hanging low like fruit on a vine, easy for the picking—although not as sweet as they used to be. Yet he saw no evidence that Sandy had tasted that sour fruit, as she too needed to absorb the finality of Megan leaving. She must have seen Megan's old room, but this time the twin bed with its frilly canopy wasn't there, nor were the dolls and stuffed animals that were usually strewn about. This whole Johnson-Robinson affair wasn't limited to the adults. Matt had already made that clear over breakfast with his need to save face among his friends because his dad had become a self-designated peacemaker on Beekman—a role no one had requested of him nor appreciated.

"I know, hon," he said, "but I'm sure the Robinsons have it decorated a little differently. Which room did you take, Julian?"

"The one over there," he answered, pointing to the room over the front door.

"If I'm not mistaken, that one is bigger than Megan's room. Smart move," Peter said, looking at Julian with a smile. Julian nodded in approval. "So what's that book you've got in your hand?"

"Oh, look at what Julian let me borrow," Sandy said, holding up a book.

"*The Count of Monte Cristo.* Hmm. I've heard that title before,"

Peter said with a wink. "Is that a good read, Julian?"

"Excellent," he said. "I just finished it yesterday." He and Peter exchanged knowing smiles. This was Sandy's discovery, all her own to enjoy.

"I can't wait to read it," Sandy said, her grin as wide as her face. Peter couldn't remember when he'd last seen her so entranced.

"Well, that's very nice of you to share the experience, Julian. Sandy, make sure you take good care of the book. I'm sure Julian would like to keep that one in his personal library."

"Oh, sure." Her excitement had yet to subside. "Then maybe I can get my own copy?"

"Your birthday's not that far off. Put it on the list. But first, you have to read it."

As usual, Sandy was their explorer, striking out and doing different things. Though she didn't suffer fools much, she also wasn't shy about making new friends, especially if they shared her passion for reading. In that sense, she was the complete opposite of her brother. Where Matt's indulgences were acutely tied to his popularity, Sandy was adventurous—as long as it was something that piqued her primal interests.

"We're gonna head out," Peter said to Jerome. "I'm hoping maybe there's a barbeque in our future once you all get settled in."

"Thanks, Peter, for everything." The emphasis on *everything* wasn't lost on Peter. Jerome had put him through the ringer with what seemed like such a simple line of questioning. It was his way of saying, "No hard feelings."

Peter waved as he and Sandy walked back across the street. "Don't forget, Jerome, I'm available to babysit," he said, pointing at the Goldwood Yellow Corvair.

They both laughed.

18

I was reclined on a teak chaise lounge, sunning myself in a modest blue-and-white bikini, hoping to achieve an even, copper-hued tan. I imagined my appearance was that of a model in a fashion magazine enjoying a lazy summer day.

My Jackie O round sunglasses probably belied my middle-class existence, but a gal can imagine, can't she? By my side on a matching teak end table sat a tall glass of iced tea with sweat beading down the sides.

Peter came to the back door and spied me through the screen and decided to join me. I barely acknowledged his arrival. The morning angst still lingered, and my escaping to the backyard was an effort to let go of its frustrations. My statuesque pose and poise was a marble edifice to the pleasures of pleasant living. Peter waited, and after an interminable pause, I finally relented and gave him a half-smile. We exchanged pleasantries.

"Did you end up buying anything at the garden nursery?" he asked.

"No, nothing new, same old stuff. How about you, what did you do this morning?"

Of course, I knew well enough how it had started, just not how it had ended. I assumed he intended to gloss over the day's untidiness. Until he leaned back in an Adirondack chair under the shade of a maple tree and measured me with his gaze.

I'd seen the look before. All women know the look. His eyes studied me as I lay in the lounge, no doubt contemplating me in another light. This was Ohio—late spring Ohio. The sight of a woman in a bikini was nowhere to be seen. Peter's stare was a hunger for intimacy on another level.

There was a time I would have been flattered, but those were different times. Instead, I closed my current read, *Middlemarch*, and contemplated Eliot's magnum opus of sublime characters I'd once idolized—a youthful discretion that appealed only to the naïve.

My first read was in my twenties, and at that age of undaunted optimism, I had only seen the one side. It was the side where Eliot's Dorothea was strident with purpose and hope, where women plied their considerable influence in ways all too common in life but rarely admitted to in conversation or on the page. But I was now on my third read, and while its wit and charm beckoned me to stroll the bucolic English countryside, my age and wisdom had long ago discerned the harsh reality that marriages were fraught with strange bedfellows; that who you married might not always be who you wanted later in life. And if one persevered, it was often with a compromise that betrayed one's naïvely youthful yearnings. It was as if one looked at themselves in the mirror expecting to see their betrothed but instead saw the face of a stranger they no longer recognized.

I felt Peter's eyes trace my long auburn hair as it spilled over my shoulders, then drift to my breasts, waist and hips. It was obvious he was still drawn to me.

"I did my run," he said, "and ended with a visit across the street. Jerome unwrapped a vintage '65 Corvair he was hiding. Reminded me of the one my dad used to have—sweet condition, sent me back in time."

His gaze made me wonder if the car was a metaphor for me or the other way around. Either way, I wasn't interested in his newfound hobby, and I had other priorities that didn't overlap with his prurient leanings. If he had intended to minimize the morning conflict, his mention of the new neighbors was a poor choice. He was now treading in deep waters. I stared at him, waiting for his next try. It was then he decided to dive deep.

"Clare, what's happened to us? We used to be able to talk through our issues. It was like we were always on the same team working to accomplish the same goals. Now I feel like we've grown apart and are working against each other. It breaks my heart that we're letting issues that have nothing to do with our marriage affect our marriage."

Despite his earlier indulgences, his look was now sanguine and earnest. I went with it. "Peter, believe me, I feel the same way. Sometimes I'm close to tears when you're not around. I just don't know who you are these days. It's like I married one guy and recently woke up to find someone else in my bed. It's driving me crazy. I don't have an answer. I've been hoping you'd find a solution, that you'd find a way to fix it all."

His stare changed yet again, this time to a steely-firm resolve. I could feel my confidence ebb. I sipped my tea, mostly to have something to do, as his eyes penetrated my veneer. I was still quite vulnerable. His sudden interest in *us* had taken me by surprise. I felt as though we were on a walking tour through life and he'd suddenly chosen to take a turn down a dark alley, leaving the family behind. And when we called out to him to get back on track, he instead wanted us to follow. It was absurd. But I was at a loss for how to change it. We were tethered for now, and all I could hope for was that this was a phase he would grow out of—like a midlife crisis, though he still had a few more years before midlife appeared on his horizon.

Peter seemed to read between the lines and went on the attack. "So I'm supposed to fix it? It's all *me*? My problem imposed on all of you? You're fifty percent of the marriage, so I think you're fifty percent of the problem—at least."

I cringed and couldn't respond. I expected him to be past the deep-seated stubbornness, but he was not easily changed, certainly not by anything I could say. It would have to find its own way. All I could do was wait.

"I don't know what to say," he went on. "I guess I have to be allowed to have my own belief in this matter. It's clear we don't see things the same on this issue, but I would like to think that you'd at least respect my feelings. Everyone has to believe in something, and if we're without a cause or unwilling to take a stand in what we believe, then we're not really worth anything, are we?"

I finally turned my head. An acknowledgment that his little soliloquy had pierced my insouciant exterior. "That sounds like something you've memorized."

He couldn't read my eyes behind the sunglasses, but my tone spoke volumes, and I'm sure it stung. I was not inclined toward charity.

"Well," he continued as if uninterrupted, "I'm trusting that time will heal these wounds. That next year at this time, we'll look back and think of it all as one big dark cloud that blinded us for a period of time until the sun broke through and guided us back to marital bliss." He smiled at his own levity. I'm sure he didn't intend to be flippant, but as usual, he couldn't help himself.

A shadowy silhouette darkened the back porch door. I knew its size and shape like the veins on the back of my hand. If Sandy had been standing there all along, I could only assume that she'd heard our conversation and was now feeling the despair that overwhelms a child when the immutable foundation of their parents' union begins to shatter. She was a statue, frozen in place. I felt a twisting knot in my stomach, the kind you got when the hurt cuts to the core. Peter and I had gone out of our way to avoid involving the kids. But that morning's row had aired the dirty laundry. It was probably the reason he'd left so abruptly, to protect the kids from a flash of anger he knew he'd regret. It was now clear the one we wanted most to protect had become a victim of the marital skirmish.

I got up and casually strolled away from Peter, whose reclined position didn't afford a view of the porch. I climbed the stairs to the back door as if calmly returning to fetch more iced tea, hoping that if I controlled my emotions, Sandy would believe things weren't really that bad. It was the parent trick that worked on toddlers after they'd taken a hard fall. But Sandy was no toddler.

As I opened the screen door, I saw that my contrived indifference was for naught. Sandy stood there sobbing quietly, a catch in her voice, sudden gasps, all an effort at trying to hold it back. Her eyes were swollen and red as tears streamed down her cheeks. She looked up at me as I came to her and fell into my arms. The sobbing lost its muteness, growing louder as she gave in to it. I closed the door behind me and held her. No words at that moment would have had meaning. Just holding her said all that needed saying.

19

Sandy woke with a fright. She bolted upright in bed, eyes wide, and surveyed the mostly dark room, squeezing her stuffed armadillo for reassurance. Shelby was a famed prize from her dad's high score at an arcade and had been her personal companion for much of her childhood. At night, the oversized amulet with supernatural powers was always within arm's reach.

The steadfast affection heaped on Shelby was apparent just by the look of it. The plushie was filthy, with grayed coloring where white stripes used to be and matted stains too numerous to count. It needed a bath in the worst way, but that was forbidden. Sandy wouldn't hear of it, fearful the water and agitation would dismember some vital appendage. The tail was already frayed and left the occasional fiber of hair throughout the house. Now that Sandy was older and Shelby was relegated to bedtime cuddling, those fibers were only found among her sheets.

Through some act of rough play long lost to memory, Shelby's plastic nose had been amputated, irreparably altering her profile. Finally, food stains added uncharacteristic spots, marking special events going back in time. Despite all that, Shelby was as much a member of the family as anyone else, sometimes requiring a several-mile return home if she was accidentally left behind when departing for a vacation. These days, she served as Sandy's nighttime confidant and protector.

The drapes were pulled, the door was shut, and the room was pitch black, save for the nightlight along the baseboard next to the dresser that lent a soft amber glow only to that part of the room. Other parts were still too dark to see, but Sandy was reassured by the quiet. Whatever it was that woken her was not part of the awake world. She knew it was a dream, though its reality seemed textured enough to make her fear there may be truth in a foreboding.

Something bad—tragic, even—had happened to someone close, someone she knew, only she didn't know who. The face had just revealed itself, but the shock of it woke her. Now, staring into the night, the image faded from her mind. Try as she might, it wouldn't return, slipping deeper and deeper into a dream that was now over.

She began to rock back and forth, her arms wrapped tightly around Shelby. The thought occurred to her that she could get to her mom and dad's room in seconds, but she feared the dream would come back to life.

What if the unknown was someone in the house? What if the first person she saw became the face now lost in her subconscious? She couldn't risk any part of her dream coming true, so she made the sacrifice—she would forgo her need for comfort for the safety of Mom and Dad.

She was trapped, rocking back and forth in the silent darkness of her room, until her eyes grew heavy, her mind slowed to blankness, and she fell back asleep.

THE BEEKMAN AFFAIR

———...———

Breakfast du jour for the Davidsons' celebration of Independence Day was none other than French toast. It seemed countercultural, or simply un-American, but the menu option was Matt's turn to decide, and he justified the choice with the historical fact that the French had supported the revolutionary effort and deserved recognition in some form or other. As French culinary feats were unsurpassed, he argued, French toast was a perfect choice for breakfast.

Such teenage sophistry was typical of Matt's way of bending the truth to win others over to his particular interest of the moment. French toast predating the French nation and being known to have existed in the Roman era was too obscure a fact for anyone else to know. What's more, his insistent tendency to debate any issue of his liking made arguing almost any point with him pointless.

Unlike the previous weekend, Matt was eager to partake in the preparation activities. The dipping and frying and flipping of egg battered bread was in keeping with his particular view of himself—exploits he would likely brag about to friends as his contribution to the day's festivities.

Sandy, oblivious to the night's terror, delicately sliced strawberries and bananas, and washed blueberries, just as she had the week before.

Peter dripped coffee and poured the orange juice while Clare enjoyed supervising from the comfort of the dining room table. She kept one eye on the flow of movement in the kitchen and the other on the *Portville Weekly*, open to a section on the planned activities for the city's celebration.

"Seems the city's going all out this year with the fireworks," Clare said. "They've got a whole twenty-minute show planned at 10 p.m. down by the river."

"They must think this is Chicago or New York," Peter said. "I'm not sure the Portville attention span will last that long." His sarcasm was laced with humor and was typical of his response to Portville trying to punch above its belt. His practical accounting side was on display.

"I'm assuming," Clare added, ignoring the attention-span gibe, "that there'll be some fancy displays. If you're gonna do a twenty-minute show, you might as well invest in some artistic fireworks, a flag, or something along those lines. That would make quite a splash. We should all plan on going, and we might as well get there early. The lookout point will be jammed by 9:30."

"I'm gonna go with my friends," Matt declared, a defiant independence that surprised no one.

Peter looked at Matt with his mouth agape and was about to pounce, but nothing came of it. Clare caught the failed gesture and was pleased he resisted the impulse to retread old issues. She sensed it was Julian again; a Matt-Julian liaison, to be precise. Peter's desire to save the world was admirable, but there was a time and place for that, and forcing his son to be who he wasn't didn't win affection—or conversion.

"I guess… it'll just be the three of us, then," Peter quietly conceded.

——— … ———

Margaret rose early, as was her habit, and descended on the kitchen while still in pajamas. The day's plans called for an early, efficient breakfast, quick showers, packed bags, and a prompt departure for Cincinnati. The family had been invited, as was usual on the Fourth of July, to barbecue with Jerome's brother and wife. Such had been the tradition for many years, and this year afforded the Robinsons an opportunity to debrief their extended family on the merits, if any, of moving farther away from Cincinnati—away to small-town Ohio, in fact.

Jerome's brother, Ted, eschewed the idea of provoking the sensibilities of small-minded towns with premature integration. Ted was content to cede suburbia to the non-progressives and keep the urban territories for everyone else. The buyout offer Jerome and Margaret had received just a week or two before closing on their house seemed to prove Ted right. But Jerome was undaunted. Such offers may have reflected concern from a small-town community, but he and Margaret were friends with many people of various backgrounds. They knew their particular interests and politics found common ground in many venues and felt they could easily win people's affection given the opportunity.

Essentially, they felt they were different from Ted, primarily in that Ted saw the world through siloed eyes. He didn't care to extend himself beyond his comfort zone, while Jerome was an extrovert in all its dimensions. Margaret was, likewise, no wallflower. Together, they received more invitations to social events from coworkers, neighbors, and social clubs than they could possibly attend. Theirs was a problem of too much integration, not too little.

It wasn't long after Margaret got started on breakfast that the aroma wafted upstairs and beckoned the men of the house to come ambling down, noses flinching with curiosity of culinary delights. One might have mistaken them for four-legged creatures with heightened olfactory senses, keen on naming all the different herbs in play.

Eggs were the primary dish frying in a skillet, but onions,

cilantro, and chives had been chopped and were already filling the kitchen with their distinct scents. Bacon and sausage were frying separately, sizzling and popping with a spray of grease on the surrounding countertops. English muffins were toasting, the orange juice was out, and the only thing not yet done was the setting of the table.

"Gentleman, you are just in time to do your duty," Margaret said, still busy hovering over three skillets as their noses led them down the stairs. "Knives and forks are already out."

"Mmm, mmm, mmm, what do we have here?" Jerome rubbed his belly as he spied the goings-on in the kitchen from mid-staircase. He could tell well enough what was on the menu, his senses in unparalleled working order.

Julian pleaded for jam with his English muffin as he raced past his dad.

"As you wish, but you're in charge of getting it out—and the butter, too. Keep an eye on the toaster for me."

The Robinson clan was soon a beehive of activity circling the kitchen island, back and forth. Margaret's tea was yet to steep. Napkins, place mats, serving platters, and juice glasses all begged for purpose. Once things got rolling, it was a well-oiled machine.

Margaret looked up at the activity and smiled. "Many hands," she said, not needing to finish the maxim.

Before long, the three settled down to breakfast. Jerome eyed the sausages and started the finger grab. Julian followed his lead.

"No fingers," admonished Margaret. "Where's the serving spoon and fork?" She looked around and, once certain they were missing, looked at Julian. "Can you be a dear and grab them?"

Julian got up slowly with a competitive glare at his dad. It would appear he was unwilling to oblige his mom, but that wasn't for lack of respect and appreciation; it was simply survival. He didn't want to leave all the food on the table unguarded. Second pickings were often slim pickings in the Robinson household. Julian was a growing teen and had a healthy appetite. His dad, however, hadn't yet adjusted to having a hungry teen competing for the portions. Julian snatched up four slices of bacon before heading off to retrieve the utensils.

"Julian, no hands, please," Margaret chided. Her gentle tone belied her criticism. She knew what was playing out and didn't really mind him Jeroma for himself after enjoying years of unfettered access to whatever quantity and cuts were on the menu. Jerome, for his part, played oblivious to all the fuss.

"I know you're not gonna deprive your mom of bacon after she came down early to put food in your belly, young man," Jerome said.

"There's enough for her," said Julian, "as long as you don't hog it all."

"Hmm," Jerome grumbled again, feigning discontent. It was the usual game they played—a family quite comfortable with itself indulging in gentle gibes without stepping on toes. The undercurrent of love and affection did not need mention. It was obvious if you watched closely, particularly the eyes. They were undeniably a path to the soul. And if you watched all that went on, it was clear—from the way Margaret chided with endearing eyes or Jerome's quizzical look when probing an issue—that Julian was ensconced in a family love story, and it was all he'd known from birth.

——— ... ———

Fred Mason was the first to rise, and he started the day the same way he did every day. His fanaticism for the morning brew was unrivaled, his monasticism akin to a Buddhist in meditation. He was an artisan of the brew, and French press was his canvas.

He took nothing for granted; everything had to be measured precisely, and each step followed without compromise. It was a simple chemical reaction that if left to nature would produce the same outcome every time. It was the human factor that disappointed. The perfect cup was the product of consistency, and Fred prided himself on being able to perform any task with perfection.

He filled the measuring cup to the brim with whole beans and poured them into his grinder. Some fell to the floor as his hand misjudged. He usually rescued the mishaps, but today he simply grumbled and trudged on. The escaped beans were free to explore a fate more salubrious than the press.

The grinder had a conical burr, a triangular device that beans had to pass along as they were pulverized into tiny specs. Fred hated the less exact blenders that chopped the beans into random chips. It was a nod to the belief that water, time, and the surface of the grind orchestrated a symphony for the perfect brew. He transferred the grinds to the French press, losing some to the counter. He picked up the kettle and poured the initial ounce or so to begin the process.

"Damn! Damn, damn, damn!" Fred cursed himself.

The water was cold. He'd forgotten to start the kettle boiling. It was a sophomoric error, a cardinal sin of the brew. It was usually his first act when he came down to the kitchen. It was now ruined. He started over, his frustration simmering. With the process now bordering on chaos—more coffee beans on the floor, more grinds on the counter—the pour was finally ready. With the water temperature exactly 200 degrees, he poured the first ounce. A hotter temperature burned the coffee and left a bitter taste. Too cold, and the brew needed longer to extract the oils from the grinds. That first ounce was the final obsession built into the morning routine.

It was the "bloom" effect, allowing gas to escape from the grinds by premixing with only an ounce of hot water.

Fred waited and watched for the bubbles, caffeinated whispers of perfection. This was, arguably, the truest evidence of Fred's coffee neurosis. However, he defended the practice as he defended his obsession with every other aspect of the process. *If you want perfection, then you must yield to nature.* Anything less was simply unpredictable and, therefore, less desirable.

After seven minutes of brewing, the pour was ready, the preheated cup was filled, and bliss was achieved. Fred performed this ritual every day of the year except when on vacation, which he considered the one barbaric compromise to leaving home. He could never trust the symphony of the brew to some random barista. He would rather forgo coffee altogether just to avoid the disappointment. Fred's particular nature about his coffee was not unlike everything else in his life. He left nothing to chance. The outcomes in life, he felt, must be predictable to have value.

Phyllis eventually made her way downstairs and was greeted with breakfast already prepared. This was not unusual; cooking was yet another of Fred's indulgences. As she took her seat before their everyday imported china, silver utensils, and linen serviettes, he served up her eggs Benedict on an English muffin dressed delicately with hollandaise sauce, a fruit bowl of diced bananas, strawberries, and kiwi. A steeped cup of her special loose tea—Earl Grey de la crème—was evidence of a holiday treat. He was a perfectionist that some might say met the diagnostic criteria for medical intervention, but Phyllis found a way to make do.

A few minutes into their morning feast, Phyllis noticed a glum-faced Fred staring down at his plate, his fork stabbing away but making no progress in ferrying food to his mouth. This was not new for him, as she'd caught him pensively passing the time on other occasions. They had already discussed it, but she could tell her previous reassurances didn't have the lasting effect she'd hoped.

"Fred, are you still obsessing again over that meeting? You've got to let it go. You know the high school band will be marching in the parade down in the village, and I have to be there as principal—and you need to be there too. It's a social responsibility, and we need to be together on this. It doesn't look good for me to appear stag at these functions. Even worse is if you show and have that sour, defeated look. What will people think of us?"

He stopped stabbing at the scrambled eggs, which were his usual, and looked up at Phyllis. She could see the pain in his eyes, the disillusionment of someone usually in control but suddenly powerless.

"I can't shake it," Fred said. "I don't know why. It's like I got knocked off my pedestal and can't get up and show my face in public. I let everyone on Beekman down. I promised I'd deliver, and I didn't. Hell, I couldn't even run my own meeting in my own damn house. Now I have to go out and sit in the stands for everyone to gawk at."

Phyllis reached over and rubbed his shoulder, as she already had once or twice before for this same issue. She gave him a firm, endearing squeeze along his neck muscles to let him know she loved him. "I really don't think anyone's thinking about that night at all. What's more, I think most people there were just as shocked as we were that some hotheads got out of control. You kept your cool, and that's the image they all remember. I'm sure of it."

Phyllis was a confident decider. Once she had pondered a situation and come to a conclusion, she never second-guessed herself. It was a weakness she'd never had and didn't admire in others. She made exceptions, of course. This being one of them. She knew

Fred had his own way of being precise, exacting, and principled. She admired him for those qualities. This was just a lapse. He'd fallen off his horse and simply needed to get back on, as if nothing had happened. Making less of a situation was the best way to keep others from perseverating over it, or so she thought. If you want them to move on, you have to move on yourself.

They pondered and discussed as they sipped and ate. Phyllis hoped she was making headway, but she had nothing to go on. "You know," she said, "for some time now you've enjoyed calling the shots on Beekman. Whenever anything went wrong or a new project was suggested, you eagerly injected yourself to lead the way. And I'm not complaining about that. You're a smart man, dedicated and generous, almost to a fault. But I can only guess that sitting on that pedestal for so many years goes to your head a little. I'm not criticizing. I'm just saying I understand why that meeting hurt the way it did. It was disrespectful, to say the least."

She knew there was a fine line between being supportive and inadvertently encouraging him to do something rash to regain his stature on Beekman. That, she didn't want.

"The problem," Phyllis continued, "is that you have a lot of clients in Portville. You can't jeopardize your law practice chasing after the approval of a bunch of yahoo goons. I hate to say it, but that's how they behaved. And I'm the principal of *the* Portville High School. There's only the one. I don't have options to transfer to some other school nearby. For me, another principal job means Cincinnati or Columbus. Neither of us want that. We have to think smart. We have to lick our wounds, hold our heads high, and move on. Time will be on our side, I'm certain of it."

"My head knows you're right," Fred said. "My heart? Well, that's another matter. I know it'll get better, eventually, but every time I drive by the Johnson house, it just churns my stomach. I feel like I need to fix it, to do something. It's such an eyesore."

"That's just the point—what *can* you do? There's nothing really. Just let it be."

——— ... ———

Maggie woke to find Dennis had slipped out in the early morning. His comings and goings were often too unpredictable to be bothered by, so she did her usual by getting dressed and going downstairs to have a bowl of cereal. As usual, she topped it with sliced bananas and the last of the blueberries that had yet to turn. She made herself a cup of instant coffee and settled onto a high stool around the kitchen island.

The *Portville Weekly* lay open at her place setting. It was disheveled with misplaced sections, suggesting Dennis had already flipped through its pages. The front page featured a photo of the mayor of Portville and her brief wish for a happy holiday celebration with the necessary concerns about unsupervised fireworks, unattended children, and safe barbequing. The following page listed the events for the day, which included the morning parade through the village square, an afternoon festival at the Portville Village Park, and the new and improved fireworks on the Ohio River. Several lookout points were listed alphabetically to allow for safe viewing by the many residents expected to attend. Part of the page had been torn out, its ragged telltale edges severing the literary work of a *Weekly* staff writer.

Dennis was here for sure, Maggie thought. She couldn't tell what article was missing so she flipped the page, and the opposite article featured an interview with Sally Jennings from the Bank of Portville titled "Real Estate Prices Decline in Portville."

Maggie read the grim news with her mouth hung open. Home

prices had dropped ten percent the year before and were on track to drop another fifteen this year. Jennings had pointed to manufacturing plant closings and other "less definable" events that she felt impacted the bottom line. Her long-term prognosis for Portville was not rosy. The future had no expected turnaround date since new jobs were not on the horizon. The article went on, but Maggie couldn't finish it. The torn section coincided with the lower half of Jennings's article.

Maggie did not know what, if any, part of the article Dennis might have read. She knew, however, that this news would not go over well with Beekman homeowners.

Where is Dennis? she wondered. *For that matter, where is Jeffrey?*

Their fifteen-year-old was usually up by now, and it was odd he hadn't made his presence known, not even the usual blaring of his radio. Maggie's curiosity finally got the better of her and she decided to check on him, just to see if maybe he'd left with his dad. She climbed the stairs expecting to hear something, maybe the faucet in the bathroom, a toilet flush, or simply the faux band leader singing in his room. He sometimes wore headphones and let loose with a solo rendition of a rock song he'd accompany, jamming with an air-guitar.

But when Maggie turned the corner, she found his bedroom door wide open. The usual mess of three days' clothes were strewn about, but no Jeffrey. They were both gone.

―― ... ――

Alice and George didn't expect to be in Portville for the holiday weekend. Their plans, which Alice eagerly shared with me and Margaret with the hope of enticing us to tag along, was to cash in some frequent flier miles for a hotel in Chicago. They intended to leave Portville at midday on Thursday to beat the traffic. It was a four-hour drive, and they hoped to be in Chicago by dinner. Friday the fourth promised to be a day of event-hopping and watching the evening fireworks at the Navy Pier on Lake Michigan.

20

The Independence Day festivities in Portville went off as planned. The marching bands acquitted themselves well, and the village festival was well attended. Fred Mason worked up enough nerve to at least keep his chin up and force a smile from time to time. For all intents and purposes, the Masons resumed their stature as civic leaders. Dennis and Jeffrey returned home bearing fresh pastries from the local bakery. We occupied ourselves between the above events and trivial household chores. Matt and Sandy also squeezed in a little time with friends before evening.

As night descended on Portville, the scheduled fireworks were beginning to take shape. Crowds teemed along the riverbanks, jockeying for position despite the obvious unlimited viewing for what was to take place hundreds of feet overhead. Unless you pre-arranged a rendezvous point, you were not likely to find anyone you wanted to sit and watch the fireworks with.

All of Portville was in attendance, which meant hundreds of families clamoring for the limited parking along the riverbank. Some families gave up on getting any closer and settled for wherever they were able to pull off the road. They kept the young ones in view while chatting up a neighbor, acquaintance, or a total stranger. Older kids pretty much had the run of the place.

Since quite a few people arrived as much as two hours early to secure a spot, most of the hubbub happened before the main event. By the time things started popping overhead, the viewing was soon over, but the general consensus was that Portville had outdone itself. The fireworks were spectacular, evidenced by the oohs and ahhs of spectators and the colorful imaginative displays. It was all of the expected twenty minutes, but it seemed to last much longer.

Everyone was engrossed in what rendition of the flag or historical person would float through the sky for brief seconds of glory. There were aerial displays of flowers, a rendition of Betsy Ross, marching Minutemen, and, of course, George Washington made an expected appearance. All in all, it was a pleasing sight.

The finale started with a *rat a tat tat* and a *pop pop pop* that went on for nearly a minute while red, white, and blue starbursts lit up the sky higher than any of the previous fireworks before them. When all was done, the black sky was left with streams of smoke floating down the river. It was a fine way to end a long, busy day of celebration. Peter and I knew that soon, the kids would be tucked in bed, and we would have an hour or two to relax and debrief the day's events. For me, it was such a nice day, one that I really needed to feel like our family was back together, that our troubles were finally behind us. It was a delusion, to be sure, for nothing had really changed on Beekman. Somehow, this respite, with our family intact, felt like a harbinger of good times ahead. I trusted that fate would intervene and bring an end to our misery.

After the fireworks, Matt was nowhere to be found. The crowds were too dense. We hoped—or expected—he would get a ride home or spend the night at a friend's. We were neither surprised nor concerned. This was typical Matt. It was not uncommon for him to do his own thing, his family simply an afterthought.

Along with the rest of Portville, we slowly made our way back to the car and began the bumper-to-bumper slog away from the riverbank. The roads in and out were few, civic planners having never expected to accommodate the hordes of people that would celebrate such an event in such a place. Many interminable minutes of absolute standstill passed, the roads frozen for no known reason. But traffic was its own unpredictable beast, and it never listened to reason. It took several intersections for the traffic to begin moving at a regular flow, allowing for a more leisurely drive home—albeit an hour or more after the fireworks ended.

It was close to 11:30 when Peter made the final turn onto Beekman. At first it seemed the typical late evening on a quiet, dimly lit street. Then Peter and I noticed a small gathering up ahead, about where we would pull into our driveway.

"Interesting," I said. "I wonder who all are hanging out tonight?"

"I don't... know," Peter answered, still trying to figure it all out.

It seemed strange. People were standing in the street, all facing in one direction: away from our house.

Away from our house, I thought again. *Away. Why away?*

It all became clear when we saw a soft, amber glow through the trees on the opposite side of the street—*away* from our house. It was the Johnson house—the Robinson house. My heart raced, and a sinking feeling in the pit of my stomach churned.

"Oh, my God!" Peter exclaimed. "Something's going on at the Robinson house. It's glowing! What the hell?"

He sped up and was able to pull into our driveway despite the crowd of ten to fifteen people loitering in the middle of the street. The three of us piled out and stared across the street. The Robinson house was in flames.

"Oh, no, no, no!" Peter cried, his anxiety reaching a fevered pitch.

The three of us walked in unison out into the street and took up position alongside the arc of onlookers. Everyone was silent, staring with vacant faces. The living room was ablaze, and the fire had already burst through the front window. Licks of flame tried desperately to grab a foothold along the front exterior and up to the porch overhang. It was the amber glow that had been visible to us as we turned onto Beekman.

Black smoke streamed out of exterior cracks from all sides of the house, a dry tornado swirling up into the sky. Fire ate through the walls, devouring chemically laden wood and insulation, savoring every morsel to feed its insatiable hunger.

I watched as the crowd grew in number, the faces all familiar, all from the block, all staring in disbelief. Some were shaking their heads, unwilling to accept what was unfolding. One or two held their hands over their mouths with tears on their cheeks. This was more than most expected—probably more than anyone expected. Most just watched, their silence a shroud to their intent. I hoped it was somehow an accident, but a part of me knew the coincidence of it being the Johnson house was wishful thinking.

"Peter," I said, "where's the siren? I don't hear the siren."

He listened. There was none.

"Hey!" Peter shouted. "Has anybody called the fire department?"

He stepped out in front of the arc formed by our neighbors, seeking some form of acknowledgment. People looked at each other, but no one responded.

"No one called? Are you all crazy? The fire is going to destroy the house!" Peter was yelling like a wild man, pacing back and forth with his hands waving as if he were leading an orchestra.

Sandy's eyes were locked on her dad. It was likely unnerving and scary for her to see him in such a mood, screaming at people we knew. And, as kids often do, she tried to appease him. As he paced and yelled, she broke away from me and ran to his side.

"Dad!" she pleaded. "Dad!"

It took a few seconds for Peter to take notice; her voice was so soft in the din of the inferno unfolding before of us.

Sandy tugged on his sleeve. "Dad!"

Peter finally looked down with a wild stare into the beseeching eyes of his little girl. "Yes honey, what is it?"

"I'll go inside and call the fire department," she said. "I'll go call them, okay?"

"Yeah, Sandy go, go! Hurry!"

I realized then that any one of us could have gone ourselves to call. Such was the confusion and trance caused by the flames. Eyes were locked on it like a living beast consuming the house, section by section. People stared without talking, stared without moving, stared without even wondering if anyone was inside the house. They just stared.

I pulled Peter back to my side, holding onto his arm. I wanted him safe. I didn't trust anyone. It was a survival instinct, a protective reflex. I now accepted that it was quite likely a nefarious act born out of the events building up over the past few weeks. I knew I was part of it, and I had to admit I had no idea of its depth or breadth.

If someone had done this, then who? How many? And what else were they going to do?

Peter was a friend of the Robinsons, and that made him a target. I hoped this was it—that nothing else would come of this tragedy. But something had been unleashed, and like a wild dog gone astray, there was no telling what to expect, or from whom.

I looked at the faces in the crowd, no longer for the comfort and reassurance of neighbors showing concern. I was now on the defensive, protecting my own—against them.

The house groaned and crackled, snapped and popped as the fire worked its way through each and every room. If you closed your eyes, it sounded almost exactly like the events down at the river just an hour before, the occasional loud boom mimicking the orchestral accompaniment to the firework crescendo.

The front was now surrendering to a wall of flames as the fire surreptitiously crept up along the shingles to the second story. It gave the appearance of making little progress, but its studious character knew the art of consumption, testing the terrain with advances in each direction until deciding on the best path of destruction.

Its wanton nature instinctively searched for crevices, outcroppings, window ledges—anything that made the grab an easy hold. Smoke was now billowing out on both sides of the house as the fire extended to the back of the first floor, consuming the kitchen and dining room furniture, while the intense heat exploded through the windows.

Any hope of saving the house was now gone. With no siren, there was no water, and the house would feed the angry beast until it was satiated or there was nothing left to consume.

I saw sudden movement from the opposite side of the crowd. It was the Robinsons coming through, pushing their way, bumping shoulders. Jerome looked back to reach Margaret's hand. The crowd's unwillingness to be disturbed from their trance-like stares meant he could easily have lost her.

It was clear Margaret already knew. She had the petrified look of fright, her hand covering her mouth, tearfully staring at her home, red flames reflecting off her watery eyes. Jerome pressed on, pushing through the crowd, his face showing the same disbelief of those standing in his way.

They got to the front of the growing semicircle of onlookers and stopped, mouths agape, taking in the full tragedy of Beekman. Jerome shook his head. And then, in a sudden look of discovery, he looked back at Margaret.

"Where's Julian? Where is Julian?" he asked her, holding both her arms as if the answer would be more forthcoming if he showed he was serious.

Margaret's eyes frantically searched Jerome's face, her arms grabbing onto him as well. "Julian! Julian!" she yelled.

She turned and looked around the crowd, searching faces in the midnight darkness.

"Julian! Julian!!" she continued to scream.

Folks moved their gazes from the house to Margaret, and some turned to look among themselves, offering to help with a glance here or there. No one left their spots. It was a concern, but not enough to distract them from the inferno that consumed their minds.

A scream rang out from the crowd. Everyone looked at the woman with her hand pointing up to the second-story window over the doorway. It was the only window not yet engulfed in flames. The billowing smoke had obscured it for several minutes, but now the smoke shifted, and the window was visible.

In the window stood the outline of a person with their hands outstretched, pressed against the glass, as a flickering glow illuminated the smoke swirling behind them. It was only for a second, but everyone saw it.

Someone was in the house—still alive.

Jerome saw it. Margaret saw it. Peter and I saw.

Jerome took a step forward. Margaret fell to her knees and

doubled over. Heaving in a deep breath of air, she let out a blood-curdling cry, calling out her son's name. "Julian! Julian! My baby! My baby!"

Jerome took another step. Margaret fell onto the street, crying—screaming—"Julian! Julian!"

Another step. Peter and I looked down at Margaret with shock and pity. She was convulsing, rolling onto her back, screaming again. "My baby! My baby!!" She held her hand up toward the window, as if it connected her soul to her son.

Another step. Peter's eyes moved from Margaret to Jerome. Another step.

Peter let go of my hand and took a step toward Jerome. They were both on opposite ends of the arc of onlookers. I saw Peter move forward, and I reached out and grabbed his arm. He flinched, pulled free, and took another step.

Jerome started moving deliberately toward the fire. Peter surged in the same direction. It happened in an instant. Peter was a blur, moving across space and time in a way that seemed inhuman.

I screamed, "Peter! No!" but he heard nothing. He moved as if in his own trance, running for his life—toward the fire.

Jerome made it to the front lawn and headed for the front door, which was itself engulfed in black smoke. Peter closed in on him with several large strides and dove across several feet to intercept him, making contact at the hips and tackling him in front of the burning porch banister.

Almost as instantly, the roof overhang collapsed in a fireball, descending on the entire porch. A booming blast spit fire out the front room and shot across the front lawn, engulfing Jerome and Peter in a flash of flames.

The entire front of the house was now a wall of fire, the whole porch and access to the front door obliterated. The window that had been briefly visible, as if the smoke had parted to allow everyone to witness the cost of indifference, was now gone.

Screams spilled from the crowd as Jerome and Peter lay still, the flames that engulfed them having receded. They didn't move.

I continued screaming, "No! No!" again and again. When I saw Peter lying lifeless, I burst into a run toward him—toward the burning house. I didn't get far. Someone grabbed me from behind to save me from what everyone thought was a likely second blast.

The sirens were now off in the distance. They grew louder until they turned onto Beekman and subsided. The firefighters dismounted their red machine and started the perfunctory duties of unraveling the hoses.

Onlookers got the attention of the firefighters and pointed to the motionless bodies of Peter and Jerome just feet from the flames. The firefighters responded with due diligence. Hoses were quickly attached to a water source, and one firefighter maintained a steady wall of water on the porch and front room while the two were carried off to the front lawn of a neighbor's house. Oxygen tanks were set up next to them, and masks put on their faces.

Peter and Jerome sat side by side as emergency personnel attended to them. I sobbed, standing back to let the paramedics perform their duties. I saw in Peter's face the lost look of dejection, a blank stare of disbelief.

That was my guy, the fool who had risked his life. For what? I was perplexed. I was drawn to him for what he'd done and frustrated for what he was putting me through. I couldn't understand him, but I couldn't understand myself, either.

I knew that when all was lost—when the thought of him as dead had descended on me like a heavy shroud—I was crushed. I had been angry with him for some time now, but in that moment, none of it mattered. He was a person who was foreign to me, yet very much vital to me. The idea was more than I was able to make sense of in that moment. I had to let it all go as something beyond my knowing.

Margaret clung to Jerome's arm, sobbing uncontrollably. The paramedics offered to take her to the hospital, but Jerome declined. He wanted her by his side. They had lost their son and needed each other. Their son had been entombed in ash, and they would not leave his side.

Matt and Sandy eventually found us. Sandy clung to Peter, who smelled of burned debris and whose face and clothes were blackened from the blast. She was unwilling to let go. She had missed the near-death event but was frightened by my emotional state and knew something bad had happened. She was relieved when she finally saw her dad. How he looked didn't matter.

When Peter saw Sandy's grave look, he took off his oxygen mask and gave her a smile. He wanted to be sure she knew he was okay. It was important to him that her worst fears were calmed. It appeared his smile was all she needed, but she stayed by his side to be sure.

Matt stood in front of Peter, looking awkward about how to behave. Guilt colored his face. Though he said nothing, it seemed he wished he could just go inside their house and mope by himself. He had much to account for, but the most obvious was how he and his dad had sparred the week before over this very issue, the Robinsons. That his dad had put his life on the line to save someone that he himself had dismissed the week prior had to be humbling.

I asked Matt where he'd been. He was the other "man of the house," and I felt ashamed that Peter had almost lost his life while Matt was off doing who knew what.

He didn't have an answer. "Nowhere," was all he offered.

The scene took on the appearance of an evening news segment. Water was put on the fire. The smoke turned from black to white. Firefighters walked along the sides of the burning structure to the back, and returned to the front. There was no access point.

Fire raged from every window. Without a ladder truck, access to the second story was limited. Julian was lost. The house was gone.

With no feasible entry point, hoses were limited to window access. They blasted water through the front and side windows and Julian's second-story window. The white smoke continued to billow out as water turned to steam and mixed with the burning chemicals of roof shingles, treated wood, furniture, and paint. The inside would burn and smolder for hours.

Peter looked at Jerome as if he wanted to say something, but I'm sure he realized that no words would do justice. In their last exchange, he hadn't been forthcoming. However it was that Julian had ended up in that house alone, Peter was certain what he'd failed to say had played a major part.

"Julian was a promise that had been sacrificed on the pyres of Beekman," Peter said in the aftermath of the tragedy. "An innocence lost to future generations."

The weight of that loss became a guilt that descended on him with a crushing emotional blow. He felt unworthy as a friend, a neighbor, and even as a husband to me. That moment marked the start of years spent rethinking, reassessing, and reworking the dialogues—the words, smiles, gestures—everything that transpired between him and Jerome, him and me, him and Fred Mason, and all the neighbors.

"How? How did it all happen," Peter would ask, "and why did I not see it clearly enough to stop it?"

It was a familiar refrain that haunted him. It had all been

preventable, and he had put himself in a pivotal position to make a difference. If he had just acted with confidence, determination, and—most of all, honesty—the outcome could have been different. But in his mind, he had failed.

21

The next day began with the usual routines: retrieving the newspaper from the front steps with a cup of coffee while still in robe and slippers, the morning jogs with a "good morning" wave to neighbors, the dogs out and about for their morning walk, and people backing out of driveways scurrying off to early morning errands. In short, it was a day like any other.

The morning sunrise also revealed the few in attendance who refused to leave the scene. The Robinsons had never left. They stood, sat, paced, cried, hugged themselves—all while watching the firemen complete their duties. Their son was still in there, buried below the ashes of Beekman, enshrined in a symbol of hate. They waited until they could retrieve their son from the wretched claws of a people capable of doing such a horrible thing.

The Robinsons understood the hatred. It had been a part of oral history for centuries and a subject of history books and historical television programming—but mostly, it was something that any person with knowledge of America's history dating back to the seventeenth century knew. Despite all that, the Robinsons still could not fathom the inhumanity. This act hearkened back to another century. A callousness that would take a thirteen-year-old's life and then go on with their day—in the twentieth century—was inconceivable.

Jerome and Margaret sat and waited for their son. They would not turn their backs on him. He was theirs.

We were also standing watch. It had become our fire as well. Peter and I pulled up lawn chairs to get through the night. The spectacle wore on for several hours before the trance-inducing flames were subdued and people slowly peeled off to get their rest. A few offered condolences to the Robinsons before departing. The transactions were well intended though rather late, coming after the show had ended.

Jerome and Margaret said nothing. Their heads hung low with occasional sobs while most folks just left for home. Peter offered them a place to stay, but they declined. I offered water or food. Margaret declined. The Robinsons were still in shock, but they were also imbued with a solemn observance of their son's life. The mourning had begun.

By late morning, a fire inspector and the city morgue van arrived on the scene. The inspector followed other firemen into the burned façade, assessing its durability. They poked at the floors and the walls with a long-spiked pike pole, making sure nothing would crash in on them. Occasionally, ceiling material came loose, revealing gaping holes into the second story.

The inspector delicately stepped through the front room where the fire was first ablaze, bending over from time to time, reaching for items in the debris with a gloved hand, smelling them, and putting them in a bag.

He kicked things over to look underneath and found more items. He then went farther into the house and out of view. After a while, movement could be seen on the upper floor. Firefighters were moving about, checking the structure from above, aware that the floor could fall out from under them at any time.

Movement eventually made its way to the room above where the front door had been. Shadows were seen congregating, and the occasional yellow fire coat passed by what was left of the window. Soon, all movement in the house disappeared.

The Robinsons had risen from the curb when the firefighters moved into the fateful front room. Now Jerome paced with a frightful look as if some new discovery was imminent, and Margaret began quietly sobbing. Eventually, the officers emerged from the side of the house through a hole that had been cut to allow entry. They carried a long black bag—the body of Julian.

Jerome looked on, tears streaming down his face, his fist thrust into his mouth in a desperate attempt to stifle the rush of emotions. He gathered up his wife, whose sobbing had now become uncontrollable, and moved toward the pallbearers.

The firefighters saw the Robinsons coming their way. They gently and respectfully laid the body on the front lawn—by chance exactly where Jerome and Peter lain lifeless the night before. A firefighter approached the Robinsons and offered her condolences. She told them they could spend as much time as they needed with their son.

With that, the officer and her colleague stepped back and allowed Jerome and Margaret to kneel by their son and cry and pray and caress the bag he lay in. It went on for several minutes; no one really kept time.

We had come over to form a second row of emotional support. Sandy and Matt also came from inside the house when they noticed the gathering. All of us stood quietly, somberly paying our respects. The matter had sunk in overnight for Matt. He now understood that words have consequences. Still, he was confused. He was a boy used to a healthy self-confidence, now suddenly thrust into a tragedy he'd been guilty of making light of. It knocked him off-kilter, and for the first time in his young life he understood that his knowledge was indeed limited—understood that things happen outside one's sphere of control, and that opinions matter.

Sandy stood by Matt's side, holding onto his arm. She remembered Julian's smile, his humor, and his generosity. She pictured the very moment he'd offered her *The Count of Monte Cristo*. He'd had a look of benevolence when he handed it to her, as if he were offering up an opportunity from something special, something that was going to change her life forever.

She turned her face away when her mind conjured up macabre images of what he must look like in the black bag. It was not a memory she wanted to imprint, a scar she knew would last forever. She turned away with the hope that Julian's smile, and the laughter they'd shared, would be the last image in her memory. But the nightmare that had haunted her two nights before was resurrected.

Although she had forgotten about the dream, it now came rushing back. She remembered it in all its clarity. The face she'd almost willed to recede into her subconscious was now clear as day. It was Julian's.

The dream would haunt her for several months to come, and she would wonder if she'd somehow caused this to happen to him. That she had dreamed it and it had happened was too real for her eleven-year-old mind to dismiss as coincidence.

22

With the body removed from the scene, the fire inspector found the right moment to approach the Robinsons. He offered his condolences.

"I'm sorry to have to ask you these questions at this time, ma'am," the inspector said, leaning toward Margaret as he spoke. "I'm Inspector McGill, and I just wanted to clarify some of my findings. I have to determine the cause of the fire, and my brief inspection didn't show any evidence of electrical shortage or stove or oven flare-ups. The heater was turned off, which is not a surprise in summer, and I don't see evidence of a gas leak. I interviewed some of the neighbors before coming over to do my inspection, and several of the early witnesses clearly pointed to the front room as the start of the fire. So I spent a lot of my time there to see if I could find a source. All I found, however, were some shards of a bottle."

Inspector McGill retrieved a plastic bag from his oversized coat pocket and showed it to Jerome and Margaret. He held it up to the light to reveal several pieces of a broken bottle, with the lower third still intact. The still-visible glass embossing suggested it was a beer bottle.

"Do either of you recognize this bottle or brand?" he asked.

"That's a beer bottle," Margaret said quickly. "We don't have beer in the house. We don't drink alcohol. None of us."

"Any chance your son purchased this or somehow got hold of it, maybe a Fourth of July thing?"

"Naw, naw," said Jerome. "That's not my kid. He doesn't do things like that. He's only thirteen. We were home all day. We were supposed to go to Cincinnati for the day, but Julian started feeling sick after breakfast. Probably ate too many pieces of bacon or something."

"Don't say that, Jerome," Margaret said, her tone admonishing. "Our son said he hadn't been feeling well from the night before. He just didn't tell us. He thought it would pass by morning. After breakfast, he took ill again, and we had to cancel the Cincinnati trip. I can tell you, Inspector, there was no beer in here today, or yesterday, or ever."

"I figured, ma'am, I just had to ask," Inspector McGill said. "I apologize for any impertinence, but was your son home alone?"

Margaret held onto Jerome's forearm as if to steady her emotions. "We... we thought since he was feeling much better by evening that maybe we could catch the fireworks. Maybe rescue something to do as a family. Julian didn't want to go, but he felt bad about keeping us from going to Cincinnati, so he encouraged us to go down to the river without him. We initially objected, but he wore us down. He's such a good boy, and we had a mobile phone, and it's only about twenty minutes away." She started sobbing. "It's... it's the worst decision we ever made."

Inspector McGill was silent for a moment, respecting Margaret's need to gradually compose herself. "I'm sorry I brought it up, ma'am," he finally said.

"You figure that bottle has something to do with how the fire started?" Jerome asked.

"Well, it's preliminary, but if it's not your bottle, then we need to investigate how it got in your front room. We'll take it down to the lab and do some forensics on it. We'll swab the insides and see what kind of chemicals we get. We might even get some DNA or fingerprints off the outside of the bottle shards. Can you give me an address of where you'll be staying so we can talk more? I'd like to keep you posted on what we find."

Jerome had to pause and think that question through. They had been living in the moment, even though their very home had gone up in flames. It was all about Julian, not the clothes, jewelry, or family heirlooms that were destroyed. *He* had been their every thought in every moment through the night. The actual loss of anyplace to stay had not dawned on them. His instinct was to just return to Cincinnati and stay with his brother, but he didn't want to leave Julian in a morgue in Portville, alone.

"What are we going to do?" Margaret asked Jerome. "We have nowhere else to stay in Portville." She, too, had no intention of leaving Julian. If she could, she would stay by his side until he was placed in the ground. Then she would visit him every day until it was her turn to join him. Margaret turned to the inspector, despondent, beseechingly. "What do people do in times like this?"

"Well, Mrs. Robinson, in these circumstances, sometimes it's best to start out in a hotel nearby. Talk to your insurance carrier, and they'll provide you with living expenses until you can make more permanent decisions. There's no need to feel squeezed into anything uncomfortable or unreasonable. You folks need time to mourn, and a hotel will at least give you a week or two to figure things out. I'll give you my card, and you can give me a call when you get settled. I should know something in a week or so." The inspector offered his condolences once more.

Margaret could see the empathy in his eyes, an empathy one would have thought had grown numb from years of investigating fires. Still, he cared, despite having seen many lives destroyed from similar tragedies. *The human heart,* she thought, *is the same in everyone. A lost soul is a lost soul.*

Soon after he met with the Robinsons, Inspector McGill interviewed Peter and Clare, especially since Peter had been involved in the evening's events. The inspector shared some of what the Robinsons had to say about not leaving for Cincinnati but held back on the bottle shards found in the house.

Everyone was guilty 'til proven innocent. The investigation was ongoing, and anyone may have been tangentially culpable.

The week turned on the second day after the fire. While the first day after was a return to routine, the second day brought the heavy shroud of guilt. An investigation was underway, and the Robinsons were not the only ones in the know. Other neighbors had watched their interview with the inspector. They saw the bag removed from a pocket, and head shaking and fingers pointing to the front of the house. It had the appearance of an interrogation of sorts. The Robinsons were essentially saying it wasn't them. Which meant it was someone else.

Beekman shut down. Children were no longer allowed to play outside. No one jogged, strolled, or walked their dogs—the backyard would have to do. With the exception of going to and from work, interrupted by a few phone calls home to check on any news flash for the day, no one did anything.

Everyone felt some form of guilt. Everyone had gone to the meetings and heard the plaintive demands that something be done. They had all agreed to the buyback of the Johnson house. They all had their fingerprints on something. The hope was that not being seen or heard would prevent anyone from remembering that they, too, had been at the Mason house for the meetings. No one wanted their name mentioned, even casually, to the wrong person.

It wasn't a coverup in the traditional sense. It was more like the hypocrisy of human arrogance, a wanting to live dangerously and getting burned in the process—then pulling back to heal, hoping no one noticed how foolish you were to begin with.

The fact of the matter was that no one on Beekman understood the social or psychological effects of mob mentality, the diminished guilt one felt when they were part of a larger group's dubious activity. They were unaware of the bell curve. That there would be a large general consensus representing the dome of the bell, but a few would be on the edges, like Peter on the dissenting side. And of course, there would also be someone else, maybe even a silent someone, just listening, not commenting, who represented the other extreme.

When discussions about what to do were suggested, the crowd chose a plan that most could agree on: The extremes, well, they're extreme; the dissenters are not likely to take part, and they may also be inclined to warn the target that an attack is imminent. The Beekman crowd had distanced themselves from Peter during the previous couple weeks because they feared that he would warn the Robinsons about their plans and encourage them to stick it out and not give in to the neighbors' demands.

The extreme in the other direction—the one who thinks the majority is not going far enough—well, that's when things get out of hand and people find themselves in a situation like Beekman's. Someone in the crowd hadn't listened to reason. Someone had heard a measured approach and decided it wasn't enough. They instead took matters into their own hands, and by doing so smeared the entire block with the guilt of having pushed things down the road toward an intolerance that resulted in the taking of a life. In murder.

People were not talking—to anyone, except maybe the police. Law enforcement made their rounds. A squad car pulled up to a house and interviewed a neighbor then drove farther down the block to another house for another interview. Information was being gathered; pieces were being put together.

The focus of the investigation was often the last to know or the last to be interviewed. The police and the fire inspector knew how to tighten the noose. You start from the outside and close the knot slowly, tighter and tighter, until the main suspect has nowhere to run. The plan was not to alert the culprit that they were being investigated. In a tight community like Beekman, it was necessary not to let anyone know who the suspect was. There was frequent use of: "No, we don't have anyone in particular we're looking at, just gathering information, for the record, you know. We have to be thorough before we close the book on this."

That last line was the teaser. It gave the witness a false sense that this was all perfunctory and would be wrapped up soon. It put the witness at ease, and then they spilled a little detail: "Well, you know, it was so busy down at the river we couldn't really tell who was there and who wasn't, but no, I didn't see him there. Oh, he was probably just a few yards down from me. There were a few hundred people there, you know, officer."

"Yes, very busy, hard to tell who attended, likely everyone was there. But who else do you remember seeing?"

It went on and on like that from house to house, a bit here and a bit there. After a few days of this, Inspector McGill and a police detective both descended on Fred Mason's house. It would have seemed he was a focal point of everyone's comments, especially since the Robinsons had been re-interviewed after a couple of days of mourning and revealed the general attitude of Beekman to their arrival.

Margaret mentioned the buyback offer signed by Fred Mason. But she didn't have a copy to show since it was in the house, and the house was gone. The investigators had been there before and were not concerned. The point was that there *was* a document, and the people who were behind it didn't know that the original was gone. The police didn't need to show anyone the copy of the buyback—just make reference to it, as if they'd seen it. The hope was that people would admit to something they were part of, which the police already knew they were part of. No sense lying to the authorities if they had the goods. At that point, one needed to hope for another way out.

Fred and Phyllis played their part convincingly. The investigators knew they had been at the fireworks. Many on Beekman had already stated that the Masons were in attendance, from early before until well after. Fred made a credible argument that he was merely a moderator and that their home had been used not because he and Phyllis were instigators but that they were the focal point of neighborhood decisions going back years. Phyllis ticked off all the block parties, street repaving petitions, signage for speed limits, and children playing. There were many, and Phyllis tried to make the point that they were simply the best hosts on Beekman, not the sole repository of ideas on how the neighborhood should decide anything.

It all sounded good, but the investigators had heard it all before. People always have a good story to tell. It's not until you hold their feet to the fire that you get the information you want, the stuff you really need to close the book.

Despite all the denials and self-abnegation, the investigators acted as though they had something on the Masons. Even if their whereabouts were accounted for, the mere hosting of the event that may have incited the fire would lead to a conspiracy charge. The Masons might worm their way out of it, but it would be in court. The charges would be made, Fred's legal practice would be in limbo, Phyllis's principal position at Portville High would be threatened, and at a minimum, a leave of absence would be necessary. Their reputations would be tarnished if not ruined. The Masons understood how the game was played. They had no problems cooperating. Thus, the tapes were produced.

Fred was no fool. He made sure to take the necessary precautions. In a large group such as the one present at the meetings he and Phyllis had hosted, things were bound to get out of control. Anyone could be responsible for leaking information to the authorities if something unpredictable happened, and who said what would easily be remembered wrong or simply misrepresented. Fred had discreetly taped the meetings to have an unimpeachable record of his position. In fact, his intentional objection to the less savory ideas on display were intended to protect him from future prosecution. He and Phyllis had too high a profile in Portville to allow the vagaries of the less restrained—and less refined—to put all they had worked for at risk.

As it turned out, it was the only way the Masons could prove that theirs was a sincere effort to do no harm. The tapes would help the investigators, but it required their exoneration. Otherwise, who else could testify that the tapes had been recorded in the Mason house? Who else would offer to identify the voices on the tapes, the yelling and threats that Fred could be heard trying to tamp down and steer back to a productive, nonviolent way of doing things? The investigators needed the tapes—they therefore needed the Masons.

The rest of the interview was to learn the agenda of the two meetings and identify the voices heard asking questions or making comments, especially the belligerent statements made by the few—the extreme.

——— ... ———

By week's end, as Inspector McGill had promised, chemical analysis identified turpentine residue lining the inside of the glass shards. Partial fingerprints were also found on the outside of the larger pieces of glass. DNA analysis of any sloughed skin cells on the glass was still pending and might take a couple of weeks. With what the investigators already knew, matching the fingerprints simply required a warrant for the more belligerent voices heard on the tape. The judge had no hesitation in ordering one.

And so it was that on the Friday following the fire, seven days after the tragic event, two police cars arrived at Dennis Thompson's lumberyard business with a warrant for his arrest. The scene occurred as it usually does in movies: Four officers got out of their police cruisers and approached the nearest workers to get the lay of the land. The employees offered their help but were quickly shown the warrant and pushed aside. A crowd followed the officers, and all eyes watched as they finally descended upon the portly man wearing a loosely tucket shirt with disheveled, graying hair, moving about with an air of authority.

"What can I do for you, officers?" the man asked with a certainty only the boss would pretend in these circumstances.

"Mr. Thompson? We have a warrant for your arrest. Please place your hands behind your back."

"Hey, wait a minute, what's the meaning of this? I haven't done anything wrong! Take your hands off me. Hey! Hey!"

The man was cuffed and strong-armed back to the cruiser.

While one officer held the door open, the other grabbed the suspect by the top of the head and pushed it down below the doorjamb, ostensibly protecting him from bumping his head.

"Somebody call my wife. Get me a lawyer," was the last thing said as the car door was slammed shut.

Once back at the station, no one talked to the accused, though he continued with a litany of questions about why he was being treated this way and protestations declaring he'd done nothing wrong. The suspect was fingerprinted and placed in a bare room with a table and two chairs opposite each other. A large mirror on one wall belied the privacy of the room; eyes were watching his every gesture for a betrayal of his professed innocence.

They left him that way for an hour or so, just to tenderize. His frustration built as he realized he was no longer in control, that his time was no longer of anyone's concern, that he was no longer a decider.

Next came the interrogation. It did not seem like an interrogation, despite the methods used to bring him in. It played out like a good cop/bad cop scenario. The warrant and handcuffs were the bad cop, making Dennis aware of the severity and that cooperation was the best game in town. Next came the good-cop approach.

"Mr. Thompson, I'm Officer Mulroney, and this is Officer Leone. We apologize for the way we brought you down here. We did have a warrant, but we mostly wanted to get your fingerprints. Sometimes just asking for them can get a bit challenging, so the warrant route smooths the way for us."

Dennis harrumphed. "Well, I'll hold back on whether I want to accept that apology. I feel manhandled! You could've just asked me to come along. Hell, you could've called me and asked me to come down. I have nothing to hide. Instead, you've made a huge spectacle in my place of business. I have customers, you know. A scene like the one you caused will cost me. I'm likely to lose clients. And for what, fingerprints?"

"I'm sorry," Officer Mulroney repeated. "If we knew a gentler way of doing it, we'd use it. It's just that we don't know how you're likely to handle a request for prints. Everyone is different. Some are likely to skip town or run and start hiding evidence. We can't allow that. You understand, Mr. Thompson, I'm not saying you've got evidence to hide, just that it's procedure and all. I gotta do it by the book or else my captain gives me hell."

"Well, I understand that, at least. I give a lot of hell to my guys all the time."

Dennis chuckled. They all chuckled together. The ice was melting.

"So, Mr. Thompson, the reason you're here is to give prints to match what we have on file. Our investigation found pieces of a bottle—a beer bottle, to be exact. The pieces were found in the Robinson house. The Robinsons are certain they don't belong to them. No one drinks alcohol in the house."

"You sure you trust those people?"

Dennis chuckled again. This time, he was alone. The officers did not see the humor. They had moved on with their strategy.

"Let me ask you, what time did you arrive and leave the fireworks show?" asked Officer Mulroney.

"Hey, are you making accusations here? Do I need an attorney?" The feeling of being manhandled came charging back. Dennis's senses were prickly, and any accusatory intention was quickly pounced on as a flagrant dereliction of duty on the part of the officers.

"We're just asking the same questions we've asked all of your neighbors," they told him. "We just want to know what you saw regarding the fire."

"Oh. Well, why didn't you just come out and say it like that? I saw the fire, but it wasn't 'til well after midnight. The firefighters had been working on it for hours by then. Wasn't much to see."

"What time did you get to the fireworks, then?" Officer Leone asked.

Dennis turned to Leone. "Early—quite early. It's the only way to get a good spot. It must have been around eight. I was hanging with my guys. Sort of a men's cigar club. My wife doesn't let me smoke around the house, so we find any reason to get together and smoke a few."

"So you were with your guys from eight until after midnight, then, huh?" asked Mulroney.

"Yup. They'll corroborate. Had a few beers while we were at it."

At that point, someone opened the door from the outside and poked their head into the interrogation room. "It's affirmative," they said and shut the door.

Mulroney and Leone looked at each other, then back at Dennis. The next step had been approved. They went to work.

"That gentleman just confirmed for us that your prints were found on the beer bottle that was in the Robinsons' front room," Mulroney said.

"Well, that's interesting, officers," Dennis said with a heavy dose of sarcasm. "What's it to me?"

"Any idea how *your* bottle got inside *their* house?" Mulroney asked.

"Beats me. Maybe someone pulled it from my trash."

"Maybe. But you can see how that looks, don't you?" said Leone.

"I don't give a rat's ass how it looks, officer, it's not really my problem."

Dennis knew well enough that the crosshairs were on him. He didn't know what they knew, but he was confident that a steady, consistent denial would win the day. He was confident his stature in the community would eventually redirect their misplaced efforts onto someone else.

——— ... ———

The plan at the Portville Police Department was to get two warrants: one for Dennis Thompson and one for Jeffrey Thompson. The reason was twofold. One set of prints on the bottle was smaller than the other. It was either a smaller female print or a teenager's print.

When officers questioned Maggie earlier in the week, she mentioned that Dennis and Jeffrey had spent the morning of the fourth together, getting pastries. Apparently, that torn section from the *Portville Weekly* that Maggie was reading turned out to be a coupon for lattes and baked sweets. Somewhere on an officer's information pad, their names were listed together. When the issue of the multiple prints came up, the two of them were naturally linked.

Thus, at the time of Dennis's interrogation, Jeffrey was served his warrant, again ostensibly to get his fingerprints into the system. The same strategy applied: a visit by two officers and a representative from Child Protective Services, the warrant shown, the handcuffs brought into play, this time with Jeffrey tearing up and calling out to his mom as they escorted him out.

"Mom, do I have to go alone? Can you come, please?"

He was only fifteen, but she couldn't. He was on his own. She watched from the curb as they pushed his head down into the back of the cruiser. She sobbed, not knowing what in the world was going on. What had Jeffrey done that could result in this?

As the police car pulled away, Maggie realized she was standing on the sidewalk in her robe. She gave a furtive glance to the houses in the vicinity, and eyes could be seen watching between the cracks of drawn curtains.

It's out, she thought. Her family were now the pariahs of the neighborhood. They had brought disrepute to Beekman. She turned and ran up the stairs to the front door and quickly closed it behind her.

Maggie stood in her living room and paced. Her eyes welled up with tears, but anger simmered as well.

This is all wrong, she thought. *How could they do this to us?*

She needed to get dressed and get to the station before Jeffrey lost it. She imagined him being dragged around a police station, shoved into a jail cell with God knew who—maybe some seedy pervert or drunkard.

I can't let my son spend one minute in that place. He needs me!

She made for the kitchen phone to call Dennis. He would know what to do. He could meet her down at the police station, and they would figure it out. It was obviously a mistake. Someone must have mentioned Jeffrey's name or had a grudge against him, or it was a case of mistaken identity. Something!

No sooner did she get her hands on the phone than it rang. It was the lumberyard manager, José, telling her that some officers had come and taken Dennis down to the station. He'd made no mention of a lawyer. José hadn't heard it; Dennis was already in the back seat of the cruiser.

Down at the station, Jeffrey's treatment was a little different. They let him sit alone, just like his dad, but when the fingerprint match was confirmed, they started by simply giving him information. He was a minor, and questioning him without a parent or lawyer was permissible after Mirandizing, but it was not preferable. It always simplified the process when a suspect spontaneously confessed, especially a minor.

"Hi, Jeffrey, I'm Officer Simpson, and this is Officer Nunez."

Jeffrey looked up at them with red eyes. He was no longer tearful, but his emotional state looked fragile. This had to be handled delicately. If they probed too deep or too aggressively, the officers feared he might just crumble into tears and cry for his mom—at which point any information obtained would be seen as the product of badgering a child, no different than fruit of the poisonous tree, the legal term for evidence not admissible due to illegal police tactics.

He was a fifteen-year-old, to be fair, but hyperbole would prejudice the courtroom, and it would simply be interpreted as extracting a confession from a child to suit the biases of the police department for the purposes of wrapping up a heinous crime they could not solve otherwise. The officers needed to think it through, several steps ahead. Theirs was a science *and* an art form. They were experts at psychological warfare.

"We know you don't want to be here, Jeffrey," Officer Simpson said, "and we're sorry about the handcuffs and all. It was protocol—department rules and all. I hope your wrists are feeling better now." Assigning a pair of female officers to his case had been no accident.

Jeffrey looked at the officer, then at his wrists. The red marks were no longer there. "I'm okay," he said.

"Great," said Officer Simpson. "I'm sure your parents are on their way here now and everything will be alright. We just want to share with you some information we have that we think you might find interesting. If you want, we'll also show it to your parents when they get here."

That last part was to bait Jeffrey into taking an interest in what they were about to reveal. He was being empowered to take control of the outcome. The hope was that he would feel less dependent on his parents' approval for his actions.

"We have a problem," Officer Simpson continued, "with some of the evidence found in the burned-out house." She purposely left out the Robinson name so as not to personalize the moment. Jeffrey perked up. "We found a bottle in the front room, and it had your fingerprints on it. We were wondering how it got there."

Officers Simpson and Nunez both studied Jeffrey, whose eyes lost contact with the officers, his gaze turning to the table before him. "I don't know," he finally said. It was a guilty response, and barely audible. The officers exchanged a glance, as if on cue.

"Officer Simpson and I were wondering," said Nunez, "if you were horsing around with some friends the morning after and maybe rode by on bikes and tossed it in there. Sort of as a prank. You know, teenagers just having fun. We were teens once ourselves." She smiled to lighten the mood.

Jeffrey glanced at Nunez with a tentative look. "How'd you know?"

Once again, the officers exchanged glances. Step two.

"We've been around, Jeffrey," said Simpson. "This isn't our first rodeo. We know that kids will be kids. So, tell us about when that morning. When did you toss the bottle?"

Jeffrey took a while to respond, appearing lost in thought for several seconds. Simpson and Nunez couldn't tell if it was real or fake. He looked up at the wall behind the officers with a quizzical look. "Sometime around ten."

"Ten, hmm, okay," said Simpson. "We have another issue that we're trying to wrap our heads around. Maybe you can help us with this one, too."

"Sure."

"Forensics found turpentine residue inside the bottle," Nunez put in. "Any idea how that got there?" Her tone was not quite as friendly as it had been before. The tide was turning.

Jeffrey's face reddened. "I don't know," came another sheepish response.

"Did you find that bottle somewhere?" asked Simpson.

"Yeah!" he answered, more quickly this time, as if seizing an opportunity.

"It wasn't your bottle or your turpentine?" Nunez clarified.

"No." Jeffrey's eagerness was now obvious.

"So, what we have here, Jeffrey, is a bottle with your fingerprints and turpentine residue, found inside the burned house, thrown there by you on the morning after the fire, around ten a.m., and you found the bottle in the trash. Is that about right?"

"Yeah," Jeffrey said, sounding confident in the summary of events.

"And where exactly did you find the bottle?"

"I don't remember."

"Was it near your house?"

"I… I don't think so."

"Was it on Beekman?" Nunez pressed rapidly.

"I'm not sure. I think I was riding around and found it on some street somewhere. I don't remember what block I was on."

"Okay," Simpson said, "we should add a couple of particulars we sort of left out. First, we didn't find a bottle in the burned house. We found fragments of a bottle. Your prints were on the fragments, but the bottle was broken and had turpentine residue. One other thing—the fragments were burned. The edges were no longer sharp. They'd been heated down to rounded edges. Once the bottle got into the Robinson house, it broke into pieces and was in a fire. Now, you've admitted to throwing the bottle into the house, but I think you got the timing wrong. I think you threw the bottle into the house at ten p.m. on the Fourth of July, not ten a.m., the day after. How does that sound? Does it jog your memory? Is there anything you want to change about your story?"

Jeffrey put his head down and was silent for a long time. When he finally looked up, he was tearful and sniffly with red, puffy eyes. He shook his head and began sobbing.

Nunez pushed a tissue box in front of him. They waited. It was important to let a person's emotional angst play out on their own time. It was an internal process that, if interrupted, could result in frayed responses. Once a suspect started to cry, you had to give them space. That was the rule.

A good five minutes later, Jeffrey had pulled himself together. Officers Simpson and Nunez were near the end of what they needed to know, but time was of the essence. At any point, Jeffrey could clam up and ask for his parents or just refuse to cooperate.

"Jeffrey, it was you who threw the bottle into the house the night of the fireworks, wasn't it?" Simpson asked.

Jeffrey nodded, his head down.

"Could you speak your answer, Jeffrey, just so we're clear what you're saying?"

"Yeah."

"Okay. We need to know, then, where'd you get the turpentine? It doesn't seem that important in the grand scheme of things, but we just need it for our report. With that, we'll be done here."

Simpson and Nunez knew nothing in Jeffrey's story had stuck, and they hoped he was intelligent enough to know telling further lies was not a smart idea. It was clear, however, that he was in too deep, and they had no confidence he would do the right thing.

Jeffrey sighed. He appeared tired and dejected. He sat with his shoulders slumped and looked every bit defeated. He then gazed back to the same spot on the wall behind the officers and said, "At the supermarket near the bank in town."

"Was that on the Fourth of July?"

"Yeah."

"In the morning of the Fourth of July?"

"Yeah."

"Are you sure?"

"Why don't you believe me?!" he yelled at them. It was an emotional outburst of another kind—a lashing out. A release of frustration and anger from not being in control, the way he was led to believe it would happen. It was clearly all sinking in. This was all a charade.

"Well," Officer Simpson said, "for one, we have no evidence of you being at that market on the Fourth of July. It was closed. When we learned the bottle fragments had turpentine residue, we collected the closed-circuit television tapes from the two other stores in Portville that *were* open on the morning of the fourth. They've been scanned. There's an image of you and another person buying turpentine at the market near the lumberyard."

Simpson pulled a photo from a manila envelope and slid it across the table. Jeffrey looked at the photo—he and his dad standing in the checkout line with the can of turpentine in front of the cashier. He said nothing.

"Did your dad put you up to this, Jeffrey?" Simpson asked.

He said nothing.

"I know this is a tough spot to be in. You're just a kid, and we can make sure things go easy on you. You shouldn't have been put in this situation. It's just not fair to you."

Jeffrey kept his head down.

"We want to see you go home with your mom, maybe even

today, if we can swing things. But that will only happen if we know who was really behind all this. We need your help. Jeffrey. You're the only one who knows the truth."

Jeffrey began to sob again. It was over. Done. There was nothing else they expected of him. Handing his dad over on a platter was a bit much. They tried, just to say they made the attempt. But they weren't going to push it. That would be crossing the line.

Once again, an officer poked his head into the room where Dennis Thompson was being questioned and asked Officer Leone for a private word. Leone got up and stepped out. Moments later, he poked his head into the room and asked Mulroney to join him.

Minutes passed. Finally, Leone and Mulroney returned. Dennis sat quietly—defiantly—with both arms on the table, his right forefinger tapping the metal surface as if he was bored.

"New development, Mr. Thompson," Leone said.

"Well, what did you bright boys figure out now? That you got the wrong guy? That you've been wasting my time and ruining my business?"

"Not quite. We have your son in the other room—"

"What the hell!" Dennis shot up from his seat, knocking his chair over in the process as he leaned into the officers with his fists planted firmly on the metal desk. "What right have you got to interfere with my family? Mark my words, I'm gonna have a field day with you all when I'm done! I'm suing and making sure the mayor fires the lot of you. I'm a tax-paying citizen here, and my company contributes significantly to your paycheck. You all work for me, you get it?!"

Dennis was fuming. His face was beet red, and his eyes were practically bulging out of their sockets. When he was finished, he pounded the table for emphasis.

"Are you done?" Leone asked calmly as he and Mulroney

remained seated, feeling no threat from the situation. "Why don't you sit back down and hear what we have to say. I'm certain you'll find it interesting."

Again, an interrogation bait to encourage compliance. To one uninitiated with the process, it would seem the police were too ingratiating, but they knew when to be kind, generous, patient—and yes, mean and threatening. They had a full deck of cards to play, and they knew exactly how and when to play them.

Dennis righted his chair and followed Leone's instructions to sit. His round, beefy face was sunburned red, and his disheveled, thinning hair hung loosely in all directions like a mad scientist too distracted with important revelations to worry about personal appearance. He was a lobster in a slow boil. He might flinch now and then, but he was being cooked from the inside—so slowly that he didn't realize his strategy of intellectual dominance and community stature wasn't quite working the way he thought it would.

Leone cleared his throat. "As I was going to say, we have your son in the room next door, and he just confessed"—Dennis's eyes bulged again—"to throwing a Molotov cocktail into the Robinson house at 10 p.m. on the Fourth of July. He admitted to it, voluntarily."

"I bet he did," Dennis snapped back. "You probably beat it out of him. It's a false testimony that won't hold up in court, you bastards."

Dennis tried to keep his rage from exploding in the hopes his temperance would paint him as a man wrongly accused. But acting wasn't his strong suit. He was too accustomed to lording it over his employees, and he certainly wasn't used to hiding his emotions. His seething indignation bled through his pores.

"My lawyer is gonna tear you to shreds." He was reaching. In fact, he knew it. But that was all he had to fight with. When in doubt, he thought, when trapped, attack the integrity of the people in charge.

"Well, there'll be time enough for all that, but it's all on tape, so a jury can decide if his rights were abrogated."

"Abrogated, huh? You trying to impress me with your education? I'll have you know I've been running my business since you were still in diapers, boy!"

The detectives let Dennis run his mouth. They had an agenda to stick to.

"We told your son," Leone continued, "his fingerprints were on the bottle in the burned-out house, and he broke down in tears and confessed. It was probably tough on him holding all that in, what with someone dying and all. That can be hard on a kid. He's only fifteen."

"Anyway," Mulroney picked up, "one of the missing pieces we haven't mentioned yet is that there was turpentine found on the inside of the bottle pieces. Seems your son got his hands on some turpentine to do the deed. I think that's pretty sophisticated, don't you? Most people don't know that turpentine will suffice for a Molotov cocktail. Most people only think in terms of gasoline. I'm kind of curious how little Jeffrey would have come by that bit of information."

"I don't buy any of this," Dennis said, glaring at each officer in turn. "I don't know anything. We have a library in town, don't we? Whoever did it had access to information. That's all I gotta say."

"Come on, Mr. Thompson, we've played nice here. It's your turn. Your son—jeez, *your* son—confessed already. And he refused to turn you in. He's a brave kid. We were nice enough not to tell him there were two sets of prints on that bottle. We only told him about his prints. If he'd known there were two, that we already knew you were the other set of prints… well, the world might have crumbled around him. We didn't want to do that to the kid. As I said, he's only fifteen."

"So, whaddaya want from me?" Dennis said with an edge, still raring for a fight.

"We want to know how Jeffrey got the turpentine, and who put him up to all this."

"Did you ask him?" Dennis yelled. It was one of those outbursts that belied his proclaimed innocence. It was the slow boil. The shell had cracked.

"Jeffrey's not budging. He won't give you up. But here's the deal. It's either him or you, and right now we can make a strong case for both of you. I know you think your alibi about being at the fireworks from eight 'til after midnight means you're off the hook, but you're not. We can make a good case that you and he conspired to commit arson, that you assisted in providing the means, that he did the arson while you protected yourself with an alibi, that there was a murder, and finally, that you are an accomplice to that murder. I believe we've got you on conspiracy to commit both arson and murder, and as an accomplice to both."

"That's a lot to prove," said Dennis. "I think you're talking out your ass. You're trying to scare me into saying something that will implicate me and my boy for something you just can't solve. I know all about this good cop/bad cop stuff. You tell my boy one thing and tell me something else. You have us both believing the other ratted us out, and that's supposed to make us come clean. Well, as I already said, I'm not buying."

Mulroney removed a photo from the envelope and shoved it across the table. Dennis looked at it and saw what Jeffrey had seen some minutes earlier: the two of them standing in line at the market with the can of turpentine.

"You paid for it with cash so as not to leave a trail. And after we picked up Jeffrey, we served your wife with a search warrant for your house. We found the can of turpentine, price sticker and all, in your garage. We measured the contents, and it's shy exactly twelve ounces of liquid. The exact amount that would fit in a beer bottle."

Dennis squirmed and grumbled and looked back and forth between Mulroney and Leone and the picture. "I want a lawyer."

23

Session 19

"Well, Dennis got his lawyer, but it didn't matter much. His fate was written in the stars," Peter said.

"And Jeffrey? What happened to him?" Anna sat on the edge of her chair, riveted by the story that had unfolded quite unexpectedly. She had grown used to Peter's avoidance of the event and had given up on him ever discussing it. But she'd asked a question she had no idea would unleash a dam of hidden emotions—anxieties and tragedies and sorrow.

"Tell me something new, Peter, that we haven't discussed before," was all she'd asked. It seemed innocuous enough. Certainly, it lacked the precision to cut to the core of the issue. It was as if simple banter was all she expected from the session, a way to gauge his temperature, not excavate a demon.

But for some reason, this time was different. She'd released control, closed her eyes, let go of the rudder, and let the ship go where it may. Peter obliged by taking her where she had wanted to go from their first meeting. The irony wasn't lost on her.

"Poor Jeffrey, just a kid," Peter said. "He paid the price for having parents that were intolerant and selfish. He went to some youth detention center in Cincinnati for twelve months. Pretty light sentence, considering."

"Quite tragic."

Anna sat to the left of the two leather chairs, with Peter on the right. Since he'd decided to change seats on this particular day, Anna had chosen to join him, face-to-face. It seemed Peter had come prepared to make a turn. Switching from his usual seat may well have signaled a change in his psyche. Sometimes, that kind of subtlety was all one had to go on.

She wondered if, subconsciously, she'd picked up on the change in chairs. In the end, it didn't really matter. If Peter was ready to talk, she figured, he would talk. "How does it feel to finally get it out?"

Peter had fallen back into his chair when the story was done. His face was tired and beaded with perspiration. He was clearly exhausted, and yet he looked at peace. Why not? This was his story, told in words he had chosen years ago. His hair was disheveled from raking his hands through it a few too many times, and those hands were now wrung to a redness of emotional distress. He had relived those details, over and over. But never with someone else. That seemed to make all the difference.

"I don't really know, Doc," he finally said. "The demons have had their way for some time now. You know, when I get lost in these obsessions, I'd sink into despair. Each time, I hoped rehashing the details in my head would eventually open a door. Maybe I'd discover an angle or insight that wasn't there before, something that would allow me some form of redemption. Only it never happened. Maybe talking about it will do some good. I guess we'll see."

Anna studied him, gauging his temperature. How was he really handling this? "I understand, Peter." She thought his answer was a bit glib, but she also knew he needed space. He needed to have whatever reaction he wanted without judgment or criticism. "I'm hoping this telling of the story will help keep your momentum going in the right direction. I've been impressed with your progress, and getting this *thing* finally out in the open has to yield dividends."

She paused again and gazed at him. He remained calm. It was all good—for now. But she was not yet convinced. Five years of haunting thoughts about a tragic event don't usually disappear in one afternoon, after one telling. She feared this might simply be a reminder of what was still lurking in the recesses of his mind—that telling it didn't banish it. It may even have given it oxygen to quicken and become a demon with more vengeance.

"I'd like to suggest we meet again next week," she said.

"You're worried about me, aren't you? I don't think you need to be."

"Well, I'm sure you're right, maybe I'm just being cautious. I'd appreciate your humoring me. How are things otherwise?"

"Good."

"Clare?"

"Better, surprisingly."

"Ah. Holding out on me, are you? Do tell."

"Well, I guess I buried the lead. I came in today with what I thought was a good sign between me and Clare. We got sidetracked, though with… you know, the story."

Anna stared attentively.

"Anyway," he continued, "one Saturday, Clare pleaded with me not to go to Cincinnati. I guess her jealousy over my time at Eaton was at a crisis point. I told her she should join me. It took her by surprise, and she didn't have an answer. I tried to encourage her that it's work that has value and purpose, and it makes me feel better… about everything. I told her to come, that we could do it together. After some hemming and hawing, she finally said she'd think about it, for the next time. I thought that was a sign—a good sign. She's deciding our marriage is worth making an investment in. On my terms, even. Whaddaya think about that, Doc?"

"Hmm," Anna mumbled, looking past him.

"What? You don't approve? Is there something going on here that I don't see?"

Peter's anxiety spiked quickly, no doubt from the fear of her exposing the raw underbelly of something hidden from his past. His facial expression was tantamount to a billboard, the trepidation and angst on full display. Coming on the heels of "the story," she realized a need to quell his anxiety before it cascaded into his usual hand-wringing and hairpulling. "The story" was too raw of a telling to let anything else crowd its presence.

"I was just thinking," she replied.

"Yeah, I know. That's when I worry the most, when you're thinking. It's usually when I get skewered by some new information that cripples me for the next couple of weeks."

"Okay, okay. I'm sorry to get you all rattled. This is just an observation—a good one. Maybe I should have just come out with it, but it was still formulating in my head, and I wanted to see where it all went before making it a concrete part of our session. Here goes. First of all, I like what I hear. In particular, for me, I like the way you handled it. You valued yourself over her judgment of how you should be spending your time. She was probably wanting you to choose her over them—Eaton, that is. But you offered to include her in the experience. That's what a responsible married person *should* do. Excellent." She allowed for a brief pause while formulating the words for what was to follow. "You know, Peter, I haven't shared my opinion on Clare for a few sessions now."

He slid forward in the chair with rapt attention, his eyes fixated on her as if there were a shoe about to fall. His hands began playing with themselves, betraying the grip of anxiety taking hold.

"But this turn of events," Anna said, "her objecting to Eaton and then considering being part of it, certainly suggests that Eaton hasn't been the primary reason for her objection all along."

Peter's bemused face now complemented his squirrely hands.

"She may have an objection to the people or the mission of Eaton," Anna continued, "but I doubt, with this development, that it's a primary issue for her. Instead, I'm beginning to think she's been struggling with her own insecurities. I know you see her as the strong-willed decider of your marriage, but I see someone navigating perilous waters, hoping to find the calm that you both once had. Essentially, she has her own issues."

"Her own issues? Like, she should be sitting here instead of me?"

"Well, if I'm right, she's been trying to cope—trying to manage, trying to force a change—but she's been unsuccessful."

"With what? What's her issue?" Peter's exasperation had developed a notable edge.

"With loss."

"Loss?"

"Yes, loss. I think, and this is obviously an educated guess about someone I haven't laid eyes on, that Clare has been experiencing loss for quite some time now. And while we all have loss at some time or another in our lives, she's had a succession of them, one after another. And based on what you've told me over our many sessions, I'd hazard a psychological guess that she's formatively at risk of not handling loss well."

"Okay, Doc. You've officially lost me—again. Formatively? What the hell is that?"

"You've kidded me in the past about my probing your childhood memories, like it's some magic trick we therapists use to solve problems—a therapy-couch trope, if you will. Well, there's possibly some application of that trope here as well. Over our many sessions, you've filled me in on how you and Clare met in college, your different backgrounds, what she was like then, and how you both evolved over time. All the while, I was forming a personality of Clare to see if I could discover her motives. In that way, I hoped to help you navigate more recent developments in your marriage.

"You've told me that Clare was an only child, that her parents were successful financially, and they used that success to dote on her—as a princess, so to speak. They were overly protective of her in childhood and high school, and even in college you said you met her mom walking the campus halls numerous times. Clare went to work for her parents when she graduated, and it was only when you got married that she slowly unlinked her dependence on Mom and Dad, forming a marriage alliance with you. You were happily married for many years, and then… you weren't. You hinted that maybe the two of you saw life differently, maybe had different values. Maybe, subconsciously, you—or she—began to pull away from the other. That's when I think her loss began. The perfect life wasn't perfect anymore. Her childhood primed her for perfection; no issue was allowed to upset Shangri-La. Clare never developed coping skills to handle what life later became for her. Those were skills you learned with your near-death incident and losing your brother in Vietnam.

"Your Beekman affair forced Clare to contend with losing her best friend, maybe the sister she never had. If that wasn't bad enough, that pseudo sister promised to protect her, mother-like, and allow for a meet-and-greet with the new neighbors. This stand-in mother didn't fulfill her promise. Worse, the interlopers who moved in didn't look anything like the Johnsons. It's possible that if the Robinsons were white, it might have mollified Clare somewhat, but I doubt her loss issues would have dissipated. Next in line, Clare loses you because you had the temerity not to see these interlopers as interlopers. You actually befriended them, which must have made her livid. Imagine living and sleeping side by side with the instigator of your torment."

Peter was now nodding along to a familiar story. His hands had calmed, but he was still engrossed.

"The two of you," Anna continued, "formed a détente, but that was far from a real marriage. Living on tenterhooks was not a substitute for what you both had in the past. The arson, the loss of life, that was all tragic. So tragic. But for Clare, the almost insurmountable loss happened when you ran toward the fire and it exploded. She was already fragile, and your act of bravery could likely have made her catatonic. I've seen similar instances result in hospitalization for post-traumatic shock. Fortunately, you both survived. You pieced your lives back together. It wasn't easy, but the true foundation, the true love between you two, was evidenced by your mutual commitment to survive that tragedy—intact. And just as Clare hoped to find herself surfacing from this string of losses, she was confronted with more. Because your recovery took longer than expected, she had to contribute more to a relationship that she'd intended to be equal, as it was in the past.

"The reason for your delayed recovery didn't help. Clare had to contend with you obsessing over the event that she had relegated to a past that had tormented her. More loss. Finally, emerging from all this comes Eaton. Five years out, when she finally sees you having success in your business, she finds you've developed an affair with someone else."

Peter raised a brow. Anna smiled.

"Yes," she said, "Eaton was your affair—your seeking refuge from the marriage, outside the marriage. It was yet another loss. She naturally resisted. Who knows if it had anything to do with Eaton, per se, or if it would have been the same with any activity outside the marriage. I'm betting on the latter, by the way."

Peter smiled. Anna continued.

"Your invitation for her to join you at Eaton was equivalent to a proposal to rekindle your marriage. She was naturally delighted. While you were concerned that she wasn't interested in the marriage, she was concerned that you weren't interested in her. Your proposal cleared the air. What's more, it begins a new page in your lives together based on a different value system. If the marriage issues you had before your friends moved stemmed from your values not overlapping, this fresh start at Eaton at least provides some balance."

Anna sat back with a confident smile, a pat on her own back for finally putting it all together. She knew Peter still had issues with the fire and what role he'd played in it, but at least his relationship with Clare could now be separated from the ordeal.

"I'm pleased," Anna concluded. "You did good."

"Ha!" Peter exclaimed. "That was quite a summation. It all makes sense. I guess another important detail is that Clare's parents died in a car crash a few years before the Beekman incident. Black ice. It was sudden, and no one was at fault, but it was likely the first domino to fall."

"Yes, of course," Anna said, "that could have been her seminal event. The beginning point of her arc of travails. Maybe after that, she had no emotional resources to tolerate any other change to her foundation. It's all speculation, but the pieces of the puzzle fit."

"Weird how I was meandering through all that, totally unaware that I was causing her pain, when all along I thought it was the other way around. By the way, starting with 'I'm pleased' would have gone a long way to keeping me off the edge of this chair for the last ten minutes." His satirical smile beamed brightly.

"I'll have to work on that," Anna said with a smile.

As she sat enjoying her epiphany about Clare, Anna's mind drifted back to what had started their session: "the story." Those had been Peter's exact words. Was he trying to minimize the tragic event—the fire? Was he distancing himself from it so soon after telling it, putting it back in the closet like an embarrassing family relic?

Maybe she was reading too much into it. All of the evidence suggested he was improving. He seemed to be enjoying his work, especially his volunteering. And things were certainly growing more optimistic with Clare. It may have been the real reason Peter felt ready to tell the story.

But a cautious foreboding still lingered. Despite the benefits of finally unburdening himself, unleashing the tragic event might also make him believe that no matter how much he improved, the reality of what happened, and his role in it, might never change. It would always be, and perhaps there would never be a remedy.

If redemption was never possible in his mind, living might not be worth it. All Anna could do was wait.

24

Nearly five years had gone by since the Beekman fire had altered lives in profound and irreversible ways. The Robinson house lay in charred ruins in the center of prideful Beekman for more than a year. It stood as a spent pyre to Julian's memory, as a reminder of the futility of foolish vanity, and as a foreboding to hate and vengefulness.

This was an epiphany shared by few on Beekman. The rest of us suffered the daily visual reminders of all that had happened, and it served as evidence that the Robinsons lacked the community spirit necessary to prove they belonged.

Sure, I felt bad for them. Losing a son is no small thing. I'd be crushed if it had happened to me. But back then, during those early months and years after the fire, I expected more from them. A bitterness still lingered. It took a while for me to see what I didn't see.

Jerome Robinson was keen to leave the shrine standing for as long as possible. He never said as much, but it was obvious. He never visited Beekman in the years following the fire. His own spite lingered for some time.

Sally Jennings reached out to him on our behalf—a Beekman

community effort, so to speak. Apparently, Margaret wanted to move on, but Jerome turned a deaf ear to her pleadings. His impulse was not to run. He eventually wanted to rebuild, to change the community day by day. He had no doubt that Beekman would be different, that sacrifices had been made and payment was due.

It was Jerome's philosophical view of human instincts, Sally said. He felt that one couldn't deprive you of all you had and not try to make amends when they realized they'd gone too far. Jerome wanted to reap the rewards; his payback was due. He and Margaret had paid the price of integration. Running now would be making the supreme sacrifice and having nothing to show for it.

Margaret could not contemplate staying in Portville, as their short time on Beekman had been so dreadful and costly. She would rue the decision to move there for the rest of her life. She made it clear that she could not live if life meant suffering a daily reminder of how Julian's life had been sacrificed to malevolent inhumanity. She needed to breathe, free of Portville air. Jerome finally acquiesced.

The banks provided the money for demolition and rebuilding. It was more than enough. In the end, Jerome negotiated to demolish, then left the property bare as a continued reminder—a scar of what had been. They sold the land years later after property values had rebounded. At very least, I had to respect his business savvy. They made a nice financial return on their investment, but it could never be equal to the loss they had suffered. In time, I came to see the world through their eyes.

In time.

The Robinsons were not the only ones to leave Beekman. Others sold their treasured homes and moved to less conspicuous areas in Portville. They could no longer live with the conflict of hypocrisy in their lives. They remembered the Mason meetings and saw in neighbors' faces a hate and indifference they were more than ready to leave behind. They needed a redemption that would not be feasible remaining on Beekman.

There was, of course, the trial. Several Beekman homeowners were less than eager to testify about comments made at the buy-back meetings or the comings and goings of neighbors on that fateful day. We were all shocked to learn the Masons had recorded everything. Fred's admonition against violence reverberated as a mythological warning, an Icarus flying too close to the sun, a hubris that in the end played out as if it were written in the stars.

The tapes were heard in court for the first time. Gasps of shock, hushed murmurs, and finger-pointing ensued. The reality that no secret ever remained secret was a lesson we learned too late. The conviviality of Saturday mornings on Beekman became shrouded with distrustful glares, muted hellos, and literally no social gatherings as the probing news cameras and marauding journalists asked children, "Did you know Julian? Did your parents tell you not to play with him?"

It was all too much to bear. Our homes were left in disrepair. My favorite garden went untended as dead, wilted flowers hung from stalks and vines, while weeds strangulated any new growth. The autumn leaves went unswept, the winter snow unshoveled. The Beekman that once sat on a precipice of pride, certainty, and resoluteness, had fallen. We were now the bane of Portville—a people of ill repute smitten by a biblical plague.

Peter and I remained. We really had no choice. Peter slipped into a near catatonic state for several weeks. He barely ate and never left home. His employer understood, at first. But after a few months with no evidence of improvement, he was no longer employed. I saw it coming and found work at the Bank of Portville. My old position became available and paid well enough to hold us over for the several months Peter needed to restart his life. Corporate accounting was now in his past, at least for the short run. Personal taxes was something he could still do, but it started slowly. Building a client base took time.

Fortunately, Beekman rose from the ashes of its former self in a renewal of purpose. During Beekman's year of purgatory, Peter was the one who bore the weight of their sins. He had preached against self and against indulgence, against self and against vanity, against self and against hypocrisy; he had spoken when speaking was betrayal; he had sacrificed marriage and fatherhood and life to uphold Beekman's undeserving reputation—a fallacy of perfection.

His sacrifice was costly. It was something no one needed telling. It existed in the air from the first day after the fire, like smoldering embers that lingered and the scent of burned memories that refused to move on. In the months that followed, Peter was the only one on Beekman who received a smile and the sheepish yet earnest, "Hello."

When it became clear he was ready to rejoin the world and that taxes would be his path, Beekman came calling. Ours was the only house people visited. To be sure, it was just the beginning. The neighborhood of three long blocks could not replace what he'd lost, but it was the confidence he needed to start again.

While Beekman embraced Peter, I did not. I couldn't see what others saw. A frayed marriage and wounded pride were complicated tendrils that prevented me from feeling the collective guilt and need for redemption that everyone else yearned for.

The ensuing years brought other, more anticipated changes. Our children grew up. Matt became a Buckeye and majored in—of all things—accounting. Reconciliation with his dad after the incident took several months to bear fruit. While Peter was consumed with a feeling he had not done enough for the Robinsons, Matt was consumed with proving himself worthy of his dad's sacrifice. His hubris was not easily tamed, but he made a modest effort. He and his dad were simply two distinctly different kinds of people. They saw the world through separate eyes and engaged it on different terms. It was hard for Peter to acknowledge that offspring didn't always mean twins.

Sandy also became a Buckeye. Her inclinations were less of a surprise. Her early penchant for reading blossomed, and she chose English as a major with an emphasis on French literature. Julian's dog-eared copy of *The Count of Monte Cristo* sat lovingly on her bookshelf on full display.

At some point in time, it was just me and Peter. The emptiness that followed was consuming, and I could no longer ignore Peter's obsessions, preoccupations, and general apathy toward engaging with life. The ultimatum for therapy was my hope for normalcy. If we were ever to find the intimate life we shared before children, a remedy was needed to leave the past in the past.

The expectation was that Peter would find a way out of a mental maze that only he could navigate. But life is complicated, and understanding it is even more complicated. His reluctance to take part in therapy morphed into an acceptance and a confidence that I was initially pleased with.

But then my skepticism began to simmer. Peter's efforts at keeping up a front with me waned. It seemed his real interests lay elsewhere. And just when I thought our marriage was done, he extended a hand. It was an offer to join him at Eaton, but I knew it was really an offer to begin again, on new terms—an offer to commit to new beginnings. I was surprised and pleased, and yet not sure I was ready. I had grown accustomed to my beleaguered life, and his abrupt offer was a change more threatening than the undesirable status quo.

One lazy Saturday morning, I showered while Peter conducted the television—a quick allegretto coordination of eyes and thumb to the music of channels. I was fortunately occupied, as I always found his maestro act an irritation to endure. He, nonetheless, was amused with his antics. For him, it was a performance—the simple act of scanning each channel for interest and pressing the remote to move on. It was an acquired skill, no doubt, that he had perfected and I abhorred as something primitive and limited to those of the male genome. All I saw when he performed these feats were blurred colors on the screen. Peter claimed to see the setting, people, clothes, and action, all within a second. It was enough to know what he usually found entertaining and what would be a dud.

Today's conducting, no doubt, began in the usual way: a start from the low numbers, moving ever higher to channels rarely watched but still paid for. It was an ever-climbing crescendo that quickened as the channels became less relevant.

On this particular day, things were different. Peter saw something that gave him a familiar feeling. He was three channels past it before it sank in. The person on the screen was not a familiar actor or television personality, as he'd first thought. He felt compelled to go back and find out who it was.

When he reached the channel, it featured a gentleman in a suit being interviewed by a woman. It was a gentleman that he knew. He was older than Peter remembered him; the man's hair was cropped shorter, and his face was a little fuller. To further complicate matters, the gentleman sported a mustache, which didn't fit with his memory. But Peter was quite sure of it. He turned up the volume and listened—and as he listened, it clicked. The man's voice cinched it. Peter knew him. It was Jerome Robinson, being interviewed by someone Peter didn't know about a topic he had yet to learn.

"Clare! Clare!" he shouted up the stairs.

I was still in the shower, insulated by tile and running water. After he'd seen enough and not having heard a peep from me, he bolted up the stairs and into our bedroom. He flicked on the television, changed the channel, and increased the volume. Then he poked his head into the bathroom, where I now stood wrapped in a towel, shower droplets running down the sides of my forehead, spying myself in the mirror and studying my facial lines for progeny.

"What's all the commotion about?" I asked.

"Come look at who's on TV." He gestured for me to join him in the bedroom.

I stepped out of the bathroom, still dripping wet, and we stood side by side, staring at the TV screen with Jerome still animated in the midst of proving a point. The interviewer was asking questions about an organization that had already been mentioned but Peter hadn't heard.

Jerome was in the group, or the head of the group. Peter stood with his mouth agape, glued to the set with a half-grin, no doubt proud to see someone he knew on television.

"So, what does your organization hope to accomplish by taking a stand on this issue?" the interviewer asked.

"We represent American values that have been lost or simply pushed aside, to accommodate a new generation that's trying to change who we are as a country," Jerome said. "We are not a belligerent group. Those that make that accusation are trying to marginalize what we stand for."

"Do you believe that gay and lesbians choose their sexual orientation? Hasn't that been debunked quite some time ago?"

"It's a choice, like everything else in life. You choose where to live, where to work, who to be friends with—and they choose who to have as a partner, no difference. It violates the God-order of things."

"So what are your members planning for the future?"

"It's no surprise. We got a permit to demonstrate during the Gay Pride Parade. We'll be there in force to tell the world that what they stand for is unnatural."

"Well, guests, we'd like to thank Jerome Robinson for spending some time with us to clarify his group's position, the Alliance for a Safe America. I'm Maureen Connor for WKMU Cincinnati."

Peter and I looked at each other and back at the screen, wondering what the hell we'd just seen.

"Alliance for a Safe America," he said. "What in the world is that?"

"You'll have to give 'em a call and find out, won't you? I'm sure they have a number somewhere. Sounds a little edgy to me, though."

"You're right. I got that vibe, as well."

"He was *your* friend at one time. Does this sound like the Jerome you knew?" I strolled back into the bathroom while continuing the conversation.

"No way. He was a straight-up sort of guy. To be fair, we pretty much talked cars most of the time, but still, he never came off as prejudiced in any way." After a brief pause, he added, "I can't believe Margaret would tolerate this. She was a salt-of-the-earth kind of person. This doesn't sound at all like her."

"Wives and husbands don't always see eye to eye, you should know that by now," I said, eyeing him through the bathroom mirror with a playful smirk.

Later that morning, Peter and I were in Cincinnati on my maiden voyage to Eaton Advocacy. As we drove the last few blocks, I furtively scanned the neighborhood streets for familiar faces. It was an awkward paranoia, like someone I knew was watching, wondering what I was doing or what this meant about me.

The old Beekman still floated like a ghost in my subconscious, lingering like mold in crevices unseen, making it hard to sterilize out of my being. I had always believed that who you associated with said something about who you were. Today I was simply a volunteer, but I felt vulnerable to people I didn't know making wild assumptions about my personhood or sexuality. Controlling who came into my life was part of an image that always needed burnishing. This was wading into muddy waters of uncertainty. I simply didn't want to be labeled as something I wasn't.

I gazed over at Peter as he maneuvered around a double-parked car, wondering how it was so easy for him. He didn't seem to care one iota about what others thought. Later, at Eaton, I watched him move casually from person to person, shaking hands and giving hugs or fist bumps. For all intents and purposes, he could have belonged to Eaton—he could have depended on their services; he could have been gay. But he wasn't.

One might have thought he was leading a double life, maybe confused about himself on some deeper level. But I knew that was not the case. Sure, some would say you just never really know about someone, but I knew. Peter was an open book to everyone he met. He had never hidden anything from me the whole time we were together. It was not his way. He had a quiet confidence that defined transparency.

No, this was something different. This was just like when he befriended a neighbor out of the blue that he knew nothing about and whom everyone else in the neighborhood had serious doubts about. Who does that? Peter does. This part of him always kept me on edge and was the reason I so often objected to his "activities." But now I was along for the ride. How did things get so twisted? How did I become an accomplice in his life choices? I had no idea.

My epiphany occurred the night Peter ran from my side to run toward the fire. An act of bravery, everyone said. I saw it as an act of recklessness. He had left me and Sandy and Matt to fend for ourselves while he put someone else's life first. From that moment on, I realized I had no real control over him. Sure, I would try to steer him, maybe at times bully him, and he'd take it, just to appease me. But over the years, and certainly over this past year, he had become more difficult to lead where I wanted him to go. I threw ultimatums at him, but they seemingly went nowhere.

I was now beginning to wonder if his deciding to follow through on the therapy may not have been my doing but his. Maybe he was ready to take that step all along, and now here I was, at a gay and lesbian outreach center, trying not to look foolish, following *his* lead. Things were certainly turned upside down, and I wasn't sure what it all meant or where it was heading.

Peter introduced me to some of his Eaton friends and asked me if I'd like to sit in on a forum where future plans addressing the gay and lesbian community were being strategized. He said it would give me a sense of the world they lived in and the issues that society unknowingly imposed on them. The only catch was that I would be doing it alone while he ran errands for the advocacy group. To me, this seemed more like trial by fire than just shadowing him around, getting a feel for what went on. To be a team player, however, I made no fuss.

It was a different vibe for me, but I convinced myself it was no different than any other community organization. I'd been to many such events over the years, and this had a familiar energy. There was Rebecca, a lawyer who knew everything and was a senior member; questions from others were always funneled in her direction. Next was Bob, a local artisan who always carried folders under his arm; he was a repository of all institutional memory. And there were groups of guys over here and gals over there—or at least people who looked like guys and gals—some dressed a little outlandish for my tastes but many others that would blend in quite well in Portville. It occurred to me that many in the room likely could be from Portville. Maybe some were. They were all moving in random motion, crisscrossing a pattern on the lobby's main floor, sketching a purpose they deeply believed in.

Peter shepherded me over to the meeting room and found me a seat next to a good friend, Moiré. She was Peter's anchor, helping him get adjusted to life at Eaton.

"Moiré, this is my wife, Clare."

I extended my hand for a friendly shake, trying to act the part as best I could.

"Nice to finally meet you, Clare. We actually wondered if there really *was* a Clare," Moiré said, throwing a sly smile at Peter. Her voice was clearly male but a higher pitch than most. "He talks about you often, but you know he doesn't ever have pictures to show, so we figured he was making it all up."

I blushed while Peter stood with pride, having proved everyone wrong.

"I tell him all the time, he needs to have pictures of his kids, at least. You'd think he was a vagabond or something," I said, siding with Moiré at Peter's expense. He seemed to take it all in stride, as if my smiling and making fun of him meant I'd do alright. The three of us continued with the pleasantries, then Peter took his leave, asking Moiré to look after me while he tended to other business.

Moiré was easily engaged, and I soon felt relaxed in Peter's absence. Moiré filled me in on some of Eaton's history and the upcoming strategy session, but she could tell that I was only partially attentive. I stared at her with an intensity that she'd likely grown only too familiar with.

"So, Clare—such a sweet name. I should have chosen that name for myself, but I guess that ship has sailed. You look like you want to ask me something. I don't often indulge people this way, but you're one of us now. So, honey, go ahead, ask away. I know there's something you're curious about."

I blushed again. I tried to avert my gaze, but Moiré's earnest look of benevolence compelled me to oblige. "I'm so embarrassed. Have I been looking at you wrong?"

"No, girl, you look like you just arrived at Disney World and don't know what to ride first. Ask, and I'll tell you."

"Well, Moiré, that name is so interesting. Where did it come from? What does it mean?"

"I don't tell people this, it's so in my past, but my given name was Bruce. It's so not me. Do I look like a Bruce? No!" She didn't wait for an answer. "I wanted something that was gender-neutral. One day, I was in a camera shop, and plastered on a big poster was a pattern of intersecting lines making this beautiful design. Moiré was written in cursive across the bottom. I loved it instantly. It's supposed to be something unique but undesirable—in a photo. I thought that was perfect."

"And your voice," I asked, "is it—female?" My embarrassment was now terminal.

"Oh, girl, ragging on my falsetto? Mm-mmm," Moiré teased with a smile. "That's just me, girl. Comes with the package. I'm what you call a transgender lesbian. The textbook says I was assigned male at birth, but what do they know? I identify as a woman.

I dress the part, and I'm only attracted to other women."

My confusion must have been obvious.

"Don't worry," she continued, "you'll get the hang of it. Peter didn't know up from down when he first came here to work. Now he's gender-fluent."

I held Moiré's arm in a show of appreciation. Embarrassment was a feeling I rarely experienced—controlling as I was. But there was something exhilarating about being out of my element.

25

It was only mid-June, yet Cincinnati was experiencing one of those high-pressure weather systems that often preceded a low, which in this case was farther out on the horizon. Indeed, the low pressure pushing down from Canada was days away, and forecasters predicted it might very well dissipate before reaching the Great Lakes. For the time being, the high pressure reigned supreme, and Cincinnati was hot. The sun, that giver of life—and taker, as well—shone high in the sky at midday. Its heat was insufferable, and its blinding glare obscured the texture of the landscape that any other time of day stood in sharp repose.

Peter left Eaton and walked south along Vine Street. The Eaton office was only two blocks from the University of Cincinnati, and walking through the campus was a favorite pastime and a shortcut, depending on his destination.

Despite the sun's heat and glare, he was energized by the optimistic start to the day. Clare had agreed the month before to eventually join him on one of his Eaton trips, but he had not been sure she would. His instinct told him that she merely wanted out of the obligation to go on that very day, so she made a promise to go sometime in the future. He fully expected her to say no the next time around, and again and again, until he stopped asking. It wouldn't have surprised him at all. In fact, it would have been in keeping with who she was and all the decisions she had made in the past. Focusing energy outside the family was not usually her purview. But she surprised him. It was beyond his capacity to know the why. He could barely understand his own actions, let alone Clare's.

Peter plowed along Vine with his head down, avoiding the sun's intensity. He had forgotten his sunglasses, so looking in any direction other than up was easier on the eyes. As he crossed over Martin Luther King Drive and continued south on Short Vine Street, he passed several eateries popular with the college crowd.

At one point, he came upon the large window of a café on his left, and he casually glanced inside, mostly with the intent of avoiding the sun's glare. In doing so, he saw the same familiar face he'd seen that day on the television at home. It was Jerome, sipping coffee and reading a newspaper.

Peter stopped in his tracks and backstepped a couple of paces just to be sure it really was him. It was. Peter knew Jerome and Margaret had moved back to the city, and it lingered in the back of his mind that he might see him, especially after having seen him on the news, but the likelihood of it seemed a stretch.

Standing just a few feet away and staring at Jerome, Peter wondered if he should go inside. It seemed a natural thing to do—old friends who hadn't seen each other for years, catching up on old times. It's what friends do. But were they friends? Peter didn't think so. His last words to Jerome had been words of confidence. They had been misleading, overly optimistic, maybe even an intentional downright lie.

From Peter's point of view, he wasn't deserving of Jerome's friendship. He was certain Jerome felt the same. Not once had

Jerome reached out to him in the aftermath of the fire. Not once had he reached out over the past five years. Jerome clearly intended to move on with his life, and it was what he did. Peter, too, had found his own way. Their lives had diverged, taking different paths.

Peter finally decided to walk on, to leave well enough alone. But after another ten feet, he stopped again. In now-typical Peter fashion, he forced himself to do the thing he avoided doing out of fear. He had grown tired of playing the puppet to fear's puppeteers and resolved to fight it at every turn. When fear reared its serpentine head, he dove in instead of retreating. While it did not eliminate his demons, it certainly forced him into situations that he surprisingly found worthwhile, though his initial instincts would have had him go in another direction. In many ways, therapy was like that for him. His instinct was always to fight against Clare's demands. In the end, success came from embracing her and inviting her to join him. It turned out to be a good, contrarian move. This time, he decided against his instinct and went back.

"Hi, Jerome." Peter stood a few feet from his long-lost pal, who had not noticed his arrival.

Jerome looked up from his paper, pulled back in surprise, and put on that wide grin Peter remembered so well. "What the hell, where've you been all these years?" Jerome said, standing up to offer a handshake.

Peter thought the situation warranted a hug, but he didn't want to come off mushy. "Been around," he said, pressing the flesh with a firm grip. "You're looking good. Life treatin' you well?"

"Sure, sure. Have a seat. Join me for some coffee?"

"Don't mind if I do."

"My, my, look at you! You haven't aged a bit."

"Yeah, all that natural organic cream I'm using to keep me young," Peter said, intending lighthearted sarcasm.

"Ha... you haven't changed much. Same Peter Davidson from Beekman. You still live there?"

"Yeah. Actually, we thought about moving but we just couldn't afford to. I lost my job. Clare started working again, but we were just getting by."

"Hmm. Those were tough times."

"You bore the brunt of it. I've got nothing to complain about."

"Can't argue with you there," Jerome said. "Margaret and I... well, it took some time. You can't imagine unless you've been through it, and I wouldn't wish that on anyone."

They sat for a while, letting the issue settle. Peter signaled the waitress for a cup of coffee. When it came, he took a sip, looked up at Jerome, and decided it was time. It was the conversation that had to happen. The conversation he'd been planning for years. The conversation he never thought he'd get the opportunity to have.

"Jerome," he said, "I owe you an apology. What you and Margaret went through... Well, it was all my fault. It didn't have to happen. Or at least, you didn't have to lose Julian."

Jerome's jovial smile turned. "What are you talking about, man? Your fault? Are you crazy? Those nuts on Beekman did what they did, that wasn't you. I think I'm a better judge of character than to believe you had anything to do with *that*."

Peter shook his head. "I've been racking my brains all these years feeling like you've got every reason to come at me with a two-by-four. You remember that conversation we had, maybe a few days or a week before the fourth? Remember?"

"No, not exactly. Remind me."

"You asked me if you had anything to worry about from the Beekman clan. You asked me, since I was on the inside, since I had gone to the meetings, and I told you it was all cool, not to worry. That was wrong. I played it down. I don't know why—I just did.

It might have been… it might have been that Clare was all hotheaded about things and I felt guilty. It might have been that I just *wanted* to believe things were better. But there were hotheads at those meetings, and I didn't tell you about it. If you'd known, if you knew what I knew… Well, maybe that night Julian wouldn't have been home alone. That's why I take responsibility for what happened."

Peter rested his emotions for a bit. Jerome didn't say anything, just stared back at him. Peter glanced out the window at a passerby and wondered again how serendipitous it was that they should meet—a one-in-a-million chance. He had never thought it would happen.

"You really shouldn't be talking with me now," Peter added. "Now that you know, and all. I'll give you your space."

Peter stood to leave, but Jerome reached for his arm. "Hey, where are you goin'? You're running crazy with ideas here, man. No one's chasing you away. Stay a while."

Feeling foolish, Peter sat back down.

"I can see you've been beating yourself up over this," Jerome said. "You've taken it on the chin, all this time, thinking that Margaret and I blame you for this whole thing."

Peter's glum look locked eyes with Jerome, betraying a dejection that had simmered for years.

"Well, isn't that something. You're something special, Peter. I don't meet too many people like you out there on the street. Everyone is running the other way when there's a fire, but you, no, you… You run straight toward the fire, save a man's life, and then take the blame for him running into the fire in the first place." Jerome shook his head and smiled. "Peter, Peter, Peter."

"What?" Peter said. "What am I not seeing straight here? It's all true, isn't it?"

"I guess it is, if you say so," Jerome said. "But you should know that what you told me didn't change my world in any big way. I mean, I did ask you with all sincerity, just to know what people were thinking. But in the business of being Black in America, the basic rule is trust no one, always be prepared, expect anything, anywhere. What you told me was nice to know, in that moment. But Margaret and I were still treated like crap by everyone on Beekman, despite our efforts at putting on the charm—being courteous and generous whenever we could, and we still trusted no one. Except for you."

"And I wasn't trustworthy, either," Peter interjected.

"Give it a rest. No matter what you say, I'm not letting you take the blame for that fire or our decision to let Julian stay behind while we went to the fireworks. That's what it was: our decision. We wish we hadn't made it. We've racked our brains for years wishing we could take it all back, but it's crazy to keep thinking like that. It's like stepping off the street corner and getting hit by a bus. If only you'd waited another second, it would've missed you. If only... if only. There's always the 'what if.' Margaret and I decided long ago to let it go. It was the only way we could move on, and we have. You need to let it go too, Peter. Take this albatross off your back and breathe for a change. You owe me nothing. Life is life, and sometimes it sucks. That's that."

They sat looking at each other. Jerome smiled at Peter's sad expression, which hadn't improved much. Peter tried to smile, but it didn't come out right. It was weak, like he didn't have his heart in it.

"So," Jerome said, changing the subject. "What brings you to Cincinnati?"

Peter tried to pull his thoughts back to the present. "Well, uh... I do some work for a place here in town, Eaton Advocacy Group.

They do community outreach."

"Eaton? I know Eaton. They're that gay group, aren't they?"

Peter was taken aback by the remark, but then he recalled the television interview. "Yeah, that's them."

"Are you... are you gay?"

"No," Peter said, his tone regaining confidence.

"So what are you doing wrestling with the boys?"

Peter paused to let the pejorative settle. He'd already heard many of the terms straight people used to malign the gay community. Moiré and others back at Eaton had once taken turns throwing out as many as they could, to try and shock Peter with how much he didn't know about the culture he lived in. It was eye opening. He lived his culture—the majority culture—but knew little of the ways it used language to denigrate others.

Despite the crudeness of Jerome's comment, Peter let it pass. Jerome had just demonstrated a magnanimous attitude about Peter's own misdeeds on Beekman. The least he could do was to cut the man some slack.

Peter tried to refocus and answer the question, sans sidebar commentary. "Eaton? It goes back a few years, when I lost my job, way back when... I had to reinvent myself."

"Into a gay man?" Jerome said, snorting a chuckle.

"Ha-ha." Peter now turned derisive. "No, I had to start doing taxes for anyone that would have me. I cold called a lot of companies in Cincinnati, the nonprofits in particular, since their taxes are easiest and they have the least amount of money to spend. I thought I could get my foot in the door if my services came cheap. I didn't know what they were about just by the name. By the time I found out the whole deal about them, they'd offered to let me do their taxes. Either way, I wouldn't have cared. They're nice people."

"So, you're doing their taxes?"

"Well, I do more than that now. I do a fair amount of volunteering for them. I enjoy the work, and it's actually helped me cope with the mess my life became after the fire."

"You sure you're not gay?"

"I think I'd know if I were gay," Peter said.

"I don't know. I hear a lot of people decide that's the life for them when they get older, sort of like a midlife crisis. 'Let me try something new,' kinda."

"I'm quite happy with who I am, Jerome."

"Well, then, why the hell spend time with these queer weirdos?" Jerome's face transformed into a mocking, clownish expression.

"We can't all be classic car enthusiasts, Jerome. I'm not an artist or anything, but I can at least give my time. It's what I have to give, so I give it. And they're not weirdos," he added with contempt. "They're people, like everyone else. They have their issues. They struggle and need a community outreach to help them survive in an inhospitable world. I'd think you, of all people, would get it." Peter shook his head in disbelief.

"I get it, only… I don't see it quite the way you do. I see a bunch of people doing unnatural things and hoping to get everyone else to turn a blind eye. Or, better yet, to sign off on it by giving them employment and housing rights so no one can keep them out of the workplace or out of their own neighborhood."

"I take it you were a supporter of Article Twelve?" Peter asked.

"Yeah, I was. Too bad it got overturned. The city is going belly-up as far as values," Jerome said. "The left has taken over."

"That sounds like something I've heard before. That's a Bill Burrey line, isn't it? It's exactly the kind of thing he'd say. I think he's just pissed off that Article Twelve didn't last very long, that people got savvy—or more tolerant—and voted it down. You know, Cincinnati has the worst record in the country on gay rights. That article banning any legal protection for gay and lesbians who are being treated like second-class citizens is un-American, at a minimum. It's inhumane. Can you believe it—1993, and they were legalizing job and housing discrimination against people? That wasn't 1963. It was '93. It's the kind of thing any person of color should've been against."

"Peter, we're gonna have to agree to disagree here. I'm curious, though, are either of your kids gay? I mean, where is all this militancy coming from?"

"It's just basic humanity, Jerome. I care. You should too. I just don't get it."

"I'm a religious man. What those people do just doesn't sit right with me. It's against God's intended purpose."

"As *you* know it to be," Peter said, waxing testy and sardonic. "You know, Clare and I saw you on television this morning. We watched you defend a position that seemed very much out of character with who we thought you were. Alliance for a Safe America? That's no different than Burrey's Citizens for Common Causes. It's all smooth talk for locking people up, shutting them down, silencing them, kicking them into a corner. It's a caste system, right here in America. And you know what happens when you get everyone to go along with all that, don't you?"

"What?" Jerome smirked.

"You get crazies burning down someone's home. All you need is one."

Jerome's subtle shake of the head signaled his disapproval as Peter's soliloquy came to a close. He glanced out the window as if to gather his thoughts, or maybe to decide if he wanted to go there. This conversation had turned into something familiar. He'd been here before. It was the need to school every person who fell into this trap, this errant thinking, this presumption of knowing that only the privileged fell victim to. It was a burden he felt unfairly afflicted with.

He glared back at Peter. The innocent face of ignorance stared back at him. It was an unknowing innocence, which was the worst kind. Was it Peter's fault he was so ignorant? How would he ever learn unless someone punched him in the face with the truth—with the uncomfortable, dirty reality of the world that never fit quite so perfectly into innocent expectations?

"Oh, I see," Jerome said, "you think because I'm Black, I should feel some solidarity with gays and lesbians. Because I'm Black, I am supposed to forever play the victim and have empathy for all other victims. Because I'm Black, I'm never supposed to be a real, full human being with my own likes and dislikes. You've categorized me as a Black man, stereotyped me as someone always disposed toward minorities—any minority. Well, you've got it all wrong. Black is just a color to me, it's not a culture. I am not locked into some fixed way of thinking and talking and being. Your stereotyping me is no better than those idiots on Beekman. You're no different. You just hide it better, play both sides when it suits you. Do you believe in anything, with your whole heart, independent of what everyone else is saying? Or do you just parrot along, finding the path of least resistance?"

Jerome paused, knowing he may have reached a bit over the mark. Peter had stood up for him and his family when no one else was willing, and that took courage. But he refused to be boxed into someone else's expectations. He was his own person. It was the only way he could have self-respect, to be a man deserving of the title.

"You know, Peter, not everyone thinks like you. Yeah, sure, there's injustice in the world, but I'm not the only one who suffers from it. You suffer from injustice. We all suffer from injustice. Some of us more than others. Just because the injustice I suffered had race attached to it doesn't mean others don't suffer from a similar horrible fate on some other level. I just refuse to live my life by that. I refuse to let it define me."

Jerome's comment stung; Peter had no comeback. He'd gone from feeling foolish—looking for redemption from the one guy he thought could give it to him—to attacking the guy's politics and way of life. He was now on edge and off-kilter and needed to get away.

"I gotta run some errands," Peter said quickly. "There's a Pride Parade coming up and permits to be gotten."

"You're going to that? That's not such a good idea, Peter." Jerome's sarcasm turned authoritative. "You don't want to be seen out there."

"There's something I need to know, Jerome. Is the Alliance for a Safe America… are they planning… Is it gonna get violent?"

"Well, no, of course not. It's just not a family-friendly parade. A lot of unseemly people will be strutting around. That kinda stuff."

Peter saw the crack in Jerome's armor. He was hiding something. His true intentions were not in sync with his words. "I remember you once said something about people, and how the de facto law is what people want—what they believe—not what's on the books. Well, the people of Cincinnati spoke, and gay rights is the law because it's what people want. Your Alliance thing is a lame effort to reverse history. And as for their dancing and prancing, I think I can handle it. People strutting around enjoying life seems like something we should be encouraging, not banning," Peter replied. "I guess I'll see you there." He stood, this time with more conviction, and walked away.

26

I was deep in conversation with a group of women when I noticed Peter had returned to Eaton. He found an obscure spot to observe me in action. The meeting had ended, and the social hour had begun. I sipped coffee and smiled at him while still in animated conversation with my new friends. A door had opened, and I had decided to step through. I could tell Peter was pleased that I had let my guard down enough to see that people were people—they could be different, but still worthy of friendship.

Later, I regaled him with stories about Moiré and her friends—how they had complained about partners wearing their clothes or moving in with lovers after just a few dates, how they had discussed their mood swings when they got their periods, and how they had endured crappy treatment from straight people whenever they went to certain parts of Cincinnati.

"No offense, Clare," was proffered to excuse me from guilt by association. I was amused. I shared my own tales of college and a sloppy roommate who had stretched out many of my blouses and favorite sweaters. In the end, I was surprised how easily I fit in. I wasn't wearing extravagant clothes, piercings, or ear spacers, but those things didn't define the person, did they? Inside, they were like anyone else, struggling with life's ups and downs.

I knew this was no great epiphany, trite as it was. When I retold some of the stories to Peter, my mind wandered. I remembered how I'd felt on the drive into Cincinnati, how I was nervous and embarrassed to be seen anywhere in the vicinity of Eaton. That was the real embarrassment. I'd been here before—that pivotal moment when you realize how silly you've been and how the world doesn't turn on the axis you thought. It's just that you never gave yourself the opportunity to see things differently.

I knew this from issues I had dealt with back in Portville—parent-teacher committees with the kids' school, or civic issues that cropped up from time to time. My sometimes bullheaded approach had to learn nuance. But how quickly I forgot. Like a muscle infrequently used, if you don't use it, you lose it. I was pleased to have opened myself up to a new experience, but also pleased that I was able to keep my ignorance to myself. I realized then that Peter had something I didn't. He was naturally accepting of people, while I was more discriminating. So be it. One step at a time.

27

On the other side of town, the Robinsons settled down for dinner in their usual fashion. The table was set. The mushrooms of chicken marsala and garlic sautéed string beans melted the air, while a lingering sweetness of butternut squash baked to perfection made its own pleasant presence.

The mood was mellowed with the soft, jazzy saxophone of Coleman Hawkins playing "Quintessence." The prayer was said, then Jerome served Margaret before serving himself. This was an evening ritual, with Jerome helping Margaret dice vegetables, peel potatoes, and prepare a rub. He was the sous-chef to Margaret's creative culinary genius.

He set the table, picked the music, and served his queen before himself. He adhered to a tradition of chivalry almost by instinct. Since a young man, he'd taught himself to respect women in a way that harkened back to the Victorian era. It had become such an ingrained behavior that he couldn't tell how or why he'd started doing it. He seemed to know what was expected of a man brought up with the right courtesies and traditions and wished to present that image to the world as a sign of proper upbringing. Appearances mattered. He always held the door and walked behind or on the outside of Margaret when in public. He held her chair when at a restaurant, and of course, he never raised his voice or criticized her meals.

After the initial indulgences and the meal was underway, Jerome looked at Margaret and smiled. She smiled back at him, but she sensed there was more to it than simple affection.

"Okay, what's on your mind?" she asked.

"I wasn't sure if I should bring it up. A blast from the past, you might say. I saw Peter today. Remember him, Peter Davidson?"

"Peter? Beekman Peter?"

"The one and only."

"My, my. How did that happen?"

"I was over at the coffee shop near the university, minding my own, when he showed up out of the blue. We sat for a bit. He joined me for coffee."

"And?" Margaret probed.

Jerome hesitated.

"Come on, Jerome. I can tell when there's more."

"It was weird. He was apologizing for Beekman."

"Beekman? That's silly. I always thought he was such a kind man, through and through. You don't meet too many like that. What's he got to apologize for?"

"He seems to think he didn't do enough to prevent the fire."

Margaret fell silent.

"I didn't mention it since it was such a small thing," Jerome continued, "but back then, he and I talked a few days before the fire, and I asked him if we had anything to worry about. You know, about the Beekman folks. He told me, after some backpedaling, that all was good. He said the neighbors just needed time. I figured there must have been a reason he struggled to answer, but I took him at face value. I agree, he's got a genuine side to him."

Margaret stared at Jerome without blinking.

"Anyway," Jerome continued, "he saw me in the coffee shop and felt the need to apologize. Said he should have said something different, something to warn us."

Jerome finally noticed that Margaret wasn't really listening. She had gone to that place. It might be something someone said or something she saw—and when it happened, she just *left*. All Jerome could do at those times was let her return when she was ready. He knew where she had gone, and he respected her time there.

After a few minutes, Margaret blinked, her stare regained its focus, and she looked at Jerome with a blushing half-smile. She always knew when she'd been away, and she always felt a touch self-conscious when she returned.

"How is he?" Jerome asked softly.

"Oh, fine," she said, still blushing.

It was a familiar exchange. Jerome knew that Margaret had visited with Julian, but he didn't know the particulars—whether it had been at his gravesite, or if they had been walking together, laughing the way they often did when Julian had still been around. It didn't matter to Jerome. It was her special time. It eased the pain of a loss that no mother should ever endure. While he threw himself into his work with numbing determination, Margaret needed to keep the connection alive.

"Well, as I was saying," Jerome went on, "Peter's a little confused that he didn't warn us *adequately*. Isn't that ridiculous?"

"He's such a sweetheart, Jerome. He just really cares. I hope you didn't make him feel bad about the whole thing?"

"No, not at all. I did tell him he was crazy to think that way. He was wanting forgiveness. Isn't that something?"

"Well, did you?"

"Did I what?"

"Forgive him. That was what he was asking for, right?"

"Well... no. I guess I didn't. I told him he was, in so many words, ridiculous to think he needed it, to think we relied solely on his assessment of Beekman to decide how to manage our affairs."

"Jerome, a man asks for forgiveness, you give him forgiveness. It's what the Good Book tells us to do."

"Aw, now, don't go beating me up over this thing. I just thought he was screwed up in the head over it. You know, he's been hanging on to this for going on six years. Six years!"

"And you didn't forgive him? After his waiting six years to get it, you didn't give it? What am I gonna do with you?" Margaret shook her head in disapproval.

"Okay, okay, I get it. I just couldn't understand why he was so worked up over the whole thing."

They both tried to get some food in before it cooled. Jerome was happy to put it behind him. But no sooner had he forgotten the first Peter topic than he recalled the other. "Oh, and guess what? Peter's going to the Gay Pride Parade, and he's not even gay. Go figure."

"Maybe he knows someone?"

"Asked. He said no."

"Well, maybe it's an issue he cares about."

"Seems ungodly to me."

"Jerome, you need to stop trying to figure people out. Just let them be. Don't you have enough on your own plate? Do you have to go poking your fork in everyone else's?"

"I just like everything in its place. What's the harm in that?"

"You know," Margaret said, "it wasn't too long ago that *we* were the ones everyone wanted kept in their place. Remember Beekman? That was like yesterday. Things change, but things don't change, if you know what I'm getting at."

"Well things have changed—for us. We're doing quite well. Our business is successful, we have employees to help run things, we could retire whenever we want. We're pillars of the community, you might say. We get invites to all the grand openings, we have a couple of friends on the city council, and just last month we went to that mayor's gala. Margaret, we have arrived. This ain't Beekman anymore."

"Well, those are just things, and don't think Beekman ain't anymore. This country has had a cyclical history of recreating the Beekman affair. First it was the Irish, then the Germans, then the Italians, Poles, the Greeks. We've put them all down when they were new to our country. All the while, Blacks were in the background, never making progress. Did I forget the Chinese? They've been around for some time, also never really making progress. Might as well throw in the Mexicans and Japanese. If you've got any color in you, it takes a bit longer for people to see you as people—as one of *them*. Seems we move forward as a society, but we still have a way of finding people to make a Beekman out of. I say, if gay is the way God made you, then so be it. Frankly, I'm not interested in singling anyone out for anything but being a nice person."

"Well, you're an angel, Margaret, that's why I married you, so I don't have to be." He let out a hearty laugh.

"I'll make an angel outta you yet," Margaret said, "if it's the last thing I do in this world." She gave him her familiar, loving smile, though there was no denying the confident, determined resolve in her expression.

28

"Hi, Peter, my secretary told me you called and wanted to talk. I have fifteen minutes. What's on your mind?"

"Hi, Doc, thanks for calling me back. I had a new development a few days ago, and it's been gnawing at me to the point I decided to get the proverbial second opinion."

"Okay, let's hear it."

"Last Saturday, I bumped into Jerome, of all people, at a coffee house in Cincinnati. It was weird. I was just walking by and happened to notice him through the window. I hesitated, but eventually decided to confront my demons and go talk with him."

"Excellent, Peter. I'm proud of you. Jerome is the… the dad of the boy, right?"

"Right. So we got to talking. I tried to make the big apology—you know, the thing I've been beating myself up over all these years. I expected anger, yelling, maybe even physical injury. I'd be lying if I didn't admit that it scared the crap out of me."

"To be expected. So, how'd it go?"

"Not too bad, actually. He told me, in so many words, that I was crazy for holding onto things for so long, that he and his wife moved on long ago, and that I should do the same. I tried to make the point that because I lied to him about the Beekman meetings, he didn't take the necessary precautions to protect his son, and that if I'd told him the truth back when he asked what to expect from people, maybe his son would still be alive. Well, he didn't buy it. He told me I was obsessing for too long over something that's just life. He misses his son, mind you, but they've had to let go of the 'what-ifs.' That life just sucks."

"I'd say he recovered remarkably well from something that often destroys marriages and people themselves. You're lucky to call him your friend."

"Well, that gets to my second issue. We got to talking about other stuff and it came up that he's a homophobe. That's my word for him, not his. He's part of some group that demonstrates against the gay and lesbians in the world. They call themselves Alliance for a Safe America."

"Interesting. How'd you handle that?"

"Well, it pissed me off. We got into an argument over it all. Not yelling or anything, but I chastised him for being… well, you know, Black, and not sticking up for people being discriminated against. It's like it's okay to hate others, just don't hate me. It's downright hypocritical, don't you think? I don't handle hypocrisy well. It's the worst human trait there is, in my opinion."

"I can see you feel strongly about this issue."

"You think I went overboard?"

"No. Not at all. It's a good thing to have passions in life. It's especially nice when our passions don't deny other people their passions, as well. I'm proud of you for defending your beliefs."

"So, here's the rub. I mentioned the Gay Pride Parade was coming up, and he warned me not to go. He said there's a lot of weird people that attend, but I think he was hiding something. I think he knows there's gonna be a lot of anti-Pride demonstrators. If I didn't know better, I'd say he expects violence."

"Okay. So, what's the rub?"

"I plan on going."

"To watch?"

"No, to participate."

"Why would you participate if you're not a member of Eaton?"

"Well, I'm an honorary member. I know they'd like me to walk with them."

"And the problem, then, is?"

"Well, the problem is Clare doesn't want me to go, Jerome doesn't want me to go, and I want to go. And I can feel that their not wanting me to go makes me want to go even more. I'm questioning my authenticity here. Am I going for the right reasons?"

"Peter, you certainly find yourself in interesting psychological dilemmas, don't you? I definitely make my money's worth with you." (Peter laughs.) "Do you feel that some sort of violence is possible, or even likely?"

"To be honest with myself, I'd have to say yes."

"Why is that?"

"Well, Jerome seemed to hint at it, if you read between the lines. Also, I saw him interviewed on television, and he tried to deny that the Alliance for a Safe America is a violent group. Well, that to me means others have criticized them for being violent. His telling me to stay away has a peculiar motive, wouldn't you say?"

"Yes, I'd agree. So knowing that violence may ensue, why do you still want to go?"

"I feel like I'd be abandoning my Eaton friends if I don't. I've been supporting them for years, and I feel now's not the time to run and hide."

"What happened at last year's Pride Parade?"

"It went off okay. I think the Eaton crowd marched up in the

Northside neighborhood. It's much less controversial up there. It's their territory. This march will be downtown, at the Fountain Square."

"You know, Peter, I applaud your courage and commitment to your Eaton friends, but not all decisions to get involved mean support—and not all decisions to leave mean abandonment. As you already seem to be aware of, sometimes intentions are not authentic. Support can be for selfish reasons or simply from guilt, in which case it's not with sincere intent. Likewise, deciding not to go can be for noble purposes. In this case, a noble reason not to go would be to support your wife. This will sound funny coming from me since I've always preached that I'm not your marriage counselor, but I know responsible acts when I see them. A decision to support one's spouse when they're scared is always a good thing—a noble thing. In this case, you have dueling allegiances, but you wear the ring of commitment to one of those allegiances. It would be appropriate, kind, generous, and loving to support your marriage by supporting your wife in this instance. If I thought her wanting you not to attend was for selfish reasons—say she was intent on subjugating you to her will—then I'd have to evaluate the decision based on the violent threat alone. But in this case, her concerns are valid, based on your assessment, and she's been very willing to accept your view on volunteering at Eaton in general. I'd say her position is sincere."

"That puts me in a tough situation."

"How so?"

"Well, I've pretty much decided to go."

"I thought I was your second opinion. It's sounding more like I'm just a sounding board you hoped would rubber-stamp whatever you wanted to do. I think you may have underestimated me. This act of yours is classic *Aegrescit medendo*."

"I'm not even gonna pretend I know what you're talking about, Doc."

"It's Latin for 'the cure is worse than the disease.' You're stuck on a way forward that is dangerous to you and your family and still, you want to proceed, all for a redemption you feel deserving of for something you did not do. Of course, that's my opinion speaking."

"I believe you may be right."

"Peter, I didn't tell you this before, but I'll tell you now. When you told me the details of the incident back in May, the full story of the fire, I was struck by one important theme. The story was tragic, no doubt, but I'm your therapist, and I listened from that perspective. How you told the story was very important. You essentially admitted to knowing you were making a fateful decision when you lied to Jerome, but you did it anyway. You mollified your guilt with excuses, but in the end, it seemed to me by your telling that you knew the consequences. Now, I know Jerome has exonerated you by saying life is more complicated than that one exchange between you two, and he may be right. But your part of that exchange fits a pattern. It goes back to that seminal event we talked about some time ago at the river. The reverse-reward issue seems to come up with you in critical moments in your life.

"With Jerome, you again chose to do the wrong thing, hoping to get the positive reward. I'm not talking about welcoming the Robinsons despite Beekman's rejection of them. That was noble and honorable. I'm talking about the lie. A lie told for personal gain at a time you believed it could put Jerome at risk. You did it anyway. I think what made that event so catastrophic for you was that it didn't work out the way it had in the past. This time, you took the risk, and you were wrong. A bad thing happened, and you were unprepared to deal with the consequences.

"You continued to make these types of decisions when you

ignored your wife to work at Eaton. You had my encouragement to volunteer, but you seemed to take a little too much delight in your wife's angst over the whole ordeal. As if causing her pain was part of the motivation. And now, here you are again, with a choice between what most people would consider is the right choice—the noble choice versus a more reckless choice. You seem intent on taking chances, hoping for the thrill, the reverse-reward. It would seem you like living on the edge, only you put yourself on the edge intentionally and hope you'll land heads up instead of… well, you get the point. Your behavior actually has some hallmarks of an obsessive-compulsive disorder. But one thing I can say with certainty, you are a Promethean Greek tragedy playing out in slow motion.

"There's one other thing. I know you had a strong attachment to your brother, Dave. He was heroic in his last act, but he didn't choose to be where he was when he made that decision. It was imposed on him. You don't have to put yourself in harm's way to honor his memory. You feel like you never truly mourned him, and I'm concerned you may be punishing yourself for something you couldn't control—your emotions over his loss."

The line fell silent. Peter was again sitting in a Rodin *Thinker* pose, his hair tousled from repeatedly hand-fisting clumps, anxiously anticipating Anna's opinion. She was direct and unyielding. It seemed he needed that to get shocked back to reality. His heart sank with the truth that she was right and he was wrong. He had been growing giddy with the idea of going to the march. He dismissed Clare's concerns and was defying Jerome in a man-to-man standoff. He now wondered if his giddiness was from the excitement of the march or the thrill of defying his wife and erstwhile friend.

"Peter, you there?"

"Yeah, I'm here. Just thinking. You're not telling me what I want to hear, but I guess it's what I need to hear. I just can't seem to shake it, Doc. You told me once that redemption was a good thing. It's been nearly six years, and I still feel I haven't turned the corner. As much as I'm trying to get my head right about my past, I know I won't live forever, so I have to spend what time I have making a difference. I guess what I'm trying to say is, on some level, I think I need to go, even if it's for all the wrong reasons."

"If you're doing it for all the wrong reasons, Peter, you may not get the redemption you're looking for. After that May session, I planned on waiting 'til you were in a better state of mind to debrief you on my perspective. Now seemed right. Hope this all sits well with you. And remember, it's a misconception that the big events in our life are what gives meaning to our existence. In my experience, my truth is that we make decisions every day that seem meaningless, inconsequential, but they add up. The sheer magnitude of these small decisions over time is way more consequential to our long-term happiness than any one event alone. The real value to your life is your marriage to Clare, not the Pride Parade. And finding that elusive redemption you're looking for can only come from within. You have to forgive yourself. Redemption is not out there somewhere lurking in the shadows, waiting to bestow itself on you. Think about it, Peter."

29

Peter woke at the break of dawn in a cold sweat, his undershirt stuck to the sheet as if glue had bonded them together. It didn't matter. His mind was somewhere else, frozen in place by a dream he could no longer remember. His heart raced from a fright that gripped his psyche. With eyes wide open, he glared at a ceiling barely illuminated by the predawn light. His gaze traced the hieroglyphic swirls of paint in an attempt to divine answers, but it was to no end. He finally relented, closed his eyes—and only then, in a moment of reprieve, did his memory capitulate.

The dream had been a conflict between him and Clare, him and Jerome, him and Doc. They all wanted something… something he had but could not give, could not part with. It was his to give, but he was not inclined to give it. They encircled him, asking, begging, railing against him from all sides. Pleading turned to shouts; shouts turned to anger. They yelled, called him names, denounced him as a coward, as he crouched in place and pulled at his hair yelling, "No. No! No!"

His panting grew heavy but eventually subsided. His heart settled. His fists released balled-up sheets as he sank back into the bed, finally letting go until he fell back to sleep.

30

I woke to find Peter's side of the bed empty. I listened for the shower, but it was quiet. I strained to hear the sounds in the kitchen, a blender or fridge opening or faucet running, anything—but all was silent.

Where is he?

I thought of all the errands he might have run, but since I hadn't made a list, I came up short. I lay back down, thinking he was probably sipping coffee and reading the newspaper in the family room.

I reached for the remote and clicked on the television to check the weather report. I tuned in just in time to see the familiar face of meteorologist Jennifer Martinez.

"Today is going to have a bit of everything except sunshine, folks," she was saying. "There'll be gray skies, rain, wind, lightning, and thunderclaps at times."

She pointed to the map of Cincinnati, which showed an intense green mass extending across the Canadian border, its long, sinister arm reaching into the heart of the Midwest.

"You won't want to be outdoors when this system comes barreling through. For those of you planning on going to the Gay

Pride Parade, bring your wet-weather gear. You may see some action."

I bolted upright when I heard "parade" and turned up the volume.

"We'll have gray, overcast skies for pretty much the whole day, but we expect the rain to arrive in the early afternoon, and for the heaviest part to hit Cincinnati by late afternoon. Of course, anything can happen. The system doesn't to be moving quickly through Indiana and Michigan, so my predicted times may need updating as the day progresses. The Pride Parade is expected to start at ten a.m., so many of the marchers may miss the rain, but I'd come prepared with an umbrella, and if the wind kicks up, a hooded raincoat is a must if you decide to 'weather' it out."

I jumped out of bed and ran to the stairs. "Peter? Peter? Are you down there?"

There was no response. I ran down the stairs and into the family room, but no Peter. I circled through the dining room into the kitchen and back toward the porch. Still no Peter.

I looked out all the windows, starting with the back of the house and coming around to the front. Braking to a halt, I saw what would have answered my fears from the start: His car was gone. He was gone. He'd promised me he wasn't going. Or maybe he'd just *said* he wasn't going. But he had to know it would come across as a promise. He knew I was afraid of what might happen after hearing what Jerome had said… or implied. Peter had to know I wouldn't be happy with his going. And yet, he'd gone.

I ran back upstairs and found my mobile phone by the end table. Just as I reached for it, it rang. It was Peter.

"Hi, hon, are you awake yet? I waited to call so you could sleep in." He was practically shouting into the phone to be heard over the din of highway noise.

"You're going to the Pride Parade! After all we talked about. And in this weather? Peter, how could you?"

He was silent. Though he hadn't mentioned where he was going, it was obvious. He must have realized his predicament—the early departure without explanation, and his decision to go to the parade. It was all a sneaky betrayal, and it stung. Especially now that we were on the road to understanding each other so well.

"I don't know how to explain it," Peter said. "I'm not sure I really understand it myself. I had a dream last night. More like a nightmare. I woke in a cold sweat, frozen with fear. It wasn't obvious what it was all about… but you, Jerome, and Doc, were all at me for something. You were all hounding me, badgering, bullying me into doing something my mind didn't want me to do. In the dream, I broke down. I couldn't handle it."

He paused, and when the traffic noise subsided, he continued in a softer voice. "When I got up this morning, it took some time for me to piece it together, but the nightmare finally made sense. I know I promised I wasn't going for the reasons we agreed on. But something wasn't right. I guess there's some part of me that needs to go. My mind won't be at peace if I don't. There must be something I need to resolve in myself that I can only do by going."

"I… I wish…" My voice fell off. Then, after a moment, I tried again. "Peter, I… I just wish you had…"

I had nothing to say. What could I say? He had decided this was his fate—without me.

"Clare, I think I need to do this to finally solve my issues. I think that's why I had that nightmare. It was telling me that if I don't go, I'll have a longer road ahead to getting the Beekman thing behind me."

He paused again. I didn't fill the void. I remained silent.

"If you don't want me to go," he said, "I'll turn around. Right now, I'll turn around. But if I go, I won't stay long. I promise. I can't let down my friends. Not again. I'll hang out for an hour, no more, just so they know I made it, that I wasn't afraid to be by their side. Then I'll head home." There was more emptiness on the line. "Clare?"

"You'll come home right away? Just an hour?" I asked, trying to quiet my sobbing.

"Just an hour."

"Peter?"

"Yes, hon."

"Don't do anything stupid."

"I won't, dear."

31

Peter could hear sniffling from the receiver of his phone, then a gasp, and then silence. He knew all was not well. That Clare was on an edge. He had pushed her too far, beyond her ability to cope. It was the first time in years that she'd let her guard down around him, and at that moment he felt like a cad.

Doc had warned him not to abandon Clare, that she was his primary commitment and going to the parade jeopardized a sacred trust. He also remembered Doc's earlier suggestion that Clare had loss issues. This blundering, idiotic move was likely only exacerbating her one vulnerability.

A sinking feeling churned in his gut. Hurting Clare in this instance pricked his pride, and it surprised him. Though he'd accepted therapy when she'd made her ultimatum, he was otherwise inured to her complaints about his obsession antics. However, something changed.

Clare being distraught instead of angry about the parade had an opposite effect on him. This wasn't the usual dismissal of him as weak, which sometimes bordered on anger or even disrespect. No. This was different. Now she was emotionally invested. She cared enough about them that she didn't want to lose him.

It was how he would have felt back in the days when the kids were knee-high and he and Clare didn't have a care in the world—when their love for each other, their expectations and generosity toward each other, was reminiscent of their college days. This was the Clare he had fallen in love with a long time ago.

Peter smiled. In that moment, he desperately wanted to appease her. It was like they were new lovers, thinking only of each other, not letting go of the embrace, breathing each other's air. It was an odd irony, but he knew then that his marriage would survive.

He felt a renewed passion to get right in his head, to stop obsessing about the past and finally move on with his life. He now understood how his impulses were pushing him to an extreme. Not that his values were wrong, but it was the way he carried them—the way he stubbornly stood apart from others, judging them to a fault, Clare in particular. The thrill-seeking behavior, that reverse-reward thing Doc always talked about, would have to end. His promise would be sincere. He'd leave in an hour. He'd be home by noon—at the latest.

—— ... ——

Predicting the weather is as much an art as it is a science, or so some would have you believe. Forecasting is never perfect, often wrong, and sometimes disastrous. In fact, that weather forecasters are never right is an axiom that usually goes unchallenged. But on that Saturday in June, the dark, foreboding sky looming over the Midwest like a blanket had been accurately predicted. The rain had yet to be unleashed, but it had been likewise predicted. One only needed to gaze up at the sky to concede an unyielding truth that no one can deny nature her due.

Washington Park served as the staging area for Eaton's Pride

Parade. It was all of six acres in the center of Cincinnati, its history dating back to the early 1800s when it was the grounds for a Presbyterian and Episcopalian cemetery. After the Civil War, it became a memorial with numerous artifacts commemorating those who'd sacrificed to preserve the Union. It was quite fitting that this was the location for the planning of a march to claim civil rights for a displaced people—an event fulfilling its rightful place in history. Many would agree it would have made the city's ancestry proud.

For Peter, such sentiments were not part of his focus. His was the more immediate crisis of finding a place to park. Like any large old city, parking was scarce in the center of town. Several blocks north of the park was the closest he could get, and even that, he considered lucky. With thousands of visitors expected to celebrate the occasion, parking would be just one of many frustrations to contend with. Engorged sidewalks bustled with soon-to-be marchers and onlookers, dancing and singing and waving flags. People crossed streets at any point that was convenient, slowing traffic to a standstill. Cars honked and the occasional police siren blared with the impossible attempt to clear the streets of loiterers. It was a celebration before the celebration.

To be sure, there would be more than just the marchers and their approving onlookers. The Pride Parade was certain to bring another element into the city, despite the expected foul weather: the people who felt compelled to be heard, who felt they alone stood between a life of their choosing and a life that others chose for themselves.

Once again, a long tradition in human history was playing out—one group of people deciding how other people should live. Both sides of this social struggle knew the other element existed and would make themselves known, but the Pride marchers had a planned route. Their march had been advertised, and permits to march stipulated a path that was in the public record weeks in advance.

The plan was to start at Washington Park, march down Elm to Fifth Street, then over to Fountain Square, meeting up with the official Cincinnati Gay Pride Parade. This was the Eaton Northside contingent of the Pride Parade. As the self-designated gay community in Cincinnati, they warranted their own recognition. The route was ten blocks—some short, some long, all heading into the heart of downtown Cincinnati.

The demonstrators kept their plans a secret. It was not part of the public record, so only they knew where and when they would make themselves known. The festive occasion was thus marred with an undercurrent of foreboding. The marchers knew that every corner was a possible flash point for conflict. The hope was that enough supporters would be present to provide a buffer to the rants from parade detractors. The police planned to protect the route, but they were not planning a presence in riot gear. They simply stood as street corner sentinels, keeping cars from crossing through or onlookers from blocking the path of the marchers.

By the time the Eaton group met on the southside of Washington Park, the rain had begun to fall. It was a light drizzle, but it was also two to three hours ahead of schedule. Many marchers immediately donned clear plastic ponchos with hoods. Others, who didn't want to mar their stylish dress for the occasion, went without.

The mood remained festive in spite of the weather. Hooping and chanting was a recurrent chorus. Placards were held high, waving in the drizzling rain with all sorts of slogans: "Be Proud, Be Gay," "Civil Rights for All," "Loud and Queer."

Peter felt he was part of something bigger than himself. It was something bigger than he'd ever experienced. This was about people, at their core, fighting to live. One's purpose couldn't be any clearer. He felt he was where he needed to be.

As he scanned the crowd, he noticed older women carrying placards with "Mothers for Gay Rights!" and "PFLAG." He was told the P stood for parents. It only then dawned on him that if he was there, why not parents? Their presence made even more sense than his, and for some reason unclear to him at the moment, he felt a belonging and a knowing that progress takes sacrifice by more than just those being victimized.

Eaton's lead organizer, Rebecca, signaled the start. People eagerly lined up in predetermined lines. Placards were waved, a boom box blared, and everyone smiled in unison, dancing in the streets.

Peter was elated. He felt every bit a part of Eaton despite not being a real member. As they began their stroll down Elm, a few scattered people on sidewalks turned to watch them pass. The marchers were about forty in number, spread out four to five abreast, easily covering more than half a block.

By the second block, spectators were sitting in folding chairs with umbrellas or wearing rain gear while others were standing and waving mini rainbow flags. The onlookers were men and women, women and women, men and men, and families with children, all waving and smiling. The Eaton marchers waved back.

Peter's eyes locked in on a cheery toddler with rosy cheeks sitting in a mini lawn chair. She had on a white sailor's cap, pink overalls, and the tiniest little white sneakers to match her hat. The glee in her eyes was infectious as she waved her rainbow flag to a beat of her own choosing.

"We're getting a good reception," Peter said, throwing a giddy smile to Moiré. She marched along with him and a few others with interlocking arms.

"So far, so good. This is a lot like last year in Northside." She had to yell a bit to be heard over the boom box jamming music out to the masses. "I hope the crazies are home in bed right now," she added with a half-grin. She wore a simple outfit of jeans, a waterproof windbreaker, a plain white T-shirt, and white low-top Converse sneakers. She was never much for excess, but this time she had a rainbow painted on her right cheek. When she smiled, it retracted into a furling flag.

Peter thought about what she was actually saying, that there might be demonstrators, crazies, who would demonstrate against them. Though all of the Eaton crowd knew to expect resistance—something they already encountered during much of their lives—Peter was taken aback. Maybe it was denial, or wishful thinking that all would go well. He had been warned by Jerome, Doc, and his wife that this march was not likely to be benign. Still, he allowed himself to think the best of people. After all, he was in a crowd, and the police were out on every corner.

"What if the crazies aren't in bed?" he asked Moiré. "Do we have a plan if they make trouble? Do we end the march?"

Moiré threw him a chastising glare, which then softened as she unlocked her arm from his and placed it around his shoulder to engender a more caring sentiment.

"Sometimes, Peter," she said, leaning in to be heard over the din, "the best resistance is to just be. To be yourself in the face of those idiots who don't like you and don't want your presence. Just *being* forces them to make space, physically and mentally. That presence. That's really what forces change. It's slow, I'd agree, but it's the only type of change that gets into their hearts—against their will, despite not really being forced on them. When you share your space with someone, when you breathe the same air as them, you give them time to acknowledge your existence. It's only then that they actually see you for who you are. It's only then that they know you're really no different from them. You can't have acceptance without that. You can legislate behavior, as Martin Luther King once said, but you can't change someone's heart until they breathe your air."

Peter stared back in awe. This was his Moiré, preaching to him on a level he was barely capable of understanding. *Presence breeds change.* How arrogant he'd been, assuming his ambitions were the same as Moiré's. But he'd been wrong. Very wrong. She was in this for survival. He, on the other hand, was trying not to betray any sense of fear, though he could feel the natural fight-or-flight instinct rearing up inside him.

The flight side of things was the primary urge. He had a growing sense that he was in deeper than he intended, that he was not really aware of the desperation at stake for his Eaton friends, a desperation that was willing to take risks. He imagined himself wading in the shallows at the beach when suddenly a surging wave crashed in, the sand washing out from under him, leaving him standing chest-high in a surf he'd thought was only knee-deep. He was now on the frontline of life-changing issues in ways he had never thought he would. His involvement in college demonstrations had never been violent, and never about survival in the face of hatred.

Where was the arrogant boldness that I confronted Jordan with in the coffee shop just a couple weeks ago? Peter wondered.

Moiré patted him on the shoulder a couple times to signal the need to focus ahead as they continued the march. For her, it was all business as usual.

By the third block, the rain was falling at a steady pace. Any chance that it was just an early, temporary shower ahead of the storm front was now a lost hope. Still, the crowd of supporters decided the rain was not an issue. If anything, as the Eaton marchers continued their stride down Elm, the onlookers increased in number, standing shoulder to shoulder and two to three deep, their enthusiasm undeterred.

By the fifth block, the marchers paused to allow police to subdue a streaker running through the crowd. The commotion created enough distraction that supporters cleared off the sidewalks and into the street, blocking the parade. The energy level of the crowd was intensifying. Placid, smiling onlookers waving flags were now speckled with army surplus wanderers moving about with intentions other than support for the passing colors of the rainbow.

Moiré leaned into Peter and half-yelled, "The beginning of the crazies. They always make it to the party."

This time her face was serious as she locked in on the mini melee taking place just ahead of them to the right. The police were struggling a bit with the streaker, who intentionally wanted to make his removal from the crowd a spectacle in itself. He thrashed on the sidewalk while being subdued and had to be carried off, arms and legs held by four officers.

As the marchers crossed Sixth Street, the rain intensity was determined to have its say. The path ahead to Fifth meant traveling between two relatively tall buildings, the Regal Hotel on the left and the Albert B. Sabin Convention Center on the right.

From the vantage point of the Sixth Street intersection, it looked like traversing through a valley. The tall façades closed in, funneling into the next intersection.

The clouds were dark and the rain grew heavy, and though it was only eleven a.m., it looked and felt like sundown. The most ominous change was the onlookers. Flags waved, but not the rainbow ones Peter had seen on the previous blocks. These were American flags—and yet children were conspicuously absent. The whole mood of the parade changed in that one intersection.

Rebecca, who held the front line of marchers together, turned back to Moiré and shouted something Peter didn't hear. Moiré nodded. She turned back and called out to Bob, whose line was a couple behind theirs.

"Okay, get ready!"

Peter peered over his shoulder to see what the Eaton formation looked like behind him. They held their ranks, locked arm in arm, side by side, still marching in formation and with determination. The only notable change were the missing exuberant smiles and singing that had been on display in the block before. The faces of Eaton were now pensive, glaring, and confrontational. One would have thought this was really the purpose of the march—to take on the crazies. To prove their pride was stronger than prejudice.

"What's going on?" Peter asked. His tone and urgency betrayed his fraying nerves.

"Well, as we expected, the crazies are out in number, and it looks like they came to tango," Moiré said with a wry smile. "I hope you brought your dancing shoes."

"Tango?" Peter asked as if he didn't understand. But he knew. He knew exactly what Moiré meant. "Shouldn't we make a turn, then, maybe go down Sixth instead of heading to Fifth?"

"Not on your life. We don't deviate. It's our calling to be here. Running from oppression only strengthens them. If we're to get any respect, we have to stand as one and confront our enemy— the intolerant bastards!"

Moiré's calm militant, demeanor in any other situation would have inspired Peter to jump from a skyscraper. But having slowly simmered in the near boiling water of the upcoming fracas, the brawl that he could see up ahead, Peter wondered if she was a borderline lunatic.

His skin began to crawl. He had lost his nerve in just the last couple of blocks. Moiré's lecture about presence being the most effective form of resistance evaporated with the angry mob now chanting slurs and waving the American flag. He understood Moiré's sentiment, but he was now realizing his understanding was from the comfort of an armchair in a living room conversation where only his opinion mattered. He was now in the moment. The weight of that opinion loomed before him. He could see it, and it didn't look pretty. This would be a costly justice.

The marchers proceeded through the Sixth Street intersection into the dark, gloomy, windswept rain. Chanting from the sidelines tried to drown out the boom box. The music was turned up.

The chanting got louder. The wind blew in gusts. Rain pelted sideways. Flags unfurled. Eggs fell at marchers' feet. Tomatoes flew overhead, some finding their mark. Marchers forced smiles. Angry tirades ensued.

"Sodom and Gomorrah, not in America!"

"Queers clear out!"

"Lesbos and fruitcakes are deviants!"

The slurs were a nonstop cacophony of noise drowning out the music, which itself didn't matter anymore. The marchers were in defensive mode. Their objective was to simply get to Fifth Street and turn the march toward Fountain Square, where a heavier police presence was expected.

The dancing had ceased—so, too, the waving of the rainbow flags. The intensifying rain had dampened their enthusiasm before Sixth. After Sixth, everyone was simply on the lookout for flying objects.

Thunder rumbled a low-pitched groan from overhead, attempting to declare a peace among the marchers and protesters, but it found no takers. A man broke loose from the sidelines and ran between the marching lines. He got in the face of Brad, Eaton's social work coordinator, who was linked arm in arm with others, and screamed, "Faggot, faggot, faggot!" over and over. The man stood nose to nose with Brad, who froze, hoping not to be the cause of the whole march descending into chaos.

Two police officers quickly interceded and dragged the protester away kicking and screaming, "Faggot! Faggot!"

The marchers pressed on. So did the thunder, chanting, and tirades. The police were outnumbered as more protesters broke from the sidelines and wormed their way through the marchers, singling them out individually with pithy, dehumanizing comments—bumping them, pushing them down, and moving onto other marching victims.

More police showed up and formed a line, a separation between the marchers and protesters. The mood of the impending chaos was undaunted. In fact, the marchers, now with better police protection, contributed to the verbal melee with their own chants.

"Gay and proud!"

"Queer from birth!"

"Stop the hate!"

The entire street was now blocked. Marchers stood face-to-face with the protesters; one line of police stood between them. The yelling and screaming continued. The rain also continued, unabated in size and intensity. If anything, it had grown worse.

Peter saw in the faces of the other side a vitriol he had never seen in a person. It seemed like the stuff of movies, but it was all happening in real time. He felt out of place. He understood the cause but didn't feel the cause the way his comrades did. It was apparent he was personally and emotionally less invested, but it wasn't his choice to be less invested. It was simply the comparison he could now easily see as he looked at the marchers on one side screaming into the faces of hate on the other. He didn't feel that intense anger in his heart, and much as he supported the cause, he understood how you have to live the cause to feel the true weight of the oppression.

Still, he was where he wanted to be. He found a renewed purpose in the steely faces of his Eaton comrades and would not turn and run. He was in the moment, and all else was swept from his mind.

He scanned the faces on the other side and saw anger. He took a step back to widen his view and noticed a person of color near the far end on the left side. It looked like Jerome.

Peter moved in that direction, winding himself between the marchers that were shouting and chanting as loud as the demonstrators. He drew closer and saw more clearly. It was Jerome. He pressed through the crowd, calling out, "Hey, Jerome. Jerome!"

Jerome turned to the sound of his name and saw Peter. Jerome pressed forward to the front of the police line and leaned in between their shoulders.

"Peter, what are you doing here?" he shouted over the din. "I told you not to come. I told you it would be… dangerous."

"You never quite said, 'dangerous,' Jerome. Weird, maybe, but you denied violence!"

"These things take on a life of their own," Jerome said. "You can't control what happens. I warned you. Get out of here now before things take a turn." He looked to the left and the right, keeping an eye on how his side was handling the standoff.

"I'm not running, Jerome. These are my people. I belong with them."

"They're not your people, Peter. They chose their lives. Whatever happens to them is their fault. It's God's retribution."

This was the man Peter had once admired and held in awe. Jerome believed in a society willing to follow that arc of justice to a better place. His conviction and determination in the face of a

Beekman betrayal had been inspiring. And now, this. A polar opposite, an abyss of sincerity turned vile, embodied in the same person. It didn't make sense. It didn't seem possible.

"Jerome, they're no different than you moving into our neighborhood. This is just like the Beekman thing all over again." Peter had to shout to be heard. "I stood up for you, and I'm standing up for them. You should be over here with me. This should be your cause as much as mine."

Jerome saw the face of an earnest man trying to find meaning, his plaintive look still expecting to make a convert of him at this late hour. His eyes were asking for Jerome to show doubt or hesitation, anything to prove he was getting through.

"You're a lost soul trying to find a purpose," Jerome said. "You're on the wrong side of history—the wrong side of God on this one. Beekman was another place and time. This ain't no Beekman. Get out of here before it's too late."

The shove came from behind Jerome. It knocked him into the police line. The police shoved him back, but more pushing followed. People lost their footing, and before long, the police line had fractured right in front of Peter.

Protesters pushed through, having replaced their placards and flags with sticks and bats. They charged at the marchers, inflicting pain on anything that moved.

The marchers fought back with whatever they had. Their placards and flags were now weapons of justice, though benign in comparison to bat-wielding anarchists.

Some fought back with just their hands. Their commitment to the cause was eternal. Some marchers ran to find cover, and Peter ran with them. These were marchers with no defensive weapons who felt they were no match for crazies with bats.

When Peter looked back, Jerome was gone and pandemonium

had replaced the fragile détente. Bodies on the ground were being struck by protesters while others were running or being chased.

The hotel on one side and the convention center on the other limited where people could go. The protesters' plan to mount their offensive on this block of the march revealed the extent of their malevolent strategy. They knew the advantages of the block. The tall buildings with no easy escape routes meant they could exact as much punishment as possible. It was an unsuspecting offering of sacrifice by Eaton marchers who were called to change the face of society against those obsessed with preserving a macabre view of exclusion and dominance.

The sight was a circus of hell, a purgatory of injustice.

Jerome stood in the center of the street and looked in every direction, as a leader on a battlefield stands tall, oblivious to being shot at, strategizing his next attack.

He was looking for the innocent, the one who didn't belong, the one who should easily stand out, cowering in a corner somewhere. All he saw was mayhem—his people on top of the enemy, exacting punishment for crimes of indecency, and in another direction, Eaton marchers cornering and lashing out at his mob of do-gooders.

Twenty minutes seemed like an eternity. In that span of time, the organized marching parade became a cultural battleground. People lay bleeding, curled up and writhing in the street. The beating continued unabated.

The police tried to break up the melee, but they were woefully outnumbered, pushed and shoved aside like play dolls in uniform. Blood ran in streams away from bodies as the pelting rain tried to hide evidence of the carnage.

Peter ran. He tripped, fell, got up, and ran again. A glass bottle crashed at his feet, another broke against a wall overhead. The shards coated the pavement and sidewalk. Blood oozed from his hands.

It was planned that any fall would bleed. He tried to rescue others who had fallen in his path, but then they would both fall again, often over another fallen comrade. At one point, the only safe path was an alley that served as a service entrance for the convention center.

Peter had no choice but to run in that direction, hoping there would be another way out.

―― ... ――

News camera crews that had been recording the parade were still running live footage as events deteriorated. More station crews arrived to provide coverage from all vantage points. "The commotion," as it was now called, was broadcast into people's homes throughout the Cincinnati metropolis.

I sat cross-legged in bed, glued to the television, watching for any sign of Peter. My emotions had seesawed throughout the morning, back and forth over his choice to march.

My early tearful shock gave way to guarded caution, and then a growing curiosity to watch the parade from home. I was pleased that the event started on time, and that the supporters were friendly faces waving rainbow flags and little children with cute faces also waving their own baby rainbows.

At one point, I almost wished I'd gone. It reminded me of the many Thanksgiving parades that took place in Portville, some of which I had participated in with the kids in tow.

When the rain came, I decided staying home was probably the better choice.

There was no longer a clear delineation between sides. Between Sixth and Fifth Street, people were running in every direction. Though a boom box still blared upbeat dance music, no one listened; it was now a melodic backdrop to brutality.

Jerome continued his search for Peter, but he couldn't find him anywhere. As far as he was concerned, if Peter got away unscathed, it would be the only good thing to come of all this.

The whole event, as he'd planned it, had backfired. The sentiments had grown hotter than he'd expected, and his own protesters had come ready for a war that he did not plan on.

If Peter was not a victim of this colossal misjudgment, then he could at least live with himself.

——— ... ———

I moved to the edge of the bed, gripping the sheets in a tight fist as the coverage of the parade gradually shifted from light and cheerful to an isolated outburst, then a few outbursts, until it was all-out chaos. The heavy rain did not let up. Peter should have left by now.

Why hasn't he called? Where is he?

——— ... ———

Peter reached the end of the alley. Only then did he realize it was a dead end. There was no fence to climb. The walls were too high to scale.

He turned back to the street and saw two protesters standing at the alley entrance. They were quite aware of his predicament. One of them had long, wiry hair. He wore army surplus fatigues and carried a stick. The other was stocky, bald, and sported a distinct lion's mane beard. He wore a simple white T-shirt, jeans, and combat boots. His beefy arms swung a baseball bat from side to side as if he were stepping up to home plate, ready to swing at a pitch.

The men looked at each other and grinned. Peter backed up to the wall, which was all of three or four feet behind him. The two men closed in on him from thirty or forty feet away.

Peter had no plan. He had fallen victim to a decision that his parade comrades had known not to do. Never head into a closed alley. If you don't know it's closed, assume it is. Always stay in the open, and if you must run, run toward the police or camera crews. That way, any attack is witnessed by someone who can do something about it, or at least by people watching on television—the hope being that if the perpetrators can't be arrested on the spot, they can at least be identified at a later time.

Essentially, stay in the open. It's a moral confrontation, and enlisting the guilt of onlookers is necessary to turn the tide of public sentiment. You don't get anything from being attacked alone in an alley. It's just you. You could have fallen, been robbed, anything other than what had really taken place.

Peter waited until the two men close enough for him to reason with. "Hey, we're just marching for fairness, for equal rights," he pleaded. "This doesn't have to get ugly. We can all be reasonable here, can't we?"

The men looked at each other and again grinned, slapping the stick and bat into their open hands, signifying their ultimate intent.

"Come on, guys, this isn't necessary," Peter said.

"One less queer to worry about, I'd say."

They moved closer.

"This isn't going to change anything, you know," Peter said.

"There's still gonna be gay and lesbian people in the world. You can't beat people into changing something they can't change."

"That doesn't really matter now, does it? This is just you and us, and I think we're gonna feel pretty good when we're done with you."

Peter tried to dash in between the two, but it didn't go well. The bearded man expected him to make a run for it and simply stuck his leg, sending Peter sprawling. The blows came just as he hit the ground. The first landed on his thigh, the next on his shoulder. The final blow came to the head.

They continued beating him despite Peter's lifeless body putting up no resistance. They were in it for pleasure, not just to prove a point.

Jerome turned the corner of the alley and saw the brutality taking place. It was his worst nightmare—a protest turned violent.

He couldn't tell who the two guys were beating, but he hadn't found Peter anywhere else. His heart sank with the prospect that this was Peter lying in a heap on the ground, being batted to a pulp.

Jerome's rage reared, and he started his charge. His initial grunts turned to growls. He was a bull at top speed with no intention of slowing on impact, aiming for the stocky guy wielding the bat.

After twenty feet, his two-hundred-pound frame was traveling at close to twenty miles per hour. In the last five steps before impact, he let go a searing scream.

"You son of a bitch!"

The attacker in mid-swing barely had time to look up from his victim when Jerome's body slammed into him, throwing him back against the alley wall, smashing his head into concrete. The bat flew out of the man's hands as his body crumpled to the ground unconscious.

Jerome picked up the bat and turned on the second offender,

who looked him in the eye and saw something he was not prepared to deal with. He turned and ran.

——— ... ———

I searched every scene of the news footage for any evidence of Peter. I held the bedsheet balled up in one hand, biting into it for relief while clicking the remote with the other, up and down, down and up, trying to find a station with an angle on the protest that might show something different—or *someone* different.

It all looked the same. It seemed they had nothing new to show, so they all focused on the same shots. I sensed, however, that it would not turn out well. Every scene on that block was someone being chased, beaten, or battered. I tried to hold out hope, but it was slipping away.

Finally, I landed on a station that panned away from a policeman trying to subdue two protesters singlehandedly, a scene I'd seen over and over, to a man walking slowly out of an alley.

I stood to take a closer look. The rain and wind made it hard to see anything with clarity. Identifying a person was difficult. The shape didn't look like Peter, though it was hard to tell.

The man walked toward the camera. He must have been a hundred or more feet away. As the distance grew shorter, it was clear he was carrying something. He moved closer and I could see that something was someone.

He was carrying a body.

A lifeless body.

It hung with its legs dangling to one side, head and arms hanging free. The man continued to walk while people ran, fell, and fought all around him. I could tell the man was Black, but the body he was carrying was not.

Tears began to well in my eyes. The jacket on the body was red. It was the windbreaker I had bought Peter years earlier.

There was no denying it. All hope was gone. I fell back on the bed and curled in a screaming sob.

32

I was standing in the corner of the room when Anna arrived. Neither of us had ever laid eyes on each other, but Anna had the advantage. She had been directed to the room, and although she had never seen a picture of me, it seemed she recognized me immediately.

"Hello," she said, stepping into the room and holding out her hand. "I'm Anna Dietrich."

"Oh, hello. I'm Clare, Clare Davidson." I was confused. "Your name sounds familiar."

"I was your husband's therapist."

My confusion turned to surprise. Anna was not expected, and Peter had barely ever mentioned her. His therapy was his thing. He never discussed it with me.

"I realize my coming down here is a little unusual," Anna said, "but under the circumstances, I wanted to express my condolences."

"That's kind of you. Thank you."

I didn't have much to follow with. I turned away momentarily, and she did the same. Then I looked back at her with the intent to ask a question, but I hesitated. She picked up on the attempt but remained silent.

"Peter did mention you to me," I finally said, "but it was several months ago. He never spoke of you much. Dietrich, did you say?"

"Yes."

"Isn't that a... German name?"

"Yes."

"But you don't look a bit German to me. I just assumed..." I didn't finish. I had trapped myself in an embarrassing moment.

"I also have some Jamaican and Irish floating around in the final product," she said, offering to make light of my faux pas.

I guess it was my fault. A lingering need for people to fit into quaint categories. That Peter hadn't said anything to me about it also was no surprise. He saw past the typical boundaries that stymied others.

Despite Anna's efforts, I still felt chastened. I looked away again, gathering my thoughts. "Dr. Dietrich, did you talk to my husband about this parade thing?"

I knew the question crossed the line, that what happened in therapy stayed in therapy. Anna wore a perfectly unreadable expression. She was probably debating the best way forward, hoping to appease me while doing no harm. She finally relented.

"Mrs. Davidson, I'm sure you must understand that it's highly irregular for me to discuss patient sessions."

I stared at her with a stern but beseeching look. I needed answers and was willing to make that clear. "He must have said something to you. I don't understand why he had to go. I couldn't get him to listen to reason. And now this."

"I'm sorry for your pain," was all she would say.

Tears welled up in my eyes. I was searching, searching for meaning to the whole tragedy.

"Mrs. Davidson, I think under the circumstances, it would be alright for me to say that we did talk about it." She spoke quietly, giving the limited amount she needed to remain polite.

"So, you knew he planned on going?"

"Well, yes."

"And you didn't think to stop him?" The timbre of my voice changed mid-sentence. It was now an accusation.

"No."

"Why not, for God's sake?" I exclaimed, growing defiant, my irritation on the rise.

"I'm his therapist," she said with a calm, understated tone, hoping to bring my emotions down a notch. "My job is to help him think through his issues. I can't decide for him. It's his choice to make the final decision."

"That sounds like a lot of crap," I snapped.

"It does, and I'm sorry. I didn't want my presence to add to your pain."

She was trying to be polite, but her minimalist approach wasn't working. I could tell she knew more was needed. A long silence followed. When I almost thought nothing would come of it, she relented again.

"Mrs. Davidson, your husband struggled with this decision. He called me for advice. It wasn't a traditional sit-down session. Nonetheless, I gave him my input, but it seemed to me he'd already made up his mind. It was as if he had some inner drive, some kind of calling, to go to the parade. I can't explain it. If I had to make a professional guess, I'd say he was looking for redemption. That thing that happened six years ago haunted him, and he wanted—needed—to prove to himself that he was worthy."

"Worthy? Worthy of what?" An emotional quaver betrayed my anger.

"I've only heard the story told once, but you lived through it. You probably understand him better than I do. As best I can tell, from what I've learned over these past few months, Peter felt that he was the cause of a teenager dying in a fire. I think you already know this, but he felt he could have prevented it. He lied to the father about how safe Beekman was, and he believed it was the reason the boy died. He felt the tragic loss as if it were his own, and he felt he was the only one who understood the magnitude of his betrayal."

I stared at her with more confusion. It took a while for me to realize she was not the enemy, that she actually hadn't wanted Peter to go. I sobbed as the idea sank in and the reality hit home.

"But... but..." I cried. "It wasn't him! It was me!" My voice was pleading, as if I were in a courtroom trying to convince a jury of Peter's innocence. "It was me!" I shook my hands in her face to prove the point. "I was the one who refused to give him redemption. I stood in the way. I refused to acknowledge his pain." My face burned, and my tears began to flow.

The emotional seesaw had become a regular occurrence for me over the past several days. Nothing had gone the way I had hoped, the way I'd expected.

I was at a point of dismal despair that all was lost. She saw I was barely holding on and tried to comfort me by placing an arm around my shoulders.

Across the room, Jerome and Margaret sat in vigil. They were accompanied by Rebecca and Moiré, who shared the same bench that ran along the far wall.

Pastor Smith stood nearby with watchful attentiveness, keeping Sandy and Matt occupied in small talk.

Jerome had heard the conversation, despite Anna's attempt at privacy. He thought back to the coffee shop confrontation with Peter and wondered why his old neighbor had been so intent on going to the Pride Parade despite his warning.

Peter had wanted forgiveness for the fire, and Jerome would not give it. Instead, he'd dismissed the whole event out of hand as an act of evilness that Peter could never have stopped. Peter had lived for the better half of a decade needing redemption, and Jerome had stood in the way of that. He, the one person who could have given it, had withheld it. Jerome now knew that Peter's need for redemption and going to the parade had been one and the same.

Although Peter's true intentions were still a mystery to him, one thing was clear. The Peter who had confronted him at the police line in the midst of imminent mayhem was a Peter with true conviction. He had been speaking from the heart in the coffee shop, and it was clear he was speaking from the heart out on the line, defending a cause he believed in.

Jerome could only admire him for that. Whatever his motives may have been, Peter had stood up for people when others had not—Jerome included.

Tears filled Jerome's eyes as his bewilderment seeped to a deeper level. It was an emotion he was unaccustomed to, a feeling he often dismissed as weakness. But here he was, feeling a kinship for this insistent, scrawny guy who believed what he believed and could not be dissuaded in any way from his version of the truth. A man who had put his life on the line for others—twice.

Jerome remembered the Beekman mob, the crowd gawking at his burning inferno of a home, and the son that was taken because of intolerance. He realized that he too had a mob, and he too could have caused a loss of life due to a similar intolerance.

The thought churned his guts. He wiped the tear from his eye and turned away from the gathering to collect himself.

——— ... ———

Something was different. There were voices; whispering voices. Voices, but no faces. He could hear them, but he couldn't see them. Why was it so dark? Nothing seemed right.

There. There! That voice is familiar, but who's that one? They don't belong.
The confusion was exhausting, and he drifted away.

Again, it happened—voices; the disorientation. His eyes opened suddenly, as if they were a new appendage he'd just discovered.

He was in a room, a bed—but... where... how? His arms and legs hurt; his whole body was sore.

Blurred outlines of people gradually came into focus. He saw Clare and Doc standing at the foot of his bed in conversation. His eyes darted to the wall where Rebecca, Jerome, and the kids were all nodding and smiling at one another. And more voices.

It was confusing; it was too much. He began coughing and thrashing his head back and forth. Alarms immediately filled the room with irritating sounds. His ventilator breathing tube filled with fluid secretions.

Nurses, respiratory therapists, and a doctor quickly ran into the small hospital room that had been home to Peter for the past seven days. They assessed the situation. The breathing tube had dislodged with all the commotion and was now entirely out. A few quick maneuvers by the medical team disconnected him from the ventilator. The alarms were finally silenced.

Peter, now calm and breathing quietly on his own, fell back asleep.

——— ... ———

I stood at the foot of the bed strangled with fear, watching a possessed Peter thrashing his head while staring into space. What was happening?

I was barely on the edge of keeping my sanity after Peter unexpectedly woke. For me, the vigil was expected to end with his death. The fright in his eyes, the alarms, the coughing—I had no idea what it all meant. Was he coming back to me, or was the doctor giving up on him? Was Peter going to live or die?

My quiet sobbing now intensified, crying jags interrupted by exasperated screams. "No, Peter! No!"

It went on like this, over and over, until I wore myself out. I eventually fell silent, surrendering to fate with soft murmurs.

"Please, don't take him. Please, please, please."

Sandy, Margaret, and Moiré joined Anna to be by my side. They held me, consoled me, and mourned with me.

It had been a challenging week. When Peter arrived at the hospital, he was rushed into the operating room for a skull fracture with blood pressing on a brain that was rapidly swelling. Two other surgeries repaired fractures in both arms and his right thigh. Pneumonia and a wound infection rounded out his maladies for the week.

He lay in intensive care, his head wrapped in a white turban, casts on both arms, and metal rods protruding from his right thigh stabilizing the femur fracture. It was expected the brain trauma was too extensive for him to wake from and that he would eventually succumb.

An hour passed before Peter finally opened his eyes again. He lay there, calmly looking about, almost forgotten by those in the room. Most of us women were still huddled together while Jerome, Rebecca, Pastor, and Matt covered the left flank of the room.

We were all in conversation at the very moment Peter's eyes started canvassing. He smiled, but it too went unnoticed. Finally, he cleared his sore throat, catching everyone's attention. I quickly made for his bedside, threw my arms around him, sobbing—but now with the realization that he would live.

"Peter, Peter…" I began, then suddenly mid-sentence, I pulled back to look him square on. "I'm so mad at you for what you did!" It came flying out in a burst of frustration, although I think it was clear I was ecstatic with the sudden turn of events. My cries of despair were now tears of joy.

Everyone in the room donned smiles. Jerome clapped a few times and announced, "Awesome, Peter."

"Ahem," Peter said in a raspy whisper, his throat obviously raw and burning, "I'm sorry to disturb you all… It looks like quite… a social… gathering." He strained to form his words. "All my favorite people in one place."

We all looked at each other, smiling and nodding. Peter's witticism told us he was indeed back. He had sized up the situation with just a glance. In his hospital room were all the people who either didn't get along or didn't see eye to eye. And now, here we were, gathered together for a purpose—a true purpose, a noble purpose.

"I'm glad," Peter said, "that I was able to find a way to bring us all together."

He smiled at his own cleverness. I stroked his cheeks then reached down and kissed him.

"Touché!" Jerome said.

Epilogue

Two Years Later

I once read that time heals all wounds, a balm that soothes the ailing heart. It covered all manner of misdeeds and tragedies and loved ones who passed away. But did it?

I would readily agree that time healed *most* physical wounds, but emotional wounds were something else. Time simply made these wounds less raw, allowing me and Peter to move on and be productive in the business of living. The emotional scars still lurked deep in our subconscious, distant from the surface of our day-to-day activities, its presence a lens through which we would always see the world.

And so it was that life moved on with time, but our family was not the same. We had seen the dark blight on the soul of humanity, a burden we would always carry. We still found happiness from time to time, but we were now the copper with a green patina, showing we had weathered the storm and now stood sturdy—a testament that one could survive life's misfortunes and laugh and love and cherish once more.

This was most true for Matt and Sandy. Their youth offered an optimism unique to their generation. Matt visited home a few times a year from New York City. His ambition, as ever, was a defining quality to his character. Still, Peter and I saw his soft side, a compassion that gave him pause to notice others in need. He volunteered at a YMCA in the Bronx, coaching basketball to junior high school kids.

Sandy was even more transparent. We were pleased that she settled in Cleveland, close enough for monthly visits back to Portville. She became a celebrated high school English teacher, and was proud to have learned enough French to own a copy of *The Count of Monte Cristo* in its original language.

Peter and I were, of course, delighted that our kids could endure the tragedies of Beekman and still thrive. We were no longer blind, however, to the realities of "skeletons in the closet," that what befalls us in our youth can sometimes still haunt us in later years. For this, we simply needed to trust, to have faith, to always be there for them as best we could, and hope that their relationship with each other was the best gift Peter and I had given them.

Eaton Advocacy also continued to thrive. It bustled with activity as the June Pride Parade was fast approaching, and because it had grown over the past two years, an extraordinary coordination required weeks of planning for a perfect event.

Parade floats were assembled in sections, making the lobby and many of the conference rooms resemble a stage set for *Alice in Wonderland*. Other parade costumes were still in the design stages—thus, fabric and costume accessories were ferried from one part of the building to another.

Some hustled upstairs to a second level of work rooms while others scrambled down, hoping to avoid anyone carrying a precariously balanced load. Still others worked the phones, which rang incessantly. The irony peculiar to Eaton was that the movement itself appeared to resemble a play with an ensemble of actors in costume portraying the very deeds they were actually performing. Such was the vigor and flare and eccentricity in dress and hair color and jewelry. At any moment, one might expect to hear "Cut!" and all the performers would stop in their tracks and slowly walk to the periphery of the stage to await further instructions. But these were real people playing out on a stage of life their most fervent dreams of freedom, acceptance, and personhood.

Peter sat in a quiet corner of Eaton, in a room to himself, while I busied myself with other activities in preparation for the parade. This was now our regular pastime. All those years of ribbing him about his dull accounting skills—who would have known that combining his acumen with my banking and development skills would make us a dynamic duo? We both spent many hours a week helping with big and small events, community outreach, marketing, and anything we could to further the cause.

Today, Peter tackled the final legal and civic aspects of the parade, not to mention the financial element: Significant funding from corporate and private donations needed to be accounted for, and the appropriate tax filings planned in advance. Though his desk was strewn with papers that represented three months of preparation, there was more order than a first glance would assume.

But that was all behind him now. The necessary work had been done. His real reason for stealing away in private was to indulge a new vice: reading. I quite liked that something of my preferred indulgence seemed to have found its way into his idea of quiet meditation. If that wasn't a unique marital exchange, I don't know what was.

His most recent read, *The Human Factor*, he had regaled with much fanfare. It was a gift, an incidental find from an old bookstore still struggling to exist. Little did I know it would become his raison d'être . The story weaved a quilt of his essence, in all its glory, as he was quick to share. When the book came to a close, he was smugly satisfied that its message of sacrifice and dedication summed him up in one reading.

I had to agree, with some insincere hesitation, that he was probably right. The book confirmed all he had been through—the angst and grief, and the remorse and regret that had once colored the lines of his existence. He had made decisions on impulse, always choosing what he thought was noble or merely instinctual, sometimes making enemies of those in his family despite treasuring his family more than anything else. He didn't weigh the outcome of one versus the other in his choosing. He simply acted from the heart, sometimes hurting those he loved most.

Peter found solace in Graham Greene's depiction of Castle, a double agent spy who likewise sacrificed all for one cause: his wife and child, or even more, for a just humanity in the faces of those who were victims of apartheid. Much to the chagrin of those who would have preferred he choose country over love, it was not his conviction. Likewise, Peter couldn't help but choose people over patriotism, or the marginalized over the elite. Was he a traitor, as Castle had become to those with more nationalistic fervor? Did it really matter? Both he and Castle were bonded in the hope that tomorrow would come and that the heart knew no wrong.

There was a knock at the door. "Daddy, there's someone here for you."

Peter looked up and smiled. There stood Lira, with a serious look of carrying out important business. Lira was a biracial nonbinary thirteen-year-old. They wore a colorful costume of denim with brightly colored patchwork and a striped tank top that was landscape to at least a half dozen beaded necklaces. Lira wore black lipstick and had reddish-pink streaks dyed in their hair.

In any other venue, Lira might have been mistaken for an iconoclast who followed no rules and leaned bohemian or free spirit. That would be a wrong assessment. Lira took the work of Eaton to a serious level. For Lira, Eaton personified all that was right with the world.

Peter peered over his half-rimmed "accountant" readers at our tall new teenager. The long, slender arms and womanly hands belied the still child-at-heart he knew required tenderness.

"Hi, honey, there's who?"

"There's someone here to see you. It's that family you know. I don't remember their name."

The adoption papers had been finalized in the past few months—Peter and I were no longer empty nesters. Lira had taken to family life like a fish to water. They came from a lifetime of struggle that eventually resulted in foster care. It was no surprise that finding a family to adopt a preteen would always be a challenge, but the adoption agency assigned to Lira had even less expectation of finding a permanent home for a preteen with a nontraditional sexual identity.

But luck would shine on Lira. A midlevel manager in the adoption agency knew of Eaton Advocacy and involved them in the search for placement. It was not long before my now regular presence at Eaton placed me in a meeting where Lira's name was mentioned. I knew at once that I had to be the solution.

That was how the story was told to family and friends: "Bolt-of-lightning idea," I'd say. "It just had to happen."

I was not exactly wrong. The feeling grew during the meeting, from a fleeting thought to a possibility to a serious consideration. Before the meeting was over, I—who had ignored the last twenty minutes of banter on odd subjects—was consumed with anticipation and excitement over what I now saw as a must.

I broached the subject with Peter, and fate weaved its delicate web of fortune. Peter, of course, was quite pleased—after recovering from an initial stupefaction. Just as he was growing accustomed to my simply feeling comfortable at Eaton, this new turn of events cemented my commitment to the cause. Nothing embodied the renewal of our marriage vows better than my taking the lead on defining our new life together.

For me, it was a surprising development, this new self that I was quite unfamiliar with, like trying on a new sweater and running my hands over the colorful threads that changed the pattern of my life. When the epiphany finally settled in my heart, I sat still with a near permanent grin on my face. I knew well enough who I had been and who I would become, and I knew exactly when the change had begun.

My first visit to Eaton had been fraught with anxiety and trepidation. I'd feared my well-honed identity would be tainted if someone of my ilk happened to notice my new indulgence and whispered it among my Beekman regulars. But just the simple act of going to Eaton, over and over, had a peculiar way of changing my heart on the matter. Certain things, I simply cared less for; other things, I began to care for more. It was a matter of where I spent my time, and with whom.

Peter got up and glanced toward the front lobby. There stood Jerome and Margaret, conversing with Moiré. "Well, look at that," he said. "The Robinsons are here."

Despite his feigning surprise, he really wasn't that shocked to see his old friends in the lobby. The Robinsons had made appearances on more than a few occasions over the past two years. Jerome's company had performed extensive electrical repairs for Eaton as a donation to the cause, and both he and Margaret had come to a number of celebratory events that were open to the public. In fact, they had become regular supporters of Eaton Advocacy in a way that influenced even city council members to take notice, making Eaton one of the many nonprofit organizations Cincinnati held in high esteem.

More to the point, Margaret was pleased to play an invaluable role in helping me streamline the adoption process, a typically daunting task under normal circumstances. Her contacts from working with at-risk children as a Court Appointed Special Advocate meant she routinely worked with the many officials involved in vetting the process.

I didn't warm to the idea of Margaret's help quite as easily as one would have thought. Though Margaret made the offer in person at one of the events we both attended, my perfunctory acknowledgment and show of appreciation was meant more to appease than to engage. It was not that I didn't appreciate the offer—it was that I was embarrassed to take it. I had spent so many years denying the full weight of events on Beekman that I now wore it as an albatross around my neck. I simply felt undeserving of Margaret's largess.

Margaret, however, was used to converts, those who were lukewarm to the plight of Blacks in America only to later embrace her as an equal, if not as family. She said that if she ever was inclined to hold a grudge, many she counted as her closest friends would instead be mere acquaintances. Margaret simply moved on. She left the past in the past. She let it be.

When my situation became apparent to Margaret, she plied her influences wherever she could, even without my knowledge. Indeed, often I was informed our credentials were approved in advance because of references already submitted.

In due time, Margaret and I became close friends, a friendship not unlike the special bond I'd had with Sarah Johnson many years before. The irony was not lost on me—the swapping out of one friend for the other. And despite the differences between Margaret and Sarah, the special regard I felt for Margaret was much the same as the one I'd felt for Sarah, though for different reasons.

Margaret had a genuineness that I never thought I would ever find admirable. My career in finance was not so much predicated on sincerity as it was on transparency, and there was a difference. One was emotional, the other legal. I relegated emotions to the unpredictable and irrational. They were considered a precursor to undermining one's own financial solvency, not to mention the client. When it came to the business of making money, my resolve was as cold as steel in the dead of winter. And I would be the first to admit that that resolve had a way of bleeding into my personal life.

I had to finally admit that it was why I'd never warmed to Peter's view of the Beekman affair—until recently. It was also why the weight of denial weighed so heavy on my shoulders. But Margaret had a way of lifting that load. Her simple genuine way of being lightened my heart and removed the burden of guilt and denial. It needed no explanation, no exorcism, no therapeutic intervention. Just being in her company was enough to effect a change. And in quiet moments, in the stillness of my heart, I would have a fleeting vision, an epiphany of understanding that Margaret and Sarah were very much the same. I had seen in Sarah what I wanted to see. I had projected my own values onto Sarah and thus created a sisterhood out of an illusion.

Suffice it to say, my time spent with Margaret was a sea change from my former self. My initial tepid indifference gradually warmed under Margaret's unyielding generosity and limitless caring for those in her presence.

When it was clear we were in need of her insight and connections, Margaret gave. My timid hesitancy finally relented. When I had doubts that my initial impulse to adopt a biracial, nonbinary teen was maybe too impulsive, maybe not something I was ready for, Margaret's soothing reassurance worked its balm of confidence that all would be right.

"It's your calling," Margaret would say. "You are the perfect choice for Lira. Don't worry about the things that could be, just love them and everything will figure itself out."

I found myself believing without understanding how or why. My anxieties just slipped away.

Margaret's largess did have help along the way. Judge David Meyers, a quiet admirer of her singular dedication to children in need, made every effort to expedite the process. Lira and I were soon to be mother and daughter.

"Well, Lira," Peter said, "let's go see what all the fuss is about."

The two strolled to the center oval of the lobby and mixed in with the small crowd already there.

"Hi Margaret," Peter said, greeting her with a hug. "Hey, Jerome, what brings you guys down today?"

Margaret and Jerome exchanged looks. "You might as well tell him," Margaret nudged.

"It was your idea, Margaret."

"Yes, but it's your car," Margaret chided.

"Car?" asked Peter.

Margaret and Jerome exchanged glances again. Finally, Margaret said, "Peter, you know we've been planning this missionary trip to Africa."

"Yeah, in about a month or so, right?" Peter said.

"That's right," Margaret replied. "So Jerome has a problem, and I found the solution for him, but he thinks it's too much of an imposition. I told him he's being foolish. I guess you'll have to decide who's right."

"Okay," Peter said, "the suspense here is killing me."

I joined the crowd, standing between Lira and Margaret, not speaking a word, though the expression on my face probably gave away that I already knew what was about to unfold.

"Ahem," Jerome started. "Well, as Margaret said, we're going to Africa, and we plan to be gone for about a year, maybe more." He pointed through the glass doors of Eaton to his convertible Corvair parked right outside. "I can't box that up and take it, and I can't just let it sit around unused. The engine will seize up. It needs to be driven—regularly. I want you to take the car."

Peter gasped. His throat closed up, preventing him from saying a word. Finally, after a long minute, he spoke. "Jerome, are you sick or something? You can't give up that car. You must have some classic car friends that can keep an eye on it for you?"

"I want you, Peter. You appreciate that car more than anyone I know. It has special meaning for you. I can't think of a better home than yours."

Peter shook his head, looked back outside, then went to the front door, pushed it open, and walked to the car. It looked as beautiful as the first day he'd set eyes on it. Though he had seen it many times since, especially in the last two years when we had dinner invitations at the Robinsons, something about this time around brought all the memories back to those first few days when he and Jerome had become friends. The nostalgia of it all hit him like an emotional gut punch.

Everyone else had spilled outside, flanking him on both sides. Lira held onto his left arm in a show of support. Peter wiped away a tear before anyone could see it fall, and he shook his head one more time. "You can't mean this."

"Yeah, I can, and I do," Jerome said.

"Just for a year. I'll keep the engine running until you return."

"Well, we'll see. Margaret and I have been planning to downsize. We're selling the house, and when we return, we'll be renters. It's not smart to have a car like this and park it on the street. The car will be yours, Peter, and don't even think of money. It's our gift to you. You saved my life and helped me to refocus on what I value most. The car also needs a proper home. Hey, maybe when I get back, you'll let me take it for a spin every now and then."

Peter was speechless. The tears returned, welling up in his eyes before he could mask them with a wipe of the forearm. He wrapped Margaret and Jerome in a firm embrace.

"I... I love you guys," Peter said, his voice breaking with emotion. "I'm such a blubbering idiot. Okay, okay. I'll take very good care of her. It'll be *our* car, sitting in my driveway. That's the only way I'll sign off."

"Fair enough, Peter," said Jerome, "fair enough."

——— ... ———

A few weeks into June, Peter and I heard the clarion call that it was time to go. It was the day of the Pride Parade, and the excitement for one person in the household was beyond expectation. It would be Lira's first time at an event that celebrated people exactly like them. That Lira was proud to be among their own barely touched the truth of how they felt—the unconditional love was palpable in everything they did—except maybe having patience with their parents.

"I'm in the car," Lira yelled from the front door.

I stood alongside Peter in the bathroom, grinning at Lira's antics while brushing the last few strokes of my hair. I added a light shade of lipstick and noticed Peter staring at my reflection in the mirror.

His eyes were gentle yet earnest. He took my hand in his. My blush was instant; it was a sudden feeling of vulnerability. I tried to turn away but couldn't resist the pull of his gaze. A car horn blared from the front driveway, and our smiles widened. Then we laughed.

"That kid waits for nobody," Peter said.

"They're just so excited," I added. "I don't think I've ever seen them this happy."

I held his gaze in the mirror, now seeing myself through his eyes. I was naked. My wants, needs, and simply my being—he saw it all. It was certainty in life's uncertainty.

In the driveway, Lira had the top down on the Corvair and had claimed the shotgun seat. I climbed into the back, but not without commentary. "I guess we now know why Lira was the first outside." I threw a wry grin as Lira leaned forward to allow me access to the rear.

"Do you want to sit up front, Mom? I just figured your hair would like it better back there." Lira's apology was sincere, but something in the guilty smile betrayed their belief that this day was meant for them, and the seat of honor should obviously be theirs. Sitting in the front had become a norm for Lira. A Sunday drive was the new favorite pastime, exclusive to Lira and Peter. He had put Lira through the paces the way his dad had done with him.

"It's alright, Lira, I knew it had to be for considerate reasons," I playfully jabbed back.

Peter started the engine, and the Corvair responded with a throaty rumble that simmered to a purr. He backed out of the driveway, and we glided past the other Beekman homes. One would never have known the tragic history that lurked in this Absalom of Portville—where vanity, greed, and fratricide were all its undoing.

The trees still lined the block with branches overhanging the road. Front yards again burst with colors of flowers in bloom. Lawns were perfectly manicured. But not everything had returned to its old form. Something was different.

Alice waved to us as we drove by, and Lira enthusiastically waved back. In Lira's brief time in our family, the neighbors had adopted Lira as one of their own.

Peter came up to the first corner intersecting with Beekman and looked over to Lira—and Lira, to him. He nodded, and Lira slid the gearshift from first to second. Peter gave her more gas, and the Corvair powered into the turn, shooting out onto the adjacent street.

When we got to the Ohio River Scenic Byway, again Peter looked over to Lira as the engine strained to make it up the on-ramp. Lira heard and timed it perfectly with Peter's press of the clutch—second to third.

The Corvair surged up the ramp, merged into traffic, and Peter looked at Lira, who wore an ear-to-ear grin, a rainbow flag furled on their left cheek. He gave the final nod. Lira, ever so gently, slid the stick back into fourth. The Corvair shot forward, pressing us back into our seats. Lira's hair flew over the seat into the back as she surfed the wind with her right hand outside the car.

Fourth gear was always the most exhilarating in a manual shift, but for Peter, it was the getting there that he loved the most. The final throw of the stick said something about life that he had always envied, a final letting go of anxiety, a not holding back, a living without hesitation, and a trust that the world was a safe place to be.

The sun was still early, its midday summit a few hours off. Golden rays shimmered on the Ohio, casting a regal glow. Peter glanced into the rearview mirror to find me, and our eyes met. I smiled and quickly wiped a tear. My emotions had succumbed to a gradual turning of the lens until my life found focus. Everything had crystallized in that moment. For me, success was always a means to an end. Having the best—of anything—was simply the best of everything, a de rigueur rule to live by. But that indulgence had become an anathema—and all the while, I had worn a grotesque mask that hid me from myself. My life had become a lie, and only now did I realize how exhausting it all was. I was now free to start again.

Peter nodded, and I wondered if he knew—if our sentiments were in sync; if my tears had spoken.

Acknowledgments

I am indebted to my parents for not only encouraging me to view others with empathy, but also for showing me through their own example how compassion is integral to a common humanity. Likewise, I am fortunate to have met and married a woman who ceaselessly pushes me to be a better person. Susan is the light of my life, with both an endearing love and as a guide toward true happiness. I am indebted to her critical insight, and her endurance and patience of my ongoing distractions while writing this book.

My children—Anna, Christopher, and Sophie—have lent a critical eye, providing a youthful generational perspective that I might otherwise have overlooked. Their continued support and encouragement has buoyed my confidence during times of doubt.

I would also like to acknowledge George Rangel, Amy Valdez, and Alexandra Kharazi for reading various versions of my writing and providing valuable feedback.

Finally, but in no way least, I would like to acknowledge the outstanding professional services of Vince Font for editing the manuscript with a fine eye toward grammar, usage, and colloquialisms. As a debut author, my challenges extended well beyond the creative. I owe the fabulous book cover design to the graphic artistry of Judith San Nicolas of Judith S. Design & Creativity.

About the Author

Eric Clark is a native of New York City, born of Jamaican immigrants seeking the American dream. Though his career steered toward medicine, which he continues to practice in San Diego, his formative years in the rich cultural diversity of New York left an indelible mark. Navigating the wonders of such varied ethnicities compelled him to see beyond his Caribbean roots. His Italian best friend, Irish neighbors, and Puerto Rican classmates all told the same story: that who he was and what he knew was undoubtedly linked to the people in his life. The more diverse those people were, the more rich and rewarding his life had become. *The Beekman Affair* captures this essence of America's rich tapestry, compelling us to see beyond, into a future of promising dreams.

Eric's personal life is filled with family affairs. He is dedicated to the simple pleasures of walks on the beach with his wife and their retriever, Luna. Otherwise, he's pulling weeds, planting bulbs, or harvesting fruit. Some things Jamaican never change.

www.ingramcontent.com/pod-product-compliance
Lightning Source LLC
LaVergne TN
LVHW040132080526
838202LV00042B/2886